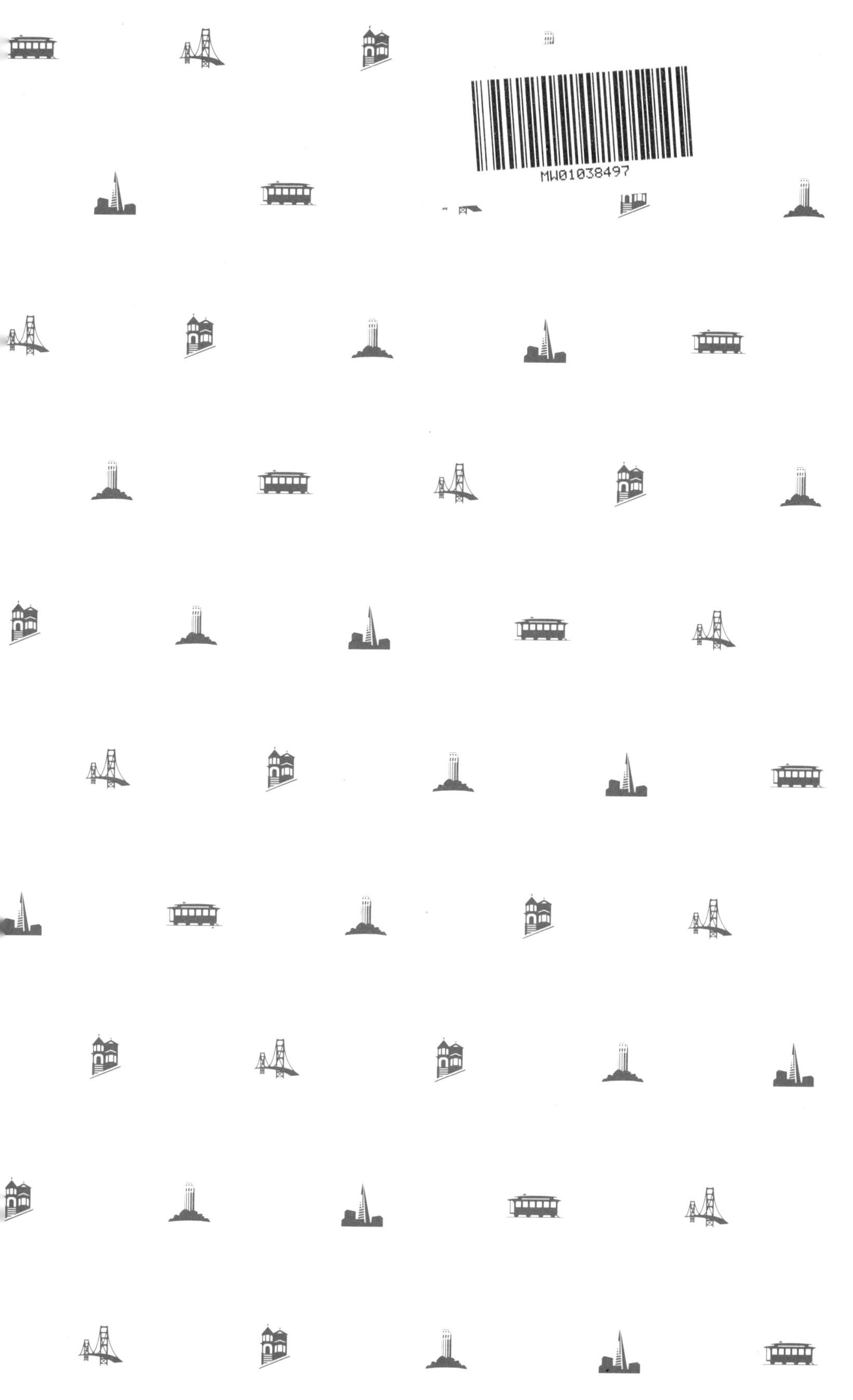
MW01038497

HERB CAEN'S

SAN FRANCISCO

1976-1991

Books by Herb Caen

THE SAN FRANCISCO BOOK
BAGHDAD-BY-THE-BAY
BAGHDAD '51
DON'T CALL IT FRISCO
ONLY IN SAN FRANCISCO
HERB CAEN'S GUIDE TO SAN FRANCISCO AND THE BAY AREA
SAN FRANCISCO, CITY ON GOLDEN HILLS
(WITH DONG KINGMAN)
THE CABLE CAR AND THE DRAGON
ONE MAN'S SAN FRANCISCO
THE BEST OF HERB CAEN 1960–1975
HERB CAEN'S SAN FRANCISCO 1976–1991

★ ★ ★

HERB CAEN'S
SAN FRANCISCO
1976–1991

SELECTED BY IRENE MECCHI

CHRONICLE BOOKS • SAN FRANCISCO

First edition 1992.

Printed in the United States of America.

Library of Congress Cataloging-in-Publication Data

Caen, Herb, 1916-
Herb Caen's San Francisco, 1976-1991 / selected by Irene Mecchi,
p. cm.
ISBN 0-8118-0060-1
1. Daily morning chronicle (San Francisco, Calif.) 2. American newspapers—Sections, columns, etc. I. Mecchi, Irene. II. Title.
PN4874.C2A25 1992
814'.54—dc20 92-1087
CIP

Book and cover design: Kathy Warinner
Composition: On Line Typography

Distributed in Canada by Raincoast Books,
112 East Third Avenue, Vancouver, B.C. V5T 1C8

10 9 8 7 6 5 4 3 2 1

Chronicle Books
275 Fifth Street
San Francisco, CA 94103

For Christopher and Ann, shining constants in a swirling galaxy.

Preface

Last year, Chronicle Books published *The Best of Herb Caen: 1960–1975*. The "Best" was the publisher's idea. I resisted it on the grounds that it implied I had peaked as a columnist during those 15 years, but my plea was rejected as bordering on the paranoid, which I am at all times.

The book, which did well enough to pay off a few outstanding bills, consisted of various *San Francisco Chronicle* columns and wisps of hopeful wit and wisdom compiled by a young woman named Irene Mecchi, who may be described as a serious student of my output. Being unable to judge my own work as anything but marginally printable on a slow news day, I am deeply indebted to her for her ability to pick and choose without doubt or hesitation.

Our discussions were usually quite short. After reviewing her selections, I'd say about a certain column, "Gee, Irene, I think this one really stinks," at which she would respond, "I think it's brilliant." I confess, not without shame, that I usually found myself able to go along with her decision.

This book covers the 15-year period from 1976 to 1991. This you know already from reading the title, which makes no claim to being "the best" of anything. It is, however, a more than fair representation of the daily work I perform, like a trained seal or perhaps a dog on its hind legs, for my compassionate and understanding employer, The Chronicle.

Every word was written under daily deadline pressure and no attempt has been made to remove the warts or polish the prose, which is as it should be. Of necessity, a journalist writes fast and has no time whatever to rewrite. The wonder of it all is how well journalists manage to write under these hellish conditions. "Some of the best writing in America today is to be found in its daily newspapers." I made up that quote at this very moment—I am writing this preface against a very tight deadline—but somebody distinguished may have said something like that. It has the ring of truth.

Once again, the faithful and tireless Miss Mecchi has pored through 15 years of columns to make her selections. This time around I offered no arguments. In the past couple of years she has gone through 50 years of columns and knows my stuff better than I do. After all, I have been writing a daily column in and about San Francisco since July 5, 1938, and have forgotten much or maybe even most of what I've written. "Did I really write this?" I would say occasionally to Miss Mecchi, forgetting that it was written at a different time in a different city by a person I have some difficulty identifying with.

The city is like a snake, shedding its skin, changing constantly, moving about in unexpected directions. However, if it is a great city, which San Francisco forever is, it retains its basic qualities—a sense of adventure, a delight in its own history, an air of freedom and a rare tolerance for divergent views and actions. The city dances on its hills and unashamedly enjoys its own beauty, which has survived many a long night of excesses, both joyous and tragic.

San Francisco, a great writers' town—tantalizing, just out of reach in its misty aloofness. A city so small and yet so varied, from block to block. Cross a street and enter a different world. Every writer about San Francisco strives to capture its essence and, on occasion, feels he has succeeded—but the city is always one step ahead, laughing, disappearing into the fog.

Looking at the city in 15-year segments, as we are doing, is instructive. The changes are there and they come and go so swiftly that only a daily newspaper can try to keep the record, not always with historical accuracy, of course, but always with the urgency and sense of drama that come with deadlines and headlines.

For San Francisco, 1976–1991 was a trying period, high among the most difficult in its history. The assassinations of Mayor George Moscone and Supervisor Harvey Milk, the bizarre tragedy of the Reverend Jim Jones and his followers, the onslaught of the AIDS epidemic, the dizzying rise in drug-related crimes, an earthquake whose aftershocks are being felt to this day, a housing and economic crisis that put thousands of homeless people on the streets, a subtle but pervasive change in the city's vaunted reputation for compassion and generosity—all these monumental events produced and continue to produce problems that sometimes seem to defy solution.

The city that has survived so much continues to survive, of course, and even flourish in the worldly amenities of a civilized place (one small example: this may be the golden era of San Francisco restaurants, and the emergence of the South of Market area as a night-life center is a pleasurable success). After the 1906 earthquake, the journalist who wrote about it most feelingly, Will Irwin, immediately described San Francisco in the past tense, as "The City That Was." "The most pleasure-loving city of the western world is dead," he reported, but San Francisco rose from the ruins to more acclaim than ever before. And now it is being put to the test again. History is on the side of the optimists.

Of considerably less importance to everybody but me, I had my 75th birthday on April 3, 1991. Hold your applause. It's not a great accomplishment—all you have to do is live long enough. On July 5, 1988, my column became 50 years old, making it a trivia footnote: the longest-running daily newspaper column in the country. Of even more trivial interest, I am writing these words on what I continue to call, rather archly, my Loyal Royal, a noble typewriter at least 30 years old.

Around The Chronicle, I'm the last of an ignoble breed, the only person still writing daily on a typewriter. Someone younger and definitely more intelligent then puts it into "the system," the computers that produce the daily paper in a manner completely incomprehensible to me. I will never win a Pulitzer but I do hope the Loyal Royal ends up in the Smithsonian.

May you enjoy these bits and pieces about San Francisco.

And, loved and/or hated, a great life it is in the enchanting, troubled, gallant little city by the bay. I feel like the luckiest guy on earth to have been a part of the excitement, deadline after deadline, for so many remarkable years.

Herb Caen
San Francisco
January 25, 1992

★ ★ ★

1976

★ ★ ★

Brave New Year

Well, how do you like it so far? The new year, I mean. Year of the Big Fly (that's "moscone" in Italian), the Bicentennial Year (on Polk, sniggers Lawyer Walter Winter, they're calling it the Bisextennial Year), the year of a new President (I can dream, can't I?). Ring out the old desk calendars, ring in the new—all those blank pages waiting to be filled with the scribbles and scrawls that mark our scrabbling progress through life. Literally, the turning over of new leaves, the making of resolutions to break. In 1976 I Will Be a Better Person! Mister Nice Guy, even, helping Little Old Ladies cross Market St. as they pluck my wallet. No more nitpicking, nagging and needling of my betters. Where once I went for the karate chop, I will lie down with lamb chops. I will go on the wagon; Portia Faces Life, sober. I will even spell the names right, not to mention learning the Hustle and Bump. I will learn to love Howard Cosell . . . Scratch that.

★ ★ ★

This week, a new Mayor will be sworn in, after which he will be sworn at. Poor Big Fly, so much to do, so much debris left behind by the great streetsweeper of Presidio Terrace. But it is still a city among cities, a pearl among piglets, a place where a love of life covers a multitude of skins. Under the previous administrator, the center did not hold. A city that once could be called a family, of sorts, broke off into warring factions. The name of the game became power, and a beautiful city started to turn a little ugly. Buildings and the crime rate rose not altogether coincidentally. The texture changed from a community of San Franciscans—we, the luckiest people!—into a Balkanized "us" against "them" and you stay on your side of the street, see?

★ ★ ★

The last few years have been an education and a revelation, even some kind of revolution. Lord knows the old San Francisco was far from efficient, but there was a civilized warmth about the laissez-fairness and an awareness that we were living in a special, delicate place—disturb the balance at your own risk! Well, the balance was disturbed. Out from under the rocks they came, the movers, the shakers, the anything-for-a-buckers. We were shown the underside of the city, and it was not a pretty sight. If you were part of the power group, you had the green light all the way—otherwise, forget it. If you couldn't push, you got shoved. Patriots who sang the National Anthem with their hand over their heart (instead of their mouth) turned out to be liars, playing fast and loose with a sacred object thousands have died for. The vote. And the leader of the people said, "Who cares? It goes on all the time. It has been going on for years."

★ ★ ★

When we were all young and dumb, it was an article of faith that there were only two Real Cities in the land—New York and San Francisco. So much in common: tall buildings, nightlife, good food, excitement, a mixture of races living in comparative harmony, most people at least Caring. We still have so much in common: tall buildings, mounting debts, good food, too much excitement in the streets, and a shared feeling that we are headed in the wrong direction. San Francisco has a new skyline, new millionaires, acres of empty blocks, declining population, increasing traffic—what's it all about? It matters not how you feel about the new buildings, esthetically. They're not doing the job we were promised. As the high-rises went up, the taxes would come down, right? Ha.

★ ★ ★

Under the outgoing regime, we learned more than we care to know about the application of pressure, the pitting of faction against faction (positively Machiavellian), the untidy spectacle of promoters and unions and civil servants grabbing the buck above all else. There must be something else and it has to come from the leadership. That something else is integrity, a belief in the city and its people, a sentimental feeling for tradition, a decent regard for the past and its visible signs: old buildings, old customs, old landmarks, old people. The No. 1 priority in San Francisco is—

San Francisco, the survival of a civilized city in a world going dark. Anybody can make a buck, as so many creeps have demonstrated during the past eight years, but how many can keep the dream alive and the flame from flickering out? A romantic city, and this is, needs romantics. The stony-hearts have provided us with enough heartless stones to last us the rest of our days.

⋆ ⋆ ⋆

Poor Big Fly. He takes over a city that is falling apart under the dead weight of a bureaucracy as expensive as that of our one-time inspiration. Today, Manhattanization means going broke. We have more and more people doing less and less, until finally nothing gets done, and yet the bureaucrats continue to offer the same old excuse: "not enough money, not enough manpower." It is to laugh to keep from crying. Even the sacred grove, Golden Gate Park, is showing wear and tear. San Francisco is fables and fog, legends and legerdemain, but somebody has to keep the streets clean, too, and water the flowers. What we have learned in eight years is that cronyism won't do it, arrogance won't do it, and a cheapness of style is not enough. What it takes is dedication, and let's hope there's enough left to go around. One more time.

January 4, 1976

Nobody Asked Me, But...

I miss: Tea dances (but not the creamed seagull in a patty shell that served as the "main" and only course) . . . Mayors who wore carnations in their buttonholes and liked to drive streetcars . . . Long leggy blondes sporting orchid corsages on their lynx chubbies, wearing anklets of hearts entwined and smelling more than faintly of Tabu—"The Forbidden Perfume!" . . . Betting parlors—like Tom Kyne's in Opal Place—where you'd see Mayor Rolph and Police Chief O'Brien laying a bet and discussing the odds, cool as you please . . . Such Runyonesque characters as Louie the Litvak, who ran a gambling joint downtown, welched on a few bets and turned up missing one day. He never reappeared but several people did mention, en passant, a fresh stretch of cement sidewalk in San Bruno.

I wonder what's become of: All those Sallies who danced in chorus lines at Joe Merello's Club Moderne, Joaquin Garay's Copa and the Music Box . . . Bootblacks who snapped their rags over your shoes, brushed you with a big whiskbroom, sprayed you with cheap cologne (unless you were quick) and displayed gardenia corsages—"For your lady, sah!"—on the washstands . . . Elevator starters who clicked castanets to get the lifts off the ground, and Little Old Lady operators who wore one glove, on the hand they used to manipulate the door . . . Men who wore homburgs, chesterfields, spats and dove-gray gloves.

Memories that bless and burn: Loud cries of "Nine-Star Final!" . . . Sitting alone in the top row at Seals Stadium on a Sunday morning, watching the Seals play the Oaks and feeling utterly, blissfully content . . . Picnicking in the Park before moseying into Kezar to watch the 49ers' all-time greatest backfield—Y.A. Tittle, Joe Perry, Hugh McElhenny, John Henry Johnson (and it didn't matter who won, it was such fun) . . . The fables we wanted to believe were true: "The Lady of the Lake"—the long-haired nymph who appeared at midnight, aglow, in the still waters of Stow Lake—and the tunnel that ran under California St. from the Pacific-Union Club to a maison de joie, and the headless ghost of Little Pete running through foggy Waverly Place, where he was murdered so many years ago.

I can hear, taste, see and smell them now: the "Small Blacks" (coffee-flavored candy) you'd buy at the Golden Pheasant at Powell and Geary before going to a matinee at the Orpheum on O'Farrell . . . Screams as the "Big Dipper" roller coaster went into its first vertical dive at Playland, and the recurrent fable we DIDN'T want to believe: that a car once shot off the tracks and into the street, killing all occupants, "but the story was hushed up" . . . The "I Was Hit" lapel pin proudly worn by ferryboat commuters used as a target by a seagull—although seagulls are said to be unable to bomb in flight (another fable?).

⋆ ⋆ ⋆

I don't miss: Cesar Romero movies . . . Corny bands like Shep Fields' Rippling Rhythm . . . Spittoons, and those who used them—badly . . . Songs like "Don't Sit Under the Apple Tree," sung by finger-snapping girl trios . . . Rudy Vallee's megaphone, the Saturday Evening Post, Liberty mag, and "One Man's Family," a serial as corny as its locale, which was Sea Cliff . . . Pedal pushers, clamdiggers and ankle-strap wedgies.

⋆ ⋆ ⋆

I can live without: Wax museums . . . The unlikely combination of steak and lobster known as "Turf 'n' Surf" . . . Pie-faced Catherine Deneuve (but Brigitte Bardot can stick around, no matter what her age) . . . Fat-bellied policemen . . . Salad bars, especially those so dark you can't tell the Roquefort dressing, which contains no Roquefort, from the French dressing, unknown in France . . . Dining in some restaurant's so-called wine cellar, a gloomy and funereal way to make a few bucks out of an otherwise unproductive basement . . . Tennis dresses with sequins . . . The All-American clean-cut look—short hair, old school ties, conservative suits—on Washington "intelligence" types known to have committed every crime in the book.

You are only as big as the things that annoy you, and therefore I am minuscule, especially about those who spell it "miniscule" . . . Not to mention writers who underline their own cleverness with "pun intended" . . . Commercial TV shows that are "brought to you by the folks at ———" . . . Savings & loan and/or bank commercials featuring heavenly choirs and/or Judy Collinsish folksingers . . . Candlelight dinners of squid and octopus on rice . . . T-shirts that plug something, anything . . . San Franciscans who say that they are going "up to Las Vegas" when South is "down," isn't it? . . . People who cut their meat into small pieces before taking the first bite, and butter their entire roll before eating it . . . People who say "Have a nice weekend" on Wednesday . . . Hot air blowers, in public washrooms, that don't even begin to dry your hands.

Adjective-laden menus on which the salads are forever "crispy," the steak "tender and sizzling," and the fish "fresh from the seas" . . . Letter writers who consider it "unpatriotic" to criticize the FBI, CIA or the President—you know whose side THEY would have been on in 1776, don't you? *February 1, 1976*

Meet the people: English-born Jacky Kaukonen—of the Jefferson Airplane-Starship Kaukonens—just became a U.S. citizen after 12 years as an "alien resident," a term, she giggles, "that always made me wish I had green skin, webbed feet, scales and at least one horn!" . . . As part of her initiation into the rites of Americanism, she was given, for study, a 93-page booklet with five key questions, one of which was "Who is Mayor of California?" The correct answer turns out to be "George Moscone" . . . Admit it. You didn't know that. Of course, George didn't, either. *March 28, 1976*

Tag, You're It!

As you have noticed, April Fool's Day isn't what it used to be, either. No wallet on a string, to be yanked away by guffawing youngsters as you reach down to pick it off the sidewalk. No phone messages to call a "Mr. Lyon" at a number that turns out to be the zoo—hoo-boy—and no rubber spiders in your bed. "All Fool's Day" is like Halloween, an annual event steeped in mystery, "origins unknown," but at least Halloween has been revivified as the Gays' New Year's Eve, when the clothes of the opposite sex may be worn with impunity and a generous dab of cheap cologne. Within my laggard memory, April Fool called for considerable work and ingenuity, such as nailing a woman's handbag to the Powell cable's wooden turntable and watching one "fool" after another try to make off with it. Maybe April Fool's day is dying out because we are beginning to realize the joke is on us, and always has been.

* * *

If I sound more bittersweet than evergreen today it is because I have just passed another pole in the Grand Prix of life, climbed another rung on the ladder to nowhere, cut another notch in the belt that conveys us closer and closer to the buzzsaw of eternity. Awright, so I just had another birthday, big deal. No digits, rigid or otherwise, shall be specified. Let us just say it's a big round number with a rather lugubrious look to it. What's a kid from Sackamenna doing in an old, cold place like this? Enough to give one the shivers . . . But remember, folks, that we do not walk alone toward the distant horizon, where angels frolic (do angels have sex and don't their wings get in the way?) and where the future is forever bright, so remember to bring your Sleep Shade. We are all, every man Jill of us, getting older. As Robert Cole has kindly pointed out, I share a birthday with Marlon Brando and Wayne Newton, the manchild whose voice never changed. Surely I have not lived in vain, nor even San Bruno. Colma may be another story.

* * *

To have been so close to All Fool's Day, origins unknown, makes one doubly aware of life's buffooneries. I suppose. Actually, I never thought about it before, but it has a deep and satisfying ring to it. The image is rather appealing: fool's cap and bells, the Elizabethan doublet, the shrewd old eyes darting about, the voice cackling puns and rhymes, barbs and shafts. I feel like that timeless character on occasion, forever playing the fool, churning out the daily dollop of half-witticisms. It is only when I try to be serious that I find I have ventured out beyond my shallow.

As one grows older—actually, one shrinks older—the sense of the ridiculous, or the futile, becomes stronger. In that sense it is the only sense that does. The vision of life as a "practical joke in the worst possible taste" becomes quite clear. The eyes dim but the perspective improves—now that's odd, isn't it? Priorities fall into place in more or less the right order. What seemed so frightfully important a quarter of a century or so ago is now long forgotten. Or relegated to the end of the line.

The rat race, the furious battle with yourself, goes on to the end, but meanwhile, some small victories may be claimed. Just to be here is something, especially when more friends are dead than alive. I continue to be amazed, as a man of consistently bad judgments and decisions, that I have been lucky enough all these years to live in this most delightful of cities. Dear San Francisco—"with all its faults I love it still" is the phrase that follows immediately when I am feeling particularly loving about this city.

⋆ ⋆ ⋆

Happy Birthday, April fools everywhere. Spring perfume is in the air, the bud is on the branch, and as for those two in the bush—well, THAT form of outdoor activity is not supposed to begin until the First of May, hooray-hooray. Happy Birthday, United States of America (I do wish politicians would stop saying "We must keep America strong!" when they mean the good old U.S. of A.) and happy 200th to San Francisco, a slightly mean April Fool's joke played upon some unsuspecting Indians by Spanish crown and Roman church. Not that it hasn't worked out to everybody's satisfaction except the Indians'. The church remains strong, bells peal, choirs sing and the sign of the cross mingles comfortably with the dollar sign. The Spanish Presidio is green and beautiful if a bit military. Still, "we must keep America strong," with guns pointed at the Golden Gate, and the military does keep the builders of schlock at bay.

⋆ ⋆ ⋆

How does this April fool feel as another decade clicks past with the deadly rattle of a snake? Nice of you to inquire, old chum, and life IS a cabaret, long after midnight, most of the waiters already gone, the ones still around starting to stack the chairs on the tables. I feel quite well, actually. Like all native Californians, I am not allowed to grow old. I must stay middle-aged, continuing to work on my tennis game until I drop dead, and that is not a bad way to go. Not that I expect to be called by The Great Scorekeeper in the Sky till I have perfected my backhand and volley. That could take some time. *April 4, 1976*

The light under the bushel: Percy Pinkney, the dynamic black S.F. street organizer who now is an aide to Gov. Jerry Brown, was asked one day last week what he would describe as Jerry's outstanding quality. "Well," ventured Percy, searching carefully for just the right words, "he has—uh—you know—hidden charisma!"

May 11, 1976

Historical offshoot: Marguerite Pendergrast, browsing through a book of Balkan folklore titled "They Gypsies," by one J. P. Clebert, came across something that may shed further dark on this subject. "In some Romanian provinces," relates Clebert, "the people celebrate the Martini, which are days consecrated to the god Mars. In the course of festivities, the sick are brought to a position where they are placed to be trodden under the feet of tame bears." All devout martini drinkers know that feeling. *May 16, 1976*

They wouldn't even let him die in peace: On Powell, near the Orange Julius stand, the thermometer showing 87, the old man slowly sank to a sitting position. You could tell he was going fast—that deathly waxy yellowish pallor, those eyes gradually blanking out. Word flashed down to the mob waiting for the cable at Market: "Hey, somethin's happenin', Mabel!" They crowded around in their Bermuda shorts and sandals, the fat-bellied natives and tourists, sucking on Frosties and watching the old man die . . . The Traffic Controller up at O'Farrell did a great job with an oxygen mask and tank, but the old man kept fading. Now and then he looked around apologetically, embarrassed to be causing so much trouble. "Stand back!" but the Frisbee-slurpers crowded in. Death in the city! A sympathetic woman put a wet towel on the old man's head. A Fire Dept. crew arrived, all business, cool, sharp. A city ambulance screamed up with its sirens scratching fingernails across your brain . . . "Come on, Harry," a woman in pedal pushers (pedal pushers!) kept saying, tugging at her husband, a dashing figure in his undershirt, "we're gonna miss our cable car." The old man's eyes were closed. The look of death was upon him. The crowd dispersed reluctantly, having denied him the chance to die with dignity. A cable car rattled past, headed halfway to the stars, with Harry and Mabel clinging to the outside step, happy . . . They were having a full day on the old man's last. *June 16, 1976*

Requiem for a dead heavyweight: And so another legendary figure leaves the scene to become part of the San Francisco mythology—that Stonehenge of fact and fancy forever outlined against the Pacific sun. Paul C. Smith, dead at 67 in a Peninsula convalescent home; even those of us who worshiped him, after our own fashion, didn't consider him immortal, but the news still came as a jolt on a sunny Wednesday. Paul, the boy editor who once ran this paper with such dash, the mover and shaker who made this "Paul Smith's town" a generation ago, the bachelor whose parties and extravagance were legendary. He was the protege of Conservative Herbert Hoover and Radical Lincoln Steffens; this accounted for a certain confusion, his romantic fantasy that "I will die in the revolution, caught between the barricades, wondering which side to run to." He would lunch at the Pacific-Union, drink in a saloon with Harry Bridges, make the late rounds with Saroyan and Steinbeck . . . Now it is over, and Wednesday night I looked up at his old Telegraph Hill aerie, above Julius' Castle, and remembered Gertrude Lawrence's laughter, Dorothy Parker's quips, Noel Coward at the piano, Clare Booth Luce floating across the terrace, and Paul, like Gatsby, moving through the crowd, inevitable Scotch and cigarette in hand, smile on face, the center of this heady swirl . . . All of you who are saying "Paul who?" missed a rare experience, a bright and shining San Francisco chapter with a downbeat ending.

June 17, 1976

Summer in the City

Do you remember it, young-timer? I mean "Summer in the City," that fine Big Beat song recorded by one of the best of the early rock bands, the Lovin' Spoonful, back around when—'69? Don't have the album handy, but I suppose John Sebastian wrote it. He did all those super tunes for the Spoonful: "Do You Believe in Magic," "You're a Big Boy Now." I think of "Summer in the City" every year at this time, for there is something Very San Francisco about its spirit of abandon, its raunchiness, its restrained hysteria. Restrained hysteria? A lame oxymoron, true, but I do feel that San Francisco Today is on the verge of a prolonged scream. The constant sirens and screeching brakes and raucous voices are only a prelude to breakdown. Around City Hall they say "the city is cool, daddy," but don't you believe it. Just below the surface, right behind the frustration, under the gloss of glittery decadence, the city is seething.

⋆ ⋆ ⋆

At times like this, when nothing seems to work right, from BART to the Planning Commission to the port to the cable cars, I'm thankful for the tradition, however spurious, that San Franciscans are sophisticated and civilized, deep down. As we, the inheritors of legend, can't seem to get off our duffs and get on with the job of saving the city, neither would we be so gauche as to riot in the streets, or—you know—Make a Fuss. That would be embarrassing, going the little bit too far that just isn't done in Baghdad-by-the-Bay. Not if we are to continue with the great game of pretending we are everybody's favorite run-down-at-the-heels city.

⋆ ⋆ ⋆

"Nostalgia is crying over spilt milk," critic John Simon has observed, but it serves a purpose, especially in this memory-wracked pleasure dome with very definite cracks in the ceiling. We don't even have to look back very far for our jollies, these days. This mild thought struck me when a young man barked at the Park-Rec Commission that "such events are in the great tradition of Golden Gate Park!" He wasn't talking about the Midwinter Fair of '94, or John Philip Sousa playing "Stars and Stripes Forever" in the band concourse—he was talking about the free rock concerts there in the 1960s, and seeking a permit for one next month; in the great tradition of San Francisco Today, he was turned down.

Spilt milk, not yet turning sour; you may have forgotten that the aforementioned Lovin' Spoonful played at a joint on Broadway, circa '67, working for pre-Carter peanuts; they bombed. It was only yesterday, at the hungry i, that Mort Sahl followed Bob Newhart who followed Nichols and May who followed Shelley Berman who followed Lenny Bruce, and we thought it would go on forever. If you want to go back two decades, Mort broke in at the ORIGINAL hungry i, in the cellar of the Columbus Ave. building now owned by Francis Ford Coppola, where he got second billing to a black folk singer named Stan Wilson. Hair was still short, ties were still narrow, but all that shall come back.

By the way, young-timer, a young black pianist played and sang nightly in The Other Room at the hungry i, barely heard over the chatter of dinner conversation and clatter of cutlery. His name: Bobby Short. He wasn't big enough then to get his name up in paint. (The club didn't have a marquee—headliners' names were daubed on the walls).

⋆ ⋆ ⋆

A tricky business, nostalgia. A decade from now, what will we look back on in awe and wonderment, asking where did it all go? It's impossible to know when a Golden Age, or even moment, is taking place, with you smack in the middle of it, but I would venture that nothing much is going on here right now. Except complaints. I was astonished when "The Question Man" column asked seven San Franciscans of various ages, "Has S.F. Changed For Better or Worse?" and got seven "Worse"s. Sample comments: "You don't see children out playing anymore," "Downtown's a bummer," "We're all afraid to go out of the house," "I've been here 54 years and the people, they're different," "Dirty and tacky," "You can blame it all on that last mayor we had, Alioto" . . . Around City Hall, they shuffle papers and scratch heads and say, "What can we do?" Well, for starters, we can make life more pleasant for our most valuable asset, the tourists, standing in line, shivering, for an hour on Powell and Market, waiting for a cable car. Serve them free coffee! Hand out maps! Hire street musicians! Give the ladies a posy! Don't let these visitors just stand there with Fortress Woolworth on one side, vacant Moar's cafeteria on the other, and freaks on all sides.

⋆ ⋆ ⋆

Not that there's anything wrong with slobs, which most of us are, and dirty streets. This is a windy city: in da Nort' Beach voinaculah, da breeze stirs up debris. I was uncharmed the other lunchtime to hear a group of Texans rattle on about "Frisco's dirty streets" and how clean it is in Houston and Dallas because "our people have pride in their cities." They also have more trash containers, no doubt, and less to throw away and no wind to whip it around. At times like that, I'm proud to be part of this community of windswept oddballs, even though our problems are piling up faster than the garbage. We've had golden ages before, maybe another one is right around the corner, and let Houston have clean streets, who cares? *August 8, 1976*

Local angle: Richard Cooley, Pres. of Wells Fargo Bank, had an audience in Madrid recently with King Juan Carlos, and the conversational ice was broken immediately. As Dick started to describe his bank's important role in San Francisco's history, the King smiled, "But I am well aware of both subjects already—I wear a Wells Fargo buckle with my Levi Strauss jeans!"

August 25, 1976

Live and Learn

Far back as I can remember, San Franciscans have prided themselves on this city's cultural and racial diversity, painting pretty pictures of a golden "melting pot" shining with rainbow colors. The facts, of course, have been a little different and not at all pretty; still, the myth persists.

"Tolerance" is an uncomfortable word, but the old-timers imagined themselves to be filled with it, beaming (down) paternally at "our Chinese" at the same time they were ordering "flied lice with beetlejuice" in Chinatown restaurants. Some of the more sensitive Caucasians, or "round-eyes" to the Chinese, may have shuddered and understood why the waiter's smile was thin and cold. The Chinese Exclusion Act and shouts of "The Chinese must go!" weren't all THAT long ago, after all.

The deportation of "our" Japanese Americans after Pearl Harbor put a permanent stain on the flag of freedom. Never before, or since, has an entire race been treated as potential traitors; it is futile to try to make amends, for none will suffice. But we, we enlightened San Franciscans, still think of the Japanese in our midst as "cute," especially when they substitute "r"s for "l"s in their speech.

The way Orientals drive is pretty funny, too. Only a short time back I quoted a Caucasian as saying "If you're not a racist when you drive in Chinatown, you will be by the time you drive out the other end, if you do." There is no shortage of bad Caucasian drivers, but about them we say "What a lousy driver!" When we run into a bad Chinese driver, you may be sure we say CHINESE driver.

* * *

I become depressed when I think about the narrowness of my life in this racially speckled city. Six deadlines a week don't allow much time for getting to know the far streets and distant people of this tiny city—a fact that may also be a copout—but I do know the white-sided Northern slopes. Here, the old-timers speak in code. "The war ruined this city" means too many minorities discovered San Francisco, and "Remember the fun we used to have in the old Fillmore?" means we have too many blacks now, and the streets are dangerous. The phones and the mail bring an endless string of horror stories about "those awful Muni bus drivers," most of whom are black. Most of them are also OK, but you seldom hear about their patience and kindness in the face of a public that can be abusive.

Some of my best friends are black, Oriental, Armenian, check one or all. Also politicians who say "the blacks are making great strides"—mainly to the unemployment line, so far as I can see. "Last hired, first fired" is still the sad fact. Once again, City Hall looks away. You don't have to learn to love your Muni bus driver, but it's a place to start. For both of you.

⋆ ⋆ ⋆

Culture gap. Generation gap. Nationalism in the air, Third World stirring, demanding its fair share. Insensitivity clashing abrasively with sensitivities that surface only when touched by carelessness.

A case in point: an item in this column on September 8 that proved to be insulting to the Samoan community. The item itself does not bear repeating since it was of interest, if at all, to the aforementioned Northern slopes of the city. But my offhand and slighting reference to a 300-pound Samoan insulted all Samoans. For that, and to them, I apologize. The fact that I meant no insult is not mitigating; it merely illustrates the width and depth of my own culture gap. I was doing what I deplore in others: treating people as objects, poking fun at what was not funny.

However, there is a good side. Since that unfortunate item, I have met some of the leaders of the local Samoan community, men of great dignity, and pride in their ancient civilization. The chiefs and ministers are serious, eloquent people. When they speak of the "scar" I have inflicted on the Samoans, I can only hope that it will heal, and soon. They showed me anger, and goodwill, and a world far different from mine. I have a new awareness of and respect for that world.

⋆ ⋆ ⋆

Live and learn. My generation was brought up in a welter of ethnic jokes and ethnic slurs, and we developed thick skins at a tender age. Even in "enlightened" today, ethnic jokes flourish, but the damage is minimal because the targets have become toughened through the years. Most Poles can laugh at Polish jokes because there really is no anti-Polish feeling in this country. Same with Italians, Irish, Swedes, Germans. The Jewish joke seems to have gone out of style, which is not to say that anti-Semitism has disappeared.

Most of us are developing fresh awareness even as San Francisco becomes more and more divided into economic and racial enclaves. Another new code is "neighborhood," as in power and pressure on City Hall. We have a city of minorities, each crying out for a piece of the action. The feeling of oneness, the "We're all San Franciscans" spirit, however shaky its foundations, is disappearing. Our next earthquake may come when all these different factions and races, balanced delicately against each other, come tumbling down.

Mea culpa: I have been as guilty as anyone, and guiltier than some, in keeping alive the cultural stereotypes, but if we lose our sense of humor, we are truly lost. Love and understanding are marvelous virtues, and respect is vital. So is the ability to laugh at one another, and especially at oneself. *September 20, 1976*

My Kind of Town

Nice on these summer-in-October days: the open windows at Le Central, the pleasant Bush St. bistro. Sitting there, toying with an Americano, you can watch the world, especially the world of girls. Passersby stop and chat with the streetside lunchers. Here comes Artist Dong Kingman, carrying his jacket, pausing to smile at Wilkes Bashford. There's Oliver (Hobbs) Merle, of the pioneer family, reaching through the window to shake hands with Chub Feeney, President of the National League. George the Bartender makes an especially good Americano, topping it with an orange slice, a bright color against the purple Campari. George can't stop smiling. "I'm on top of the world!" he exults. "Up on Potrero Hill, we've been celebrating all week." Why? Because their beloved 49ers beat the hated L.A. Rams last Monday night. Life can be sweet. And simple.

★ ★ ★

This is a city of super bartenders and almost unfailingly pleasant waiters and waitresses. I can't prove it, but I've always felt you can tell the caliber of a restaurant by how long the help has been around. Trader Vic has some terrific waiters who've been with him from the start of his legend, and he even knows some of them by name. Jack's, the Poodle Dog, Bardelli's, La Bourgogne and other steady old places keep the same steady old crews. In a world of rapid changes, a little continuity is reassuring.

⋆ ⋆ ⋆

I wandered around the town, playing tourist. The visitors are correct: our streets ARE dirty and we don't have enough trash containers and those we do have seem always to be overflowing. Clean streets are not Priority A on anybody's list, but neither should it take inordinate amounts of time, money and effort to do the job. This is not a subject Mayor Moscone is too interested in, and I agree, it is a bit of a bore. Not a sexy item at all, and my occasional references to it, say the pop psychiatrists, mark me as anal-retentive. I've never been quite sure what that means, but I think I'd rather be retentive than whatever's the opposite.

⋆ ⋆ ⋆

When people ask plaintively about this city, "Isn't anything better than it used to be?" I always start off with the Old Mint at Fifth and Mish'. That's much better than it used to be. Worth a visit, if you don't mind stepping over a few winos fermenting away on the steps. Up the street at Seventh, the Main Post Office: old Federal Heavy at its heaviest, but showing signs of wear. At opposite corners across the street, the Grand Southern Hotel and the Atlanta Hotel—mysterious choice of names, even though this IS South o' Market.

Over at Blanche's on Channel St. at Fourth, the crowd was lined up to the drawbridge. Blanche of the eternal sweet smile, and shrimps almost as sweet. Down below, an old guy in a wide-brimmed hat was balancing on a piling, fishing for shiners. He had a coffee canful. "Whaddya gonna do with 'em?" I called down. "Eat 'em," he gruffed. Not much of a meal. Two blocks away at Fourth and Brannan, the restaurant critics were discovering Ruby's, a fine little eating place devised by Douglas Arrowsmith with his chums. Tasteful in both senses.

I paused on the Fourth St. bridge to look over at the old Southern Pacific station on Third, partially torn down. Its California Mission towers are gone, revealing a carcass of plaster and lathe. Old-timers got sore at me for not helping to "Save the Old SP Station!" but hell it was only a temporary structure in the first place. And the "bells" in the bell tower were made of wood. A friend shot a BB gun at the bells one night to prove it. No clang.

⋆ ⋆ ⋆

Funny old town. Edgar Allan Poe's "Annabelle Lee" is painted on several pillars under the freeway to Second and Harrison, which, as Juliana Davidson says, "is distinctly peculiar." Indeed. Jerry Johnstone, moping over a kebab martini at the Gold Mirror: "San Francisco used to be a melting pot and now kids are smoking it." But what is there to say for a martini kebab, which has an olive, onion, lime, mushroom and pickle on a toothpick, thereby displacing much too much of the precious life-giving juniper? A 4-1 gin martini straight-up, the glass beaded with frost, a perfect green olive glowing at the bottom, is a work of art. All deviations suffer.

* * *

Seeking same, I walked up Tillman Place, past Charlotte Newbegin's dear little bookstore, and found myself in the Templebar. A bit ersatzy—was there ever an excuse for flocked wallpaper?—but not too bad. The guy on my left was saying to an earnest-looking woman, "Of course there is no justice but there IS a telephone company." She nodded dolefully.

When I said "Nice back bar," the bartender took me for a tourist. "Rosewood and birch," he said. "Came around the Horn in the '90s and was saved in the Big Fire." I wonder how many bars that has been said about, usually inaccurately, in San Francisco? He gave me some literature about the old Templebar. Most of the names were misspelled. On the back bar, a bowl of hard-boiled eggs stood alongside a Silex containing coffee strong enough to run a nuclear power plant. I drank my straight-up and left.

"Have a good stay in San Francisco," called out the bartender. Like all good barmen, he looked like he could get you a cab, a girl, a fix, an abortion, a lawyer, a bail bondsman. Anything. The town's not running any too well—you know, streets all dirty and so forth—but it would be worse without old pros like this guy.

October 17, 1976

Nostalgia spoken here: North Beach was a simple place BD (Before Doda). You argued about whether to eat at New Joe's or Vanessi's, or go for a pizza at Lupo's. After that there was a beer at the Red Garter, the Bocce Ball for an operatic aria, cappuccino at Tosca's. If you had tourists in tow, you could astonish them at Finocchio's ("You mean they are all MEN?") or Mona's ("You mean they are all WOMEN?") or the Black Cat ("You mean these are ARTISTS?"). Now the streets are empty when they are not dangerous. And Jack Dupen has decided to close his Red Garter on

Halloween—after 19 years. "The laughing audiences are gone," he sighs; so are his six branches. The Bocce Ball, where such greats as Jess Thomas got their start, is closed while Owner Mario Pieroni makes up his mind whether to renew his lease. "The street has changed," he said yesterday morning. A familiar refrain in the key of gloom. Typical of the older North Beach people, he was sweeping the sidewalk outside the Bocce Ball at 9 a.m. . . . Not that all is lost. Tommaso's, in Lupo's old location, is every bit as good as its predecessor. And over on Montgomery, the venerable Iron Pot is still a warm and friendly bargain—your check is likely to be less than the tab for parking across the street. In the Black Cat days, artists traded paintings for food at the Iron Pot. The paintings are still there and they are still as terrible as the food is good.

October 21, 1976

Nobody asked me, but there should have been more than a two-second pause between the Ch. 7 movie plug, "Look What's Happened to Rosemary's Baby!" and that familiar face beaming, "Hi, I'm Jimmy Carter!" *November 1, 1976*

So It Goes

Skin (human) isn't what it used to be. I mean, it's getting thinner. On the other foot, people's toes seem to be getting longer, the easier to be stepped on. Although there no longer are any majorities around here, minorities are growing daily—each minority is a majority?—and developing the sensitivities of brain surgeons or concert violinists. Well, columnists are a minority, too, and their (my) mission is to enrage as many people as possible without being downright offensive about it. As for my skin, it's exactly what it should be for a columnist—thick-thick-thick.

* * *

Lately, I have been hearing, stridently, from outraged Chico nationalists (one seldom hears from inraged people). "All in fun," I said that Chico is the kind of place where you find Velveeta in the gourmet section of the supermarket, and you wouldn't believe the reaction. "Drop dead" phone calls, cancelled subscriptions, letters pointing out stiffly that Chico now has SEVERAL supermarkets and what's wrong with Velveeta anyway unless said columnist is an un-American closet gay addicted to French cheeses?

★ ★ ★

Since the subject has turned serious, undoubtedly there are all sorts of excellent Velveeta recipes. Velveeta frostees, Velveeta fondue, Velveeta shreddies, Velveeta surprise (this contains no Velveeta) come immediately to mind, titillating palate and epiglottis alike. Besides, Chico is a pretty, thriving community. Little-known bare fact: there is nude bathing in upper Bidwell Park, where, almost 40 years ago, Errol Flynn and Olivia de Velveeta filmed the Sherwood Forest scenes for the immortal "Robin Hood." Sex fact: According to the October, 1976, issue of Playboy, Chico State University ranks No. 4 nationally in "scoring," a term that does not refer to football. And finally, a business fact from the loyal KPAY disc jockey Joe Garrett: Chico has the only store in the country specializing in the repair of overheated pacemakers.

★ ★ ★

Now that we have assuaged Chico's thin-skinned long-toes, let us turn on Bakersfield. Anita Brown says she was thinking about moving there from S.F. till she sent for a Bakersfield Chamber of Commerce brochure and found "Shakey's Pizza Parlor" listed under "Italian Restaurants."

★ ★ ★

Along with the ethnics whom I seem to offend daily without even trying, I have also had some flack from Colma, which is odd since although that town's population is about 1.5 million, only about 500 are alive, the others being safely or otherwise interred in cemeteries. What exercised the presumably living Colma thin skins was our tale of a "Colma à la Carte" cooking contest held at a local gathering, the winner being Debbie Sanguinetti for her hamburgers with peanut butter centers and tuna pancakes. ("Colma à la Carte" is not to be confused with "Chico Chic" or "Bakersfield Bravura.") At any rate, I apologize to all Colmans, including the late Ronald, especially since Valentina Degenhardt of Bolinas has found an even better "Colma à la Carte" recipe on the side of a Nabisco Shredded Wheat Box. It's for "Broil'ems," as follows: "Split 4 Shredded Wheat biscuits, add mustard, 1/4 cup butter or margarine, melted, 1 can luncheon meat, 1 8-ounce package processed American cheese (what, no Velveeta?), canned peach halves, drained and chilled, jelly." Then, I guess, you "Broil'em"! I don't know what it tastes like but it sounds like grounds for dissolution.

★ ★ ★

Nota Bene: Next time you're in Colma, with a loved or deceased one, do not fail to drop in at Molloy's, one of the last of the great Irish saloons, established in 1892 and owned by the Molloy family to this day. With only 500 live ones and a million stiffs in the neighborhood, you'd think the place would have gone out of business years ago, but, says Bartender Patrick Maguire (what else), "We are thriving." For many years, the sign on the ancient roof proclaimed "Coattails Molloy's," a name that became famous and was thought to be a colorful nickname from the old line: "He ran so fast I could have dealt cards on his coattails." Actually, the sign originally read "Cocktails" but an odd State law, post-repeal, forbade the public use of such horrid words, so Mr. Molloy thriftily changed the third and fourth letters and thereby entered the mystical world of lore and fable. On a foggy night, with wraiths weaving among the gravestones, "Coattails'" is the place to head for, even if they're fresh out of hamburgers with peanut butter centers.

December 3, 1976

★ ★ ★

1977

★ ★ ★

Tuesday night in Ghirardelli Square. Patricia Hearst and her lawyer, Albert Johnson, shadowed by two bodyguards, enter the Sea Witch for a drink. The shadows, looking around vigilantly, take a table behind them. Singer Dianne Grilley asks if anybody in the audience would care to step onstage and sing. With a smiling glance at Ms. Hearst and the bodyguards, Johnson takes the mike and sings—"Me and My Shadow." *January 14, 1977*

For the driver with the most panache, Bonnie Mills nominates the owner of the yellow Mercedes 450 SL bearing the license plates "IRS BOO." *January 24, 1977*

"Now I know why you're always broke," needled Financial Planner Phil Fein yesterday. He was referring to my lead item—about your Pacific Telephone bill arriving with "Federal Excise Tax Reduced From 6 percent to 5 percent" printed on the envelope, while inside was a notice that the S.F. tax on phones had been raised from 5 percent to 6 percent. "At least we come out even," I commented sagaciously, at which Fein snickers, "Like hell. From 6 percent to 5 percent is a 16 2/3 percent reduction, while a jump from 5 percent to 6 percent is a 20 percent increase. Las Vegas gets rich on people like you."

★ ★ ★

Droughtwatch! Or, some more exciting ways to save water, toilets and your marriage: Don't walk your dog; teach your dog to walk you. Don't wash your hair under the shower; send it to Meader's to be dry-cleaned. Brush your teeth twice a year, see your dentist twice a day. Wash your car with Gordon's quick-drying gin. Replace your lawn with AstroTurf. Drink Scotch on pet rocks. Fill your swimming pool with raspberry Jell-O. Perform a vasectomy on your creeping ranunculi. Don't wash your hands after not going to the bathroom. Use paper plates and plastic utensils; turn your dishwasher into a terrarium. Remember that a camel can go seven days without a drink; you, too, can be dumb, ugly and smelly. And finally, Roger Kovach's immortal suggestion: "Do not throw the bathwater out with the baby!" *January 28, 1977*

Was your phone jumping off the hook yesterday morning? So was mine, with calls from Igor Bivor and others who wanted to be first to report that the "Thank You Coral Sea" sign at the West entrance to the Broadway Tunnel has been cleverly altered to read "Thank You Oral Sex"; for those of you who just arrived from Ulan Bator, Sup. Quentin Kopp had those signs erected at either end of the tunnel to thank the men of the USS Coral Sea for stringing an aerial through the tunnel so your car radio shouldn't go dead for all of 11 seconds, thereby causing you to miss part of a Desenex commercial. *February 4, 1977*

Bagatelle: Riding the Muni isn't always a muniserable experience. Take the word of Barry Beeker, who was aboard a No. 19 Polk jammed with wall-to-wall people and, in the rear, the obligatory sullen dude playing a radio with the volume turned up to 10. Lots of muttering and dirty looks from the other passengers, but no action. At last the man seated next to the oaf commented "Nice radio. Care to sell it?" No reply. "No, I mean it," persisted the other, producing a $20 bill. "I'll give you 20 bucks for that radio." With a shrug, the dude handed it over and took the money. The purchaser then slid open the window and tossed the radio into the street, as casually as though he were flipping a cigarette butt. If there's a Muni Passenger of the Month, he's it.

February 9, 1977

High and Dry

"Everybody talks about the weather," etc., etc., as Mark Twain is alleged to have said, and thus a miracle has occurred. At least in the local media. You might recall that before the drought became so obvious that even politicians, Governors and editors were able to recognize it, everybody in San Francisco talked about—the crime wave. Remember The Great Crime Wave of '77? Oh, you couldn't open a newspaper or turn on the televidiots without hearing how San Francisco had become "Crime Capital of the U.S.!," or world, as the case or deadline may be. Charts were published, policemen were shifted about, police cars were repainted in a last-ditch effort, and psychologists granted long interviews to open-mouthed and/or adenoidal reporters, expounding on the "violence factor," crime as "political statement" and murder as "the ultimate acting-out of deep-seated urban hostilities." Until I read that I thought of murder as some friendly act—such as a bear hug or slap on the back with a blunt instrument—carried to extremes.

* * *

A callow journalistic fellow, and I blush, said something accidentally sensible back in 1937. When I ran a piece in The Chronicle about an incident that had occurred two months earlier, one of the principals needled, "Some scoop—that story is stale, kid," to which I riposted hotly, "Nothing is news until it's printed." (I believe that even today; I may "see" a story on the telly, but I don't really believe it till I read it in a newspaper.) As you may or may not have noticed, the crime wave is gone from the front pages. As a celebrity is someone who is well-known for being well-known, a crime wave that can generate no publicity becomes a nonevent and may even have been "solved." You may be mugged, slugged, burgled or even shot tonight, but if this unhappy event is not recorded in tomorrow's paper, it never happened.

* * *

My prescience is that of a mole at midnight in the Mississippi mud, but even I could see the Great Drought of '77 coming along, as the world's greatest crime wave was hogging the headlines. It was obvious to anyone this side of a TV weatherman that it had not rained for some time, but the rattlebrains kept rattling on about "another beautiful day." Three months ago I sat in a North Beach restaurant and murmured to a Supervisor, as a busboy filled our water glasses to overflowing, "When is someone going to declare an emergency?" "What emergency?" he scoffed. "Don't print this but between you and me San Francisco has enough water for the next two years at least and I got that straight from a Hetch Hetchy engineer." Maybe he meant two months, but even as he spoke I had visions of dried-up lakes and cocktail waitresses dead of thirst alongside wateringholes, their legs in the air, dollar bills still folded around their stiffened fingers.

★ ★ ★

The crisis, as even Gov. Less S. More has taken to calling it, is producing a predictable reaction. The media are busily discovering Things They Never Knew Till Now (when it's too late) about conservation and waste. Good People, who may make up a slim majority, have long since been cutting down voluntarily on water consumption, and urging laggards to do likewise. The wasters continue to waste—but ours not to criticize or condemn those poor souls, the victims of generations of Hard Sell in the Disposable Kingdom. In The Chronicle's men's room, I marvel at the guys who wash their already clean hands for five minutes, an exercise that would have fascinated Dr. Freud, and then rip off six paper towels when one would do the job. Around the town, thickheaded individuals and corporations continue to wash down their sidewalks till the water runs in Johnstownian floods toward the corner drains, and shrubs drown in enough water to service half of north Larkspur.

★ ★ ★

And then—another typical reaction in times of emergency—there are the jokes, tending heavily toward the scatological. This has offended some fastidious readers who cannot bear to think of themselves as, in the words of George Bernard Shaw, "human fertilizer machines." Never have I received so many letters containing every possible permutation of the words yellow, mellow, brown and down. At last count, 211. The new Marin County "wine," Poodoo Pinot, has made its way around the world as a witticism to be reckoned with. In the first flush of the crisis, I printed more of these jokes than are strictly necessary, and I blush. Nevertheless, the sheer number suggests that people are now well aware of the great water-wasters—toilet, dishwasher, clothes washer—and that may be a step ahead. The outhouse, decorated by your favorite interior designer, may be in for a revival, with a Chic Sale crescent on the door.

★ ★ ★

As the drought worsens, the nastier manic-regressives are also doing what comes naturally—blaming the Marin water crisis on conservationists, "bird-watchers," Sierra Clubbers and the like. This of a piece with outcries that Dow Chemical decided against building a $300 million chemical polluter across the Bay because "eco-freaks" opposed it. The environmentalists have been warning for years that resources are finite, that the planet is as fragile as a Ming vase, and that we had better mend our profligate ways—and nothing has come along to prove them wrong yet. Meanwhile, isn't it nice that the crime wave has ended? *March 13, 1977*

Good morning, and did you feel better after reading yesterday that a bill to restore the death penalty in California passed the State Assembly by the two-thirds majority necessary to override Gov. Brown's veto? If so, congratulations. It appears you are a member of the majority in this state, so don't be silent. Speak up! Cheer, dance in the streets, buy a round of drinks. You have just taken a giant step—backward.

Law enforcement is messy, prisons are messier, and the death penalty is the messiest of all to administer. No matter how the law is worded, no matter how strongly you may feel that it is all right there in the Bible (eye for an eye and other hogwash), some murderers will be executed and others will survive. The murder rate, as has been shown repeatedly, will not decline. It may, in fact, go up. Even you may find yourself in that little green room, strapped atop the eggs of death. If you think you aren't capable of murder, you're living in a dream world. Time, place, opportunity, motive—that's all it takes.

Capital punishment is a dark, dismal and dirty spectacle, performed in medieval secrecy. The public cries for blood but doesn't want to look at it. As a young police reporter for the Sacramento Union, I saw three men hanged by their necks until they were very dead at Folsom Prison. On each occasion, most of the witnesses, many of whom had volunteered, some of whom made nervous jokes before the event, fainted dead away after the trap had been sprung and the body dangled broken-necked at eye level. They could not face up to the brutal reality. We all came away from the prison feeling degraded.

The road to civilization has many twists and turns. At the moment, California has backed itself into an old dead end. And not one of us is a whit safer than we were day before yesterday.

May 18, 1977

Deep Purple

As I let the car engine warm up on this cool gray morning I flipped the radio to KMPX and there was Benny Goodman playing on that 1938 black Victor of "Don't Be That Way." Mind and motor idling, eyes in the middle distance, I found myself sinking into yesterday, taking that familiar old ride with the world's greatest swing band. Benny, Harry, Ziggy, Gene, Jess—they sounded as bright and saucy as the day the record was made. Playing with his customary dash, the good Dr. James did a twisting turning takeoff on the bridge. The band started into that long series of repeats, diminuendo, and I pulled over into a parking place alongside Lafayette Park, waiting for Krupa's startling single stroke roll. Once again, he played it flawlessly, ending with a triumphant bass drum boot, and the best brass section ever put together shrilled and trilled the final chorus.

* * *

I turned off the radio, lost in 1938. Terminal nostalgia, the San Francisco disease, had me in its death grip. Simply by squinting, I could ride the time machine 40 years into the past. A proper nanny, pushing a proper English pram, paraded up a pathway in the park, her head high. A woman in a classic gray felt hat—Dobbs?—and gray suit, early Chanel, walked a Schnauzer. Peeping across the street, I let my eyes sweep only so far, from the McGinnis mansion to the Magowan to the Spreckels and then up to the pink walls of the old apartment house where Bunker Vincent could stroll through his own garden a dozen stories in the sky, with a view to all creation. It's a game I play constantly, looking past the present into the past, eyes inching along.

When they pick up the distant point of the Transamerica Pyramid the game is over and I have lost.

* * *

Nostalgia. An ugly word for an ignoble weakness. There's that hint of neuralgia, which is only a short step from neurotic; nostalgia is a pain in the neck. The San Franciscan is born with it, heavy with hand-me-down memories by the time he's a dozen years ago. "Remember when—" is the beginning of too many sentences that start early and end in an alcoholic haze. I coined another ugly word once—"nostalcoholic"—in an effort to describe all of us who suffer from one of the city's 10 leading diseases, right up there along with cirrhosis, runny sinuses and a slight deafness from the banging of dice on bars.

★ ★ ★

There are those, and their number is growing, who refuse to live in the San Francisco past—that warm, snug place where everyone is young, there is such a thing as a free lunch, and the ferryboats were made of gingerbread, the girls of spice and gardenias. These strong people have broken the nostalgia habit and go around insisting that "things are better than ever"; since their motto is "Never Look Back," they do not know they are echoing Dr. Emile Coue, the Werner Erhard of the 1920s, whose incantation, echoed by thousands of devotees, was "Day by day, in every way, I am getting better and better." To those who have kicked the nostalcoholic habit, the Pyramid is our Parthenon, Irish Coffee our champagne from a slipper, and the nearest pickup bar preferable to the velvet madness of those upstairs dining rooms in the French restaurants. Who cares indeed that Oysters Kirkpatrick were invented at the Palace Hotel?

★ ★ ★

"People who are hung up on nostalgia," scoffs Victor Vecsey, "are banal-retentives." Tom Cahill, another flint-heart, says flippantly that "Nostalgia is a thing of the past," and I laugh weakly, know I am beyond redemption, a cancelled stamp on the packet of life. Merely to read, as I did the other day, that Rough Rider, maker of men's pants, has gone into bankruptcy, and I go into a funk. When I was in high school, we all wore Rough Rider corduroys, golden, cut to fit, as perfect as Gatsby's shirts. Then we got them gradually and evenly dirty until they were stiff enough to stand in a corner by themselves, smelling of puppy dogs. For some reason, it was de rigueur to wear the cleanest, whitest and starchiest shirt with these filthy pants, each sleeve rolled up exactly two turns, no more, no less. The long collar was worn open, in the style of Barrymore or Warren William. Only a fraternity pin could be worn for adornment, and that on the upper right-hand corner of the shirt pocket, NOWHERE ELSE. We were banal-anal-retentive, but since we didn't know it it still hurts.

★ ★ ★

San Francisco, city of deep purple shadows just around the corner from the latest high-rise that may lower the tax rate but does nothing to lift our hearts. It was a city of beautiful long-legged girls screaming on the Big Dipper at the beach after a night of dancing at the Mark or the Frantic and necking under Coit Tower as the amber lights of the Bay Bridge reached across dark waters that lapped against piers where white ships slumbered at the end of romantic voyages. It was a silky, Cole Porterish, Noel Cowardly, after-hours, giddy kind of city, and to have loved it once, unwisely and too well, is to love it forever, even if it means being a pain in the neck about it. But if it hurts to look back, think what there isn't to look forward to. *May 29, 1977*

"What Would You Change About San Francisco?" was The Chronicle Question Man's quizzer a few days ago, and Michael Oesterman replied, "The street signs. Why can't they all be in the same place and the same size?" A neat idea, observes Strange de Jim, who suggests we make them all eight feet by 10 feet and put them at California and Montgomery. *August 7, 1977*

Mission Implausible

Last Friday afternoon I tried to fly to Lake Tahoe from San Francisco International Airport, which is a suburb of San Bruno, and found myself on a bus to Oakland. This proves that Fate, the old crone, still has a few tricks up her tattered sleeve. Also that the best laid plans of mice and men gang aft agley, a Scottish proverb which, like haggis, is not worth thinking about too long.

The drama began to unfold when I checked in at the Air California counter for the 4 p.m. flight. Just getting to the counter is a triumph in itself, since San Bruno International Airport, a make-work project that will never be completed, is definitely a carbuncle on the neck of civilization. One wrong turn and you're in the garage, never to be heard of again. Two wrong turns and you've made the Grand Circle Tour and are back on the freeway. Stop and you get a ticket.

Devout coward that I am, I always give my car to Valet Parking since the first and last time I went into the garage I spent three days there, going up and down ramps. Valet Parking always gives the car back, eventually, so it cannot be said that nothing works.

* * *

"Have a nice day?" I said at the AirCal desk. I though I'd finesse the counter girl by saying it first, but it was no good: "It's not a nice day. The plane from Tahoe is in Oakland with engine trouble. We're going to bus all of you over there. No, we don't know how long it will take." Why not bring another plane? "Our other two planes are already in the air," she said (actually AirCal has a dozen planes, but only a few of the prop jobs that are allowed into no-jet Tahoe).

I did what I always do in such moments of stress. I ran for the newsstand and bought an espionage book. With some people, it's junk food. With me, it's junk books. ("I don't understand," I said, looking down at Pierre's dead body. "He didn't have an enemy in the world." "He had one," said the Inspector.) I grabbed the only suspenser I haven't read—something called "Double Cross, Triple Agent," by somebody called Simmel. At a riffle, it seemed to have something to do with spies going back and forth through tunnels under The Wall between East and West Berlin. "What kind of assignment?" "We mean to find out, Fraulein Szapek. That affair in Vienna—we know all about it—was phony. As for Herr Scharowski, he was a rocket specialist who'd spent many years in the Soviet Union and . . . "

OK. Familiar terrain.

* * *

Back at AirCal, people were either milling about or streaking for phones. Malcolm "Nappy" MacNaughton Jr. of Woodside, and his wife, the delectable Liza Jane, were busy chartering a private plane to Tahoe. "Want to come with us?" he asked. "The plane is on its way from Bakersfield." "Sorry, Nappy," I said with simple dignity. "My place is with the people." "I understand, old man," he nodded, clutching my arm. "Good hunting."

We filed into the bus. To Oakland. I remembered my last visit there, when someone had hit me in the face with a custard pie as I emerged from a Chinese restaurant, down the street from the Tribune Tower. Not a bad custard pie, at that. The tower was leaning to the right, as usual.

The bus driver stepped on the throttle and the engine died. "This trip is full of good omens," somebody sighed. We inched into the rush hour traffic toward the Bay Bridge, and I began reading. "It had been a long time since Bruno Knolle had first met Nelly in the ruins of Berlin . . . "

At which point the guy in the adjoining seat, smelling of booze, began muttering at me. He talked in unfunny one-liners. "Why is he drivin' dat way? Why isn't he usin' the Sammateo Bridge? Why dinn he take the 280 cutoff, ferkrissakes? Country's goin' to hell. Nothin' works any more. Willya lookit the traffic ahead? Bumpa to bumpa. Say . . . how come you don't say nothin'? You too good to talk t'me?" I looked up from my book. "OK," I said, "whaddya wanna talk about?" "Now dere's a smottass answer," he said. "Boy, I hope I don't sit next ta YOU on da plane. Watta you, a mute, or somethin'?"

I nodded mutely.

* * *

Oakland Airport, just South of an Adult Motel. A pretty place, jammed with people who have cornered the Aloha shirt market. A lot of people who shouldn't be wearing shorts were. I went to the bar and said, "Heineken's, please." "Only got Coors," said the bartender. Figures. When you drink Coors, you are making a political and sexual statement. You are telling the world you are an anti-union heterosexual. "Vodka tonic," I said, and the bartender gave me a look, trying to decide if I was a union gay.

I walked over to a Pong table and sat with Andy and Sandy and Herb and Pat, wonderful people. On their way to catch John Denver. "I really can't hack this trip," confided Andy, "but when Sandy came down for breakfast a couple of days ago wearing a T-shirt reading, 'Won't Somebody Take Me to Hear John Denver?' what could I do?" For the next hour, we played four-way Pong, at four bits a pop. Nolan Bushnell, inventor of Pong, was getting richer by the minute and he's already living on Pete Folger's big old estate in Woodside.

Our flight was called, three and half hours late, but who cares? An ennobling experience. Nappy MacNaughton's chartered plane arrived only 10 minutes before we. And the espionage book isn't half bad, especially the part about the fat woman getting stuck in the escape tunnel. *August 30, 1977*

Personalized license plates have room for only six characters, wherefore I recently saluted the holder of "UNIRB9" for squeezing the most syllables into the space. However, Doug Griffith can top that with a legitimate six-worder in six letters, on a car presumably headed for a Shakespeare Festival: "2BRO2B" . . . As for the plate on Broker Jay Schiffman's Mercedes—"YUKFOO"—he insists that's an ancient Oriental incantation given to him by three Chinese sisters over a cup of ginseng tea. *September 9, 1977*

Matters of Style

Mister Eckhard, the Fairmont's renowned hair stylist, stared at me critically. A hair stylist is a barber who charges over union scale, calls himself "Mister," and goes on ski holidays. As for the critical look, I always get that from Mister Eckhard. Secretly, he feels that I don't have enough hair to bother with, and what I do have grows the wrong way, but this time he appeared concerned about my sideburns. "It iss time zey vent," decided Mister Eckhard, who is German, tall, slender and possessed of a full head of hair—definitely an overachiever. Before I could protest that "Some of us have to grow it where we've got it," he had whipped out his straight razor. Thwick. Thwack. Gone were the sideburns. Gone was the "now" look cultivated so assiduously by this "then" person. After the shock had worn off, I stole a glance at myself in the mirror, and had to admit I felt more like me than I had in years. Once again I was hep and not ashamed to show it. No longer would I have to try to look hip.

* * *

All the foibles, fashions and fads we all live through in a life studded with anxious rapture. (Never stand in front of a three-way mirror—you'll discover that not only has somebody been gaining on you, you've been left behind.) Overage guinea pigs, we have been manipulated into acting out everybody else's fantasies. Clothes, hair, cars, "lifestyles" (awful word), language, even the way we stood or sat—all these things became symbols. We let our hair grow longer, if possible, to show we identified with the grass-puffing, free-loving kids who snickered at us. We wore jeans and opened our shirts to the Top of the Potbelly to demonstrate we were free souls when we were just the opposite. If we were largely bald, we let our sideburns creep down to our jowls. We were signaling our mistaken belief that redneckism and crew cuts are indivisible. It took a bumper sticker on a raunchy van—"Long Hair Does Not Cover a Redneck"—to tell us how wrong we were. Hair, patchouli, dirty denims and jewelry no longer were passwords. Never in history have so many crucifixes been worn by atheists dancing in discos, and badly. For the squares, it's back to square one.

* * *

Middle-aged swingers—what a sad and touching sight, with their thinning hair combed East and West, instead of North and South, as God intended. One hour a week in the stylist's chair at $35 a pop, patted, powdered, blowered and sprayed, with the result that, in Fran Lebowitz's cruelly accurate observation, "they all look like

Alan King." Even Alan King doesn't want to look like Alan King, but he does, an explosion of doubleknit swank, polyestered puffery and white shoes. Gold necklace, pinky ring, gas guzzler car, and wife to match, in Tourmaline mink. It was only yesterday that people like this epitomized Making It the American Way, but yesterday happened a long time ago. What makes it poignant is that these are NICE people.

★ ★ ★

At a gaming table in Tahoe's Nevada Club a weekend ago stood a doubleknit hairstyled man wearing patent leather shoes. Printed in black paint on the right shoe was "UP" and on the left, "CAEN." Said Dapper Dave Falk, Vice-Pres. of Grodin's, to this forthright fellow, "Let me buy you a drink—that Caen killed the white shoe business in San Francisco." If the shoe fits, wear it, as long as it's black or brown, always remembering the British nobleman who warned, "Never brown in town."

★ ★ ★

As I recall it, the so-called peacock revolution among men was started about 10 years ago by designers who had been spending all their time making women look silly. Now it was the men's turn. We who made fun of women for raising and lowering their hemlines at someone else's whim now began doing a similar number. Before you could say Bill Blass, we were wearing lapels out to our shoulders, shirts with collars that rose to our earlobes, and ties as wide as bibs. Flared pants, high heels, platform soles, fake fur trenchcoats, suede jockstraps—there was nothing that could not be stuffed up or down our gullible throats. We went to "Hair" and "Grease," learned to tell Neil Diamond from Barry Manilow (actually, they're the same person), puffed grass, and suddenly discovered we were a majority. The minority turned out to be those who stuck to their gunboat shoes, skinny ties and Brooks Brothers suits, and maybe they were right all along. There are no more symbols. Revolt today consists of jaywalking, riding skateboards the wrong way on one-way streets, and sauntering disdainfully against the "Don't Walk" sign. Big deal.

★ ★ ★

It has been a rough crossing, but perhaps we are back in smug harbor. Thanks to the taste and leadership of Wilkes Bashford, men's clothes once again look like—men's clothes, better designed (and more expensive) than ever. The designers can rededicate themselves to making women look like anything but. I've riffled through the new Vogue, fellow legmen, and the miniskirt is not coming back. We're getting boots, baggy skirts and something even more atrocious called "the layered look," under which there may or may not be a female person. Me, I'm off to Mister Eckhard to have my ears lowered. That's the way we used to describe haircuts in Sacramento, a million fads ago. *September 11, 1977*

A slice of wry: It was 10 years ago that a brash 21-year-old named Jann Wenner launched Rolling Stone magazine here in a tiny office on Brannan St.—a success story of such magnitude that on Nov. 25, CBS will present a two-hour TV special titled "Rolling Stone: The Tenth Anniversary." Among the fantastic superstars who'll appear, along with the now 31-year-old Wenner, will be Bette Midler, Donny Osmond, Jerry Lee Lewis, L.A. Police Chief Ed Davis(!), Lesley Warren, Melissa Manchester, one of the Beach Boys—and—nobody from San Francisco, where it all began. No Jefferson Starship ("We're too busy recording"). No Grateful Dead ("Complications"). No Boz Scaggs ("Just wouldn't work out"), no Steve Miller, no Bill Graham . . . When Wenner moved his magazine operation to N.Y. earlier this year, various of his aides were quoted as saying "San Francisco has become a backwater" and "San Francisco had sort of played itself out as a center of cultural change." Wenner disowns these statements, but the suspicion remains. And besides, when you can get Police Chief Davis, who needs Grace Slick? There's cultural change for you.

October 3, 1977

It happened a Saturday or two ago in a large dark downtown bldg. which houses a big and powerful corporation. A young man and woman, among the handful working that day, began commiserating about their sad Saturday fate; as one thing led to another, they ended up, as it were, on the sofa in the women's powder room—and were caught in flagrante delicioso by the young feller's wife. By Monday afternoon, the story reached command level, where it was decided that a firing was in order. By corporate decision, the sofa was discharged—unbolted and carried out as being overly conducive to lying down on the job. *October 19, 1977*

One Day in the City

At 6:03 a.m., Bobby G., a stockbroker, arises in his elegant Steiner St. apartment, squints out the window at the Dow Jones sinking in the West, and crawls back into bed. Seven minutes later, a middle-aged squirrel, known to his friends as Red, scampers across John F. Kennedy Drive in Golden Gate Park, is hit by a milk truck, dies instantly; friends are asked to contribute to the Society for the Prevention of Trucks. At 6:30, a kid puts a quarter in a Chronicle vending box on Van Ness, takes out all the papers, and sells them to people to use as rain hats while waiting for the bus. Ten minutes later, Stephanie M., having had a fight with her doctor-lover in Sausalito, stops her sportscar in the middle of the Gate Bridge, puts up the top and starts singing Gershwin's "Who Cares?" At 6:59 a.m., a kid carrying a baseball bat pauses in front of a car parked at 11th and Folsom, sets himself like Reggie Jackson, smashes a headlight and trots off to circle the bases, waving his cap.

★ ★ ★

At 7:05 a.m., a lawyer has breakfast at Sears with a labor leader who is about to be indicted, picks up the tab, and adds $100 to his fee for "consultation." Five minutes later, a dentist drinks three cups of coffee with shaking hand before going to the 450 Sutter Bldg. to make a tricky extraction that doesn't come out right. At 7:20, a gull known as Sam dives into the Bay after a shiner that turns out to be a beer can tab and tries to regain his perch with dignity in the face of birdcalls from his gull friends. Three minutes later, a teenager nicknamed Dee pauses on her way to George Washington High to light her first marijuana cigarette of the day, inhales deeply, exhales "Paaah!"

★ ★ ★

At 8:03 a.m., a jogger swings around a corner at Green and Webster, knocks a kid off his skateboard and keeps going with a panted "Sorry." On a Geary St. bus, Emil L. arises, tips his fedora and offers his seat to Ruby B., who gasps "I can't believe it—is this some kinda dream or somethin'?" A scavengers' truck stops outside the Jackson St. mansion of the W's, who had a big party the night before, and the crew finds enough leftover champagne for a slight buzz. On Sixth St., Myrtle J., lady of the night, starts her day with a beer and a belch and studies herself in the mirror with distaste; "Aw shuddup" she mutters at the radio as the late Clancy Hayes sings "I Wish I Was in Peoria" with the late Bob Scobey's band.

★ ★ ★

At 9:11 a.m., a bitter ex-member of the Pacific-Union Club looks at the flagpole and curses because the flag is not at half-staff. On the Taylor St. hill, a tourist from Peoria, in an Olds 88, panics as the light turns red, kills his engine and has a fight with his wife that lasts through three light changes. At the same moment, a side of beef falls off a meat truck on Vallejo in North Beach and is immediately dragged away by a small but surprisingly strong Chinese. At 9:29, a City Hall politico breakfasting with his secretary in the Fairmont Brasserie cautions her as he leaves, "Don't return the key to the desk—just drop it in a mailbox." Joey F., cutting school, dribbles a basketball across the lonely yard at St. Dominic's, executes a perfect layup and shouts "Awrrrrright!" to an uncaring world.

★ ★ ★

At 11:11 a.m., the line begins forming outside Mama's in Macy's basement. Under Market St., a tourist from Peoria puts a dollar bill in BART's change-making machine, gets stiffed and gives the machine a kick, scuffing his Hush Puppies. Three minutes later, at Geary and 42nd Ave., a kid who says he's a Boy Scout helps a Little Old Lady across the street, grabs her handbag at the center divider, and runs off through heavy traffic. In Union Square at noon, a Little Old Man tries to entice a pigeon into a paper bag even though he has long heard that they are too tough to eat and he is toothless anyway. The bells of Grace Cathedral float out over the city like a benediction nobody deserves.

★ ★ ★

At Olympic Lakeside, a fat contractor who saved his money for a rainy day is spending a rainy day at the bar—alone. In the Stockton Tunnel seven minutes later, a kid whips out his Magic Marker, scrawls "F—— You" on the wall, spits, looks relieved. At 1:17 p.m., a young stockbroker unbuttons his vest and takes off his Brooks Bros. hat as he enters a steam bath to meet his good friend for a box lunch. Two minutes later, an aging lawyer and a Pacific Ave. divorcee duck into the side entrance of the St. Francis and take the outside elevator to a suite his office rents for visitors from Peoria and elsewhere. At 3:15 in Cal Mart Super, a woman 20 pounds overweight grabs an It's It, unwraps it like a junkie and gulps it down in a few sharklike bites, stuffing the wrapping into her $150 I. Magnin handbag so she won't get charged.

⋆ ⋆ ⋆

At Powell and Market, a pretty young girl pleads "Any spare change?" to a truckdriver who says "Plenty, but you'll have to work your ——— off for it," and she shrugs. Up the street, a cable car pauses so the conductor can rub the meter maid's chalk mark off his parked car. In a booth at Sam's, the Mayor shakes dice expertly for the check, wins easily, saunters out. At Blanche's, the gull known as Sam snatches three shrimp off Herbert G.'s plate. At dusk, a Russian freighter clears the Gate, the crew looking back with longing as the city begins to light up for the long night. Sam the gull sniffs the Soviet's wake and wheels back toward Fisherman's Wharf. *January 22, 1978*

Aloha: It is slowly dawning on a number of people that when PFEL's SS Mariposa ends its current cruise in April and joins the already retired SS Monterey, there will no longer be any passenger ship service between here and Honolulu. End of an era, and all that, especially for oldish-timers who remember the glamor and excitement of "Ship Day," pop of champagne corks in staterooms aboard the gleaming white Matsonia and Lurline, suntanned beauties standing on the stern to throw their orchid leis overboard as the ships headed back to Fogdad-by-the-Bay. There was even a pretty legend: if the lei floated ashore, she would return some day to rejoin her lover on the sands of Waikiki . . . Making love in the sand is high among life's overrated pleasures, such as breakfast in bed and reading in the bathtub, but that is indeed another story. *February 3, 1978*

New Worlds: A lot of people have asked whether I believe in biorhythms, and honey 'deed I do. In fact, I asked John W. Snider of Medford, Ore., a recognized authority, to prepare my Computerized Biorhythm Chart for March, since February is such a bummer, and it just arrived. I will bore you only with what he underlines as Double Critical Days:

March 9th: You will pass a kidney stone the size of a duck egg. Plan on screaming a lot that day.

13th: You will be found dead in a sleazy motel with the Queen of England. Expect some unfavorable publicity over this incident.

16th: You will be trampled by a herd of wild goats. Try not to laugh any more than you have to while this is happening because goats are easily infuriated if they think they are being ridiculed.

22nd: Today would be a good day to assume the fetal position and spend the entire day under your bed. Ignore this warning and you will find yourself stark naked in a cheese factory in Pennsylvania.

24th: Everything falls into place for you today. It will be a smashing day to rob a bank, take out your own appendix or tell the Internal Revenue Service to go screw itself.

30th: Today is a good day to avoid people who get mad when they lose at Russian roulette.

I think I'll take March off. *February 24, 1978*

'The City'—In Quotes

The fog, always the fog, "gray and opaque as a roll of undeveloped film" (Anon.). It crept in "on little cat feet" (Sandburg) and mushroomed along Robert Louis Stevenson's "citied hills" above the Bay—"an immense arm of the sea which penetrated into the land as far as the eye could see" (Padre Juan Crespi). Padre Crespi goes back to the very beginning of the city, when the principal occupants were Costanoan Indians whose big 18th century hit—and very contemporary it sounds—was a song titled "Dancing on the Brink of the World."

The fog, "like the cold breath of old men" (V.S. Pritchett), devoured the Golden Gate Bridge, "the car-strangled spanner" (Anon.). "Why are the bridge towers so high, father?" asked the small boy. Replied the father: "So the red lights on top can be seen by airplanes, my son." The old finger piers far below jutted out "like black dogs standing knee-deep in the water." The revolving light on "America's Devil's Island" was blotted out. Not even "a dime's worth of sunlight" trickled through.

All that could be heard, reverberating above the lonely bleating of the horns, was "the man-city and its snarling roar" (Jack London). "Somewhere a long time ago summer ended," wrote William S. Burroughs in "Port of Saints," a book not about this port of sinners in "a city that has lost its soul" (Billy Graham on his first visit, sounding like Anita Bryant).

* * *

I walk down Kearny, street of small stores, restaurants, fringes of Chinatown and North Beach—mundane now, once athrob with life and color. "In the space of one block on Kearny," an adventurer claimed in the 1890s, "I could raise a gang to hijack a schooner, topple a statue, rob a bank or set off for a treasure hunt in the Galapagos." In 1889, Rudyard Kipling found the city to be a place "where humanity was going to the Devil with laughter and shouting and dancing and song and the rattle of dice boxes." The rattle-slam of dice is still heard on Kearny, and in the nearby alleys of Chinatown, where the tourists wander. "To this day," I once wrote, "when I hear a Chinese and a Texan in conversation, it's the Texan who sounds foreign."

* * *

Third and Market, where Wm. Randolph Hearst by-jingo'd the Spanish-American War from his beautiful loggia-topped building, an ornament of the Belle Epoque doomed to die in '06. On the city room wall were inscribed his hypocritical words of inspiration to his writers: "Get It First But First Get It Right!" Beneath which a cynic, more mindful of deadlines than the Old Man, had inscribed, "Don't Get It Right, Get It Written!" Bitter Bierce, Sterling, London—the original Bohemian Club gang—roared over that.

A writers' city. "Such room of sea! Such room of sky! Such room to live, such room to die," bellowed Joaquin Miller, beatnik before his time. "There are three storybook cities in America," said Frank Norris. "New York, New Orleans, and best of all, San Francisco." The Depression came, but the writers weren't depressed, especially ebullient Bill Saroyan, sitting in a small room on Carl St., "writing a letter to the common people, telling them in simple language things they already know."

We who grew up during The Great Depression can attest to the truth of Robert Lowell's words. "Being old in good times is worse than being young in the worst."

* * *

Crowded, jumbled city, where "parking is such street sorrow"

(Anon.) and the garages present "a Sorry-Full situation" (Price Hall). "What San Francisco needs is another earthquake," growled the curmudgeonly architect, Frank Lloyd Wright, while Irvin S. Cobb saw only "monotonous miles of narrow-chested high-shouldered jimber-jawed houses." But they were a minority.

"This city is so beautiful I hesitate to preach about Heaven while I'm here!" (Billy Graham, on a later visit), while Herbert Mye my-my'd "It's a good thing the early settlers landed on the East Coast; if they'd landed in San Francisco first, the rest of the country would still be uninhabited." "Here," decided a visiting Britisher, "there are fewer people one either pities or envies," and Alathea Siddons of London was moved to "feel sorry for children not born here. How disappointing to grow up and discover the whole world is not like this." "It's a lot like Hong Kong," added Corey Ford, the humorist, "but I like it better. After all Hong Kong doesn't have a Chinatown."

Still, it's not perfect. The Muni, dirty streets, Yerba Buena, the entire litany of projects that never got off the ground. "One can't expect everything to be perfect now," warned Evelyn Waugh, 40 years ago. "In the old days, if there was one thing wrong, it spoiled everything; from now on, for all our lives, if one thing is right, the day is made." At least the rains came. "The only time it rains enough in S.F. is when it rains too much," (Milton Kreis) but "I prefer a wet San Francisco to a dry Manhattan" (Larry Geraldi).

⋆ ⋆ ⋆

As the city retreats behind barred windows and iron gates, remember these words, inscribed over the entrance to Noel Sullivan's house on Russian Hill 50 years ago: "Hail Guest! We ask not what you art; if Friend, we greet thee, hand and heart; if Stranger, such no longer be; if Foe, our love shall conquer thee." Has the spirit of the city of St. Francis ever been expressed better?

March 12, 1978

The way we are: You know about Dr. Meyer (Mike) Friedman? He's the heart specialist—director of the Harold Brunn Institute at Mt. Zion—who divides people into "Type A" and "Type B." The former are the hard-driving, deadline-ridden overachievers—like us—who get most of the heart attacks, whereas the latter are relaxed souls who sort of amble through life, not even feeling guilty about goofing off, which is definitely SICK. . . Anyway, Mike Friedman recently got federal funds to pursue his theories in a big way: a five-year research program involving 900 volunteers—450 "Type A's" and 450 "B's"—who've already had heart attacks. The 450 "B's" were obtained without a hitch. However, only some 300 "A's" have agreed to participate. All the others contacted so far have begged off as being "too busy." *April 5, 1978*

Big city nightmares: You walk across a sidewalk elevator that suddenly gives way and you plunge into the black and icy Bay, never to be heard from again . . . Stuck between floors in a stalled elevator, you dial the number posted on the telephone, only to hear, "The number you have called is not in service at this time and there is no new number" . . . Strolling jaunty-jolly toward a bar for your regular 5 p.m. deep-dish martini, you see your very own beloved Porsche Targa being towed up Taylor St. at 45 miles an hour, its glorious tail emitting sparks as it drags along the pavement . . . You put a Canadian quarter in a parking meter and it immediately claps a handcuff on your wrist . . . Jogging like an antelope across a meadow in Golden Gate Park, you gradually begin sinking in up to your ankles, your knees, then your waist; as it dawns on you that you are trapped in quicksand, you call out "Helpfrrrmmmsssblurp" . . . You stick your finger into the slot of a public phone to see if maybe a coin is there and your digit is caught in a vicelike grip by something cold, powerful and monstrous that slowly drags you into the box. Your last agonized thought: "It Came From Beneath Ma Bell!" *May 28, 1978*

Beaucaens to the unknown but not unsung composer of these words on Muni streetcars, to be rendered to the tune of "Camptown Races," ready: "Oh the N street car runs all day long—Judah! Judah! The N street line is nine miles long, all the Judah day. Gonna build new tracks! New cars on the way! Paid my money, got my fast pass now, guess I'll ride on the K." Katchy.

May 31, 1978

"Well, it sure didn't take 'em long to get Dick Nixon's memoirs on television," drawled Ralph M. Heintz of Los Altos upon reading ads for "'The Bastard'—the powerful story of a young man who met rejection with a savage counterattack and battered his way to a position of power!" . . . However, Neal Coonerty, owner of Bookshop Santa Cruz, is not giving up on Nixon's $19.95 book. During the first two weeks of June, he will be selling it at $1.69 a pound, the price of bologna, "and if that doesn't work we'll drop it to 69 cents a pound, the price of turkey." *June 1, 1978*

Culture cont'd.: The pro-Muni Railway jingle published here last wk., to be sung to the tune of "Camptown Races," draws this rebuttal from Passenger Russ Miller: "Oh, the N street car broke down again—Judah! Judah! Deferred maintenance struck again on Muni's right-of-way. Waiting here all morn, might be here all day. Here's one now, it's packed to the roof—guess I'll drive today!"
June 6, 1978

Mourning becomes electric (sign on the door of Stone's Pet Shop in Pacific Grove): "Death in Family—Back in 5 Mins."

* * *

Times, sign of: And it was on Union St. that Suzanne Beauregard of J. Walter Thompson overheard a conversation that couldn't have taken place a generation ago, 12-yr.-old boy to father: "I'd like to buy a necklace." Father: "What kind?" Boy: "A BOY'S necklace, naturally." *June 12, 1978*

Nobody asked me, but NBC's controversial documentary on hedonistic Marin, "I Want It All Now," made the county appear a lot more interesting than it really is. If anybody deserves credit or blame, it's Cyra McFadden, whose year-old best-seller, "The Serial," first proposed the notion that Marin is fantastically—you know—different. Cyra: "That book is my Karen Ann Quinlan. I keep trying to cut its life support systems and it refuses to die" . . . Still, the Thurs. night special was a plus for some. On Friday, Allen Lissauer, owner of Redwood Hot Tubs in Mill Valley, was swamped with orders for his $2,500 deluxe hot tubs. Same day, reports Gert German, a loudspeakered voice at Marin's Cost Plus told the crowd: "Sorry, we are completely out of peacock feathers, but a new shipment is on the way" . . . NBC went overboard, certainly, with its loose talk about divorces and suicides. In the former category, Marin isn't even in the top 10 (first and second place "winners" are Shasta and Del Norte, where there isn't much to do except fight). And in suicides, Marin is 14th (first: Lake County!). No statistics on tickling oneself to death with peacock feathers or being overcome in hot tubs. *July 25, 1978*

Henry Doelger, who died in Italy at 82 Sunday, not only covered the Sunset sand dunes with his thousands of "Doelgerville" houses, he was a generous host and a jolly fellow who enjoyed his millions. Furthermore, his houses (one year he built so many he lost one) have weathered remarkably well, and he provided me with some good lines—"The White Cliffs of Doelger," for one, and the crack he enjoyed the most, he said: "Old Doelgers never die, they just FHAde away." He kept a huge yacht at Monaco called the Westlake, after another area he developed here, and served Dom Perignon exclusively as he showed off his seven toupees—the hair "growing" gradually till he "needed" a haircut and would return to No. 1. Cheers, Henry. *July 26, 1978*

Sodden thoughts: Who first thought of putting celery sticks in Bloody Marys and why? They either poke your eye or drip on your tie . . . If there's a wall-mounted phone in your hotel bathroom, it will have a cigarette burn on it . . . Do crocodiles play tennis, and if so, do they wear shirts with a little person over the left breast? . . . A lotta guys think it's chic to wear their sunglasses dangling on the outside of their shirts or jacket pocket. A lotta guys are wrong . . . A True San Franciscan (Definition No. 8303) wants to be right here when the next Big Earthquake hits. April 18, 1906, is the most important date in our history and those who survived it are our elite. True San Franciscans aspire to join that group, no matter what the risk.

Am I speaking only for myself when I say that? I see.

* * *

Add party guests I can live without: Those who say, in holier-than-thou tones, "I only drink wine"—and then go through three bottles of your best . . . The most boring bar conversations these nights are about the mad success of Perrier water and how many other brands are cheaper and better (uh-uh) . . . Everybody who has had enough of so-called street fairs kindly rise and holler "Horace Schmidlapp!" . . . Since a proper sidewalk cafe has tables on the sidewalk, it must be said that San Francisco has no sidewalk cafes . . . When a car with an "A" sticker is parked in another district—mine, for instance—it should get tagged after two hours. Fair's fair. *July 30, 1978*

Little stories behind big headlines! . . . (Fanfares, clashing cymbals, drumrolls, etc.) . . . One night some two years ago I wandered into Mumm's, the classy disco on Powell, and there bumped into the 49ers' star end, Gene Washington. "Ouch!" said Gene, removing most of his clothing to display the cuts, bruises and burns he had suffered the day before while catching passes on Candlestick Park's iron-hard artificial turf. "It's like landing on cement," complained Gene. "Since you smell like the most powerful man in the town, can't you do something about it?" . . . Next day, I chanced to be having lunch at Vanessi's with then Supervisor Al Nelder. When I repeated Washington's comments, the Supe's ears perked up like a friendly terrier's. That very afternoon, he began an investigation that will result in God's Own Grass replacing AstroTurf at Candlestick Park next year . . . Just think! If I hadn't gone to Mumm's that night, the city might not be stuck for $868,000 worth of natural grass. Thus we conclude this installment of—Little Stories Behind Big Headlines! (Hoots, jeers, fanfares of Whoopee Cushions.) *August 10, 1978*

Over at the Pleasanton "Correctional Facility," otherwise known as a Federal prison, Patricia Hearst is now wearing a T-shirt reading "Pardon Me" across the front—and on the back, "Being Kidnapped Means Always Having To Say You're Sorry." A gift from her younger sister, Ann . . . Grabber of a graffito in the Castro: "If all the world's a stage, San Francisco is the cast party."

August 17, 1978

Roll 'em: Another chapter in the daring, dizzying, dazzling life of Dianne Feinstein, Super Supe! As today's episode opens, we find our heroine dashing into the Noir Art Gallery at 454 Geary, breathlessly calling for "a telephone, quick—a man is being choked and shoved out the window right upstairs!" . . . Upon hearing this, Marilyn Collier, the gallery director, asked "Are you a tourist?" "Indeed not," replied Ms. Feinstein hotly, "I am a Supervisor and

I want to call the police." Ms. Collier: "No need. That's the ACT school upstairs and they do things like that all the time. Just a rehearsal, you know" . . . Not to be deterred, our heroine marched upstairs to the American Conservatory Theater and advised the fledgling actors to stop frightening passersby. They crossed their hearts. *September 8, 1978*

And the twain shall meet: You know all about the Hunan Restaurant on Kearny. Hot. Crowded. Tiny. Authentic Hunanese stir-fry cooking. Big plugs in national mags. So! Late the other night, Janet Goldenberg dropped in just before closing time. As she was eating her Harvest Duck at the counter, the three stir-fry cooks finished their cleaning chores and headed for the refrigerator . . . The cooks, all Chinese from Burma, extracted therefrom three items: half-gallon of milk, big jar of peanut butter, bag of hot dog buns. Their rapturous exclamations as they spread the peanut butter on the buns and washed them down with great gulps of milk made one thing perfectly clear. The future of McDonald's in Mainland China is assured. *September 18, 1978*

The Walking Caen

If there really are a million stories in the naked city, I'm not getting my share. This vaguely disturbing thought strikes me as I take my daily stroll up Fifth, past the grand stairs of the Old U.S. Mint (a resting place for Old U.S. Poor), around the mean little hotel whose denizens stagger in and lurch out, and rapidly cross the alley where evil-looking but undoubtedly warm-hearted ruffians drink booze out of paper bags and thump each other around, playfully, till one or another falls to the pavement, suffering from what police reporters and personal injury lawyers call "lacerations" and "abrasions." To thee and me, cuts and bruises.

* * *

The downtown streets of the naked city are peopled with rare and exotic birds, making their various jungle sounds: mating calls ("if you don't like my sister how about my brother?"), cackles of insane mirth, pleas for help, attempts at music, poetry and sermons on stones. The scene is at once compelling and repellent—the smell of dirt and poverty, the flopsweat of desperation. If looks could kill, you in your neat suit, carrying your briefcase, hurrying along in your well-shined shoes, would have been dead a long time ago, bones left to bleach under the warm September sun blazing out of a washed denim sky.

★ ★ ★

The rise and fall, and the city settling into its familiar rut, tourist dollars stashed and cached for the winter, as a squirrel stores nuts and a nut stores squirrels. It is only coincidence that the moment the tourist season ends, good things begin—warm zephyrs, lazy Bay days, opera season, party rounds, shorter lines at the better restaurants, a seat on a bench in the sun. In the wintry blasts of July and the filtering fogs of August, the tourists have a hard time, but they keep coming back for more. Will they one day be fished out like the tiny Bay shrimp and the sardines of Monterey? Is the meaty San Francisco sucker on the verge of disappearing, too? All pray.

★ ★ ★

The Sacramento kid walks rapidly up Powell, taking exaggerated, elongated steps. You can take the boy out of the country but etc. etc. All by himself he is playing a sidewalk game he remembers from his boyhood in that hot valley town: "Step on a crack, break your mother's back." Carefully he bounces from square to square, remembering especially to hop over the engraved name of the contractor. Step on THAT and something awful happens to the entire family. He reaches Ellis safely. Stops. Watches all the people walk against the "Wait" sign. Sighs. Thinks about his German mother, the sweet singer of the Saar, and how she would stick her head out the upstairs window on 26th St. and holler in her operatic contralto, "Herrrberrrrt!" Dinner Time. All the other kids within five blocks would mimic "Herrberrrrt!" and fall upon the ground in orgies of mean-spirited delight. The Sackamenna Kid remembers her rich voice summoning him to a dinner of knockwurst, bratwurst and strudel. What a name for a law firm.

★ ★ ★

The naked city—hardly. Even with the tourists gone, it is jammed with the most mystifying mix to be found anywhere. Stockton St. in Chinatown smells like Hong Kong at high noon. Chicken feathers in the gutters, lotus children playing tag in filthy alleys, women squatting on the sidewalk over their little treasures of what may or may not be jade. On the walls, posters of Mao, his face defaced, his thoughts scribbled upon, for this is still Chiang Kai-shek country. Kuomintang land. Young gangsters stare at you coldly, contemptuously, till you look away at a glazed chicken hanging in a fly-specked window, its ceramic skin glistening.

★ ★ ★

Traffic: Fierce. Downtown has turned bumper-to-bumper, cabs shooting signals, bicycle messengers flying the wrong way, frustrated motorists brushing past pedestrians. Tall buildings rise, one much like another, casting new shadows over old streets, creating wind tunnels where the sun once fell like a blessing. It is not a good time for environmentalists. I note a right-wing group selling bumper strips reading "Save the Environment—Feed Nader to the Whales!" Is that funny? Some think so, even the young fogeys selling the strips. The environmentalists warned a decade ago that Manhattanization, "booteeked" neighborhoods, the transformation of a city into Commuter Town, and shameless wooing of tourism would create an entirely different San Francisco. So, like the liberals, they are hated. To be right is not to be popular.

★ ★ ★

"What a great town!" The words come blurting out at dusk on the night of a full moon, erasing the doubts and returning the child-like shine to eyes grown cynical. The beauty is slowly vanishing, but enough remains, more then enough, as the lights come on and the bridges turn golden and a pinkish glow softens the hard lines of the marching buildings that could almost stamp out the spirit of a great city. Almost, but not quite. *September 24, 1978*

Why do loyal San Franciscans love Jack's restaurant, down there on Sacramento St.? Let me count the ways. It has been in the same location since 1864, there is no parking, the place is noisy, the bar is too small and nothing ever changes, including the tablecloths, the menu, the waiters—and—that telephone! It's a 1920 pay phone, near the door, and all the regulars think it's cute, since A.P. Giannini, Herbert Hoover, Dashiell Hammett, Jake Ehrlich and Sunny Jim Rolph all made calls on it, not at the same time. On the other hand, Ma Bell thinks that phone is hell. It goes out of service at least once a week. Operators complain about it. A repairman griped to Jack's owner Jack Redinger that to keep that dang thing going, "I might be able to borrow parts from the Telephone Pioneer Museum. Or the phone could be destroyed in one of the annual grease fires in the kitchen ventilator—it's my only hope" . . . Jack Redinger stands firm. Every time a new set is pressed on him, he says "Nothing changes at Jack's!" The number of the old pay phone is 986-9854. If anyone answers, act surprised. *November 7, 1978*

Present Indicative

Gray skies dripped sadness and sorrow over San Francisco yesterday. Headlines told of tragedy and madness in steaming jungles. Radio stations, chattering and nattering to stay abreast of the news, fired salvoes and bulletins, interspersed with commercials for laxatives and deodorants, and taped tips on gardening. Television newsmen looked grave as they recounted the incredible turn of events. It is too grandiose to say "the people were stunned" yesterday, but conversation was not casual. It was not the usual Monday morning melange of 49er talk, opera talk, party talk. Small talk was a casualty. The thoughts could almost be seen drifting off to that faraway landing strip, to the dead, the dying and the dream that became nightmare.

★ ★ ★

"Life is a mosaic," Jerry Brown is fond of saying. Over the pain-wracked weekend, the mosaic was there, but madly askew. The bloody title of Guyana threw everything else out of kilter. As is always the case when great tragedy strikes—tomorrow is the 15th anniversary of John F. Kennedy's assassination—"normal" events turn unreal. On Sunday, KCBS newsradio tried valiantly to stay on the story that emerged so slowly from that primitive shoulder of South America. Television scrambled to catch up, and anyway, it was a football day. For once, not too many people cared. It was also the day of a grand occasion at the Opera House—Kurt Herbert Adler's 50th year in opera, 25th as our impresario. The timing was off.

★ ★ ★

How to judge the insanity surrounding the end of Rev. Jim Jones and his strange mission? A common theme is "Who could have expected THIS?" but perhaps Götterdämmerung was inevitable. Step by step, Jim Jones and his followers retreated from the comparative reality of the San Francisco ghetto to the impassible jungles, where madness could take root. Good men and women are dead—there is the sorrow. Here, politicians scurry to find new positions for themselves—a sorry sight. There are those who were impressed with Jim Jones and later changed their minds. A lesson learned.

★ ★ ★

I met Jim Jones twice. We had long lunches, early in his career here, before he became a political figure. I found him appealing—soft-spoken, modest, talking earnestly of helping people. If he was a con man, he was masterful at it, even dressing the part in a severe black "uniform," actually a leisure suit. When I wrote a couple of favorable items about him, the mail flooded in from People's Temple members, almost every letter identical, as though they had been ordered. Unnerving. Then came rumors of discontent, and Marshall Kilduff and Phil Tracy's first story in New West magazine, based on dissident testimony. I was skeptical of their story, but they were on the right track.

* * *

When Jones moved to Guyana, ostensibly so he wouldn't have to give up the son he had fathered by a Temple member who had defected, I dropped him a note, wondering why he did not return to face the growing criticism and harsh rumors.

"I felt and still feel," he replied on April 3, "that it is necessary to protect my child from being used as a pawn by people who have no real interest in him." (He also spoke of his fear that the church would lose its tax exemption over his having fathered a child out of wedlock.) "All my life, I have endured the pain of poverty, and suffered many disappointments and heartaches common to human kind. For that reason, I try to make others happy and secure. So many who are suffering are not happy unless they see others suffering as well. Perhaps that is why I have tried so hard to compensate for that factor, and make this society a joyous one that celebrates life."

* * *

In another letter, he wrote: "For many years, I have existed on the premise that I am needed, because long ago I realized what a cruel hoax life is, how false illusions are, how unjust. Even here in Guyana, a place of great physical beauty and tremendous potential, I am not 'happy.' It is too much of a responsibility to be the administrator of this socialistic society. But even if I did not have this on my shoulders, I doubt I could ever be happy knowing that two-thirds of the world's children have no future but the prospect of starvation and of lives 'nasty, brutish and short,' as Hume discerned long ago."

* * *

Further along, he reflects: "I think I will always bear the guilt of knowing that this model socialistic society should have been built in the U.S. Perhaps, if I had communicated somehow differently, I could have exposed these liars who have so callously tried to ruin what has been for many people the only chance they had to make something out of their lives . . . Many of the young people who came here were alienated, angry and frustrated. They were tired of the hypocrisy that cried over 'human rights' while they were being buried alive . . . The society we are building in Guyana has given people who were considered the refuse of urban America a new sense of pride, self-worth and dignity."

★ ★ ★

Gray day. I read and reread the long, emotional letters from this latter-day Emperor Jones of the Jungle and try to equate his words with his dark deeds that have destroyed so many good people. The mystery remains, thicker than the rain clouds over San Francisco.

November 21, 1978

Gray Day

Horror upon horror, shock upon shock . . .

What is there about November? First, the memories of a dead President, victim of a "senseless" tragedy. "Senseless" is the word we use to console ourselves that it is all too mysterious, that we as individuals are helpless, that there is random madness running wild—beyond our control, beyond our responsibility.

"The world has gone mad" is the phrase that sprang to people's minds and lips yesterday.

The vocabulary of grief and disbelief stretches only so far. The ghastliness of Guyana exhausted the pitifully few words at our command. At the end of a week of incredible headlines, all of us were left stunned, exhausted, overwhelmed by the flood of bloody, "senseless" information.

And then came the shock waves of yesterday.

The Mayor, a good man, dead. The Supervisor, a good man, dead. The suspected killer, we had been told many times by his supporters, was a good man, too.

It was all—senseless. Like the hundreds dead in Guyana. Like the young President and his brother and the great black leader. And yet there must be a thread connecting all this violence. As so-called civilized people, we must be failing, somehow.

If there is no sense to it, the world has truly gone mad. We are all dangerous, then. We who think of ourselves as sane must be deluding ourselves. Let us sit upon the ground and talk about the death of—sanity.

★ ★ ★

George Moscone and Harvey Milk had much in common. They were joyous men, celebrants of life, believers in people. They were eminently sane and reasonable. If they had any faults, they were those of generosity, of a willingness to think the best.

They loved their friends and they loved San Francisco. "I must be the luckiest guy in the world to be the Mayor of the greatest city in the world." George Moscone uttered that sentence often as he sat back on a beautiful evening looking out with shining eyes over a shining skyline that was, in a way, his.

In the best sense of the term, George was a sweet man. Harvey Milk was a sweet man. They seemed filled to overflowing with positive feelings. I didn't know Dan White, the suspect. I don't know why an insane rage possessed him . . . but once more the limits of the vocabulary of horror have been reached.

It was a "senseless" act. All death is sad. To be killed without reason is the tragedy that grips us all by the throat and renders us speechless in our bewildered grief.

★ ★ ★

Monday morning. Sirens and seagulls, the sounds and symbols of the city known around the world as beautiful, seductive, dangerous—and, in a careless phrase printed and heard constantly, "the kook capital."

We who have lived here a long time resist that description. What others call "kooks" we look upon as characters in a charade we smile at. We think we understand the show, having played our own roles for so many years. Maybe we are wrong.

Maybe there is some thread connecting it all, something unperceived that can make sense of the "senseless." We who are in the middle of it may be the last to see what it is. The mind, stunned, searches for clues.

★ ★ ★

Monday morning, Christmas bells tinkling, the shopping rush in full cry, "Joy to the World" in the background of radio commercials, the Guyana nightmare slowly receding, the world inching back toward whatever passes for normal . . .

My phone rings. It is a confidant of George Moscone's. "The Mayor will call you in a few minutes," he says. "He wants you to know that he is not going to reappoint Dan White as Supervisor. He has picked someone else. I think he'll give you his name. Stay by the phone."

A few minutes later, the phone rings. But the news is that

George Moscone and Harvey Milk are dead; Dan White has surrendered.

I think back to a conversation I had on Saturday with one who is close to the City Hall scene. "Too bad Dianne Feinstein picked this time to go on her trip to Nepal," he said. "If she had been here, she would never have allowed Dan White to resign. They were political allies. She could have talked him out of it, easily. Now we have this mess on our hands."

Now, Dianne Feinstein, as President of the Board, is the Mayor.

Now Dan White, young, clean-cut, conservative, God-fearing, a man who made speeches about "decency" and against "kookiness," is in jail, booked for investigation of the murder of a Mayor and a Supervisor.

If he had not resigned in the first place . . .

It is all—"senseless."

★ ★ ★

As I look out over the city that George Moscone and Harvey Milk loved, a flag is slowly being lowered to half staff. Two valuable, invaluable, irreplaceable people are dead, their families and friends grief-stricken. Hundreds are dead in Guyana, leaving tears and mystery in their wake. The phones are suddenly silent, the streets quiet. A pall settles over the holiday hills, Monday's mourning broken only by the siren that has become the sound of the city.

What is there about November? What is there about San Francisco? *November 28, 1978*

Uncollected Thoughts

I couldn't think of anything better to do Monday afternoon so I went for a walk through the streets of George Moscone's San Francisco. Besides, I wanted to get away from the telephones. A lot of out-of-town newspeople, scrambling desperately against their deadlines for an angle, any angle, wanted a few comments on why this is "the kook capital of the world." I don't think it is, and anyway, I was fresh out of words on the subject. "Jim Jones, these murders at City Hall, you say they could have happened anywhere but the fact is they happened in San Francisco, did they not?" pressed a radio "personality" in the resonant rounded tones of a radio "personality." Yes, they did happen in San Francisco, my mellifluous man, but it would take hours, days, years to explore the reasons and I know we only have a few seconds between commercials, so, sorry.

★ ★ ★

It was a crisp November afternoon. The shock waves from City Hall had almost emptied the streets. Drivers and pedestrians seemed more polite than usual, waiting for others to go first. It is always that way after a major tragedy: a sudden respect for life, an awareness that we need each other. Nothing brings us together, or tears us apart, like death, but we forget too soon. "Let us then be true to one another"—so many took that pledge after the great assassinations of the 1960s. We turned to our various religions. "If yours makes you kinder than mine makes me, yours is better" . . . but we would be kind, no matter what. And we weren't.

★ ★ ★

I drifted down toward the old part of town, away from what passes for architecture these days (do brutal buildings brutalize people?). I wanted to see warm brick walls and graceful arches and tall windows speaking of high ceilings, high hopes, high resolve. San Francisco, the old city, is beautiful. There is nothing crazy about the feelings and memories it evokes—taste, gentility, sense of style. I walked around Jackson Square in the thin November sunlight, the sidewalks thick with fallen leaves. It looked like George Sterling's "cool grey city of love," but Poet Sterling had killed himself in the Bohemian Club. It is still a "storybook city," as Frank Norris called it, long ago, but the stories of this November are not what he had in mind. And when George Sterling, a small-b bohemian, killed himself, "kook" had not been invented.

★ ★ ★

I walked with the first edition of Monday's Examiner under my arm. It is a collector's item. When it arrived on my desk, early that morning, I looked up at the top of the front page headline and smiled. It read "Japanese Dump Premier." We were back to "normal." For the first time in more than a week, something less than utter disaster was the biggest story in the paper. I tried to work up a little sympathy for "a stunned Prime Minister Takeo Fukuda," who had just lost his job. A few terrible minutes later, Mr. Fukuda was off the front page.

★ ★ ★

On Pacific St., terrific Pacific, I passed a few acquaintances. We nodded silently. A couple said softly, "Awful, awful." Nobody said, "Have a nice day." At Bali's, Mme. Armen Bali, crying, was shooing her luncheon patrons and locking up so she could be with her friend, Gina Moscone. Bars and stores were closing. At Jack's, the famous criminal attorney, James Martin MacInnis, looked grim. "Someone just phoned to ask me to represent Dan White," he said, sounding incensed. "The very idea. George Moscone was an old, dear friend." I returned to my car and turned on the radio. Rock sounded positively obscene, pop inane, Beethoven and Mozart appropriate, ageless. On a news station, Harvey Milk's taped voice was saying, almost cheerily, "I expect to be killed by some crazy anti-gay."

★ ★ ★

A small zircon for those sifting through the shards for clues: Jim Jones and Dan White had one thing in common—no discernible sense of humor.

★ ★ ★

And yet, and yet: Jack Casford recalls these words from the last annual meeting of the Northern California Coalition for Handgun Control: "I am concerned about the potential for terrible tragedy in a society that has no effective policy for the control or possession of handguns by private individuals." The speaker: Dan White. I fish around on the dial. A learned professor is saying, "If people enjoy violence, that is what they are going to get." George Moscone's taped voice, in 1976, explaining why he didn't want a bodyguard: "Anybody who wants to knock me off can do it." A shaken Mayor Janet Gray Hayes of San Jose makes a tearful plea for handgun control—"my mother was killed by a handgun." Archbishop Quinn is eloquent, moving. Mel Wax, the press secretary, is admirably professional. If there is a tiny ray of light, it falls on Dianne Feinstein, so suddenly the Acting Mayor. She is superb.

★ ★ ★

It was only last Friday that George Moscone turned 49. "Be prepared," he grinned to his friends. "I'm going to celebrate for two weeks because I have NO intention of celebrating my 50th," and he shuddered. And it was on Friday that he said to Gina: "I'm worried about Dan White. He's taking this hard. He's acting sort of—flaky." Ah, euphemisms. People being "snuffed" instead of killed, "passing on" instead of dying, "flaky" instead of crazy. Life goes on, and death, but will we ever learn that there is no such thing as "just a harmless kook"? *November 29, 1978*

State of the City

Jerry Brown is all heart, as in stone. Following is the Governor's full, official statement on Monday's tragedy at City Hall: "It is with deep regret that I learned of the deaths of Mayor Moscone and Harvey Milk. They were dedicated public officials devoted to serving all the people of San Francisco." That's it. All of it. "Think Small" in all its glory.

★ ★ ★

Yesterday morning, the heartbeat of the city throbbed in St. Mary's Cathedral. From the outside, the great structure at Gough and Geary does look like a washing machine agitator, as its critics will have it forevermore. But inside, there is breathtaking space, soaring to the heavens. Its ribbons of stained glass are almost too festive. A slim golden cross hangs in mid-air, under a mobile of shimmering crystal spears, alive with constant motion.

The quadrants of the upswept ceiling open onto cityscapes. City Hall dome, scene of Monday's bloody events, can be seen to the Southeast. Only a few blocks down Geary stands People's Temple. To the North rises the vaguely Oriental dome of Sherith Israel, the synagogue that served as Hall of Justice after the 1906 firequake. There, a scene of high drama, not tragedy, was enacted: the political boss of the town, Abraham Ruef, was found guilty of bribery and extortion and sentenced to San Quentin. He emerged in five years to become a real estate millionaire.

The St. Mary's Choir, augmented by 10 members of the Symphony Chorus, sings Randall Thompson's "Alleluia." It is a marvelous choir. The organ rumbles. A harp speaks thinly in ancient harmonies. A thousand eyes spill tears, unashamed. A woman, wailing, undone, is carried out, screaming, kicking. A siren echoes her agony.

★ ★ ★

Surrealism. There is no end to it. As the mourning clouds hung heavy, as the high priests called once again for a coming together in the face of the hate that kills, Ronald Reagan somehow found it necessary to point out this week that "the great majority" of Rev. Jim Jones' followers were Democrats.

★ ★ ★

Mass at St. Mary's. George Moscone was there. A priest who knew him as a young man spoke warmly and well of the martyred mayor. George Moscone was there in the silent handclasps and embraces of old friends. His political allies were there, and his political enemies. There was no getting around it: the pecking order was there, in full pecking order.

First came the captains and kings, the Mayors and former Mayors, the Governor, the Senators, the Assemblymen, the Supervisors, the powerful who stand in the shadows, pulling strings with checkbooks. Limousines came and went. Right this way, Sir. Then came the fringe dignitaries, on the proper edge of the fringe. All these complex pieces fell into place, and who makes the decisions? At last, the people were permitted to enter. The people of various sizes, shapes and colors. George Moscone's people. He would have been among them, a warm hand on their shoulders.

"Let us pray." The loud silence of thousands of minds, flitting from George to Harvey Milk to Dan White's bereaved family (let us not forget them), to Joan Baez's performance of the day before—she who always comes through—to the City of St. Francis, the Catholic and catholic city that tries to be all things to all people and, in the main, succeeds.

When it fails, we have this great sadness.

⋆ ⋆ ⋆

Simple eloquence: The velvet-draped front window of The Emporium, containing only the portraits of George Moscone and Harvey Milk, and a vase of dark red roses.

⋆ ⋆ ⋆

The mass nears its end, candles flickering, golden crosses shining, voices crying "Forgive us our sins" and "We are troubled," old and comforting words about "Our brother George, the son of the church, the father of his city." As is so often the case, it is the music, so beautifully sung, that is the most eloquent and moving. Music, the universal voice, the true unifier, the magic that reaches every heart and starts the tears coursing down the most grizzled cheeks.

The honor guards change shifts at George Moscone's casket every few minutes. In the manner of Americans, they cannot seem to march in step. Perhaps it is just as well, given the example of those who do march like automatons. The captains and the kings file out, the limousines roll, the motorcycle escorts roar. The spell is broken.

"See you when things are back to normal," mourners say to each other, gripping hands and arms, attempting smiles. "Normal." What is normal? Downtown, the Meter Maids are tagging cars and chalking tires, jaywalkers scamper, panhandlers pan for hands with money, a blind guitarist sings "God Rest Ye Merry,

Gentlemen," and the Powell Street Jazz Band serenades Stockton St. with "Santa Claus Is Coming to Town," in a most lively tempo.

* * *

That was the week that was, a normal week of life on the streets, and sudden death that mocks the Christmas cards already arriving with their messages of "Peace on earth to men of good will"—men like George and Harvey. *December 1, 1978*

Loose Ends

Uncountable millions of words have been written and spoken about San Francisco since the Guyana horrors and the City Hall slayings. In newspapers around the world, on radio and TV stations, this city has been loved and hated, praised and damned, discussed and dissected. Some of the words, and I include myself as a perpetrator, have been overblown, oversentimental, maudlin. There has been a tremendous outpouring of sympathetic concern, and a surprising (to me) amount of bitterness. There has not been this much concentrated "analysis" of San Francisco since the hippie era of the 1960s, and what emerges is the jumbled outline of the city that is all things to all people. For every person who finds this "the most civilized place in the country," there seems to be one who regards it as a cesspool and sinkhole, awaiting only the wrath of God.

* * *

A few agonizing reappraisals. In the deadline-pressurized hours and days following the deaths of Mayor Moscone and Supervisor Milk, I wrote some heartfelt words, and some foolish ones. "What is there about November? What is there about San Francisco?" are questions without answers, as well they should be. John F. Kennedy was killed in a November, the Jonestown madness transpired in November, but there is no link unless we are prepared to accept astrological mysteries. Robert Kennedy was killed in Los Angeles, Martin Luther King in Memphis, and so on. In a later column, I wrote another thoughtless line: "When will we ever learn there is no such thing as 'Just a harmless kook'?" There are harmless kooks here and everywhere. Nobody ever called Dan White a kook.

* * *

Kook is a miserable little word. It became part of the national vocabulary after the attempted assassinations of then President Gerald Ford here and in Sacramento, a city not noted for kookiness. Following these episodes, a Ford aide named James Falk described Northern California as "the kook capital of the world." The phrase stuck. The New York Times took up the cry on Sept. 26, 1975, when it published an unfunny article on the difficulty of getting anyone to run for Mayor of San Francisco because "Who wants to be Chief Kook of Kookville?" The article was written by—me.

* * *

During the past week, I have received letters, phone calls and clippings from all over the world. First came words of encouragement from those who love San Francisco, and there are many. Then came the old-timers, commiserating over the way the city has changed; a familiar refrain—"We remember when everybody dressed so well, the men in suits, the women in hats and furs and gloves." There were angry letters about Dan White, and letters supporting him—"Not that we agree with violence, but he had taken all he could take and we are not surprised something snapped."

* * *

Pundits and editorialists found much to chew on. Writing in the L.A. Herald-Examiner, Columnist Denis Hamill concluded that "Guyana and this double-murder have finally made San Francisco just another American city with a bridge." (After the assassinations, kidnappings and knee-cappings in Italy, I wonder if he wrote that Rome is just another Italian city with a Vatican.) The Journal-Star of Peoria, Ill., thundered that "If any place has earned a reputation for kookism, for a climate divorced from reality, it would seem to be California. And if any city has earned its growing reputation as Capital of Kookism, it is San Francisco . . . the nearest thing we have to Sodom and Gomorrah, a glorious preview of the wonderfully 'free,' 'compassionate' and 'open society' of the future."

* * *

Reno's Nevada State Journal is more temperate: "The People's Temple may have its roots in San Francisco, but the poor, impressionable, idealistic and easily led people who flocked around Jim Jones were not necessarily San Franciscans . . . And of course it's worth noting that it was not until they left the warm, accepting social milieu of San Francisco and settled in a strange continent that feelings of doom and paranoia began to take hold . . . Let's push away suspicions that 'something is not quite right in San Francisco' and accept the fact that it is an American city, with its share of violent, unstable, foolish, impractical people, but with a larger share of beauty, tradition, tolerance and creativity."

* * *

A riffle through the mail on my desk is dizzying. Atty. William E. Spence of Alpharetta, Ga.: "The people of San Francisco have turned their backs on God as shown by the many horrible crimes they have committed and tolerated." John Eschelbach of Novato: "Because of what I saw and heard during the memorial service for George Moscone and Harvey Milk, I am convinced San Francisco is the most civilized city in America." R.W. Walsh of Grants Pass, Ore.: "Perhaps you and others of your ilk will cease to brag and revel in the lowest of filth that permeates your so-called beautiful city. Ruin & horror will come upon you and those like you, and we who at least try can look upon you stupid clannish fools and say 'Thy Will Be Done, Oh Lord!'"

* * *

"Choose to live. Continue your unique experiment. This nation NEEDS San Francisco!" John S. Walker, a visitor from the Yukon, wrote those encouraging words when we needed them most. The time of darkness and doubt is over, and the Christmas lights are shining.

December 10, 1978

★ ★ ★

1979

★ ★ ★

Torrential downpour, icy wind whistling in from the Aleutians. People and umbrellas being turned inside out. I'm due for lunch at Le Central. Time once again for the dry-shoes dash through the drizzle. Take a deep breath and my hand and follow me:

Down ramp into Pickwick Garage, up back steps into Jesse St., hop over prostrate wino, run into back entrance of Emporium, take escalator to basement, past tennis shoes and socks to Powell St. BART station, walk up escalator (not working, as usual) into Woolworth's basement, up escalator to main floor, out Ellis St. doors, jaywalk into Ellis-O'Farrell garage, take elevator to O'Farrell side, dash across to Macy's through men's dept. and up escalator to Geary, cross Geary into Union Square Garage, exit Post St. side, cross into Hyatt Union Square (mizzerable windy-slippery plaza), execute dangerous catercorner jaywalk into Sutter-Stockton garage, take elevator to third floor, exit on Bush, slide down Bush to Le Central, arrive soaking wet.

So much for the famous dry-shoes shortcut.

February 1, 1979

ECLIPSES

Somewhere a total eclipse was darkening the skies yesterday morning, but in San Francisco, there were no signs of the phenomenon. After the rains of the night before, the 7 a.m. skies seemed unnaturally bright. The sun beat down on those celebrated San Francisco gardens with Southern exposure, but it was not the beginning of a happy day or the end of a gloomy Sunday. On KQED that night, from 10 to 11, I watched an old friend who had died a year ago face imminent death all over again. Yesterday morning at 7, I read on the front page of this paper that another old friend had died. A cloud passed over the sun and the day grew dark and cold.

★ ★ ★

Paul Jacobs, as good an investigative reporter who ever asked a tough question, died in January, 1978, of cancer, but his dying began more than 20 years earlier when he started digging into the effects of nuclear tests in the Nevada desert. In his last pain-wracked effort as a reporter, he went back to Nevada and Utah to interview those who, like himself, were dying of cancer because they, too, had been exposed to "minor" radiation. His last gallant stand has been made into a one-hour film called "Paul Jacobs and the Nuclear Gang," an unfortunately flip title. There is nothing light or amusing about any of it: KQED, which has surrounded this important document with disclaimers that reek of gutlessness, will repeat the film at 5 p.m. Saturday. One hopes.

★ ★ ★

The mystical meanderings of fate and coincidence, the life lines that intersect unexpectedly and add up to—nothing and everything: Paul Jacobs and John L. Wasserman were friends, compatriots, two of the good guys in a world they looked at with jaundiced and amused eye. Shortly before Paul, long dead, came to life on Channel 9, John was dying—one must say it: meaninglessly—in a car crash on a freeway. They were so different, so much alike and both irreplaceable. Paul bulldogged his way through one serious investigation after another. John pursued with equal seriousness the light story, the original line, the back-breaking art of making it all look easy. He was the most amusing writer on this paper and his batting average was astronomical (but it's the Pete Roses who make the money).

★ ★ ★

It occurs to me that newspaper people seldom write about one another except under tragic circumstances. To paraphrase the critics of the press, we are only news when the news is bad. And yet people like John L. Wasserman and Paul Jacobs are household words. Thousands must be interested in them. They are certainly as worthy of interviews, comments, criticism or gossip as, say, Farrah Fawcett Majors or Bianca Jagger. But who writes about the writers? There is some unspoken rule there whose delicacy escapes me. I can only say that John and Paul were more newsworthy than most of the people I write about, and I realize what faint praise that is.

⋆ ⋆ ⋆

John L. Wasserman was the liveliest man around this paper. He didn't walk, he hustled. When he entered a room, it came alive. He talked, listened, argued. Like most cynics, he was sentimental, an easy laugher and crier. He lived in a rambling "pad," the only possible term, above the Boarding House on Bush (it can now be revealed that he is listed in the phone book as "Joaquin Bandersnatch"). Like Paul Jacobs, he enjoyed beautiful women, eclectic crowds, good wine, bad jokes. Neither cared about clothes. Both cared about people.

⋆ ⋆ ⋆

They were always surrounded by crowds. It was not unusual to walk into the Wasserman "pad" and find Joan Baez, Sammy Davis, Decca Mitford, Ann Getty and Willie Brown mingling with rock musicians and Ultra Room starlets from the Mitchell Brothers. Paul, who lived in a big old green house on the Greenwich ledge of Pacific Heights, would be entertaining on the same evening Shana Alexander, C. K. McClatchy, Jules Feiffer, and William F. Buckley Jr., along with an itinerant rabbi and a Palestinian guerrilla. John couldn't fry an egg. Paul was an expert and enthusiastic cook. John was a bachelor. Paul slid close to the end of his rope when his wife, Ruth, died of a heart attack shortly before his own death.

⋆ ⋆ ⋆

John L. Wasserman and Paul Jacobs leave a legacy and a gap. Where are the replacements for people of such rare talents? John's hilarious reviews of bad, really bad movies are classics of journalism, and should be collected into a book. Paul's last work, the film on his fellow victims of radiation, deserves to be shown and reshown, no matter how bitterly the nuclear industry complains. It was heartbreaking to see him Sunday night, wasting away, just short of death, spending what little energy remained to interview those who were dying, too, as a result of Government callousness and inadequate safeguards. It is heartbreaking to remember John L. Wasserman bustling out of The Chronicle building just last Friday, wearing his usual black, carrying his usual overflowing armload of records, books, papers—"Ogawd I've got so much to DO!" were his last words, half-camp, half-serious.

⋆ ⋆ ⋆

"A pussycat." That was John Wasserman's supreme compliment.

He was one. So was Paul Jacobs. In this dog-eat-dog world, we need them desperately, purring one moment, slashing the next.

February 27, 1979

THE WALKING CAEN

Waiting for the Muni. Spent some of the best years of my life waiting for the Muni at corner of Five and Mish', where at is situated this pillar of veracity. It's like Richard Armour's catsup bottle—at first none will come and then a lot'll. Credited that couplet once to Ogden Nash, but I'm a fast learner on back burner. While waiting for Muni, must think about other things. Anything. "They're doing the best they can," is OK thought. Also true. One thing you mustn't do, after, say, about 15 minutes, is step into street and look for buses that aren't there. Watched bus never boils into view. When you look up street for buses and don't see any, get very depressed. Wonder if a strike has been called and nobody mentioned it. You think about writing your District Supervisor, whoever he or she may be if at all. Kick mailbox, which is dumb.

⋆ ⋆ ⋆

Sequence is as follows. After 10 minutes, during which you gaze steadily at Old Mint (not a bar), your peripheral vision detects bus approaching. Between Sixth and Fifth, it will turn left and disappear behind Old Mint, never to be seen again. Lose a lot of buses that way. Next bus arrives. As you climb step, driver says "Turning right at Fourth." Disembark. Following bus is a SamTrans from Sammateo. Only bus service with a first name. Sam can't do a thing for you. Then three trolley buses and a Diesel arrive at same moment, trunk to tail. They all say "Ferry." If you're transferring at Third to No. 15, any one you select will get there just as 15 is leaving. That takes planning.

⋆ ⋆ ⋆

Lot of people surprised that I ride Muni. Think I have a limo with a driver played by Tony Curtis. He calls me "J.J.," I call him "Sidney," or didn't you see "Sweet Smell of Success"? I ride Muni to get closer to The People, who I wish would get closer to deodorants. Keep hand on wallet and examine scenery. Yerba Buena Center! Community College! A real only-in-Ess Effer: behind St. Patrick's Church, a Florentine palace designed by Willis Polk as a PG&E substation, a red brick masterpiece drowning in sea of parked cars. Passed Rincon Annex, named for Abraham Rincon, and dodged traffic over to Ferry Building.

★ ★ ★

Lunched at World Trade Club with Mover & Shaker. Charlie Mover, Irving Shaker. Beautiful room, pleasant service. Spectacular view of Bay spoiled by two gray and white gulls seated on railing just outside window, staring at me. Waiting for handout. Tried to explain by sign language that I couldn't feed them through plate glass. Gulls unmoved, kept watching me eat prawn salad. Glad I hadn't ordered squab. Looking past gulls, noticed that million-dollar restaurant now being built atop BART ventilation shaft. Place has no name yet, but Top o' the BART is no good. Will open in November. With BART boob tube having so much trouble with ventilation, will restaurant help? You want cooking odors in your tube? Decided on cheese for dessert. Camembert. "Is it runny?" I asked waiter. "Oh NO sir," he assured me. Alas.

★ ★ ★

Took trolley back up Market. Old devil, built in '47 by St. Louis Car Company. Seat patched, window cracked, but a smooth ride. Debarked at Fifth and ran into Melvin Belli, large ornate barrister. Belli jowls shaking with rage. His legal opponent in case involving transsexual (Belli's client) had announced a settlement in "nickels and dimes." "I know inflation is rampant," thundered Mellifluous, "but since when is $325,000 nickels and dimes? It ain't millions but I've had worse settlements." He huffed off. "Any spare change?" asked hippie. "How about $325,000?" snapped Bellicose.

★ ★ ★

In next few hours, did any number of mad things. At "Splendor of Dresden" in Legion of Honor, saw a Crocker (Charles), a Flood (James) and a Hearst (Catherine) in same room. Spendors of San Francisco history. Dropped in at Old Mint for Presidio Hill School's annual Author's Night. Everybody kept asking "Where's Ferlinghetti?" No Ferling, but lots of bad champagne and sounds of glasses breaking. Cigarette burns appearing on white ledges. Old Mint too beautiful to be treated this way. Ninety percent of people there had never before been IN the place. Steep front steps discouraging, but you must see it before social events ruin it. Building survived 1906 earthquake. Good place to head for when next one strikes.

★ ★ ★

Minarets of Alhambra Theater on Polk summoned me to "Murder By Decree." Sherlock Holmes tale. Biggest dog since hound of

Baskervilles. Title should be "Death By Ennui." So depressed I went on sudden junk food binge, starting with double whammy at the Noble Frankfurter with onions, sauerkraut, relish, chili beans (latter "homemade," perhaps on Rue Morgue). Stumbled on to Double Rainbow for butter pecan cone and fudge cake. Still hungry for decent movie, took 55 Sacramento up to Fillmore and French flick at Clay, "Get Out Your Hankies." It asks question: "Can a 13-yr.-old boy find sexual satisfaction with a married woman twice his age?" Yes, if you're French. Parental guidance suggested, kid, in case you don't know where to start.

⋆ ⋆ ⋆

Out at Zohn Artman's house (he's Bill Graham's amanuensis), a wake in progress for late, great John L. Wasserman. Only champagne served because that was Wassy's favorite drink. Several people said "John would have wanted it this way." "John would rather have been here," I said, running for 24 Divisadero. Missed it but there'll be another in a few days. *March 6, 1979*

Newspaper Stuff

It just occurred to me, with the usual thull dud, that "etaoin shrdlu" is dead. If you are under a certain age, this will mean nothing to you, more's the pity. If you are over that age, and are a print-freak besides, the mere mention of "etaoin shrdlu" may bring a tear to your peepers—the same tear that is drawn by the mere mention of such words as "running board," "25-cent martini" and, well, okay, "peepers." In the pioneer days of print journalism, the intriguing "etaoin shrdlu," pronounced roughly "Etwan Sherdlu," was the most famous and frequent of all typographical errors. And needless to say, The Old Chronical had more than its share.

⋆ ⋆ ⋆

Once upon a time, children, reporters wrote their stories on typewriters. The result, called "copy" or "jeez that's awful," depending, was edited by copy editors (drunk, grizzled) using pencils. The copy, ruined or vastly improved by editing, depending, went to the composing room, where it was set into type by Linotype machines. These machines made wonderful, delicate, tinkling noises as the operators' skilled fingers flew over the keys. The machines' hot lead, in great pots, was transformed into columns of type. The type, beautiful to see and touch, was transferred in trays to a metal frame, where compositors arranged it into a page, the layout of which had been sketched by a makeup editor, grizzled, drunk.

★ ★ ★

Every now and then, a Linotype operator would make a mistake, causing him to say expletive deleted. He would then run his fingers down the two left-hand columns of the lowercase keyboard, producing the matrices "etaoin shrdlu," which filled out one line. Or, these words would be used as a guide on a galley of type, under the slug, say, of "Caen." Caen the slug, a phrase that lives to this day, was thus identified to the compositor as the writer, a term that died. Under it would appear "etaoin shrdlu." The compositor, a fellow who could read type upside down and backward but no other way, was supposed to remove the slug and the "etaoin shrdlu." But in many cases, after too many trips to Hanno's, the M&M of Breen's, the compositor would forget. And a front page story would read: "The Mayor, shocked at reports that he would be indicted for mopery, called in reporters and said etaoin shrdlu." Or "Bryant Townsend II, socialite sportsman, announced his engagement to Miss etaoin shrdlu." The Chronicle became so famous for these it was sometimes called The Daily Shrdlu.

Like everything else, the newspaper business has changed. For one thing, it became a business. It used to be "the newspaper game," a term that made us feel better about our ridiculous wages. Who gets paid for having fun except ballplayers and maybe some hookers? (Hookers are "turned out" and newspaper people are "broken in" but otherwise there isn't much difference, hence the term presstitute.) In the old days we pounded out the copy with two fingers and hollered "Boy!" to rush this hot stuff to the composing room. Today you yell "Boy!" and a girl arrives along with a member of the union grievance committee. It's silly to holler "Person!" so nobody yells any more. City rooms are as quiet as N. Gray, no matter what you see on "Lou Grant."

★ ★ ★

Gone the magnificent men on their Linotype machines, gone the galley proofs smelling of fresh ink, gone the paperweights with your name in 90-point type, the gift of a friendly printer. Gone the "Boy!"s of yesteryear, gone with the wind, gone with the Winchell, gone with the demon rewrite man with phone cradled to ear and cigarette burning his lips as he pounds out a perfect, tight, noneditable "new lede" (never "lead") on a fast-breaking story. Gone—yes—the very TYPEWRITERS!

★ ★ ★

When the cold type replaced hot lead and electronic scanners doomed the Rube Goldbergian fantasy of the Linotype, the manual typewriter was doomed. The scanner—ours, at least—would "accept" only IBM Selectric, which doesn't have keys that jam, like a proper typewriter, but a golfball device that runs back and forth like a mouse in a maze. I say if God had meant typewriters to have balls He would not have invented the movable carriage. Now, the Selectric is being phased out for VDTs, which is not polite shorthand for someone with a social disease plus the shakes. The initials stand for Video Display Terminal. The hapless reporter, already denied the pleasure of hollering "Boy!" sets his own "copy" in what appears to be type and edits it with an electronic "cursor." This last spells the end of the copy pencil as we have known it to break for so many generations.

⋆ ⋆ ⋆

Although I am generally spineless, I rose off my knees in protest at both the Selectric and the VDT. Old dog, new tricks and all that. Since I do use only two fingers while typing, the Selectric is too much machine for me, and the VDT is either above or below contempt, I forget which. I have thus been allowed to go on using my ancient and beloved Royal manual—metal, not plastic—and living in the past. I edit my copy with an Eagle 314, just as in the old days. I go on writing, and yelling "Boy!" as though it were still 1941. You may have noticed. Where have you gone, etaoin shrdlu? Operator, gimme rewrite! Stop the press—uh, scanner—I gotta story here that'll shake this old town right off its foundations! Boy! Boy? Uh . . . *March 11, 1979*

Speaking of keeping one's cool, Janet (Mrs. Mortimer) Fleishhacker was the epitome of grace under pressure during the $100,000 armed robbery of the glitterati at a Sea Cliff cocktail party last Thurs. night. Janet was stripped of her rings and handbag, and, like the other victims, ordered to lie on the floor, but she kept her priorities straight anyway. Scrunching around, she gazed up at one of the bandits and asked, "Could I please have my ballet tickets?" He said no in unprintable language.

March 19, 1979

Espee faces life: Slowly, ponderously, with appropriate dignity, the Southern Pacific is coming to grips with reality. For the first time since the turn of the century, observes Atty. Hal Mickelson, the fine print on the back of the 20-ride Peninsula commute ticket has been changed. It now "is valid for use of purchaser and/or any member of his or her immediate family." Up until last month, the ticket read, grandly, "Valid for use of purchaser, his wife, his children, his relatives and domestic household servants." Now a collector's item, along with servants. *March 30, 1979*

Also nominated for a True San Franciscan Award: Trisha Benedict, who remembers the cream cheese and jelly sandwiches at the Raphael Weill Room of the old White House department store. You may also qualify if you remember the warm raisin toast served in snowy napkins in the Palace's Garden Court, Townsend's creamed spinach, the Golden Pheasant's small blacks, the original Blum's milkshakes (too thick for a straw) and North Beach minestrone you could stand a spoon in. And how about the first time you had a barbecued rib at the original Trader Vic's at 65th and San Pablo in Emeryville? No love like first love. *April 15, 1979*

The Moving Finger

The spacious San Francisco skies were overcast yesterday, matching the mood of the city. Faces were sullen, the atmosphere suddenly Southern and heavy. You could almost imagine lynch mobs. People stood around on downtown street corners, talking about The Verdict That Shook the World, or parts thereof. Matters that had seemed so pressing only the day before—the gas crisis (fake or real?), the Giants (weak up the middle?), "Apocalypse Now" (triumph or tragedy?)—faded away. The sound of sirens waffled continuously, from Hunters Point through the Castro to Polk. The city of love was undergoing another agony of hate, doubt and confusion.

* * *

Monday night, we cave dwellers went through the familiar ritual, gathering around our TV sets to observe the wall paintings of our advanced civilization. "LIVE," it said on the screen. In videoland, the opposite is not "DEAD," but the dead, George Moscone and Harvey Milk, were very much there, alive and on tape, while Dan White was very much alive and will remain so. A local reporter had written a few days ago, in an excess of underthink, that three people had died on that day last November—Moscone, Milk and White—but only White is being taped now for future release, perhaps in as few as five years. George and Harvey are on tape forever.

* * *

"What is there about San Francisco?" That question swept the country after the assassinations and the Götterdämmerung of Jim Jones. The question concerned itself with our permissiveness, our free-and-easy leadership, the wild manic-depressive swings, our supposed liberality. In San Francisco, ran the myth, things always go better with coke and/or martinis, and when they don't we head straight for the bridge and jump, thereby becoming a star-studded statistic. Join the Golden Gate Suicide Club—Be More Than Just a Number! All the evidence was trotted out again. From VD to cirrhosis, we were right up there among the biggies. We were proud and ashamed. After George and Harvey, as after Jack and Bobby, we were determined to be better. We all sat around and said, "I'll drink to that."

* * *

"What's wrong with San Francisco?" was being asked again yesterday, again for all the right and wrong reasons. A middle-class jury, not a bunch of kooks by any stretch, had decided one can kill, twice, complete with coup de grace, and get away with it. The grateful defendant was a staunch defender of law and order, a man who, quote, believed in "the good old American virtues." He believed in the death penalty. He believed in paying the price for your sins and mistakes. A religious man who went straight to church after he killed. If he had been in full possession of his faculties—and we now know, officially, that he wasn't, for it is on the record—he would have been appalled at the sentence handed down by what the Dan Whites like to think of as a soft-hearted judge and soft-headed jury.

* * *

Monday night was Ugly Night. "Gay," a term that has never been felicitous, seemed miles off the mark. Out in the Castro, gays turned grim, then mean, finally violent. Disbelief to sorrow to vengeance, a progression helped along, predictably, by "the electronic media." Only a few minutes after the verdict had been announced, a KRON reporter in the Castro kept asking, hopefully, "Do you think there'll be violence?" The replies moved up the scale from no to I don't know to you never know to could be to damn right there'll be violence. A fateful crescendo.

★ ★ ★

This is a city of undercurrents, not all of them well hidden. Many police made an open secret of their support for Dan White and their dislike (understatement) of homosexuals. The gays distrust the cops and blame Dianne Feinstein, a straight arrow, for the harassment they have been experiencing lately. If ever the stage was set for a confrontation, it was the Dan White verdict. The gays were itching to yell "Dump Dianne!" and let the world know that they are still second-class citizens, even in the city of Anything Goes. The police were itching to crack a few heads, and if some members of the press got in the way, that's fine. Police and press have an edgy relationship, too.

★ ★ ★

And so battle cries were heard in the Castro, as cameras and microphones delightedly sharpened their eyes and ears. "Out of the bars and into the streets" is not a phrase that will live in history, like "Aux barricades!" and "Sic semper tyrannis," but it got the fateful show on the road. The rest is bad history: burning police cars, broken windows and heads, an assault on the very City Hall that once symbolized "permissive San Francisco," which this city isn't, one layer down. What we have is a divided city, and the Dan White juror who cried helplessly, "All we wanted to do is bring people together again," failed in her innocence.

★ ★ ★

Dan White, the man who liked junk food ("The Twinkies Insanity Defense," one lawyer called it). The jury, sending out regularly for soda pop, candy and other white sugar products. Cynics predicted a Dan White Sugar verdict: "They'll find him guilty of hypoglycemia," said a bitter Peter Kuehl. "The Three Mile Island of murder trials," snapped Charles Graham. In high irony, Dan White's strong belief in capital punishment has found thousands of new converts. From now on, a lot of people will die because Dan White lives. *September 23, 1979*

Entree news: In this desiccated age of diets, jogging, "health" foods and the like, it's an occasional pleasure for a foodaholic to take lunch at The Hoffman Grill on Market. The Hoffman has been right there since 1891, and the menu faithfully reflects that year, when a paunch was something to be proud of—a pot belly was called "a corporation"—and cholesterol had not yet been invented . . . Since man cannot live by Lecithin alone, I dropped in at The

Hoffman one noon last week and browsed with pleasure over the day's specials. What an array! German meat balls and potato, Hungarian Goulash with noodles, Roast Pork with mashed potatoes and applesauce, roast Tom turkey with dressing, breaded veal cutlets with country gravy and French fries, Yankee pot roast with taglierini, sausage with sweet potatoes or Boston baked beans, frankfurters and sauerkraut with boiled potatoes—and on and on . . . The closest thing to a "diet special," an abomination eschewed by The Hoffman, may have been a jelly omelette or breaded oysters. Brushing the calories off the menu—they are thicker than the sawdust on the floor—I selected the Chili con Carne with ravioli, a bargain at $4.25. *August 27, 1979*

The Way We Are

These may not be the best of times, but they could be among the worst. Nothing like that certain morning in April, 1906, of course, and one has to wonder how the San Franciscans of today would deal with a catastrophe of similar proportions. If the evidence is to be believed, our forerunners faced that disaster with a smile and a Jeanette MacDonald song, and, whistling while they worked, built a city even more glittering and glamorous than its doomed predecessor. Out of the ashes rose the cliché about the phoenix bird that would haunt cub reporters forevermore. "Like the phoenix bird, the Milpitas Mustangs rose out of the ashes of defeat to"—to what? To make the boozy old copy reader spit on the floor in disgust as he applied his big blue pencil.

★ ★ ★

As I wrote recently, there was a time when everything seemed to work. These days, nothing does, starting with the workers. How is our little world of a city-state falling apart? Let me enumerate the ways: BART and ferries and teachers on strike. Bay heavily polluted again. Golden Gate Park falling apart. Cable lines shut down for months, maybe years, maybe forever. Streets more cluttered with debris than at any time within memory of the oldest writer of letters to the editor ("I put pen to paper to protest," etc.). Union Square, "the heart of one of the few real downtowns," strewn with flotsam here, jetsam there, here flot, there jet, everywhere flotjet. Fisherman's Wharf with hardly enough fishing boats to bless—right, padre? Worst Giants' season since they came west. The 49ers zip–five. Traffic? Please, not while I'm eating breakfast. Bacon?

Please, not till they get the nitrites out.

★ ★ ★

Even Pollyandy, the Glad Boy, a role I sometimes assume, would be hard put to find an optimistic word. Oh, at certain times of the day—dusk, for instance—the city looks hunky-dory (that's a small Hungarian boat), but we can hardly claim credit for this glorious profusion of hills, water, splendid weather, and our very own mountain, Tamalpa, the Indian maiden, gazing serenely toward the heavens. All this was here before us, when every prospect was pleasing. Vile white man arrived soon enough, and before they knew it, the Indians were a minority.

★ ★ ★

Today everybody is a minority, in a majority of cases. The city itself, once a faceted jewel we could admire from all sides, has broken into bits and pieces. Critics of San Francisco find it as difficult to define us now as we do. All in one recent issue of a Southern California magazine, we were "smug and stodgy" as well as "the kook capital of the world." We are "living in the past," a charge first leveled about 100 years ago, while "the wave of the future" crashes on the southern shores. We are all things to all people, or maybe nothing. It's hard to tell.

★ ★ ★

The city is a mess for a lot of reasons, only some of them fiscal. Proposition 13 has been the catchall excuse. "Lack of leadership" is another. Ex-Mayor George Christopher warned two years ago that "deferred maintenance"—putting off repairs and upkeep to keep budgets down—was a dirty bird that would come home to roost, and it has. Scratch one phoenix, sub one dirty bird. To become slightly amorphous, there is a lack of civic pride. People who love their city don't foul and defile it. They don't slash the very Muni bus seats they have to sit on. They don't run red lights. One reason they do is that they know they can get away with it.

★ ★ ★

The city is breaking down, literally and otherwise. In 40-odd years of writing about this place so many people love, I can't remember a more divided community. The great strength of San Francisco used to be its tolerance for diversity. Well, "tolerance" is a dated word, and maybe a dated concept. Whites I once thought of as enlightened mutter about "the Orient express"—the buses jammed with Chinese—and about trilingual signs, ballots, a dozen languages filling the air and covering the walls. "My parents came from Lithuania," an Old San Franciscan complained the other day, "and the first thing they had to do was learn English or they would have starved." "I guess they had no lobby," half-smiled Wise Willie Brown.

★ ★ ★

All the criticisms leveled at San Francisco are true enough, to varying degrees. The Old Guard is smug and stodgy. Also ingrown and frightened stiff, to the point of arthritis, about new people and new ideas. Some of the newcomers are indeed pushers & shovers, as well as movers & shakers, and show little sensitivity to what is precious to old-timers. Still, there is no excuse for the xenophobia of that holiest of local creatures, Native San Franciscans (all rise). Pride of birth and place is all very well, but like our hills and views, it is a circumstance over which they had no control. If there were ever a time for them to demonstrate their vaunted sophistication—their "understanding" of exotic and/or difficult people from faraway places—it is now.

★ ★ ★

"With all its faults I love it still," sings Pollyandy the Glad Boy, making his favorite double pun on earthquakes. Our beautiful women, our restaurants and bars, the downtown stores, the steely power of the financial district, the people with Good Taste to match their Old Money—OK, there is still time. But from where I sit, the hands on the Ferry Building clock stand at five minutes to midnight.

October 7, 1979

BAGHDAD-BY-THE-BAY

That mystical mythical clear day when you can see forever, far beyond the Farallones, out to infinity and one step beyond. A biting North wind down from the Yukon, stretching the sky so tight you can almost see through it. San Francisco with pink cheeks, chapped lips, fog on its breath, eyes straining across the next hill, sharply etched wonders to behold. On a day like this, everything is close enough to touch: Angel Island only a giant leap away, Alcatraz across the street from Buena Vista. The views are so foreshortened that the city seems one-dimensional, flattened against a wall of space. Out on the blue-black Bay, the sailboats scud along as though on a single string. By employing The Selective Eye, you could say the city has never looked more beautiful. The Selective Eye blocks out the blunt buildings with their squared-off tops—uninspiring, literally—that desecrate one of the world's great cityscapes. They rise without soaring. They lack that certain grace. They scrape the cold sky and leave it raw. Through the open wound, a screaming gull soars to a landing atop a piling on the dead waterfront, alive with the ghosts of clipper ships.

★ ★ ★

There is no place like the city, even one that flirts daily with a dozen disasters. Walk along the streets, alone in the swirling crowd, and wonder which ones will still be alive 24 hours from now. In a city, life and the people move fast. Slow down and be trampled. Look vulnerable, and you are dead. There are people who exude fear and will not be around much longer, and there are those who walk defiantly through the darkest alley and come out the other end in one piece. At Fifth and Market, I watch an Indochinese woman cross the street, against the light. She is old but her back is straight, her chin high. Barefoot, a bright cloth around her head, she carries tragedy on her shoulders as she once carried children and the pitiful baggage of refugees. As she walks against the light, looking neither right nor left, traffic slams to a halt. A cop watches her, whistle unblown. She is grand, oh so grand. She has survived, she will survive.

★ ★ ★

City of infinite riches, endless poverty. Bits and pieces—that's why a city like San Francisco never becomes boring. Dormer windows and stained glass, laughter floating out of a bar, a far-off saxophone wailing "Can't Get Started," the never-ending song of the siren (notes of hysteria, rising, falling), Greek columns, Corinthian excesses, Victorian prissiness, the bleating beep of a bus turning a corner, a hand on your heels. On the tattered fringes of the Tenderloin, always a passed-out drunk to step over. How soon we become accustomed to the sight. No thought of calling for help. Besides, he wears a reasonably happy expression, and if he died, he died happy. The Tenderloin, world in transition. The old Bay Meadows Hotel coming down, the Paddock and Ringside bars closed. Once it was a haunt of horse players, gamblers and fighters who fought clean even in the gutters. Now the punks walk along swinging baseball bats. No hero. I cross to the other side and pay my last respects to Newman's Gym.

★ ★ ★

Art Deco, Art Nouveau, Art Moderne, Art this and Art that—the examples are everywhere. The well-built well-kept old apartment houses, still with proper uniformed doormen and white-jacketed houseboys who walk the Shih-Tzsus and the snuffling Pekes.

Nurses with prams in Lafayette Park, formerly Square—a little time-warpy, a sight like that. Out along the rich streets, the trees are thicker, the streets cleaner, the children better kept. A few blocks away, the reverse side of the coin and con of capitalism. In a city this small, the contrasts are so facile and obvious as to be corny. Limousines and lice, violins and violence, furry rats and ratty furs and lost souls rooting around in garbage cans, leaning far in for a one-handed catch at the bottom. Dignity is the first casualty. An empty stomach makes its own rules.

* * *

It is hard to stay depressed in San Francisco, on a crisp November afternoon, with flowers and pretzels for sale on the street corners and the tourists going Instamatically mad at the bright wonder of it all. We are so lucky to have a proper downtown, where people can parade. And they do parade, playing dress-up like so many children, eyeing each other as they pass. The great stores are jammed. Their show-windows are cunning, brilliant, a cornucopia of earthly delights. Buy now, pray later. At dusk, even the Bank of America behemoth grows light and bright, standing on tiptoes to peek down into Embarcadero Center, our most enthralling urban space. Pre-Christmas karma: tiny lights, by the thousands, flickering like fireflies along landscaped walkways. Pedestrian bridges over rivers of traffic. Great statues rising alongside chic little restaurants and cozy little bars, all in the shadow of buildings as sharp and thin and dangerous as a knife. Call it what you will—High Tech, hard edge, Tomorrowland Today—there is a hint of craziness in the sterile air. But not a flower, not a leaf, not a tile out of place.

* * *

Nearby, the Ferry Building, bright in its 1915 Exposition lights, stands guard over the gingerbread fleet that sailed for the last time so long ago. It stands straight, held aloft by a great American Flag starched flat against the sky by the North winds. A garish postcard to shake one's head over, but let us never be afraid to be sentimental in this most cat-graceful dog-dangerous of cities.

November 25, 1979

Goodbye and Hello

Look, Ma, a year is dying, and we are about to start dancing on its grave, but so what? They don't make years the way they used to.

Old '79 came with the usual 12-month guarantee and it went faster than a runaway cable car. This year must have been made under water by natives in Taiwan. It looked all right from a distance but the plastic fantastic cracked under the strain, and we know for sure now that the hostages will not be home for the holidays. They didn't get their Christmas wish. May 1980 bring them what they want most—a one-way ticket home, nonstop, first class all the way.

★ ★ ★

Unless you listen to the nitpickers, it is also the end of a decade, or at least of the Seventies, for bookkeeping purposes. The nitpickers will tell you the 1970s will end on Dec. 31, 1980, but again, so what? Life is not a series of neatly labeled cubicles. It is a matter of ages, golden and otherwise. I can tell you from personal experience that the Edwardian Era lasted till World War I, when my birth in Sacramento caused a temporary truce and the troops emerged from the trenches to exchange gifts. The Roaring Twenties came to premature ejaculation (unprintable) in October of '29, and the Great Depression didn't really end till the Japanese bombed Pearl. In the 1960s, Pearl meant Janis Joplin, who was bombed most of the time, too, poor soul. Rock once meant Hudson, then Bill Graham, now punk.

★ ★ ★

The Seventies are about to go down in history, and the farther down the better. Your basic crummy decade: the Texas Chain Saw Massacre—that was a good one. A sick man named White got away with murder. We still have Nixon to kick around, but let us also berate famous men like Jeb Magruder, Egil (Bud) Krogh and Bert Lance. The Symbionese Liberation Army, People's Temple, CB radio ("Ten-four" yourself, good buddy my foot), the Werner Erhard scampaigns, the fall of Chuck Dederich, the sadsacks who looked for answers at Esalen without asking the right questions. There is no difference between eyeball contact and rude staring, and no, I do not wish to encounter you. Take a number and wait your turn.

★ ★ ★

The Seventies, sinking slowly into the primordial snooze, taking with them the ashes of the Symbionese Liberation Army and all those posters of Patricia Hearst, which outsold all those posters of Huey Newton, both of which were outsold by posters of Cheryl Tiegs. 'Bye-bye, Cheryl, here comes Bo Derek, and therrrre goes Bo Derek. We have short attention spans—fortunately. What became of the Killer Bee invasion from South America? Stung again. If you were a Born Again Christian, would you want your daughter to marry a Jew for Christ? For the 1980s, I predict an end to lightbulb and Perrier jokes. I wish I could be as optimistic about blow cards in magazines.

* * *

San Francisco during the Great Holidays, a fat cat sprawled over its seven, 14 or 41 hills, spent (and overspent) on Christmas excesses, and awaiting the new year, Maalox and aspirin at the ready. What is there to say about something that ends with dyspepsia and starts with a hangover? Above the city floats a haze of turkey, champagne and garbage. Underfoot, gift wrapping and Scotch tape, stuck to your sole. Still, the parties were fine. At the Cotillion, three generations pecked cheeks. Pat and Jack Falvey took over the Mark and created Instant 1947. Everybody sat in the Lower Bar, stared glumly at the bleached bricks (Instant San Carlos) and wailed, "Why did they ever change it?"

* * *

It has been instructive to read the newspapers during the Great Holidays. All of us flailing away in the annual futile attempts to say something Meaningful, or, failing that, Amusing, my dear. The fatuous Christmas gift lists ("For Al Davis, someone else's fingernails to chew on. Dianne Feinstein: The blouse can stay, but the beau has gotta go"). Sentimentality: "At this time of year, I remember Mama, an angel with flour on her cheek. Heavenly cooking smells floated through the old house whose walls spoke to me of times past." Nobody remembers Papa at Christmas time. Then there are the columns reprinted annually "by request" of nobody, and the clinker of a "poem" with rhyming names. With each passing year, "'Twas the night before Christmas" and "Yes, Virginia, There Is a Santa Claus" look better.

* * *

All things considered, the city is in good shape, considering the shape it's in. Who else could afford a $2 billion sewer system, or can we? Something smells here, certainly, but we dopes are not on the ropes yet. Christmas is always a boggling reminder that there's a lot of money floating around. Day before Christmas, the cars were double-parked for miles outside Jurgensen's, the Tiffany of grocery stores, as customers ran in to pick up their caviar (Russian, from the Caspian, $450 a pound, not Iranian, that wouldn't be patriotic). Tiffany, the Jurgensen's of jewelry stores, was as jammed as the Marina Safeway on Saturday morning, or Cala

Foods at midnight, and that's either astonishing or inflation. A jewelry store with a fast lane for nine items or less?

* * *

And so another decade winds down without my finding out what a "semi-conductor" is. A part-time Muni worker? I'm not too sure about rack-and-pinion steering either. Oh well, I could care less or should it be I couldn't care less? Either way, happy new year—all 12 months. *December 31, 1979*

Playing Fields of Eatin'

Everybody used to say that San Francisco is "a great show town." Maybe it still is. I don't know any other place where the audience applauds the scenery to show that it Cares. This is also a good sports town (30,000 to see the Giants vs. Houston on a freezing night), a good drinking town (the statistics are frightening) and a good eating town. This last is true for a lot of reasons, some of them obvious. From the beginning, meaning the Gold Rush, San Francisco has been a city that goes out at night. Lonely guys living downtown and looking for a little action—I mean, where else are they going to go besides Out? Then the hookers arrived from New Orleans and you remember the rest of it. A thoroughbred doggerel: "The miners came in '49, the whores in '51; and when they got together they produced the Native Son."

★ ★ ★

Food. Any light remark one is inclined to make about the Donner Party is guaranteed to be in bad taste. Even to use the phrase "bad taste" about the Donner Party is in bad taste. Nevertheless, Grey's Toll Station Restaurant in Truckee boasts that Chief Truckee was the last cook with the Donner Party, an 1847 disaster. This is not too appetizing. There was some cannibalism, but George Donner himself died of blood poisoning in his hand and was not eaten. His wife was. The Toll Station's present cook, Doug Lindsay, claims to be George's direct descendant. Don't order Tripes à la Mode de Donner unless you're in a party mood.

★ ★ ★

Everybody talks about food in San Francisco. When strangers eye each other across a crowded room, it is not love or sex they have in mind—one wants to tell the other about the great little restaurant he just found, down an alley, cheap, undiscovered, great ambience. We are all ambience chasers. The town is full of restaurant critics, most of them blessedly free of criticism. Every other day a new restaurant guide comes out, listing places everybody already knows about, like the Fourth Street Grill in Berkeley, which gets discovered regularly. San Francisco magazine this month lists "365 Selected Restaurants," whatever that means. Were they selected because they were good or because they bought an ad? The implication is that they are good. Who would "select" a bad restaurant? There aren't 365 good restaurants in the world, but the popular conceit around here is that "you can't get a bad meal in San Francisco." A harmless hyperbole unless you find yourself in an indifferent restaurant.

★ ★ ★

San Francisco is one remarkable small city, and getting smaller. I hate the doleful fact that the population is diminishing but there are ever fewer places to park. Have residents taken to having cars instead of children? I know a lot of two-car no-kid families these days (hi guys). Still, the variety is dizzying. From Hunters Point to Sea Cliff and from Lake Merced to Telegraph Hill isn't all that far, and what a lot of action takes place in between! Here's Tinytown USA with big league baseball and football, major league opera and ballet and symphony, big theater, little theater, a thousand clowns in a thousand bars, world-class hotels, a financial district with 500 banks . . . and all . . . those . . . restaurants. And it all started because a gold miner needed a place to eat and a homesick Frenchman needed a place to cook.

★ ★ ★

Trader Vic was the first innovative restaurant man I met, circa '36 or '37. He was and is a genius, a guy who'd try anything, including a gardenia in your rum drink. "It doesn't hurt the rum any," he used to chortle, "and the public seems to like it." Scorpion, Missionary's Revenge, Sufferin' Bastard—he had a flair for names. What did he serve? Simple. "Grog and Chow." Back before World War II, I was able to report that "the best restaurant in San Francisco is in Oakland." That was when there was only one Vic's, the mother church at 65th and San Pablo. Vic has a sense of style and arrangement—and a helluva staff. His place here might not be the best restaurant in town, and I'm not saying it isn't, but it's always fun. A place to see people and have some strong grog and good chow.

★ ★ ★

When people ask me to name my favorite restaurants, I say "Vic's and any four places you like." Any good restaurant where you know the captain (and the captain knows you) is going to be your place. When you walk in and the bartender starts mixing your favorite drink before you can order it—well, you're home. "The best restaurant in town" is a foolish phrase, considering the differences in taste (and budget, let us never forget that), and besides, it depends on your mood. Sometimes, on a sunny day, with the carillon ringing out from nearby Grace Cathedral, the little Nob Hill Cafe is the best. Sometimes, Todays on Stockton, especially when the tuna is fresh and you can look out the window at Union Square and dream of El Prado, the long-gone luncheon hangout that turns out to have been irreplaceable. Sometimes it's Jack's, the noisiest and authentically oldest place around. You can eat alone at Jack's and not feel lonely. The waiters treat you like a member of the family, and you know most of the regulars to begin with.

★ ★ ★

San Francisco can be a perfectly maddening city. But when there's a good bar across the street, almost any street, and a decent restaurant around almost any corner, we are not yet a lost civilization.

August 17, 1980

Well, tourismos and touristas, confused by San Francisco's sometimes drizmal weather? So was I, most of my life, till Michael Castleman produced a new vocabulary appropriate to the city's range of precipitation. "Meteorologists can't do it," he says, "and they're always wrong anyway. Therefore I propose the following lexicon in ascending order of wetness":

IZZLE—Light form of precipitation. It seems to come from nowhere, often on relatively sunny days. You can hardly feel it; you can't see it. But it's THERE.

MIZZLE—Izzle from visible fog or mist. You feel wetness without the sensation of real droplets.

FIZZLE—You FEEL droplets, but can't see them.

VIZZLE—The droplets become visible.

DRIZZLE—Standard definition.

DRAIN—More than drizzle, less than rain.

RAIN—Standard definition.

RAINING DOG POOP—A substitution for "raining cats and

dogs," which is anachronistic. Cats die under the wheels of onrushing cars, dog poop is everywhere.

★ ★ ★

What every San Franciscan wants: A stop sign at his corner. Two uniformed cops patroling his block 24 hours a day. A guaranteed parking space in front of his house. A North view and a South garden. Right around the corner: good school, good park, good little restaurant, drugstore, cleaner, shoe repair, grocery. Not a swimming pool or tennis court, but friends who have them. The pleasure of a sailboat without the trouble and expense of owning one. All the benefits and services of a big city without paying the taxes for them. *August 24, 1980*

A Star Is Born

"What did you do in the war, Daddy?": You may have missed the opening of the Opera House in 1932—not having been born yet is an acceptable excuse—but you really should have been at the launching of Louise M. Davies Symphony Hall Tuesday night. So you didn't have $1000 or even $100—certainly there is some Federal agency around to take care of small contingencies like that. Urbane Renewal, perhaps. Besides, it's all "reduckable fum de ovahead," as Amos used to say to Andy . . . If you really weren't there for the Opera House opening, Claudia Muzio starred as "Tosca," and Socialite Tallant Tubbs, taken in illegal French wine, fell asleep two minutes 47 seconds after the curtain rose, establishing himself as a Famous First on that Great Snoreboard in the Sky.

★ ★ ★

"Launching" seems like the proper term for the opening of what I suppose we will be calling Davies Hall, or Chez Louise. The atmosphere Tuesday evening was strangely shiplike, akin to sailing day. As gongs sounded and the uniformed crew scurried around in circles, the Titanic came fitfully to mind, the main difference being that the Titanic didn't run out of ice. The main hall resembles a ship's salon, curving prowlike, while the steep-steep grand staircase, rising halfway to the stars, is definitely lineresque. Or perhaps it is more like Cardiac Hill at Candlestick. Any funds left over for escalators?

★ ★ ★

San Franciscans are extremely good at giving parties, and this was a great party, with more body contact than a 49er game. "Pickpocket heaven," somebody murmured, putting a hand on my wallet (I gave at the office). Moet Chandon champagne was spilled on $4,000 Givenchy gowns. Stuffed shirts buckled and groaned, studs popping. Diamond baubles rolled underfoot, their owners on all fours in hot pursuit. Spirits were high and giddy—"San Francisco has done it again!"—and self-congratulation the order of the day. When ship's gongs started ringing to announce that the concert was about to begin, several wags inquired archly, "Oh, is there music, too?" Not as funny a question as it sounds, for The Sound soon became Topic A through Y, Topic Z being "Where are you going afterward?"

★ ★ ★

Edo De Waart does a great "Star Spangled Banner," up-tempo with a definite swing. The audience, filled with pride and pâté over its newest toy, sang lustily, as though to test the acoustics. The Berlioz was LOUD, man. Then came David Del Tredici's "Happy Voices," commissioned especially for the occasion by the indefatigable Louise Davies. (Item: she paid him a flat $15,000 for the composition, so he DOESN'T work on commission, see?) A hand-cranked wind machine seemed the highlight of the piece, which John Dahlquist described as "a ripoff of 'Le Jazz,' written by Bohuslav Martinů in the '20s." I forgot to tell you that San Franciscans know their music. In the Mendelssohn, Rudolf Serkin missed a lot of notes but there are more than necessary to begin with.

★ ★ ★

"How does it sound where you're sitting?" was THE question during intermission, along with "Where is the nearest bar?" and "Where did you get that divine dessert?" (The St. Francis catered the affair and very well, too.) It was people-watching's finest hour, but not Dianne Feinstein's. "Where DID she get that dress?" became the question of the moment as she displayed a purple thing with puffed sleeves inflated to 50 pounds pressure. Tony Kent suggested that the designer was Mr. Blackwell, he being the L.A. badmouth that ranked LaBelle Dianne only No. 7 on his annual list of worst-dressed women, despite her "ding-a-ling bows" and "macho stiff-shouldered suits." So why not first? Upon being asked whether his boss was indeed wearing a Blackwell, Mel Wax, her faithful press secretary, hollered "bull——!" Actually, it was an Oscar de la Renta, or perhaps I misunderstood. If she got it from Oscar the Renter, it can be returned.

★ ★ ★

The sound, the sound, the horror, the horror. Suppose we built a

$30 million symphony hall that sounded awful? This was the unspoken thought that brought out the flopsweat among some of our most important citizens. "How was it where you were sitting?" indeed. "Fine," replied one woman. "I was in the powder room." Where I was sitting, the sound was muffled. Others found it "too live," still others "juuuust right," like Baby Bear. Critics fell back on such evasions as "Well, you can't tell at one hearing," or you can't hear at one telling. I guess a hall, like a new car, has to be broken in. Item: the reflectors over the stage, which can be moved, were stuck. The vaunted banners, which can be raised and lowered, didn't seem to make much difference. Let's just say it was a whole new sound.

* * *

As he has so often through the best musical years of our lives, old Lewdveeg van saved the night. Edo conducted a Beethoven Fifth for the ages, and the crowd, finally finding something to sink its teeth into besides a cream puff, went away happy. (A Sousa march would have been nice, by the way.) The main thing is that nobody wants to, or should, knock Chez Louise at this point. It's not nice, and besides, the hall has yet to be completed. Thanks to Louise for her $5 million, thanks to us taxpayers for OUR $5 million, and thanks for the future memories. Just think, some day you can qualify as an Old San Franciscan simply by sighing, "Remember when the Symphony played in the Opera House?" I'm not saying those were the good old days . . . yet. *September 18, 1980*

House on the Corner

Bernice Bergquest, my old friend and one-time neighbor in Sacramento, tells me that the old house I was reared in there is on the market for $126,500. How my late father would have loved THAT! He bought the house in 1919 for $6000, lost it in the depths of the Depression, and went to his grave thinking of himself as a guy who hadn't quite made it in this country. Lucien Caen—or "Lou," "Louie" or "Frenchy," as he was sometimes known among Sacramento's rougher trade—never wanted to be a millionaire but he always thought "about $100,000 would be nice." He never came close to that once-imposing figure, but now it turns out he was living in a $100,000 house and never knew it. His pale blue eyes would have danced with delight as he hauled a kitchen match out of a pants pocket and lit his El Stinko cigar. I loved that old Frenchman but he did smoke lousy cigars.

★ ★ ★

The current ad for my old house—at 26th and Q streets—talks about its "traditional elegance," a quality I seem to have overlooked during the 17 years I lived there. It is also "a rare treat," which seems accurate enough. "Three bedrooms." Yes, I remember those. Hot in the summer, cold in the winter, but that was Sacramento. The coolest bedroom, in the front of the house, had a proper dressing room, mirrored. That went to the star of the family—my sister, Estelle, a talented pianist who went on to Juilliard and a reputation as a fine teacher. My parents occupied the middle bedroom, with an excellent view of a vacant lot. I was consigned to the "sleeping porch," facing East. The sun and I both got up early. In the style of those times, there was only one bathroom, but we got by. Nicely.

★ ★ ★

The ad goes on to mention a "sewing room," which I don't recall (it sounds grand, however), and a "sunporch," which might be my old bedroom. There is no mention of the basement, a dungeon of frightening, flickering shadows, acrawl with black widow spiders. What I remember was a huffing, chuffing furnace, with more arms than an octopus, squatted like a monster in our dark netherworld. Every winter night, my German mother would say, "Herbert shovel some more coal on the fire." Down the rickety wooden stairs I'd go, staring around fearfully. The ghosts and dragons were all in my mind but the spiders were real enough. On occasion, equipped with a candle on the end of a long stick, I'd be dispatched on a spider-killing expedition. Even now, goose pimples rise at the thought.

★ ★ ★

By any standards, it was a comfortable if not imposing house, its good-sized "backyard" filled with roses. It stood on a corner, with lawns on two sides. Every two weeks, it was "Herbert, mow the lawn," and always when a REALLY important baseball game was under way in the lot across the street. A marvelous catalpa tree flourished in front, blossoming whitely in the spring and producing long cigar-like pods that we tried to smoke. On hot summer nights, we rocked on the front porch, the wicker furniture creaking, as my sister practiced at the Everett piano. Now and then my mother, who had been an operatic mezzo in Germany, would sing Schubert's "The Erl King," setting the windows to rattling a block around, while the next-door neighbors would counter by playing Sousa marches on their windup phonograph.

⋆ ⋆ ⋆

A good, sturdy house in a good, sturdy neighborhood, the kind that has largely ceased to exist. We knew everybody within a four-block radius, and they knew us. When my sister, still in her early teens, gave a recital, they all turned out, nodding wisely and saying "What a talented sister, you must be proud," and I was. The Boyer kids, next door, dragged me off to Catholic mass on Sundays at the twin-domed church across from Sutter's Fort. It was an Irish-Catholic neighborhood that produced a lot of tough, freckled kids who liked to beat on me. Whatever happened to freckled kids and "Four-Eyes" and "Skinny" and "Fatty"? And the rich girl around the corner who wore taffeta dresses to school, and white silk knee socks, and shiny patent leather shoes?

⋆ ⋆ ⋆

My father was proud of the old house at 26th and Q and a corner house, at that. It represented a major achievement for the immigrant who had left his village near Metz in Lorraine, at 17, and come to San Francisco in 1895, to work for an aunt and uncle. Then he became a whiskey salesman out of Sacramento, proudly peddling Hanover Rye up and down the state, in a horse and buggy, and by all accounts he was one of the best. With his ready smile, his sense of humor, his charm, how could he miss? And a dandy he was, too: wing collars, diamond stickpin, double-breasted vest, spats. When Prohibition came, he obediently turned in his barrels of whiskey and opened a handsome billiard parlor—"not a pool hall, mind you," he would say severely—on K Street.

⋆ ⋆ ⋆

For a while, business was good. But times and styles change. Billiards (and prosperity) became a thing of the past, the stock market crashed, and the Great Depression stole slowly up the shaded streets of Sacramento, arriving eventually, like a blight, at the corner of 26th and Q. As she packed for the move to a small apartment, my mother wept silently and constantly. My father tried to smile but his eyes were wet, and he shook his head a lot. He would never again own another house, but for a while there, he had made it in the New World, a good man in every way.

September 21, 1980

Farewell: What was once described by cocky San Franciscans as "the ninth wonder of the world!" will soon be buried, never to be seen again except perhaps by archaeologists a century hence. Unfortunately, I am not referring to Candlestick Park. That's the ninth blunder of the world. We're talking about Fleishhacker Pool, the once-watery white elephant out there near what was once Fleishhacker Zoo. The new billion-dollar sewer project in that area will create tons of dirt and sand, and an apparently irrevocable decision has been made to dump it into what was once "the world's biggest outdoor saltwater swimming pool!"

Actually, Fleishhacker Pool never made much sense, but what did in those heady days of 1925, when it was built? In the glorious Twenties, a foolanthropist, and his money were soon parted, and there was no greater giver than Banker Herbie Fleishhacker. The pool, 1,000 feet long, was so vast it had to be patroled by lifeguards in rowboats—yep, you've seen the photos—and on a warm day, it would be asplash with 4,000 kids of all ages. There weren't all that many warm days, of course, and besides, the pool was right next to an even bigger pool, the Pacific Ocean.

No, it made no sense, but it was another marvelous relic of an era when San Francisco thought BIG, and hang the expense. Shortly after the first of the year, the long-unused watermark will become just another buried treasure. You may shed a tear. One.

October 8, 1980

Staying with It

The late Paul C. Smith, one-time "boy wonder" editor of The Chronicle, made and ruined me as a columnist. It was 42 years ago that he deeded me this space in what appears to be perpetuity (cross fingers), but then he had to go spoil it by giving me a last-second piece of advice. As I was floating out of his office, aglow at getting A Column Of My Very Own, he said, "Oh, by the way, kid"—I was seven years younger—"try to be entertaining. I like to be amused in the morning. And don't stay on one subject too long. I am easily bored. Please keep that in mind."

* * *

Paul Smith, my mentor and hero, died in 1976, but not a day goes by that I don't remember those fateful (to me) words. Maybe he didn't mean to be taken so literally, but halfway through a long and increasingly tedious story, I say to myself, "Paul ain't gonna like this!" When I try to be serious—always bearing in mind that my serious is not necessarily a serious person's serious—I wonder if I am violating the sacred trust, this strip of white space, that he entrusted to me. "Be entertaining!" if it kills you. The world will little note the inside story of yet another scandal in the Housing Authority, but a good one-liner could put you into Bartlett's Familiar Duck-Billed Platitudes. Paul was probably right, and anyway, by now my brain is hopelessly riddled with three-dotulism . . . the fatal disease only a columnist can live with.

* * *

The world of Paul Smith is long gone. He and we knew what we wanted and we had it—our own well-ordered, snug, smug life in a city that was more accurately a village. If there were problems on the horizon any larger than a man's fist, we were almost unaware of them. The cops were getting rich running the town but the story was treated as an in-family joke. "Sure, run the story, Curt, but keep it short and off the front page." Everybody was white, middle-class and vaguely related. Families intermarried and only a divorce was a scandal—really!—in this Catholic town. The few blacks ran bars in the Fillmore or played jazz, as God intended (this is meant as irony—can't be too careful THESE days), and the Chinese, like the cable car crews, were content to be quaint and colorful. The joke may have been on us but we laughed a lot and I wrote it all down. "You're doing OK, kid," said Paul, smiling faintly over the torrent of one-liners between those three . . . little . . . dots.

* * *

Everything (and everybody) goes out of style eventually, and at the moment, San Francisco (and those who have devoted a lifetime to writing about it) may be as old hat as a bowler. Once we were content to say "it's the greatest city in the world" and let it go at that. No questions raised, asked or answered. Cable cars were mystical and emblematic, not a $60 million problem. Our streets weren't covered with trash and filth, they led to the stars. Along them strolled "colorful" characters, not people who are desperate, demented, armed and dangerous. "Careful now," Ambrose Bierce said (and I thank Michael Grieg for recalling these words). "We're dealing here with Myth. This city is a point upon a map of fog: Lemuria in a sea unknown: like us it doesn't quite exist . . . "

* * *

Reality is too much with us these days, except on strange mornings when the sun rises like a fireball out of the East and then floats in the midday mist like a misplaced moon; except when the Golden Gate Bridge towers disappear even as you are moving beneath them; except when the top of the Mt. Sutro tower floats on an ocean-spawned land-sea like a clipper ship rounding the Horn; except when wind chimes tinkle in shadowy Chinatown alleys and mah-jongg tiles rattle behind barred doors . . .

⋆ ⋆ ⋆

But all this is nonsense, sentimental drip. Paul Smith would not be entertained. "What mean?" he would sometimes scribble on a proof, alongside a piece of writing he didn't understand. However, he did like to meet new people and listen to new ideas. The idea of "punk"—as in punk or New Wave rock—might have entertained him. He definitely would have enjoyed Pheno Barbidoll, my informant in the Punk World. "In New Wave circles," she tells me, very much a mentor, "there is almost never anything 'amusing.' A smile is seldom seen here. Dour is the password, scowl the chic mode. Pay attention! I feel your interest is waning. You try your best, I know, but there is much more to San Francisco than cute little jokes. Stay pale. Stay hungry." Warns her friend, Roscoe Guiltiboy, "One must never laugh."

⋆ ⋆ ⋆

Now this is all most provocative. Pheno Barbidoll's words explain a lot about what is happening in Punk City, a part of San Francisco that may be on the rise. Punk is more than being gross and shocking on purpose—the group called The Dead Kennedys, for example. Punk is a philosophy, beyond funk and beat and existential. It is all around us, an attitude toward life: run a signal, knock over an old lady, walk slowly into the swirl of traffic, tear this down, break that up and above all stay very, very cool. It is a way of death in a city Paul Smith would never recognize. But maybe he would understand, now, why it is not always possible to "be entertaining." I can't even find that "cute little joke" for the bottom of the column. Sorry, Paul, and I guess you win, Pheno Barbidoll. *October 26, 1980*

Five minutes on Nob Hill: Here's Bob Jones, the Mark Hopkins' credit mgr., walking his standard poodle in Huntington Square. His poodle is named Eliza Doolittle because "I found her on the street and made a lady out of her." Along comes an attractive woman walking her Yorkie. As proper Nob Hill folk, the dog-walkers nod and Jones says, pointing to his poodle, "This is Eliza

Doolittle." "Oh, I knew that when I finally met her she'd turn out to be a dog!" giggles Mrs. Rex Harrison, for it is indeed she . . .

November 5, 1980

Questions Before the House

Granted, there's a fine line between nostalgia and reality, but where do we draw it? Where, exactly, does old San Francisco end and The City of Today (and, God willing, Tomorrow) begin? Is Coit Tower worth fighting for, or shall we actually convert it to that long-discussed reservoir of brown gravy, serving the restaurants of North Beach by gravity, if not levity? Are you willing to throw your almost perfect body in front of the bulldozers before they raze the Ferry Building, tower and all? As for the proposal to pave Golden Gate Park and turn it into the world's largest roller rink, where do you stand, prone or supine?

★ ★ ★

We have already lost so much that meant so little to so many. We nostalgics are a dying lot—it's built in at the factory. Memories are not for the young, except in very special cases, and in this careless city—careless of lives and dreams and treasures—the blessed memories are for burning. Once we stood around, secure in our greatness, and poked fun at the Jack Tar Hotel. Even as I was joining in the derision, I wrote forgettably that "Some day we will look upon the Jack Tar as our Parthenon," and don't you forget it. That day is almost upon us. We had an old Hall of Justice in the shape of a Renaissance palace, and we let it crash into rubble—pillars, pilasters, ghosts and all. We had a Montgomery Block whose rooms and halls spoke of Ambrose Bierce and George Sterling, and we buried those voices under monumental ugliness. We had ships and piers and honest buildings like the Fitzhugh . . .

★ ★ ★

But we still have the cable cars. More or less. If you can read between the lines and behind the headlines, you can tell that a battle is brewing. The skirmishers are out, spreading alarums and excursions: the system is falling apart. It is inherently and demonstrably dangerous. It will take at least two years and $60 million to restore it to proper working order. Think of that, folks! Can it possibly be worth $60 million to save an archaic, repeat ARCHAIC means of transportation? Why, imagine the libraries and schools and housing that $60 million would buy! This is a favorite argument and about as germane as "Eat your spinach, think of the starving children." Don't eat your spinach and they will still starve, alas. And if we pave over the cable car slots in favor of more stinkpot buses, not a single new house or library or school will be built as a direct result. You can count on it.

★ ★ ★

I prefer to think that $60 million would buy half a B-1 bomber. Couldn't the Pentagon do without half a bomber so we can keep our cable car system? They could but they won't and it wouldn't make any difference anyway. The bureaucracy doesn't work that way.

★ ★ ★

In a simpler and more sentimental time, a comedian named Phil Baker said that "San Francisco without its cable cars would be like a kid without his yo-yo." These days, the manic-progressives, and how manically depressing they are, consider any cable car supporter to be a yo-yo. Thus do terms and times change. It could well be provably true that a cable car system, a system that has not changed since 1872, is unrealistic. Good heavens, man, you don't see any horsecars around, do you? Or gas streetlamps? We have sent men to the moon, this is the age of the computer and the microchip—advance, old friend, into the soon-to-be 21st century! To which I say, in my best 1927 manner, "Sez you, buddy!" I have seen the future and it doesn't work; the cables run every bit as well as BART and are beloved around the world, to boot. I won't even go into Muni Metro, literally or otherwise.

★ ★ ★

Cable cars have nothing to do with reality and everything to do with the myth of San Francisco, a city that once was colorful and "different" without working at it. Now it takes a bit of effort. This is the age of blockbusters and viewblockers, of commuters and traffic jams, of fast food and furious pace. In this supercharged speeded-up San Francisco, who has time for a piece of Victorian gimcrackery that goes nine miles an hour, the same speed it traveled at 100 years ago? Of course, says Mr. Sly Boots, with an evil smile, they run a lot faster—downhill and out of control, eh? Unsafe at any speed, right, Mr. Nader? Amazing the Feds didn't ban the damn things years ago.

★ ★ ★

A cable car may be the last surviving piece of public transportation that is still fun to ride. You see people actually smiling aboard them. You see people standing in LINE with a smile, just to ride them. A bus is a chore, a streetcar is infinitely better and a cable car is unarguably in a class by itself, being unique. I wrote long ago that the justification for the cable car can be found in the bright and shiny eyes of a child awaiting his first ride; today, say the cynics, you see that bright and shiny look in the eyes of personal injury lawyers, awaiting the next accident. I think most of us are willing to take our chances on the outside step of a cable, simply because it IS outside. The wind, the air, the view of San Francisco passing slowly by, to be savored—no other public transport provides these lifts to the sagging urban soul.

⋆ ⋆ ⋆

Sixty million. A lot of money. Yet how do we measure the worth and value of a lovable, cantankerous device that, to millions of people, is the very essence of San Francisco? The cable car bell is one of the authentic sounds of the city, as the cable itself is a very real tie to the past. Take them away, and we will pay a price this city can no longer afford, the price of ordinariness.

November 9, 1980

Do Not Write in This Space

Malcolm Muggeridge, the British curmudgeon, once coined the wonderful word "Newzak" to describe columns like this one. "Newzak," he said, "bears the same relation to news as Muzak to music." Once upon a time, when I was prickly as a cactus and easily nettled, I would have fought back with such sophistries as "Well, what is news, Muggeridge? Define your terms," but I know what he is talking about. Trivia is trivia, no matter how thin you slice it or fine you write it, and trivia is my business. Not, mind you, that I believe the real news of the world comes anywhere near the front page or the six o'clock news. The real news happens out there somewhere, usually behind locked doors in a bug-proofed room, and eventually makes the headlines—when it is too late to do anything about it.

⋆ ⋆ ⋆

Trivia is more than a barroom game or fillers at the bottom of a page. When I was wet behind the ears, a phrase I still find slightly mystifying, I tried to make a case for trivia being more important than anything else in the public prints, comic strips excepted. "When archeologists a century hence poke through the shards of what we laughingly call our civilization," I would write in my most earnest English Lit style, "they will learn more about us from the gossip columns than from the perorations of a Walter Lippmann." While that may well be true, it doesn't say anything, and at some length, too.

★ ★ ★

San Francisco is a city that lends itself nicely to trivia. Parks built on sand, monuments dedicated to firehouse groupies, hills named Russian for no easily discernible reason, streets (Turk, for instance) that start in the Tenderloin and mysteriously become "boulevards," hungry i's and Old Spaghetti Factories and Original Cold Day Restaurants, the first martini and the last ferry—these are the stuff of which civilized conversations are made. Why did our most distinguished architect, Willis Polk, have this irresistible desire to stand on his head in public? How did Lucius Beebe get away with it when he loudly asked the most revered matron in town, in the crowded drawing room of her ornate mansion on California, "Madam, when may we expect the girls to come downstairs?" From what floor of the Mark Hopkins did George Vanderbilt throw himself to death, and why, and who remarked to the Mark's owner, "Your scion fell down"? This is heavy trivia, as opposed to light news of alleged front page significance.

★ ★ ★

There has never been much real news in San Francisco anyway, give or take a gold rush or major earthquake. The Comstock Lode and the peccadilloes of Sharon and Ralston were good scandalous stuff, to be sure, but I wonder when we will be allowed to hear the real story of who did what to whom (Sharon does look like a villain but you know what they say about appearances). There hasn't been a decent scandal in this town in years—just gossip and insinuendoes, or, if you will, Newzak, spilled over the tables at Trader Vic's and Jack's. Armies of "investigative" reporters have tried to Get Something on that particularly flamboyant politician, always without luck because the feller turns out to be—honest, frevvinsakes. He answers indirect questions directly. Oh, what a bad show, oh for the days of crooked politicians who could be trusted to stay bought.

★ ★ ★

Mr. Muggeridge's Newzak may be garbage to you but it's bread and butter to me, and which old-time scavenger outfit used that as its slogan? Or "Satisfaction Guaranteed Or Double Your Garbage Back"? On these gloomy December nights, the news breaks on unseen shores, unheard, unreported. Now and then it surfaces willy-nilly, through the police reports, jail blotters, official files. A crazed killer rustles through the underbrush of Marin County, stalking his victims, and gone, at last, is the Newzak image of Marin, fun-filled never-neverland of hot tubbies, mantra chanters and "laid-back" loonies. Sometimes the real news can do that, and then the trivia not only looks like garbage, it emits a distinct odor. But the real news doesn't happen that often. There are all those newsless days running one into another, enlivened only by an occasional joke, a bright one-liner, a notable quotable quote. Then it's the Newzak that pays the bills and fills the space alongside the ads.

* * *

In San Francisco, as in every taut and troubled city, the news goes on, 24 hours a day, hidden from the so-called newsgatherers. The quiet man gazing across the tiny living room out there in Sunset, wondering whether to kill himself or his wife, or both. The woman with the breadknife in her Vuitton bag, ready to plunge it into the back of her two-timing married lover. The jazzed-up kid with the gun, poised to commit murder for the few bucks that may help him get another fix. The angry drunk behind the wheel of his Mercedes on the Gate Bridge, tempted to turn head-on into the oncoming traffic—all these are part of the nightly "news" that stops short of becoming news because they didn't happen. But in the city, they will, sooner or later. Meanwhile, the deadlines come and go, the presses roll, the Newzak lands on your breakfast table, and you yawn, "Nothin' in the paper today, nothin'."

* * *

The trivia of our lives—funny names, funny places, funny lives—goes on day after day while the news skulks in dark corners. Let the Newzak drone on. It will be drowned out soon enough when the world falls apart and the real news crashes down on the last reader.

December 7, 1980

The true nostalgia: at this time of year, it's hard not to give a moment's thought to City of Paris, the long-dead store whose magnificent tree in the rotunda seemed the very spirit of Christmas downtown. Memories of the beauty salon, whose manager, heavily tinted and rouged, left a vapor trail of perfume that took 15 minutes to dissipate. "Deposed royalty," was the way she described herself. On the main floor, the ethereal old lady with blue hair, constantly folding scarves and stacking gloves. Normandy Lane: undying smell of croissants and fresh roasted chicken, cheese, coffees, spices. Paris newspapers, magazines, posters on a kiosk . . . And let us not forget the old elevator starter, an actor with the style of Chevalier. The day after he was told that push-button elevators were being installed, and his services would no longer be needed, he died of a broken spirit, as did his beloved store.

December 24, 1980

★ ★ ★

1981

★ ★ ★

State of the City

Mayor Feinstein is mad as hell and she isn't going to take it any longer. The murder of a Muni bus driver last week was the last straw "and I have had it up to here," she says, asking for millions of dollars to fight crime. We can but applaud her sentiments and support her efforts, knowing the futility of it all. Still, we have to start somewhere, even if it means going back to the old liberal philosophy of throwing money at problems. Politicians have been vowing that they'll "get tough on crime" for a long time now, with negligible results. Increasing the penalties is one place to start; as the Mayor says, eloquently: "Life is cheap but the price is going up." It's a good line that will go unheeded and probably unread by the roving packs of punks and killers who have taken over large parts of San Francisco.

★ ★ ★

We have restored capital punishment but that doesn't make it any easier to find a jury with the stomach to send a person to the gas chamber. Since we are backing inexorably into the Dark Ages, perhaps it's time to return to Middle Ages punishment. First violators could be dunked in Stow Lake in Golden Gate Park. More serious offenders belong in stocks installed at the various downtown street corners, replacing the flower stands that are a gentle reminder of more civilized times. For murderers, I have long recommended public hangings in Union Square, with mothers holding up their babies to see the sight, as pickpockets roam through the crowd, fleecing the unwary. After a few years of this we may even experience a New Renaissance.

★ ★ ★

A hate-filled "cool gray city of love" is an obvious anomaly. This beautiful, intelligent, prosperous and famous city is being stolen from the law-abiding, piece by piece. Newcomers may scoff, but within the lifetime of many of us, it was literally safe to go anywhere in San Francisco. We walked the night streets without looking over our shoulders. In a way that rings false today but was true then, we felt a kinship with all San Franciscans and had reason to believe the sentiment was returned.

★ ★ ★

Now there are entire sections of the city that are off-limits to those of the wrong color, age, style. At sundown, it is High Noon on the Streets of San Francisco. The parks that were once our glory are places to avoid. You "enjoy" the view from Twin Peaks at your own risk. Life is lived behind locked gates and barred windows.

★ ★ ★

Mayor Feinstein is rightfully angry, but putting more cops in cars will make a small difference, if any. The police-to-civilian ratio in the S.F. of the '30s and '40s was about the same as it is today, but the people were different. There is a difference between the irreverence and anarchy. This city has always been cocky and not particularly awed by "the majesty of the law," but most of us got to know the cop on the beat, and liked him. There existed a reasonable, if not overweening, respect for the law. And there were the imponderables: the "all in the same boat" bond of the Great Depression, the optimism miraculously generated by Franklin Roosevelt, the mutual concern over war clouds darkening, and a real affection for the city we lived in, a very different city from today's.

★ ★ ★

The level of violence is rising everywhere, not just in San Francisco, but it is this city that concerns us most, of course. Criminologists, sociologists and psychiatrists, who have answers for everything, are hard put to explain it. It is not hard for the layman to recognize the symptoms, however. You can experience it daily, on the streets, in the buses. People drive murderously, anarchically, knuckles white on the steering wheel, eyes blazing hatred. "If looks could kill," most of us would be dead. It is now possible to imagine a nut firing a gun, or at least pulling one, over a parking space or a jumped signal. Everybody has a gun. Hardly anybody has a place to park.

★ ★ ★

In my lifetime, I've watched the level of violence rise from a shaken fist to a muttered expletive to The Finger to the use of weapons in a way that suggests mass insanity. To some, shooting has become as natural as breathing. As the Mayor says, "Life is cheap." Said the teenager after the execution of a 16-year-old in the once-peaceful Crocker-Amazon district: "Yeah, we wasted him. Only the strong survive." If only the macho punks survive, the trouble is only beginning. But where does this kind of crazed philosophy come from? Why was the city truly different only a comparatively short time ago? Can it be something as simple as movies glorifying punks, the random inanities of television, the carelessness of the press, the downgrading of the schools? Is it the tragedies like Vietnam, weak leadership, inflation, joblessness—and hopelessness?

⋆ ⋆ ⋆

This at last may be closest to the mark. Jobs for kids may not be the answer, but it's a beginning; putting teenagers to work is infinitely more important than placing neutron bombs in Europe. This city that was once one city has become a nest of armed enclaves. On the North side, the power brokers go about their ingrown business as though the other side of San Francisco didn't exist. Priorities are skewed: we have so many Meter Maids that they run into each other in their eagerness to tag cars that are parked and not bothering anyone. The much-reviled Muni driver is indeed "a sitting duck" and one is now dead. There will be more. Have a nice day and avoid the night. There are more of Them than Us.

February 9, 1981

Mister Nite Life: Bali's was the place to be early yesterday morn. There on the dance floor was the world's greatest male dancer, Mikhail Baryshnikov, circling disconsolately on one foot; the other has a sprained toe, which means he's out of the extravaganza at the Opera House this week. Snaking around him sensuously: Joan Baez, swathed in white scarves. Leaping through the air: Martine van Hamel, who would rank as the best woman dancer there if Natalia Makarova had not been nearby, fluffing her new blonde hair. At the bar, Sam Shepard, the Pulitzer Prizewinning playwright, was making goo-goo eyes at a raving beauty from South America. In a knot: Alexander Godunov, Sasha Filipov, Joel Grey. Looking on: Gerald van der Kemp, ex-curator of Versailles. In other words, S.F.'s greatest party-giver, Ann Getty, was at it again, and it was caviar and vodka all the way . . . Across the room, Judge J. Anthony Kline, former legal adviser to Jerry Brown, was raving about the wonders of Sacramento, "a real and exciting city." After a few minutes of this, Atty. Jeremiah Hallisey announced slowly and clearly, "The only difference between Sacramento and Boise, Idaho, is that Boise is six hours from anywhere and Sacramento is only two." *February 11, 1981*

Oh what a guy was the late Lefty O'Doul, who'll be honored tonight by inclusion in the Bay Area Sports Hall of Fame at a banquet at the St. Francis. Not too long before his death, word spread that Lefty was flat broke, a condition not unknown to the great baseball slugger. So Politico Morris "Mighty Mo" Bernstein asked 50 San Franciscans to contribute $100, no more, no less. Late one night, at Lefty's bar on Geary, Mo slipped O'Doul a check for $5,000. And next day, Lefty gave it to the S.F. Boys' Club.

March 5, 1981

Days of Our Years

At Grodin's clothing store on Stockton St. a few days ago, Vice Pres. Dave Falk summoned a young employee, handed him a package, and said, "Take this over to the Flood building, please." The young man, a recent arrival in S.F., looked momentarily confused. "Flood building?" he echoed. "I knew there'd been an earthquake and a fire here, but I never heard about the flood."

★ ★ ★

And so it goes, the handing down of lore and legend that gives a city its fiber, its texture, its continuity. Years from now, the young man, grown gray, will laugh over his gaffe about the flood that never happened. By that time, he may even have learned about Bonanza Jim Flood, whose rocklike fortress of a building survived the earthquake, and about Jimmy Phelan, and the rest of the gathering clans—Tobins, Hearsts, Sterns, Zellerbachs, Crockers—who built a foggy outpost into a city that still fires the imagination.

★ ★ ★

Yesterday marked the 75th anniversary of the earthquaking even whose tremors are felt to this day. Today is Easter, an abundance of flowers and joy, exultant songs and the peal of organs. There is a nice symmetry in this, the triumphant rising from ashes, the promise of new and better worlds, more to life than mundane dailiness, etc., etc., besides which the grave is not the goal. You can get as symbolic as you want over this juxtaposition. Both are events that cry out for empurpled prose, and are seldom disappointed.

* * *

Nostalgia for a catastrophe may seem odd, but this is an odd city. We glory in our past while busily tearing down the evidence of it. Those who truly care about San Francisco know in their bones that there was something very special about The Founding Fathers, those grave, bearded, hang-the-expense types who built a world city overnight, saw most of it go up in smoke, and started all over again without, seemingly, a whimper. We try not to think about another earthquake of the magnitude of 1906's. When we do, we wonder if we could measure up to our forebears' courage and high-flown spirits. The dead city of 1906 put on a Portola Festival in 1909 that, by all accounts, was "glittering and perfectly mad," as befits a perfectly mad place. In 1915, one of the most glorious Expositions in history capped the climax.

* * *

When the last survivor of the '06 firequake dies, will the nostalgia die, too? We will find out soon enough, for the old crowd is disappearing fast, the survivors still marvelously chipper, shiny of eye, sharp of memory. Like veterans of a long-ago war, they remember the events of April, 1906, as the best days and nights of their young lives. Some of their recollections are captured nicely in a new book by Friends of the Public Library, "1906 Remembered," in which old-timers reminisce with Editor Patricia Turner:

* * *

"I was only eight at the time, and to me it was a great spectacle. They were dynamiting one building after another. We had a fine time" (Alvin Greenberg). "I was watching people go by. A woman came by in her beautiful evening gown with her Japanese houseboy. They didn't have a thing. A man went by carrying a bird cage with a cat in it. I said, 'Why have you got the cat in the cage?' He said, 'The cat ate the canary'" (Edna Laurel Calhan). "Everybody was out in the street. A big three-story hotel, about 1100 Howard, was just as flat as two pancakes. People were running up and down the street stark naked because in getting out of the building, the night gowns, they didn't wear pajamas then, were torn off" (Walter Herman).

* * *

The tales go on and on, but one theme prevails. San Francisco was a city, a community. There was an instant sharing of food and only a small amount of looting. The troops, indeed, looked the other way as people helped themselves in doomed grocery stores that stood in the way of onrushing flames. The kids seemed to have had a great time, for school was out: "All good things in a youngster's life must end," recalls John Conlon, "and about October 1, our April-October vacation was over. The principal (at Jackson Primary, Oak near Stanyan) overlooked our glum looks. May the children of San Francisco never again enjoy such an experience." Silver-gold lining dept.: "My father, a painter, made money hand over fist" in the rebuilding of the city. "I would build bridges and houses and whatnots with gold pieces. People didn't pay by check in those days. Everything was in cash—silver and gold pieces. Imagine that!" (Lilas Mugg, born 1898).

⋆ ⋆ ⋆

Chimneys tumbled, fires sprang up everywhere, streets split, buildings collapsed, but most people survived, to become the true aristocracy. They knew The City That Was and the city that was to be, only partially recognizable today. Over all, despite the bravado, the experience was, in the main, terrifying. Retired Fire Chief Bill Murray, six in '06: "I'm still frightened if I feel an earthquake. Puts the fear of God into you. You don't know when it's gonna stop. Now that thing only lasted 48 seconds and look at all the damage it did."

⋆ ⋆ ⋆

Forty-eight seconds that shook the little world of San Francisco as never before or since. The next one could happen today, next year or never. I don't have to tell you which one to pray for on this blessed Easter.

April 19, 1981

Gray Day in May

"To what do you attribute your longevity?" a young interviewer asked Author William Saroyan a few years ago. "Not dying," replied Bill promptly. Despite the flip reply, he used the phrase as a book title, for, like most people of a certain age, he was more than a little obsessed with death. What turned out to be his last published book is called "Obituaries," in which he rambled on and on, in his usual entertaining fashion, about friends who had gone to their reward, passed away, passed on or otherwise disappeared from the temporal scene. The book had a point, eventually arrived at. "Don't die," he advised.

* * *

Through no fault of his own, Bill Saroyan, old chum of antediluvian times in preplastic San Francisco, was unable to take his own advice. The first phone call I received yesterday morning brought the news that he had died of cancer at the age of 72 in the Veterans Hospital at Fresno. Although he had achieved a reasonably great age, it didn't seem right. It is hard to think of Bill Saroyan dead—he was always so full of life. No one else I can think of seems to have so much of it, or enjoy it more.

* * *

It so happens I had been thinking of death—not obsessively, of course—when the phone rang. Another old friend, Richie Gladstein, also 72, had died Saturday. Richie and Bill were not only the same age, they were often to be seen on the nightly rounds that led from Izzy Gomez's to the Backyard to the Black Cat in the era called "bohemian." What bothered me slightly yesterday morning was that someone who doesn't know much about San Francisco had labeled Richie's obituary: "Israel R. Gladstein." Israel, indeed. Nobody ever knew he was an Israel. He was and always will be Richie, a short, smart, tough guy who ably defended Harry Bridges against a variety of silly charges, and had his political neck stuck out at all times. You don't see people like Saroyan, Gladstein or Bridges around the town these days, and that is a great loss. We get a lot of born-againers and born-againsters and Werner Erhardians, but those old guys really cared about quaint things like social justice.

* * *

If you never met Bill Saroyan, you missed an experience. First you heard him. He bellowed like a bull, laughed frequently at window-rattling levels, and had an engaging manner. "Eye contact" was a phrase foreign to him, but he had it. His piercing brown eyes locked on the person he was talking to and stayed locked. His roaring voice may have been due to increasing deafness, a weakness he denied as he disclaimed all physical weaknesses. "I'm not deaf," he shouted at me one night at Bali's. "You just don't talk loud enough!" He had a great head, with a shock of black hair and a wild moustache. He didn't walk into a room, he invaded it. All that energy gone forever—hard to believe.

* * *

Bill Saroyan, Armenian. He never let you forget his roots. In the days when I was addicted to word coinages, no matter how strained, I called him a "Charmenian." "That's lousy," he said equivocally. Nor was he amused when I said he was suffering from "pernicious Armenia," a much better pun. I had just published my second book, "Baghdad-by-the-Bay," when I ran into him one midnight at John's Rendezvous, "I read your book," he said. "It stinks." We had a drink on that, and I agreed the book wasn't very good, deferring to an expert. When Bill described himself as "The world's greatest living author," he was only half-kidding.

★ ★ ★

I first met Bill at one of his hangouts, the late George Mardikian's Omar Khayyam's on O'Farrell (now closed, too). He was in the process of borrowing some money from George, another nationalistic Armenian. I soon discovered that Bill was always on the shorts, mainly from gambling. He bet on the horses at a bookie joint in Opera Alley (now gone, too), a dead end off Third and Mission. When he wasn't losing there, he was playing idiotically bad poker behind New Joe's in North Beach. Not only did he not possess a poker face, in spades, he usually revealed his hand. In seven-card stud, he'd say "Don't bet against me, I got aces back to back!" He was not lying.

★ ★ ★

Money, clothes, cars, houses—they meant nothing to Bill. When he made his first big stake—$60,000 from Louis B. Mayer for "The Human Comedy"—he gave $10,000 to each of six relatives he was supporting. He was immediately drafted by the Army, which had deferred him as the relatives' sole support. By that time, he had married his lifelong love, Carol Marcus, now Mrs. Walter Matthau. I don't think he ever got over her, and yet after they were married, circa 1942, he treated her in the old-time old-country style: she stayed home in the Sunset, he went out. She phoned me at the office one day and said, "How about taking me to the Top o' the Mark? I've been living here for three months now and I haven't seen a THING." On the troop ship that took him to Europe during World War II, Bill lay on a top bunk and wrote "Carol" over and over, thousands of times, on bulkhead and overhead.

★ ★ ★

Bill Saroyan was born to write, and he wrote constantly, obsessively, excessively, disdaining rewrites or editing. His San Francisco was a foggy fantasy of hookers with hearts of gold, good guy gamblers and starving artists, leading bewildered lives of touching innocence. In the end, that's what he was: an innocent, abroad and at home, as guileless, and sometimes as annoying, as a child. A lovable child, to be sure. *May 19, 1981*

Distant Trumpets

We who were born during the Great War of 1914–18 were in for a wild ride—and, in too many cases, a short one. The surviving members of our class look back in wonderment at a landscape unlike any other: war against enemies that became friends, the death of empires and innocence, a wild prosperity followed by an economic depression that scarred us all, horse-drawn vehicles metamorphosing into rockets to the moon, "timeless" traditions scattered to the winds, changes coming so fast as to leave the past an unexplored mystery. We became different people, clinging to lost values or searching for new ones. We knew vaguely where we had been, we had no idea where we were, and completely in the dark as to where we were going.

⋆ ⋆ ⋆

Our only signposts were tragedies or trivia. The haze over the ruins parted here and there to reveal an Armistice or your first drink in a speakeasy, a lynching in San Jose or your first ride across a spanking new Bridge. Gertrude Stein's "You are all a lost generation" appealed to us, even when we were still so young as to be merely confused. "The Beautiful and Damned"—yes, Scott, that was it. Damned and doomed from here to eternity. Our fathers had had their war and now we wanted ours. When the lights went down for the last time on the Treasure Island exposition of 1940, we had a premonition that we would never again be so joyously young. When Pearl Harbor exploded the following year, we knew our youth was over.

⋆ ⋆ ⋆

We of the Class of '16 or thereabouts have lost all concept of time, tending to divide our lives into two equal parts—Before the War and After the War. Of course it isn't that way at all. It is becoming increasingly difficult to remember the young strangers we were—young for such a short time, middle-aged for such a long time, now old enough to realize we know so little. Tomorrow is the 40th anniversary of Pearl Harbor! Most of us think we remember it vividly—one of those moments you "never forget," like exactly what you were doing when John F. Kennedy was killed—but the details are beginning to blur. Four decades is a long time.

★ ★ ★

The summer and fall of 1941, San Francisco had never been gayer, a small town of infinite pleasures, from Bimbo's all-night gambling palace on Market to the wild roller coaster at Playland and one-buck dinners at the Cliff House. At Seals Stadium, "America's finest minor league ballpark," we cheered for "Cocky" Fain, Joe Sprinz and Sad Sam Gibson. The opera, led by Gaetano Merola, had an all-star lineup that puts this year's to shame: Grace Moore, Gladys Swarthout, Lily Pons, Lotte Lehmann, Bidu Sayao, Rise Stevens, Licia Albanese, Jan Peerce, Lauritz Melchior, Ezio Pinza, Lawrence Tibbett—immortals we took for granted, and even slept through.

★ ★ ★

December 7, 1941, dawned clear and warm, the sky an innocent blue. We arose painfully with hangovers after a long night at Amelio's and the Bal Tabarin, after-hours' nightcaps at Chez Paree, a 4 a.m. snack at Tiny's, the all-night Powell St. waffle shop that, inexplicably, had become a hangout for The Crowd. The hangover was soon forgotten. By unspoken consent, we all drove out to Ocean Beach—thousands of us, standing along the sea wall and on the sand, gazing silently to the West, as though we might see the smoke rising from Pearl. Then came the unforgivable reprisals against the Japanese Americans, a national disgrace we carry to this day. The Sunday patriots were beating up Chinese, too. Soon the latter would be wearing big buttons reading "I AM CHINESE." That prime racist remark, "They all look alike to me," never had more tragic overtones. In May of '42, The Chronicle reported that "for the first time in 81 years, not a single Japanese is walking the streets of San Francisco tonight." They had all been moved to an "assembly center," and the new world of euphemisms began.

★ ★ ★

And so we had our war, we who had been born in the middle of one, who thrilled to the tales of Château-Thierry and the Argonne, who observed Armistice Day every November 11 at 11 a.m. by a minute of silence in our classrooms. We grew up on John Gilbert in "The Big Parade" and Buddy Rogers in "Wings" and "All Quiet on the Western Front." We tipped our overseas caps to a jaunty angle, lighted a cigarette and itched to get Over There and Over the Top. We hadn't yet read Wilfred Owen, the great British poet of World War I, who knew what war was like: "If you could hear, at every jolt, the blood come gargling from the froth-corrupted lungs . . . My friend, you would not tell with such high zest/To children ardent for some desperate glory/The Old Lie: *Dulce et decorum est/Pro patria mori.*"

★ ★ ★

In the far distance, a ghostly trumpeter sounds "Taps" over the graves of those who may or may not have agreed with Horace that "it is sweet and fitting to die for one's country." Old Horace could have imagined the world that died on December 7, 1941, but not the age that began with Hiroshima and Nagasaki. When we remember Pearl Harbor, let us not forget that.

December 6, 1981

Chills and Fever

January is usually the month of quiet desperation, but San Francisco is on a roller-coaster ride, a cable car on the loose, a city on an upper. While one tries to resist the notion of investing much emotion in a game played and supported by amiable maniacs, there is no doubt the 49ers have put joy into January, especially after the "killer storm." How fast our spirits fall and rise: Monday was Disaster City and Tuesday dusk brought a golden sunset that made the skyline look better than it really is. The street people were back to smiling at one another, and a small army of fresh-faced kids began singing hymns at Hallidie Plaza, where every other "bum" is a plainclothes cop. Games city people play: identifying undercover policemen, spotting "unmarked" cars, pointing fingers at decoys, winking at transvestites, watching the midnight shadows on drawn curtains in cheap hotels.

★ ★ ★

Well, what is there to say about this "49er fever" that has a great city in its grip? In its grippe, I should say, if it truly is a fever. A city is not a football team, and vice versa, and I find it hard to identify completely with players from Georgia and owners from Ohio, but this is a whole new world. The hometown team doesn't have to be made up of hometown heroes—that is a concept from the past. Lefty is long gone and Frankie a millionaire who lives down the Peninsula. "Show me a hero and I'll write you a tragedy," said F. Scott Fitzgerald, and let us raise our glasses, gingerly, to the plunging fullbacks of yesteryore who drank themselves out on Skid Road, slippery when wet. Sure, you knew them well—handsome blond bull married to the millionaire's daughter, the equally handsome dark brooder who ended up in a wheelchair, pawing over his yellowed clippings. Nice guys who never grew up, but that's too glib.

★ ★ ★

People don't grow up, they grow old. One fateful way to counteract that is to live in the past, the occupational hazard of San Franciscans. The success of the Niners has the graybeards mumbling in their bristles about Strike and Bruno and Leo the Lion and a lot of other terrific local guys who wound up selling used cars for a living. All that adulation on all those Sundays, and then "Say, didn't you used to be—?" You have to prepare for it early: the stadium grows empty and dark in a hurry, and there is no echo. Only those tantalizing clippings that you can't resist looking at through a glass, dreamily. You may even have tender memories of Kezar Stadium, that mess of a place that grows more beloved by the year. Sentimentalists have rotten memories.

★ ★ ★

"Baseball is what we were, football is what we've become." Columnist Mary McGrory, I believe, composed that line. It is not only neat and tidy, it stands up fairly well. Baseball is a synonym for gentler times and lazy afternoons. Time doesn't matter—one game could go on forever—and yet baseball has changed too. When was the last time you saw a real felt cap, and as for those plastic helmets with the earflaps—But Mary is right: football is more in tune with the terrifying tempo of time itself, the countdown, the obsession with life ticking away on the field of battle. Football is war-like, high-tech, computerized and very, very hard. It is also fun to watch, let there be no doubt of that. It is the perfect creature and even creation of the TV age. Cheap thrills, vicarious tortures and the beauty of the perfect pass, caught forever in midstride. There are no replays in the game of life, but TV allows you to relive the passion, ebbing slightly with each showing, orgasm and afterglow.

★ ★ ★

I keep reading about and even meeting people who "live and die with the 49ers." Maybe I even envy them. Are these the true fans, the real patriots, filled with the right stuff? Some of these are the same people who say, fiercely, challengingly, that "San Francisco is the greatest city in the world, buddy, and don't you forget it." They sound like they are ready to fight over this proposition, no matter how hastily you agree. No use suggesting that San Francisco was the greatest city in the world long before a professional football team came along. No use making jokes that we had Caruso singing opera here before we became "a major league city," whatever that means. A major league city is the sum of its parts, and the so-called major leagues are only a small part—sometimes even a subtraction.

⋆ ⋆ ⋆

Madame Mayor and other politicians, solidly aboard the bandwagon, extol the 49ers for "what they have done for the city." They have indeed done a lot, not a pun on Ronnie Lott. It is not unpleasant to hear San Francisco talked about on the networks, by learned commentators and other gamblers. It may even be good for business that San Francisco has a winning team, but business wasn't all that bad when the Niners were losing. It just wasn't all that good for the ownership. San Francisco has done a lot for the 49ers. This is a great day for those who "live and die" with the team, and have for years. This day belongs to them—long may they live, especially after today's game.

⋆ ⋆ ⋆

Rich is better than poor, thin is better than fat, winning is better than losing, but let us try to keep our wits about us. Root for the Niners, but if Dallas wins today, it will not be the end of the world—just the end of a very successful season—and San Francisco will continue to be the greatest city in the world and don't you forget it, buddy.

January 10, 1982

Madam Queen

If you live long enough in the newspaper racket, you can spend most of your time writing obituaries. I said that before, no doubt, and I say it again. The passing parade never stops: Last week, there was Dr. Russ Lee, who lived a long and fruitful life. And Joan Hitchcock, a good-hearted soul, Dorothy Parker's "Big Blonde" right down to the tragic ending, a drinker who drank herself out. Sunday, the remarkable artist, Wilfried Satty, who lived a surrealistic life in a subterranean cavern on Powell in North Beach, fell off a ladder and killed himself. It was an ending as bizarre as any of the Hieronymous-like illustrations he was famous for.

And then, early yesterday, there was Sally Stanford, or whatever her name was. It didn't matter when she was riding high and it doesn't matter now.

★ ★ ★

Sally Stanford (a.k.a. Mabel or Marsha Owen Gump Kenna, etc., etc.) was part of our own era of wonderful nonsense, the 1930s, when the police ran the town and everybody played for pay. In the Tenderloin, the doors never closed. Every other little hotel was a house of ill fame, as the journals of the time like to call them. You could drink all night in a dozen after-hours joints. The payoffs were good. A lot of cops, several politicians and a few madams, Sally Stanford, Dolly Fine and Mabel Malotte among them, got rich.

★ ★ ★

The Great Depression was in full cry, but San Francisco was never more exciting. The mindless city stayed up all night, partying, from the penthouses of Nob Hill, where Socialite Anita Howard reigned, down to the Black Cat, over to Finocchio's and on to Mona's, a lesbian joint rivaling anything in Paris. And a lot of people ended their evenings at Sally Stanford's, where the champagne flowed all night and Sally herself would whip up a batch of dawnside eggs for this guy from Pebble Beach, that one from the Pacific-Union Club, and the City Hall playboy, who would be right down.

★ ★ ★

Wonderful nonsense is right: Sally's first bed-a-whee, one of my lesser coinages, was the Russian Hill mansion owned by Paul Verdier, elegant proprietor of the City of Paris department store. It became so famous a landmark that it was included on sightseeing tours. Now and then Sally would allow the hayseeds to come right in and meet "my girls," all of them demurely attired in silk kimonos and wearing gardenia corsages. "Every one a former Junior Leaguer," Sally would assure the rubes. A tour of the mansion revealed that every bedroom had a fireplace, "at no extra cost," twinkled Sally.

★ ★ ★

She created her own legend. About her name: "I was walking down Kearny Street in the rain, alone, friendless, when I saw the headline, 'Stanford Wins Big Game.' That's for me, I said to myself. No more Marsha Owen—I'm going after big game." The story grew more polished by the year. Why Sally? "Well, Sally, Irene and Mary were famous hooker names," she explained, "and Sally went best with Stanford." When she married Robert Gump, grandson of Solomon Gump, founder of Gump's famous store, and brother of the noted art dealer, Richard Gump, a reporter asked her,

"How does it feel to marry into such a distinguished family?" Sniffed Sally: "The Stanfords are MUCH older." She loved telling the story of the eager young cop, son of a police captain, who burst into her house and shouted, "I'm bustin' this place!" "Before you do that, buster," replied Sally coolly, "I suggest you go out to the kitchen and talk to your dad—we were just having a cup of coffee."

* * *

Sally's most famous place was 1144 Pine, an old mansion with great iron gates and a sunken bathtub off the drawing room where Anna Held allegedly had her famous milk baths. The story didn't check out but Sally went on telling it and everybody wanted to believe it. "I love this place," she would say dreamily, looking around at the Charles Addamsy decor. "It's a real mausoleum. I wouldn't mind being buried here." Among her visitors one time was her equally famous New York counterpart, Polly Adler, who wrote "A House Is Not a Home." Some of the conversation was quite delicious. Polly: "You know the madam's lament—everybody goes upstairs but us." And "It's a relief to get out of the business. No more opening the door and looking first at the man's feet, you know?" Sally: "Yeah. Right. Big feet. Cops."

* * *

"Do you really have a heart of gold?" I once asked Sally. "If I did," she snapped, "it'd be in a safe-deposit box." She was tough, shrewd and conservative. After the cops finally shut her down in 1949 in a fit of morality, she opened the Valhalla restaurant in Sausalito. Her maitre d'hotel, Leon Galleto, reminisced yesterday about the time she had one of her many heart attacks, and he had to drive her to the St. Francis Hospital in S.F. As he slowed down at the Golden Gate Bridge toll plaza, she called weakly from the back seat, where she was stretched out: "Don't forget to get a receipt, honey." In a crooked world, Sally Stanford always had her priorities straight.

February 2, 1982

Keeper of the Flame

If you want to see the past in San Francisco, you have to squint. Narrowing my eyes like Humphrey Bogart peering through a scrim of Camel smoke, I walked down Market toward the Ferry Building, one of the last repositories of The True City. The day was gray and misty. In other words, perfect. By squinching, which is bad for the eyeballs, I was able to block out the Dambarcadero Freeway, shooting cars back and forth beneath the Ferry Building's Blessed Clock. Two proper seagulls, the gray and white kind, screamed overhead like F-16s after a Libyan (why don't we fight somebody our own size?).

★ ★ ★

If you have reached a certain age, you'll remember when the gray and white gull—"seagull" is redundant and inaccurate—was the San Francisco symbol, a sticker that you carried proudly on the windshield of your Nash or Studebaker or Shovenrollit, as we were wont to call Chevrolets in Year One. The sticker carried no message. Just the wheeling gull, caught in flight. But everybody knew that meant San Francisco, the dream city, where the fog misted your eyeglasses and the Embarcadero was still East St. and Little Pete and his bodyguards shuffled along Waverly Place at midnight to avenge a tong murder with yet another.

★ ★ ★

The aging boy columnist squinches his eyes away from the Ferry Building, a monument he would kill for, and locks onto Blind Tilden's bronze mechanics, still trying to punch a hole into a metal plate. "What's new?" he asks plaintively, ballpoint poised over spiral-bound notebook. "Nothing," comes the routine answer. "Same old thing." But it's never the same old thing in what used to be Baghdad-by-the-Bay, now Icetrays-in-the-Sky. The city changes and grows away from itself. The green aquarium of Crown Zellerbach, once Mr. Skidmore's finest piece of architecture, is already obsolete, perhaps doomed. Shaklee Terraces rises sliver-thin and slick out of the muck of Market, antiseptic, faceless, perfect. Philip Johnson's 48-story cylinder built by Texas millions, has now grown to its full height on a full block at California and Front, across from Tadich's. San Franciscans know how to bring a building down to size. "Where's that new round tower that Johnson is building?" "Across the street from Tadich's." "Oh yeah—thanks."

★ ★ ★

Dozens of small buildings died so the Big Silo in the Sky could rise—bars, restaurants, stationery stores, cheap hotels, drug stores, newsstands, mom 'n' pop lunch counters, even the not inconsiderable and fairly historic Dollar Building. The texture of a neighborhood is ground to dust when a blockbuster rises. A lot of little people are sent scattering, usually to the suburbs. A lot of new little people come in from the suburbs to work in the blockbuster but it isn't an even trade. At night, a neighborhood that was once a community turns dark, silent and dangerous, or even worse. Dead.

★ ★ ★

Granted, there's an excitement to a downtown bristling with skyscrapers. We associate prosperity and progress with these heartless and sometimes joyless monsters, and turn away from critics who warn of gridlock and shadowed streets that become wind tunnels. What was once a small, warm and friendly little city, the darling of world travelers, comes dangerously close to Lookalike City. And so we cling desperately to what remains of the past. We change our mind about the Pyramid because at least it takes a smaller bite of sky than most of its neighbors. Our new heroes are the realistic dreamers who will bring an old building back to life, against all the odds.

★ ★ ★

One such is a youngish man named Dusan Mills, a Yugoslav reared in Australia who now lives in Sausalito. He is the new owner of The Building That Refused To Die—the French-style Audiffred Building at Mission and the Embarcadero, built by Hippolite d'Audiffred in 1889, a landmark that has survived fires, earthquakes, tides that move in and out of its basement daily, the waterfront strikes of 1934 and '36 (two longshoremen were killed there), threats of demolition by various boards, commissions and "sensible" developers. At Tadich's, over the best French bread in town and a bottle of Fetzer's Chardonnay, Dusan, pronounced "Du-shan," grimaced, "I put all the facts and figures through my computer, and it said 'Tear it down.' But I couldn't. When I bought the building, the walls were caving in and the floors were falling into the basement. I'm spending millions to bring that old Frenchman's building back to life and I feel good about it. I'm giving something to the city that has given a lot to me. This is a wonderful place."

★ ★ ★

Time stands still at Tadich's. I sat there in the booth and listened to the rattle of dice cups, part of the San Francisco luncheon tradition for a century. Honest wood on the walls, thick tablecloths, slabs of French fries and old waiters who seem to know everybody's name. I ate a Hangtown Fry, wondering for the thousandth time how the Placerville gold miners managed to get their hands on Olympia oysters, and then walked out into the gray afternoon. A cable car festooned with gay balloons rattled past, heading toward the hill where the Mark and the Fairmont are still king of the mountain. "Survive!" is the word for the 1980s, and it's a miracle that so much that is special about San Francisco is managing to do just that, no matter what the computers say. *March 14, 1982*

At last, proof that our intrepid Meter Maids can smell fresh paint a mile away! Last Thurs. morning, a city crew began painting the hitherto virginal curbs at Levi's Plaza—a couple of yellows here, a blue there, a lot of red at the corners—finishing the job at noon. Within 45 minutes, two Meter Maids were on the scene, happily tagging cars that had been parked legally only a couple of hours earlier. How greedy can the city get? *April 28, 1982*

Shortsnort: Bill O'Connor, the retired police capt., cracked up Charlie Bulanti with the story (true) of the plainclothes cop who cruises the Tenderloin in an unmarked car, nailing male and female hookers. Few days ago, on Turk, the cop got the high sign from a tall male, so he stopped and rolled down the window. "Wanna date?" asked the guy. When the cop nodded and asked how much, the feller said "Twenty bucks." They finally agreed on $10, whereupon the young man got into the car and was immediately handcuffed. The prisoner stared at the bracelets. "Into bondage, eh?" he said. "That will be $5 extra." You have to like his style. *December 3, 1982*

No escape, even in the boonies: Claire Hundley and her husband were driving through Garberville when their car broke down, so they went to a bar called The Cellar to wait out repairs. In the ladies' room, Claire discovered that the toilet tank lid had been covered with sandpaper, and inquired why. "Too many women chopping and snorting lines of coke in there," explained the bartender. "Now they can't use the toilet top. Cheaper than hiring a policewoman." In the men's room, Mr. Hundley found that the tank lid had been removed entirely. So had all the doors. Garberville???

★ ★ ★

Ah mothers!: Jim Cvitanich, a bartender at a gay saloon in the Castro, went home to So. Cal. to visit his mother, who complained as usual about the way he dressed—so he showed her a photo of himself in drag for a Halloween ball. "Well," she sniffed, "at least you dress better as a woman than as a man!" *January 25, 1983*

One of my squirrelier spies filched the following memo from the files of Ed Hardy, Pres. of the Yosemite Park & Curry Co. It concerns the impending visit of Queen Elizabeth II and Prince Philip, and reads as follows:

"Gahl Bothe called from the White House to say that the Queen and her party will need all of the Ahwahnee (Hotel). She also said that the Queen normally travels with a chef team to prepare her food; however, they were so favorably impressed with the Ahwahnee and our chefs that they may not be bringing their chef team to Yosemite. She said the Queen drinks red Dubonnet, prefers white wine over red, very dry martinis and gin and tonic."

At least we know what she carries in those oversized handbags.

January 27, 1983

For the past couple of days, BART passengers have been buzzing about a new example of monumental nonsensicality—printed notices, in almost every car, about What To Do In Case of a Nuclear Attack. These are not only a triumph of pithy advice, they are fetchingly illustrated, the whole subject being so amusing . . . Here we go: "Stay calm." No problem there. "Avert eyes from flash." Since, if you are lucky, you will be in a BART car at the bottom of the bay, that can be handled, too. "Brace for blast. Duck and cover. Place newspaper over head." This last is illustrated by a figure with what appears to be The Chronicle over its head. The Chronicle always provides ample coverage. "Reserve medical attention for high priority evacuees." That is, if Queen Elizabeth or Dianne Feinstein are aboard, they get out first. "Have food and water for several weeks of isolation." Waitaminnit! How long are we gonna be here at the bottom of the bay? "Comfort the dying." Anybody know any good stories? And finally, "Isolate corpses to prevent spread of diseases." This shows two BART cars, one with people standing, the other with people prone. You live or you die.

* * *

Yesterday, BART workers were busily removing these notices. Embarrassed BART officials claim they were printed and put up by person or persons unknown as a "very well done" joke. But the point is that most passengers took them seriously, so insane is the nuclear threat.

February 3, 1983

Eye to Eye With the Queen and Nancy

OK. I met the queen last night in the receiving line at the de Young Museum. In her champagne-colored gown, probably designed by Hardy Amies, she was cool but gracious. The president looked me right in the eye and said, "Hello." Mrs. Reagan looked surprised to see me but was interrupted by the prince, who said, "Hello," not knowing I was among the uninvited. Inside Hearst Court I looked for a no-show so I could pop into a seat but it was like musical chairs and I was the loser. I slunk out. In the press room, British reporters who have followed the queen on her West Coast tour, said, "San Francisco has done it again. The Los Angeles show was tacky. In San Francisco she has found real elegance and is having the time of her life." And I say hooray for us.

★ ★ ★

Sup. Harry Britt, old True Britt, who boycotted the Mayor's reception yesterday at Davies Hall, keeps complaining about the money the Queen's visit is costing us. Actually, it is costing very little, thanks to many a private donation, including the $7,500 worth of flowers that decorated Davies yesterday (a gift from a certain Mr. G.). Florissimo Bob Bell decorated the cable car that stood across the street in the Opera House driveway. A published and broadcast report that the de Young Museum spent $20,000 to convert the men's room into the Queen's powder room is balderdash. "I can give you the exact figure," says Gus Teller of the museum staff. "It's $1,060, mainly labor. We cut the cubicles down to three, screened off the urinals and put in a lounge." That money can be reclaimed easily by converting the cubicles to pay toilets, with an appropriate sign. In good taste, of course.

★ ★ ★

Evening the score: The London gutter press has been ragging the responsible American media for getting things wrong in matters of protocol, titles and whatnot. Well, how about the BBC man who told his listeners that the royal couple would "rest up at Yosemite Park in the Rocky Mountains"?

★ ★ ★

Wednesday night, about 7:30. A few people were seated in the window of the San Raku Japanese restaurant on Sutter, near Taylor, chopsticking their teriyaki and staring out at a wet, empty street. Suddenly all hell broke loose. Squadrons of motorcycle cops roared up, battalions of Tac Squadders took up positions in the middle of the street, clubs held menacingly at port arms. The rooftops came alive with Secret Service men, sharpshooters and people barking into walkie-talkies. Ah, security. The people in the San Raku stopped eating and looked both curious and frightened. They hadn't realized they were across the street from the rear entrance to Trader Vic's. They were not aware that the Queen of England was about to arrive.

★ ★ ★

A long wait. I stood in the drizzle with James Whitaker, famous royalty watcher for the London Daily Mirror. He pursed his lips and shook his head. "Oh, she (the Queen) is not going to like this," he said. "She is not going to like this at all. She hates a fuss being made. Oh, dear." Presently, a cavalcade came around the corner: motorcycles, limos, outriders, inriders and, at the end, an ambulance. Ambulance? In case somebody got a bad fortune cookie? Goof: Mrs. Reagan was on the sidewalk side of the limo and darted into Vic's. The Queen debarked in the middle of Sutter and had to walk around the rear of the car. We shuddered. If ever there was a time ———. After she had gone inside, a Tac Squadder said fiercely, "All right, back on the sidewalk. Did you hear me? BACK ON THE SIDEWALK." All right, all right, but how about Her Majesty standing alone in the middle of Sutter St.?

★ ★ ★

Nobody can figure out how Trader Vic's was picked, aside from the fact that it's world-famous and near the St. Francis. "It wasn't my idea," said Nancy Reagan yesterday. "She wanted to go to a restaurant—any restaurant. You can't believe how excited she was! I don't know who selected Vic's exactly. The food was marvelous, by the way." The Examiner reported that the Queen drank a daiquiri. That's what comes of phoning in stories. She and the Prince had Tanqueray gin martinis over ice. Nancy Reagan had a Shirley Temple made of real Shirley Temple. No, that's a joke. She had a screwdriver . . . The 80 cops working the Union Square beat ate well, too. Bob Mendes, owner of the McDonald's at 1041 Market, sent over 160 quarter-pounders, free.

★ ★ ★

Yesterday morning, I walked down Polk toward Davies Hall to get the feel of the city. The Queen would have loved it. A jogger flashed past wearing naught but a Union Jack. The Stallion bar was jammed with a merry, even gay, throng at 9 a.m. Shocking. Sukkers Likkers, which usually displays irreverent marquees, played it straight: "God Save the Queen!" A crowd was filing into the corner bar that dares to call itself the Irish Embassy. A mob near City Hall chanted "IRA All the Way!" over and over. Life as football game. A banner outside the S.F. Museum of Modern Art read "Long Live the Queen and the Rest of Us—Freeze Nuclear Weapons."

★ ★ ★

The line of people waiting to get into Davies for the Mayor's reception stretched for a block and a half. "I didn't realize Dianne knew this many people," murmured Claude Rouas. His brother Maurice's restaurant, Fleur de Lys, on Sutter, in the same block as Trader Vic's, had closed the night before. "Too much security," lamented Maurice. "They wouldn't even let my doorman park cars." Said Modesto Lanzone: "I'm not hurt. I knew the Queen wouldn't come to my restaurant. She hates spaghetti." Prince Philip got off a sharp line to a local: "I hear all your animals are not in the zoo!"

* * *

At last, the royal party settled down for the show, produced by Steve Silver, and wonderfully corny it was. Schmaltzy in the best sense of the word. You just can't beat good corn: Mary Martin singing "Getting to Know You," as Yul Brynner beamed from a box. Tony Bennett, in exceptionally good voice, singing "I Left My Heart," carefully changing the tense to "Where little cable cars CLIMBED"—wink—"halfway to the stars." Prince Philip appeared knocked out by a super Steve Silver hat—Steve is a devil with hats—that showed Buckingham Palace (complete with marching guards), Tower of London and a Big Ben tower that opened to disclose photos of the royal family. The Prince was, in fact, ecstatic, leaning over to point out details to the Queen, who seemed bemused. Jose Simon, who studied Her Majesty throughout the wonderful show, said at the end: "I still say that's not the Queen, that's Dustin Hoffman."

* * *

And so it's off to Sacramento for a meal catered by the Nut Tree. That sounds funny even if it isn't, but rully, darling, croissants with crepes? The Queen looks like a pleasant lady, somebody's sister, cozy, fun to talk with over a cuppa tea, and it was nice of her to drop in. The Prince, too. *March 4, 1983*

"It couldn't happen in a million years," but it did: Air Force Two, the Presidential plane that flew Queen Elizabeth II and Prince Philip to Seattle last Saturday, took off without the Queen's luggage, which contained some of the most valuable jewels. "In the incredible confusion," to quote an SFO worker, the vanload of royal bags was left behind—and so were six members of her staff. They and the bags were flown to Seattle in a chartered plane—paid for by us, no doubt—and let us hope Her Majesty remembered to keep her baggage checks . . . *March 9, 1983*

The last sailboat of the day scuttling into the safety of the St. Francis Yacht Club, like a kid being called home to supper; the two-story conference hall atop the great gray bulk of the old Standard Oil building, where mysterious deals are cut and distant thrones are made to tremble; Cesar Ascarrunz's samba-mambo palace in the heart of the Mission, oozing raw sex, strange rhythms that may or may not be a misdemeanor, high adventure amid the low-riders; the Dixieland beat of beat-up old Pier 23 barrelhousing up the eastern slope of Will Irwin's "Tellygraft Hill"; the faded sign on the side of a Market St. building, "Gas and Credit Given"—a memory of Painless Parker, who extracted teeth and money with equal proficiency.

★ ★ ★

More facets than a gem: Brink's guards carrying bags of money past penniless bag ladies; the $100 million Ramada Renaissance hotel rising noisily on the grave of The Pit, a remarkable saloon that was both black and gay; punks with pink hair pouting their way through red lights on jerky Turk, daring you to hit them, perhaps wanting you to; hookers in hotpants trying to thumb rides from the three-piece button-down squares heading home to Middle-Class Manor, out there in the Richmond; Polk St.'s leathery-tough gays, handcuffs and chains jangling on their belts, eyes hollow, lives desperate, mouths spitting hatred at any straight who looks twice.

★ ★ ★

Passing parade: The Salvation Army lassie (Lily) who is straight out of "Guys and Dolls" as she passes her tambourine in South o' Market deadfalls; the flower peddler making her bar-to-bar rounds in North Beach, her gardenias turning brown as the clock nears midnight; Bill Swan, the super doorman at the Fairmont, a man who finds parking spaces where none exist, a candidate for Mayor of Nob Hill; Mr. Purcell, the proper newsie at Powell and O'Farrell, whose very presence brings back memories of Herbert's Bachelor Grill, the old Orpheum (Sophie Tucker and Jack Benny on the same bill), Coffee Dan's in the basement across the street (you entered via a slide), Gamboleer Benny Jackson and the bookies gathering in John's Grill at 10 a.m. to split the take over bacon and eggs.

★ ★ ★

Little big town: The rich deadness of Sea Cliff, where you seldom see a pedestrian; the odd enclave of Presidio Terrace, whose primordial silence screams "Keep Out!"; the bosky steps leading down the Baker St. hill between the Lewis and de Wildt mansions, traversed by those who like the smell of money and the most expensive view of the bay; Beniamino Bufano's eloquent mother penguin raising her bill skyward at the Powell-Pine corner of Stanford Court, imploring the heavens to be kind; up the street, the turreted wall, which is all that is left of Madame Mark Hopkins' mad explosion of Victorian bad taste.

★ ★ ★

Roving eye: The 11 a.m. line forming faithfully outside Tadich Grill, the nonstop domino games at Enrico's "family table" (where there are feuds with the food), the ancient cappuccino machine barely holding together at Tosca (as Caruso sings tinny on the jukebox), Henri Lenoir heading up Columbus toward a mirage of the Black Cat (no man wears a beret with more flair), the doll-tiny doorman at Tommy Toy's Imperial Palace, wearing a uniform three times too big, a hat that comes down over his ears, an appropriately worried look.

★ ★ ★

Quickshots: The rickety steps leading to Macondray Lane, whose leafy enchantment now seems dark and sometimes dangerous; the marvelous stained-glass entrance to Bardelli's, once Charles' Fashion, a survivor of the Gilded Age, never cracked, never broken; Wednesday matinee at ACT's Geary Theater, with the children spilling out into Geary and looking for a place to go for a soda (oh, where are you now, Golden Pheasant!); the lovely old Curran, everybody's idea of what a "legit" theater should look like; across the street, the lost and almost prehistoric world of piano bars, a whiff of disinfectant, a hint of broken dreams and careers gone sour.

★ ★ ★

Calliopes and kaleidoscopes: The carousel at the zoo, spinning its mournful sounds of children who grew up long ago and took their songs with them; Maxfield Parrish's marvelously restored painting in the Palace's Pied Piper bar, a clubby place of old gaffers looking through a glass darkly at Parrish's bright youngsters, forever following the foolish dream; Stan the Man, the dice-shaking barman at Le Central, who pays his losses out of his own pocket and never whines; Ed Moose, the big, shambling, friendly guy who gives the Washington Sq. Barngrill its special ambience; the city within a city that is the UC/SF Med Center, a tapestry of lights climbing out of Parnassus toward Sutro Forest, all darkly alive with the scampering of bandit-eyed raccoons.

* * *

The way it is and was: Bank of America's black monolith turning silver-light and surprisingly graceful at dusk; the day's wash fluttering on the fire escapes of Broadway and Vallejo near Stockton, where Chinatown fuses with North Beach in a clash of cultures, crash of bumpers, flare of tempers; walking the bridges through Embarcadero Center, catching glimpses of secret lives, treasures like the Ferry Building, shadows of the past that are restlessly alive in the haunted hills we call home. *March 13, 1983*

The Vertical Earthquake

It's not polite to say "I told you so." In fact, it is definitely lacking in charm. Yet we who have consistently opposed the overbuilding of San Francisco have been treated a bit shabbily too. "No-growth kooks"—an odd phrase but often used. We cared more about petunias than progress. Not only that, we were environmental elitists: Because we got here first, or early, we thought the views belonged to us. We had an "unnatural" aversion and hostility to the hard-driving newcomers from Elsewhere who threw up (a term I use advisedly) the blockbusters that robbed us of those views. We were the "little San Francisco" people who wanted the most pleasant, livable, human-scale city in the country to stay that way.

* * *

Dean Macris, the city planning director, is at last facing the bleak fact that San Francisco is not New York or Chicago. San Francisco is a small, delicate and infinitely precious place that has to be handled with care, precision and a lot of love, including love of a mystique that cannot always be expressed in words. Macris' latest plan for downtown calls for a year's moratorium on new buildings, a general downsizing, and a definite end to the aptly named blockbuster, with its straight lines and flat roof. This is a big step ahead, but it won't bring the city back to 1945 or even 1967. In fact, it may already be too late to "save" San Francisco. If you would see the irreparable damage that has been done, simply look about you.

* * *

"The vertical earthquake," as I termed it in a piece 15 years ago, did more to change San Francisco than the cataclysmic events of

April, 1906. In '06, a vital young city dug itself out of the ruins and built pleasing variations on the theme of what had been there before. What emerged was something handsome and proud. The people of those times, that "different breed" we look back on with something like awe, couldn't wait to show off the New San Francisco by means of a World's Fair. The vertical earthquake of the 1970s and '80s destroyed what was left of a tradition and covered it with a new city that bears no resemblance to what had gone before. The piledrivers were singing the song of the big buck. The cranes rose high over downtown, looking at times like vultures. Anybody who dared raise a voice in protest was "a carbuncle on the butt of progress," to quote a leading architect.

* * *

Although Dean Macris and his planners—not to mention the Mayor—don't come right out and say so, it's obvious that a Big Mistake has been made. With their new plan to "save" an already shellshocked downtown, they are implying as much. How long it takes some people to learn, and how painful the lessons. A distinguished architectural critic wrote just recently, as though discovering the fact for the first time, that a proliferation of skyscrapers causes changes in the climate, shadows to fall over open space, and traffic to increase disastrously. Sunny streets become cold and dark. The wind whistles up and down the sterile canyons. The nightmare of gridlock becomes a reality. Late on a Friday afternoon, gridlock is here: Horns blow, tempers explode, signals go through their timed phases, and traffic moves not an inch.

* * *

Why San Francisco would try to emulate Manhattan is a mystery to all but those who see dollars in them thar skyscrapers. Manhattan is a natural highrise city, though it, too, is paying a dreadful price for overbuilding; gridlock is there to stay. San Francisco, on the other hand, already had its breathtaking vistas, its sacred view corridors, its wide-open expanses of bay and ocean that lifted the spirit and made the heart sing. The view corridors didn't stay sacred for long. A blockbuster appeared at the foot of Post. A hotel rose on Third to block the sightlines along Kearny. The most exciting city in the land was about to be imprisoned behind fortress walls.

* * *

A few people kept up the fight. Not many. Nobody wanted to stop the developers dead in their tracks, but there is such a thing as unreasonable growth. There is also such a thing as having a feeling for a city, and few developers ever expressed much. Most of them merely complained about red tape, height limits and safety precautions. To them, San Francisco is just another place to exploit, and it is sad to add that they found plenty of San Franciscans eager to help them cut the red tape. "Anything for a buck" is not confined to auslanders. In the last decade, the face of a beautiful city has been changed beyond recognition, and it didn't have to be that way. It turned out that the style, the charm, the elegance of San Francisco had no bearing on the case. A unique city turned into a look-alike for any other skyscraper-plagued metropolis. Coit Tower, the Ferry Building, Willis Polk's Hallidie Building and Mills Tower became monuments to the city that was. Everything old and graceful was threatened, if not already doomed.

⋆ ⋆ ⋆

So now we have a breathing spell, a year in which to count up our profits and tragic losses. It is no longer the beloved city that poets rhapsodized over, visitors fell in love with and natives worshipped. Gone are the spires and minarets of Baghdad-by-the-Bay. The fight now is to save what is left, and fortunately, there is still a lot worth fighting for. If ever a city had an embarrassment of riches, it is this one, even after the squandering. *September 4, 1983*

The Lotus Grows No More

Last Friday started out gray and drizzily and it didn't get any better. The phone rang all day with people who wanted to commiserate over Don Sherwood, found dead that morning in his Russian Hill aerie. "I'm dying, Herb, going fast," he kept saying at Enrico's, his favorite hangout the past few months, and then he'd go into his trademark dirty laugh, followed by a hacking, wracking cough, and you knew he wasn't kidding. It was sad and painful for old "Donny-babe," as he used to call himself, dying of emphysema, breathing by means of an oxygen machine, smoking one cigarette after another. Don, the legend. His tongue was in his cheek when he called himself "The World's Greatest Disc Jockey," but he was and wasn't. Wasn't a disc jock, I mean. The records he played on KSFO didn't matter. His patter did: Wry, funny, serious, mean (the nastiness always softened by that famous chuckle), delivered in The World's Greatest Radio Voice, a voice the mike loved, a voice that filled the speaker. "Out of the mud grows the lotus," he said at the end of each show. The muck and mire of commercial radio produces a rare species like Don Sherwood once in a lifetime, and the lifetime is over. It was all too short, but god it was fun while it lasted.

★ ★ ★

I could go on and on about Don, but by the time you read this, the story will have been well and fully covered. He crossed me up right down to the end, dying on a Friday. I have no Saturday column, the Sunday column is locked up on Wednesday, and here it is Monday. I can hear him laughing now, and rolling his eyes: "Scooped again, eh?" It was only a week ago that, uncharacteristically, he hired a Rolls-Royce limo and driver. I say uncharacteristic because he hated any kind of flash. He dressed like a guy who didn't care how he looked, and he didn't. He drove old, beatup cars, which is not a bad idea in this town. In fact, he was a careful guy with a buck—even tight, you might say, except that no rules applied to him. When a guy is a life-enhancer, as Sherwood was, who cares who picks up the tab? Anyway, here he was with his rented Rolls, outside Enrico's, and asking Enrico to drive up to Coit Tower with him. "Just want to look around," he said, but Enrico was busy. It turned out that Don had had himself driven all over San Francisco, to drink in the views, soak up the old sights, for what turned out to be the last time. "Only a few days left," he called out to Enrico, who must be feeling especially downcast, not having gone for that ride to Coit Tower.

★ ★ ★

It's hard to explain Don Sherwood, and the hold he had on this town, to people who never heard him. There was something essentially "San Francisco" in his manner, or so we like to think. A certain breeziness, a wary way of looking at life, a lack of pretentiousness. There was an appealing honesty and disingenuousness. On matters political or complicated, he was sometimes appallingly simple-minded, but his humor continually saved him. His style was at once sentimental and cynical—two qualities, or lack of them, that aren't all that far apart.

★ ★ ★

Whatever it was, it worked like nothing else worked in local radio and it lasted a long time, from the 1950s to the mid-'70s with a lot of time out in between. He was almost as famous for his no-shows as he was for his almost-daily appearances. When he was fighting with the station or suffering with a hangover—both frequent occurrences—he'd say "the hell with it," turn over and go back to sleep (the management at KSFO was remarkably patient, but losing a rare bird like Sherwood was unthinkable). His fans loved him even when he let them down. He was the naughty little kid, Peck's Bad Boy, Peter Pan and Don Quixote all wrapped up in one rumpled bundle. "Nobody shoves old Donny-babe around," they'd say when he'd be off the air in yet another salary dispute. They stuck by him through all the pitfalls of his pitted life: drunk-driving arrests, car accidents, paternity suits, divorces. The self-mocking laugh persisted but he was having a hard time, the celebrity who hated being one, the lonely guy in the crowd.

★ ★ ★

Don Sherwood, who was making well over $100,000 a year when that was real money, who lived in penthouses (and hated it), who had the highest radio ratings ever scored in this town, never quite could pull himself together. He tried everything, from Zen Buddhism to health foods to psychiatry. Characteristically, he called his psychiatrist "The Dirty Doctor." He didn't have a high regard for himself or his calling. The radio show was "silly," but when he tried to go serious, on issues ranging from Indian rights to the destruction of the Bay, his listeners rebelled. They liked "Just Plain Rosita," a hilarious ongoing soap opera that Sherwood ad libbed to Spanish language records. They liked it when he reminded them, on foggy mornings, to be sure their headlights were off after they'd parked. When he commanded commuters to blow their horns at the same time, the Bayshore, Nimitz and 101 in Marin sounded like New Year's Eve.

★ ★ ★

Don, real name Danny Cohelan. When the real Don Sherwood opened a sports shop on Grant, radio's Sherwood mused, "How can I get him to change his name to Danny Cohelan?" Then he'd laugh that laugh which, if it could be put into words, would be unprintable. The late John Wasserman, another who killed himself in the fast lane, once asked Don to define the meaning of life, and he replied: "Shakespeare said it—a tale told by an idiot, full of sound and fury, signifying nothing." Pause. "But it's the only game in town." And now it's over. *November 7, 1983*

Lily Dechamp has decided to retire, and thus ends another colorful chapter of Old Sanfranciscana. If you frequent the better downtown and South o' Market saloons, you've seen her—a bright-eyed, irresistible lady in a Salvation Army uniform, rattling her tambourine for contributions. Lily, now 84, has spent most of the last 44 years making the rounds for the Army, "and my legs are tired," she says. "Besides, South o' Market isn't what it used to be. Third Street has really gone downhill. Used to be so many nice places, like Breen's, and now they've been wiped out." Sorry, Meridien Hotel. You don't quite meet Lily Dechamp's standards.

December 6, 1983

★ ★ ★

1984

★ ★ ★

Brief Encounter

Last night I ran into the guy who used to be me.

He looked about 30, or a young 35. About 160 pounds, 14 of it curly hair, beginning to recede at the temples. It made me feel better to realize that by the time he was my age, he'd be close to bald.

"You're lookin' sharp, young Herb," I said, taking in the Oxxford suit, the Johnston & Murphy wingtips, the Countess Mara tie and the round-collar shirt. "And I like that tie bar."

"Gift from BG," he said offhandedly. "You know, Benny Goodman. He gave it to me after he finished his gig at the '39 Fair on Treasure Island. 'Here, kid, thanks for the help,' he said. He tossed it to me and walked off. That's the way he is. See? On the back it says "HC from BG 1939 SF."

He walked over to his car, a white Caddy convertible with red leather seats and a blonde showgirl. "This is Sally Wickman," said young Herb. "Helluva girl. Dances at the Music Box. A million laughs. Say something funny, Sally." "Something funny," she said. "See?" roared the guy who used to be me. "Get in, let's take a spin around the town we're in and have a little din-din."

A poet. The bard of Baghdad-by-the-Bay.

★ ★ ★

A brash youngish fellow. I wasn't too sure I liked him. Big nose, big mouth, the beginning of a double chin, and overweening confidence. "They call me the Winchell of the West," he said as we drove up Powell, past Bernstein's Fish Grotto, past the Golden Pheasant.

He honked at a handsome man in a homburg and chesterfield, carrying a silver-headed cane. "That's Dan London, manager of the St. Francis. We play bridge together. Helluva guy. I call the St. Francis the American Embassy because Dan is, you know, like an ambassador." He slowed down outside the Sir Francis Drake to say hello to a good-looking All-American boy. "Don Burger," explained young Herb, obviously a man who knew his hotel managers. "Runs the Drake. He built the Persian Room—best pickup spot in town, I'd say. What do you say, Sally?" "You pick up everything except the check," said Sally. Young Herb, easy laugher, let out a howl. "I named the Persian Room the Snake Pit, and the name really caught on. Don doesn't like it, but whaddya gonna do. It IS a snake pit. Some real vipers down there, Pops, waiting to hiss. You can't miss."

"Pops?" I inquired.

"Nothing personal," chuckled young Herb, "That's hep talk. BG calls everybody Pops, even his girl singer. Swinging is my life. Bands, broads, snakes, you name it, I dig it."

* * *

We cruised over to the top of Nob Hill, where the Cal and Powell cable lines cross. Amid much clanging, young Herb made an illegal left turn, flashing a red light and laughing boyishly. "Winchell has a siren, too," he said, "but he's a real nut. Don't get me wrong. Best damn three-dot columnist in the biz, but a nut."

We went into the Mark's Lower Bar. "Got to check this joint every night," he explained. "Action place. Saroyan usually drops in with Anita Howard. They've got a thing going. Right here is where Al Marsten belted me one because I took his wife to meet Sally Stanford. What the hell. So she wanted to meet a madam. I walk in here and he blindsides me. That's Jake Ehrlich over there. The great mouthpiece. Fixes juries, puts artichokes in 'em. That's what he calls 'em—because they're plants, see?"

We moved across the street to the Fairmont's Cirque Room, where Papagayo Al Williams was having a drink. "Big fight here last night," said young Herb. "Gerry Melone came in with a certain socialite—big family—and Dick Tobin said 'Whaddya doin' with that whore?' Poor Dick. He'd had maybe two too many. Gerry is big and strong, Pops. He hit Dick so hard that Dick's head hit the wall and left a big hole in it, like somebody had thrown a bowling ball at it."

We examined the indentation. "Dick is one nice guy," said young Herb, shaking his head.

* * *

We made the rounds. "I know this town like a book, which I intend to write," the guy I used to be rambled on. He drank White Label and water steadily and smoked Pall Malls—"the red death!"—in a gold Dunhill holder. A fop. I still wasn't sure I liked him. "I make seven, eight places a night, go to the office, pound out a li'l ol' column and then hit a few of the after-hours joints, like Dutch White's, or Jack's out in the Fillmore."

We spent a few minutes at John's Rendezvous, where Bill Gilmore, a steel millionaire, was buying drinks for the house. John, the owner, walked across the dance floor in his underwear. "Hey John," hollered young Herb. "Sober up!" At the Bal Tabarin, we sat with owners Tom Gerun and Frank Martinelli as Ted Lewis sang "I'm Steppin' Out With a Memory Tonight." Young Herb wiped away a tear. A sentimentalist.

"Well, so long, Pops," said young Herb. "Gotta drop Sally at the Music Box and get to work." As his gleaming Cad vanished into the mist, it occurred to me that everybody we had met is now dead.

Of course, so is the guy I used to be. *January 22, 1984*

CHARACTER STUDY

I've known people like him all my life. Pleasant, hearty, given to telling jokes. By their own lights, honest and straightforward. Firm handshake, steady eye contact, winning smile. To the very end, they are trapped in the web of their formative years: Work hard, keep nose clean, meet right people, rise to top. The rich have power; therefore, get rich as soon as you can or hang out with them. The enemies are Communism, unions, welfare cheats, unmarried mothers and people who are "different" from the crowd; if corporations are caught breaking the law, well, "that's business." Life is basically simple: Pledge allegiance, salute flag, revere John Wayne, watch out for foreigners; they are "sneaky." When you have acquired a loving wife, big car and a house on the hill, you have made it and will enter the Kingdom of Heaven where well-off Americans get the best tables.

* * *

These are not bad people, necessarily. Ronald Reagan is one, and he became president. Unless something unlikely happens, he and his loving wife will occupy the big house on the hill for four more years. The unemployed, who don't figure much in his plans, would be well-advised to start looking for those jobs that are out there, you know, for people who really want them.

⋆ ⋆ ⋆

I can understand why Ronald Reagan is popular with most Americans. He looks more amiable than he really is, and he "speaks well." For some reason, this is very important to a lot of people. Radio announcers speak well, too, some even more mellifluously than he, but never mind. I imagine that, to most people, Mr. Reagan represents the real American that doesn't exist—a Mr. Clean, pure in heart, uncluttered of mind, yet prepared to pull his six-shooter if threatened. If he seems the wrong man for the nuclear age, consider that most people don't want to "think nuclear," nor do many of them actually believe the horror tales; it is not easy to think of planet Earth as a lifeless cinder. If the second most horrendous problem of his administration is the trillions of dollars being squandered on weapons and interest payments on deficits a Democrat could only dream of, remember that most Americans, this one included, cannot think in trillions.

⋆ ⋆ ⋆

Ronald Reagan right now is at the height of his popularity. The polls, which are devoutly to be believed, say so. This is odd, and belies the age-old wisdom that the "average" American—here we have a caricature of a squinty-eyed farmer in overalls, chewing on a straw—is one smart cookie who is not to be fooled by window dressing. He has not been fooled this time. The real Ronnie Reagan has little time for the little guy and his little problems, such as working and eating three squares. The Real Ron loves pomp and ceremony, Hollywood flash, military hardware, admirals and generals and the image of the lone cowboy destroying the evil empire. It's a good act, and for a B-movie actor he does it well.

⋆ ⋆ ⋆

The supposedly shrewd and keen-eyed "average" American is mad for Nancy Reagan, too. Even though she is palpably a snob, as her occasional slips (by Adolfo) reveal all too painfully, she is the most admired woman in the country (and No. 3 in the WORLD!). Well, why not. It's pretty obvious that Mother Teresa doesn't dress as well, and makes us a little nervous, besides, with her saintliness. Nancy and Ronald are the ideal couple in the dreams of millions of Americans—very much in love, holding hands, looking adoringly into each other's eyes. It is the movies as real life in the fictional world of 1984, and all it implies. Nobody's knocking it, but a lot of people are surprised that the romantic values of the 1930s are still apparently valid, as we plunge faster and deeper into the nuclear void. It can't be nostalgia. The other values of the 1930s are deader than Franklin and Eleanor Roosevelt.

★ ★ ★

Mr. Reagan is good. He looks good and he talks good. His speeches, no matter who writes them, are classics of simplicity and evasion. With that great eye contact of his, he appears to be telling the truth, even when he is playing around with it; his mistakes have been documented in several books lately, but nobody's perfect and the American public is forgiving to a man with a twinkle. His speeches avoid the specifics of El Salvador and Nicaragua, the senseless spending in the Pentagon, our insistence on supporting the anti-democratic side as long as the other side is anti-Communist, the national debt that is mortgaging the future.

★ ★ ★

To the Ronald Reagans, defense contractors are rich men who are members of the club and therefore can do no wrong. That's why he expresses not a word of outrage over the Pentagon buying a three-cent screw for nine dollars. A country that will pay nine bucks for a three-cent screw deserves what it gets.

February 5, 1984

This Old Town

It's Valentine's Day. I'm hunched over the Loyal Royal, staring at a likeness of the love of my life—a wall map of San Francisco. I look at it a lot, even though it doesn't do her justice. The map is yellow, a color more appropriate than it used to be, with green blotches (parkmarks on her dear old skin) and patches of blue. Blue for Lake Merced, blue for Mountain Lake. How many San Franciscans know about Mountain Lake? It's another of the half-hidden wonders that make the crazy lady worth all the inspired insanity, an enchanted pond off Lake and Funston, a few yards from the maddening bridge traffic. Funston, formerly 13th Ave. till somebody decided that was an unlucky number, and besides, General Funston was more or less a hero during the Great Shakes of 1906. This city of rogues, thieves and flimflam artists can use all the heroes it can invent.

★ ★ ★

My old flame, a good title for a song, and a good song it was, in the time of ballads to be belted by a blowsy blonde at 3 a.m. in a Turk St. deadfall. That, and "Drunk With Love," which moved many a B-girl and hooker to tears. "Sentimental fools," said Sam Spade as his upper lip twitched. Sam owned the town I loved, a mysterious gray place of small hotels and shadows on drawn curtains. It was a city of secrets and he knew all the passwords. Many's the time I walked with Sam down dead-end alleys that came alive at the push of a button you'd never notice. The door would open a crack, the sound of a jam session would burst out, and the blonde woman, played by Lilyan Tashman, would say "Come in, Sam and make it snappy—the cops come by every 15 minutes." Sam laughed as he flipped his cigarette. "You're paranoid." "Parawhat?" asked Lilyan. "You know too many fancy words, you big lug."

* * *

Yeah, the love of my life and I didn't even send her a Valentine this year. Sometimes she gets on my nerves—OK, and I on hers. Noisy, avaricious, selling out to the new guys with the sweet talk and all those Eastern bucks. Oh, she has let herself go, all right, and not always to the highest bidder. Sometimes she sells out cheap to the cheapies. For a dame who has been around the block more times than I care to think about, she can be dumber than a poker player who draws to four kings and an ace. Well, maybe that's because she has forgotten how special she was, and can still be, when the lights are just right and the savage ravages don't show.

* * *

Hard-boiled critics like Novelist John D. MacDonald write that she used to have it but she lost it: "Now she sells what she used to give away." Well hell, John, she has always been a hooker at heart from the time she was a brawling young kid on the waterfront, so salty, saucy and outgoing that she became a famous name in every port of call. A wild one "with tousled hair," I think you called her. She tried to go respectable—for a time there we were afraid she'd move down the Peninsula—but the corset was too tight. Like June, she kept bustin' out all over and she still does. She was never a snob, this party girl who is growing old but not up. From the Castro to the Bawdway, from Polk to Nob Hill, she still makes a brave stab at playing the game. Only the tourists fail to notice that she's trying too hard.

City as woman. Maybe it's not the most felicitous metaphor, and yet she is eternally seductive, sensuous, singular. She has been a man's kind of town, seemingly always ready for a drink, a dance, a frolic in the feathers. In the desperate times of fires and earthquakes, she showed the courage of a goddess, of Mother Earth. Helluva dame. City as man doesn't work. Besides, I have the gut feeling that women don't love her as men do. There's a raw sexuality. There are tales of champagne nights and upstairs rooms, bawdy jokes and an indiscreet fondness for firefighters and cops. All those things that Just Weren't Done—she did 'em. "Whaddya think, Mr. Spade?" Sam pushed the gray fedora off his forehead and let out a raspy laugh. "I think you're nuts," he said. "This is a dump, not a dame. I'm gonna get me some fresh air. If you want breakfast at John's, I'll be there."

* * *

Valentine's Day. I keep staring at the map. There's still something there. All those wonderful names: Islais Creek, China Basin, Land's End, the Excelsior and Ingleside, where you can still follow the outlines of the old racetrack. Whenever I feel "the bone-deep fatigue of urban gaiety"—a line Tom Rooney dredged up from somewhere—I walk along the Embarcadero, watching the wheeling seagulls, eyeballing Mr. Crowley's tugs, sniffing deep of the salt air. "Still a helluva city, Sam," I said to Mr. Spade at John's. He snubbed his cigarette in the scrambled eggs and got off that half-smile that means everything and nothing. "She'll do," he said, "till something better comes along, and that'll take about 10 million years, I figure." *February 19, 1984*

Entre nous: People keep asking "Who is Strange de Jim?" Although his unique whimsies appear here often, I don't know. We have a perfect relationship: He sends me his thoughts, written neatly on a small memo pad, and I either print them or toss them into the wastebasket. When I do the latter, a faint but clear "Ohhhhhh!" is heard from the depths.

Recently there has been a change in our relationship. He wrote a note that was printed in the Letters to the Editor column. I felt a pang. Perhaps I had rejected Strange, whoever he or she is, once too often. His defection produced a reaction from other Letters to the Editor people. Such as "All this while I thought that Strange de Jim was the alter ego of Herb Caen, coming out of Caen's cerebral closet every now and then. Is he for real?" signed "Familiar de Bob, Novato." ("He is for real," said the Editor. Ha.) This was followed by "No wonder Familiar de Bob questions that Strange de Jim is an alias when Huxtable Pippey writes to you," signed "Pretty Boy Floyd Hollenbeck."

And now a word from Strange de Jim: "Aside from a little too much late-night big band music, I've been very happy living inside your head all these years. However, now (evidently in a bold move to decrease circulation), the Chronicle 'Letters' editors are trying to drag me kicking and screaming into the real world. I don't know whether to give you my 30-day notice or ask you to talk to these editors and assure them I'm really imaginary. Love, Strange."

Some mysteries are better left unsolved.

* * *

Food fair: Blazing Burgers, the oddball Walnut Creek place famous for the Grossburger (a hamburger with a bite taken out of it), has two new specials—Spam and Velveeta on Wonder bread with Miracle Whip, and Oreo Soup, which is five Oreo cookies in a bowl of milk. It is only a coincidence that Owner Denny Callaway went to Chico State. *March 30, 1984*

Out to Lunch

The most important time of day is the lunch hour, which in San Francisco runs from 11 a.m., when people start lining up outside Tadich's, to sometime after 3 p.m., when you have to make the big decision at Trader Vic's: one more li'l mai tai or put in a token appearance at the office? Lunch is where the deals are made, in the curtained booths at Sam's or in the upstairs dining rooms at Jack's. Lunch is what makes or breaks a restaurant. Get two or three turnovers at lunch and you can make it through the quiet nights that afflict most financial district eating places. Lunch is an invitation or a brushoff. "Hey, long time no see! Let's have lunch one of these days." Other guy, a touch too eagerly: "Sure. When?" First guy, moving away rapidly: "I'll give you a call—we'll set something up." As Prof. C. Northcote Parkinson once put it, so wisely, so well: "Delay is the deadliest form of denial." When a Cal student asked, "What does that mean, exactly?" Parkinson replied, "I'll tell you later."

* * *

For some people, lunch is their life. Socialite Harry de Wildt, otherwise known as Sir Lunchalot, is one. He has an office downtown for one reason only: "So I'll have a place to go before lunch." It's true that "socialite" is an outmoded term, but it fits Harry: He lives well, knows the right people, speaks several languages and has no visible means of support. I'm a member of the Lunch Bunch, too. Part of my job. Get around, eavesdrop, pick up items, duck check. Actually, I'm a check-grabber. Seriously. A bad case of Sacramento insecurity.

* * *

I eat out a lot. Lunch AND dinner. As a young feller, hoping to make a noise in this racket, I thought eating out was exciting. When I was first recognized by imperious headwaiters who bowed, scraped a little and murmured, "Right this way, Mr. First-Nighter," I felt I had bridged some pinochle of success. I liked the smell of restaurants, a blend of cooking odors, coffee, linen, sourdough, a hint of perfume from the next table. At places like Vic's and Jack's and Vanessi's, it was fun to see who was there with whom and why. Not only that, this city has a terrific bunch of old-time waiters, a lot of whom own apartment houses and are richer than the people they wait on. Well, why not?

* * *

It's nice to have a place where you can lunch alone, dawdle over the food, doodle on the menu, read a paper, make lists, collect your thoughts, unwind. Maybe write a letter or postcard. Ideally, the place should be open all afternoon so you don't have waiters standing around, looking at their watches or even snatching at your plate. The food should be good and the customers trilingual, at least. The waiter must never hover, except when you want a refill on your kir. Such a place is the cafe at Sutter 500, especially when chef Hubert Keller is on duty. Good dishes: French bean salad, asparagus with green onions, fresh mussels, pasta with duck, excellent wine by the glass. The newsstand sells the London Times. I think the place is having a little financial trouble. I hope it survives.

* * *

So I sit there alone, forking my beans and feeling my oats, making little lists. The woman next to me lights a cigarette. A steady stream of smoke is directed toward my sensitive nostrils. "Pardon me," I say, "but you are contributing to the malignancy of a diner." She is not amused. I put her first on my Nominated for Oblivion list, followed by people who say "hoho" for "happy hour." Happy hours. People who say "hordoovers" for hors d'oeuvres. Auto horns that play a tune. Auto horns. Drivers who think it's OK to run a red light if they blow their horn. "Edited for Television." Restaurants that play K-101 as background music. If we need background music, give us the real Muzak. Who needs background music, jerky motorists who give you The Finger, letterhead stationery so chic it doesn't include a phone number, prices like $99.99 and $299.99—who's kidding whom?

★ ★ ★

Tiring of that I begin wondering why I am such a terrible cook. I start a list of the bachelor's kitchen friends: Aunt Penny's White Sauce, Pepperidge Farms croutons, canned tuna (oh, lots of canned tuna), Trader Vic's Javanese dressing, Skippy's peanut butter, longhorn cheddar; thus do we revert to childhood. I start a list of people who make life more pleasant but seldom get recognition: organist Ludwig Altman, Donald (Pocket Opera) Pippin, the Grace Cathedral choir, Dr. Herb Wong on KJAZ, Assoc. Concertmaster Jorja Fleezanis at the Symph, the Flying Dutchman valet parkers. I start a list of good things: big brass mailboxes and the people who shine them, a seagull standing one-legged on the head of Don Juan Bautista de Anza in Just Herman Park, a Rolex watch, a navy-blue knit tie by Polo . . .

★ ★ ★

The check, please, waiter, and here's a tip that will make you financially independent for life. No-no, no need to kiss my hand. Just put me on YOUR list. The good one. *April 8, 1984*

I'll confess I couldn't get it up during the recent feeble flap over which should be our official song. "San Francisco" or "I Left My Heart," etc. Both are representative of a city that died long ago, a city some of us try to keep alive as a form of wish fulfillment. "San Francisco" is a Hollywood version of the city, circa '06, and "I Left My Heart" is straight Convention Bureau but with slightly more appeal. Those little cable cars climbing halfway to the stars or Pine St., whichever comes first, are right out of the pamphlets, but there is a sentimentality there that touches the spurious heart—like the pagoda'd roofs of Chinatown. We know there are tenements below, so we sing louder and have more drinks than are good for anybody.

★ ★ ★

Of all the contests engendered by the official song flap, the best was run by Tim Yohannan, of Maximum Rock 'n' Roll, on KPFA. Among the entries were, of course, Scott McKenzie's fairish "San Francisco (Be Sure to Wear a Flower in Your Hair)"—yet another false media image of the city—and Eric Burdon's "San Franciscan

Nights." Then there was "Let's Go (to San Francisco)," an early (1977) punk version of the McKenzie song, with emphasis on "the weirdos" one meets here. But the best of the bunch—and the winner of the contest—was "San Francisco" by Black Randy & The Metrosquad, an original song by a 1987 Los Angeles punk rock band. Some of the lyrics: "Ran into a guy with lipstick and a beard. When he took me home it was everything I feared. He lived in a house, it was run by ferns. We sprayed their leaves and polished their urns. The ferns were anarchists quoting Chairman Mao. Now I want to leave, but I don't know how."

★ ★ ★

I should add that the runner-up was "(Let's Kill) The Muni Driver," by Sick Pleasure, an S.F. band of two years ago. Another facet of the San Francisco scene that some may consider a bit extreme. *May 13, 1984*

Whatever happened to Strange de Jim? A postcard explains: "Landed at the Greater Pittsburgh Airport, couldn't find a town to match so I flew on." (Summer fun and some aren't.) Now that he's safely back, he reports: "Whew, talk about narrow escapes. I was about to drink a bottle of cyanide this morning when I noticed the seal showed signs of tampering." *September 28, 1984*

Speaking of food, or whatever, Serena Jutokovitz found some newer-yet nouvelle cuisine on the menu of the Won Thai in Berkeley: "Yum-Spam—Spam served with lettuce in hot spicy lime juice." Not worth a special trip . . . News nugget in a Mendocino Beacon story about the CAMP (Campaign Against Marijuana Planters) raid on the fields: a lone marijuana bud on a sign reading "This Bud's for You. CAMP has the Rest" . . . Barbara Harris overheard this Marinesque dialogue in the Greenbrae Petrini's, one woman to another: "How was your summer?" Other: "Not so good. Smashed up the car." First: "Oh, yeah? Which one?" Other: "Only the Porsche, thankgawd."

★ ★ ★

Well, it's about time! Whole Earth Access in Berkeley just rec'd an order from the PG&E Corporate Library for a copy of "Understanding and Using Electricity," by Bruce A. McKenzie and Gerald L. Zachariah, 1982 second edition. We anticipate no further power failures.

★ ★ ★

Attention Chico media: A pal at Cal forwards a strange artifact produced by the United Trading Corporation of Bombay, India. It is called—the mind reels—Velveeta Toilet Paper! The only evidence that it bears some resemblance to the more celebrated product is found in these words on the box: "Velvety Texture, Strong, Absorbent."

October 1, 1984

One of a Kind

It's a thrice-told tale by now. I've told some of the stories a lot more than three times. Gradually, they've become part of the legend of San Francisco, caught between the hard covers of books, engraved in memories. It's a good story, a success story. A kid with a wooden leg opens a beer parlor on an obscure corner in Oakland almost exactly 50 years ago and becomes a world-famous millionaire restaurateur—a household word in the households that count. When his artificial leg isn't fitting properly, he grumbles "Don't get one of these things unless you really need it." Now and then he delights in frightening the ladies by plunging an ice pick into it. A real character—the kind I used to call a 14-karat karakter—tough, ribald, hearty, oozing vitality. But he's not just having fun, you know. Most of the time he's behind the bar, concocting drinks the likes of which had never been seen (but would soon be copied). Or out in the kitchen, a self-made cook making history on a tiny stove.

★ ★ ★

He oozed so much vitality, in fact, that it is still hard to believe that Victor Jules Bergeron—Trader Vic—died at 81 late last Thursday afternoon in his Hillsborough house. He'd lost a lunch earlier, he was having heart trouble, he had a stroke—"the parts are wearin' out," as he put it—but we who knew him longest and best figured he'd stomp back into his Cosmo Place restaurant this morning and resume terrorizing the staff. He used four-letter words, told dirty stories and loved to scare the people who worked for him. "Jump! Move! Run!" The staff understood and loved him. One yardstick of a person is how long the employees can stand to work for him. Vic had waiters who've been with him 35 to 40 years. They respected each other and prospered together. Real tears were shed at Trader Vic's Thursday night.

★ ★ ★

San Francisco, 1936. The city had some good restaurants—Jack's, Sam's and Tadich's, of course. The Fly Trap, named during the Spanish-American war for the flypaper dangling from the ceiling to trap the horseflies (appetizing!), was forever crowded. It was torn down to make room for the Wells Fargo building; a San Franciscan who'd been gone for a decade returned one day, gazed up at the 43-story high-rise, and said, "Phew, when they remodeled the Fly Trap they went all the way, didn't they?" The social crowd hung out at Amelio's, the politicos at Fred Solari's, the heavy hitters (like Steelmogul Bill Gilmore) at John's Rendezvous and the kids at the little North Beach places, like the Manger. But word was getting around that there was Someplace Else!

★ ★ ★

It was a pair of beaux vivants named Billy McDonnell and Charlie Dreyfus who tipped me to Trader Vic's at 65th and San Pablo in Oakland. We went over by car ferry to the Berkeley pier and drove back along San Pablo, a trip well worth the effort. The Trader was already the subject of excited conjecture. He had lost his leg to a shark. He was a South Seas smuggler. He was on the lam from the Foreign Legion. Actually, he lost his leg at 6 (tuberculosis), had never been out of the U.S., and used to run a service station up the street. He had already invented a great drink—the Banana Cow, made of rum, milk and bananas. Nobody who tasted his honey-coated ribs for the first time ever forgot the experience. The guy himself had a booming voice, a big smile and a no-nonsense style. When gourmets started to rhapsodize, he'd remind them, "Look, I serve booze and chow and that's all. Of course, it's the best damn booze and chow in the world."

★ ★ ★

Exciting times. When the Bay Bridge was completed, we Loyal Sons of Hinky Dink enthused "Hey, they built this thing just so we could get to Vic's 20 minutes faster!" Hinky Dink's was the original name of Vic's, derived from the World War I song, "Mademoiselle from Armentières (Hinky-Dinky Parlay-Voo)." When the World's Fair opened on Treasure Island in '39, Vic's became not only famous but crowded. Even we Loyal Sons had to wait at the bar but it was worth it. By this time he had invented rum drinks with gardenias, orchids and crazy names like Missionary's Downfall and Sufferin' Bastard. In the foyer was a case containing two shrunken heads. It was I who had printed the caption that was affixed beneath them: "My, that certainly WAS a dry martini!"

* * *

Vic made it big during World War II, when Scotch and bourbon were hard to get but rum was plentiful. "That took planning," he'd chuckle slyly. For a decade, the best San Francisco restaurant was in Oakland, but he was always afraid to move it here. "Kid, you think I can make it over there?" he'd fret, as I'd point out, "What's the problem—most of your customers are from San Francisco." We drove around town, looking at sites. He almost took one down near Aquatic Park. Then he found a crummy garage in a corrugated shed down an alley across from the Bohemian Club. "That's it!" he whooped. He hired the celebrated architect, Gardiner Dailey, and said "When you get through, I STILL want it to look like a shed, okay?"

* * *

Young people are surprised to learn there was a real Trader Vic. They figure he was a franchise with a name invented by some ad agency. To those who were lucky enough to follow him from the start, he will always be real and alive—a true original who left his mark on generations who had their first dates over a rum drink and a sparerib in a place that was fun. For that, in the end, was what he was all about—a man who gave his all to the joy of living.

October 11, 1984

Saturday. John Rogers playing great stuff on KJAZ—lots of Ella and the Duke (Rogers for program manager). Two great cruise ships, the nifty Noordam and the twin-sticked Independence, side by side at Pier 35. It's a measure of the way things have been going that the sight of a ship on our waterfront causes surprise and pleasure. The Noordam, preparing to back into the stream and head out, was belching some wonderful chords on her big hooters, rattling windows on T'graph Hill.

I drove across the bridge and through the rainbow tunnel into the magic land of ahs, ohs and BMWs (Basic Marin Wheels). Mist was rising from a thousand hot tubs, smoke from a thousand barbecues, but I was heading for real country. West Marin. Narrow winding roads, cow-studded hillsides, beautiful red barns, fishing boats bobbing off Bolinas (alliteration is an affliction). Near Point Reyes, traffic began getting heavy: Forget football, pandas and standing in line for movies—the great gray whales are here!

The annual migration is on. By the hundreds, the 40-foot 40-tonners are on their way from the Arctic to make whoopee in the lagoons of Mexico, and at Point Reyes, which juts miles into the ocean, you can come as close to them as you can get without a boat. The challenge is to take the long hike down the steep steps to the Point Reyes lighthouse—"Equivalent to a 30-story building," a sign warns—knowing all the way that you will have to retrace your steps.

★ ★ ★

It's worth it, every step, every aching city muscle. Saturday, the waters just offshore were alive with whales. Planes dipped low, choppers hovered, boats ventured close. Even the Noordam made a detour to give her passengers a glimpse of whales diving, sunning, spouting, even leaping. Whale-watchers being among the nicest of the smaller mammals, there was a jolly holiday atmosphere. Fresh, beautiful kids like Sharon Fawcett, Jocelyn Eisenberg and Annabel Wong (Burkettes from Burke School) kept needling "Look at that one jump! Aw, you just missed it!" That became the code, "You just missed it," but I did see three—Patty, Maxene and Laverne Whale—leap in unison and take a bow as everyone cheered. *January 8, 1985*

Two Great Games

It's important to keep in mind today that there is more to life than football. Sex, for instance. Sex has been around since Day One Year One and, all things considered, is a better game than football. Less equipment, for one thing. It's a game that is played better by amateurs than professionals, although I might get an argument on that one. Any number can play—only two, in most cases, although you know your crowd better than I. It's true that football is more of a religious experience than sex—think of all the prayers being wafted toward Heaven and Las Vegas today—but sex has wider appeal in the long run. Long after football has become as archaic as court tennis and shuttlecock, sex will be a universally popular indoor and outdoor sport. Whether it's really up there with the major spectator sports again depends on your circle of friends.

⋆ ⋆ ⋆

Not that football doesn't have its sexual aspects. Take the Super Bowl, for instance. If you're some kind of sick Freudian nut, a bowl is definitely a sex object. So is a football, if you think about it in a sick sort of way. For some people, including various residents of the Castro, the skintight pants are a turn-on. The quarterback and the center in the T-formation—what is there to say? Then there's all the grappling, the grunting, the pushing and shoving that, in some parts of the animal kingdom, come under the heading of foreplay. The blitzing linebacker locking the quarterback in passionate embrace, rolling on the greensward with him, then giving him a pat on the fanny to show there were no hard feelings. Or were there? Who's to say? We won't even think about the mounting excitement.

⋆ ⋆ ⋆

It's amazing how much football and sex have in common. In both games, the idea is to score. There are advances and retreats, probes and feints. Stubborn defenses give way to determined efforts—or, conversely, rebuff all attempts to put the old pig bladder into the end zone. When penetration is achieved, a roaring climax ensues. As Ernest Hemingway put it, the Earth moves. The crowd rises in orgasmic bliss. On the other side of the bowl, there are other aspects of the sexual dilemma: frustration, anger and a very definite pain in various parts of the posterior.

★ ★ ★

I must admit that the concept of football as sex is a new one to me. Pete (Mr. Clean) Rozelle, the all-powerful, would probably find it distasteful. Football is pure and manly, except for the occasional finger in the eye, helmet to the kidney and blow to the head. Football clean, sex dirty; lock up the beasts before the game so they shouldn't lose vital bodily fluids. Learned observers have long considered football a metaphor for war and violence, which shows how little they have learned or observed. Players climb all over each other in their eagerness to be loved. There is even this love-hate relationship on the field, as there is sometimes in the sack or wherever you choose to play. The guys out there like and respect each other. They enjoy physical contact and camaraderie. They are trapped together in a perfectly insane public exhibition. No wonder they feel a closeness.

★ ★ ★

W. C. Fields once said about sex, "I don't know if it's good and I don't know if it's bad—all I know is that there is nothing quite like it." Football and sex are crazy and beautiful. Sex, of course, is more personal. Most of us think we thought it up ourselves. It comes as a shock the first time you find out other people have figured it out, too. "Too good for the common people," sniffed Milady in Restoration England. Right. It should have been patented. Football may be the more beautiful game. The beast with two backs is, from some viewpoints, a faintly grotesque and even ludicrous figure. Nothing like a fleet halfback slithering through outstretched hands. Nothing like a wide receiver straining, straining to get his hands on the ball that is about to outfly him. Nothing like two teams at kickoff rushing toward each other with arms outstretched.

★ ★ ★

The great and sexy day is here. We will all bundle up and trundle down to the small and beautiful town of Palo Alto, with its wide streets and lawns, its pretty houses and trees, its vaguely Southern, lazy atmosphere. At least half the people will experience satisfaction—those who can make a buck on the proceedings and those who bet on the winner. Almost everybody will have fun, as befits the mating of sex and football. Despite what all the fast-buck artists of the world have done to ruin it, football survives because it is a game as primal as sex, appealing to our best and worst instincts. Man and woman locked in ecstasy, quarterback running to throw his arms around a wide receiver—these are people saying, "I love you!"

★ ★ ★

It will be a long, hard day of laughter, sadness, madness, hysteria and confusion, a microcosm of life in 1985. At the end, you will be exhausted, which is only natural. When it comes to sex and football, you get back what you put into it, so give it all you've got.

January 20, 1985

Ask a silly question: Jo Ann Muiner wonders if ladies who gobble up Danielle Steel's romantic novels suffer from heroine addiction and I'm sure I don't know. *January 31, 1985*

And now that her daughter described it as looking "like a large Ban roll-on," Joan Kirsner sighs that the Palace of Fine Arts will never look the same to her again. *March 15, 1985*

Old ferries never die: To S. F. nostalgics, "Peralta" means only one thing—the Key Systems ferry, Peralta, which dipped beneath the stormy waves as she neared the Oakland mole on February 17, 1928, dumping 30 passengers, five of whom drowned, into the icy waters. One of the darkest days in the era of the sidewheelers. Most of us thought the Peralta was long gone, but, disguised as a fish processing plant called the Kalakala, she's up there in Kodiak, Alaska, being sold at auction. A dark-starred craft, the Peralta. Expert Harre Demoro says that after the stock market crash, there were more suicides off the Peralta than any other ferry on S. F. Bay. A thoroughly bad girl. *March 19, 1985*

Wet Feet

That was a miserable rain last Tuesday. Colder than Candlestick in July. A bad day to be poor and thin in this rich city with its big hotels, smug mansions and wide boulevards. Guys with holes in their soles and not much hope in their hearts were standing on Fifth, holding out their hands silently. They were too wet and cold to talk. People with umbrellas walked the way they always walk—under the canopies, bumping into one another and cursing. This is not the cool gray city of love on a midwinter day in spring. The Easter lilies were dying on the sidewalk flower stands, and the Gray Line buses had not sights to see. Was there ever a more fitting name for a sightseeing company in San Francisco than Gray Line?

⋆ ⋆ ⋆

I tried to do my rainy-day shortcut from The Chron to Le Central and didn't get very far. The old route was through the Pickwick Hotel garage, out the back door, across Jessie into the Emporium, down the escalator to the basement, under Market St. via the BART station to Woolworth's, out the back into the Ellis-O'Farrell garage, up the elevator, across to Macy's, out the Geary side, jaywalk into Union Sq. Garage, cut through the Hyatt Union Square into the Sutter-Stockton Garage, take elevator up, exit Bush, slide down hill to Le Central. All this without taking a breath, but I was foiled at the start. The Pickwick Hotel garage—once adorned with beautiful murals of California!—now has a gate. Back door locked. And besides the Pickwick has changed its name to the Merlin. Not a magical monicker. More like dumb.

⋆ ⋆ ⋆

Frustrated, I marched squishily into Woolworth's, which is always fun in a hopeless sort of way. All those fat people always eating fattening food. There is no end of the things to eat in the world's biggest five'n'dime—or don't they call it that any more? Barbecued this and that, pastries that look like they could hold their own in a fair fight, candy in every size and color, soft drinks that light up in the dark, peanuts, popcorn, plus an overpowering smell of people whose Speed Sticks failed. Don't get me wrong—I love Woolworth's. Every visiting VIP should be given a tour of that and the Marina Safeway and Cala Foods at midnight. There's the real San Francisco, weird and freaky but not unfriendly, filled with people who need people but are afraid of them. The Safeway in the Castro is worth a look, too, although you guys know by now there is no Safeway. It's better to be Lucky unless you believe in Purity. Seven-eleven are lucky numbers, and so much for stupidmarket jokes.

★ ★ ★

I had a hot dog at Woolworth's. The doggies revolve slowly on steel rollers. It's something to look at while you are waiting for your coffee to cook in the Styrofoam cup. Some of the dogs are raw, and some are on the verge of burning. Just as one is about to turn black, the lady snatches it and pops it into a bun. Great timing. I struck up a conversation with two regulars wearing black shirts, black jeans, pointy shoes, cowboy hats and string ties. "Good doggies." "Best in town." "Yeah. Schwarz, y'know." "Yeah, all beef." "Made in South City, y'know." That stamped them as real San Franciscans, the kind who would never say South San Francisco. "I like the relish, not the onions." "Yeah. Good relish. Not too hot, not too sweet." "Juuuust right," I interjected hurriedly.

★ ★ ★

One of the regulars may have recognized me. He squinted as he chewed. "Say," he said around his bite of doggie, "you aren't gonna write about this place, are ya?" "I dunno," I shrugged. "Like you say, good doggies. Why?" "Hey, don't write about this place," said the other. "You'll ruin it for us. We know most of the people who come here. It's our little club. We'll have all kinds of people here, we won't be able to get near the counter . . ." His voice trailed off. I felt crummy because I knew that on some rainy day I'd write about it, and anyway the doggies aren't THAT good. I put down a couple bucks and told the waitress to keep the change. She didn't look up. Waitresses at Woolworth's think you're nuts if you leave a tip.

★ ★ ★

Still raining. All the street people in hiding. Cable cars empty. Across the street, workmen tearing out that old steakhouse that had meat—maybe even a steak—grilling on a revolving gadget that looked like something out of the Inquisition. The owner told me once it was the first place in the country that had steaks grilling in the window, and who cares? Not the greatest sight in the world. He didn't know what was going in, but some franchise, no doubt. Or a "gift" shop. How many gold chains can there be? I wandered half a block up Powell to a trendy-looking bar called Dashiell's. I tried to imagine Dashiell Hammett perched on a bar stool there and failed. My wet feet began to itch, and I ordered a cup of coffee. It tasted like something that would stop the itch.

March 31, 1985

Seeing is believing: Hank Dekker, the famous blind yachtsman who recently sailed alone from S.F. to Hawaii, deftly docked his sloop, the Outta Sight, at the Alameda Marina Village, tapped his way to a red Cadillac, jumped into the driver's seat and—yes!—drove off. In the passenger seat was his pal, Deming Smith of Hillsborough, who guided Hank to the Rusty Pelican, four miles away, by calling out "Four degrees right, now 30 degrees left, stop sign 100 years ahead," and so on. Dekker, who drove before he began losing his eyesight, says, "It was fun! And easy. Now I'd like to do a Cad commercial." *April 25, 1985*

EMBARRASSMENT OF RICHES

Northern (or Superior) California has it all, I reflected last Friday as I placed a bottle on a road map and gave it a spin. No matter where it ended up pointing—even to Turlock—there was a place worth visiting for a couple of days. Mountains and seashores, lakes and valleys, cunning little $200-a-day resorts—here is a wonderland that has it all and had better stop talking about it because it isn't even May and the highways are already bumper-to-sticker. On second thought, perhaps it is better to pull the covers over one's or two's heads and forget the whole thing. As W. Somerset Maugham once said with a gentle smile, "It was such a beautiful day I decided to stay in bed."

★ ★ ★

Our blessed and absolutely incomparable part of the world has always been keen on le weekend. Almost everything is within driving range for a two-night stand, which is so much classier than a one-nighter; on a two-nighter you can really establish a relationship, her socks in my tennis bag, my shorts in her jewel box, much laughter as you wait for room service. Besides, "getting away for the weekend" is such a tradition. A changing one. Now it starts on Thursday and runs to Monday. That leaves Tuesday for recovering—and exchanging underwear—and Wednesday for working. Can capitalism survive the one-day week?

★ ★ ★

The No. Calif. weekend is freighted with memories. As a kid, I listened to Capt. Dobbsie on the Shell ship of Joy, singing "Highways Are Happy Ways (When They Lead the Way to You)." An automobile ad rhapsodized on "The Call of the Open Road," a romantic idea illustrated by girls of impossible perfection, hair streaming in the wind, driving their open coo-pays (rumble seat extra) down a two-laner toward an immense setting sun. Somewhat less glamorous, we roared from Sacramento to San Francisco in a Dodge touring car with disk wheels that reverberated with wolf-like howls. The exciting destination was the Carquinez car ferry, our escape from the hot, boring valley and introduction to the excitement of lapping waves and shouting gulls. In 1939, hay still growing in my ears, I stood at the Mark bar and marveled as a young man with a great tan said on a Friday eve, "Well, so long, old sport." He'd already read Fitzgerald. "I think I'll borrow Dad's Rolls and motor down to Pebble for the weekend." I'd never heard anything so grand.

* * *

I kept spinning the bottle on the map. It pointed to Sonoma. Great place for a weekend. Only an hour away, no matter how bad the traffic. Salamanders alongside rushing creeks, David Bouverie's round pool, M.F.K. Fisher's perfect hospitality, the Kangaroos of Tom Rooney, or, as we laughingly call him, "Kanga-Rooney" and "Marse Supial." The Napa Valley and Claude Rouas adding courts and bedrooms to his Auberge du Soleil. Only Mendocino (trillium growing in Russian Gulch) and Tahoe seemed too far. At last the bottle pointed south. John Gardiner's Tennis Ranch in Carmel Valley. Pebble Beach and memories of Sam Morse—a weekend in 1938, when Salvador Dali threw a party in Sam's old Del Monte Hotel, a wrecked car stood upside down in the lobby (live naked girl underneath), Clark Gable and Ginger Rogers up from Hollywood, saloonkeeper Izzy Gomez the guest of honor. "Cost me $50,000," complained Sam. That was '38. How much in '85 dollars?

* * *

The main problem with driving south is San Jose, which threatens to become The Blob That Destroyed Northern California, if it hasn't already. How can something so nothing go on so long? Sannazay, yeah. Sannazay is probably bigger than S.F. already but who cares. Nobody goes there. It's simply "San Jose—Next 51 Exits," or whatever, on the freeway and traffic keeps right on going, albeit at about five miles an hour. Smogville North. Off to the right I could see a vestigial skyline but nothing to get excited about. Now and then a plane seemed to be headed for what the road sign called "San Jose Municipal Airport." I'll give them some points for restraint there. It's not "San Jose International." Yet.

* * *

The southern city limits of San Jose are somewhere down around

San Juan Bautista. One of these days, Sannazay is going to be bigger than Lohs' Anggalayz and it serves them right. Miles and miles of exits to nowhere. The only good thing about inching past San Jose for hours is that when you finally clear it, you're in Salinas and the world looks brighter. You can smell the soil and feel the spirit of Steinbeck. The spring countryside is beautiful, everything in proportion, the way Xavier Martinez painted it. The hills aren't too high, the trees aren't too big, the fields aren't too wide, the valleys aren't too long. The only sadness is that most of the roadside stands seem to have disappeared, their sites swallowed by the ever-widening freeways. I'll miss the hand-painted signs in farmhand shorthand: "Cukes," "Cots," "Chokes," "Bings" (cherries, not Crosbys).

⋆ ⋆ ⋆

Springsightems: a three-day-old colt frisking alongside its proud mother, a five-week-old goat dancing among a dozen ducklings, mallards waddling down a road, quail scampering across a perfect lawn. At John Gardiner's Tennis Ranch in Carmel Valley, there are 14 courts for 14 units, making it unique. A secret world with bowers of flowers (can't get more California than that) down the hill from the best highway marker anywhere, a sign reading "No Hunting or Shooting." Not a worry in the world but something dangerous is inching up the road and it may be Sannazay. *En garde,* Gardiner!

April 30, 1985

Moonbeam lives! Last Fri. night, ex-Gov. Jerry Brown wheels his black T'bird into David Tonner's Carnegie Truck Plaza in Tracy, stops at the unleaded self-service pump, inserts the nozzle into the gas tank and puts it on automatic pump. "American Express," he tells David and wanders off to make a couple of phone calls. While he is gone, the pump shuts itself off. "Nice lounge area you've got," says Jerry to David. "Thank you," says David. Jerry then signs the credit card slip, jumps behind the wheel, fires up the T'bird and zooms off with the nozzle still in the tank, ripping off the hose and causing the pump to teeter dangerously. When last seen, Ex-Gov. Moonbeam was rolling south on I-580 with 15 feet of hose dangling out of his tank. Somebody should tell him.

May 3, 1985

This Old Town

The city, love it or leave it—but for what and where? Benign or malign, it grows on you. Torpor turns terminal, resistance crumples under the pressure of the daily dailiness, the need to succeed, the struggle to survive to the next deadline. The fatal attractions, forcing you against the walls of frustration with deadly centrifugal force; the constant distractions and detractions, the ceaseless and pointless ebb and flow of a million lives playing out their secrets all around you, close enough to touch but impossible to reach. The city animal is private, frightened, looking over its shoulder at shadows in the fog.

★ ★ ★

San Francisco is an excitement and a soporific, flooding the senses with visual excesses, dulling them at the dead end of dreams that died in the dawn of reality. Little big town, running around itself in ever-tightening circles, grabbing for the gold ring and biting its own tail. A city of free souls forever paying the price of conventions decreed long ago by style setters who vanished but left indelible marks. At heart, a conservative city that tolerates the crazies because it has been dinned into them that this is what San Francisco is all about, even if it isn't. A rivulet of nonconformity survives from the Gold Rush madness, but it has been slowed to a trickle. Today's traffic stops everything but "progress," which goes on killing neighborhoods and stifling the spirit with buildings that rise but do not soar.

★ ★ ★

The cities of San Francisco, just across the street from one another and worlds apart. The miles of little businesses still surviving along the wide reaches of Geary Boulevard, onion domes of Russian churches burnished by sun and fog, restaurants of all sizes and flavors, the unique little houses of the late Henry Doelger—"The White Cliffs of Doelger"—sweeping through the Sunset District to the sunset shores of the Pacific, where here and there you can still glimpse a "Carville" streetcar under a peaked roof. A San Franciscan never ceases to marvel at so much variety in a small space: secret lives on streets winding their way over hills that bear no name, comfortable old houses alongside hidden Presidio paths, the oddly out-of-place palm trees on Mission near the splendid grass islands of Dolores, the hidden charms of Liberty Hill and the unprepossessing house that was Sunny Jim Rolph's.

★ ★ ★

The city, hard, cruel, sentimental, violent, sexy, alluring. So many blandishments to keep you going—a history of scandals and dark deeds behind drawn damask curtains, played out against the innocent CLANG of a passing cable car, a carillon ringing out from Grace Cathedral, the chimes of SS Peter & Paul's sounding the hour, which grows late. A place of disturbing counterpoints: always the fancy cars outside I. Magnin's, tended by uniformed doormen, as the beggars plead and wheedle on the sidewalk and millionaires pass them by, shaking their heads petulantly. In Union Square, the old-timers turn their faces to the Dewey Monument, picking up a little sun, thinking of past victories and Teddy Roosevelt's Great White Fleet.

★ ★ ★

At O'Farrell and Mason, I watch the bulldozers at work, breaking ground for Japan Air Lines' new hotel, a 700-roomer. Across the street, the Hilton is about to spring another tower and another 400 rooms, adding up to 2,200, biggest in the West. The Ramada Renaissance squats on 1,000 new rooms. All this within two blocks in a city holding out its heart and open palms to tourists who may or may not come. A dangerous game, building on the ruins of the very things that made the city a tourist attraction to begin with—the charming small places, the cul-de-sacs, the Golden Pheasants, the Blums, the elegance of tea dances in shirred silk cafes. Elegance is in short supply, its void filled with the braying of many voices, amplified, and the blowing of auto horns. Once it was considered very bad form to honk your horn in public unless the descendant of a Bonanza millionaire, taken in wine, was about to tumble into your path outside the P-U Club.

★ ★ ★

A remarkable panoply, a city. Between meals, white-hatted chefs standing at their kitchen doors, getting a breath of the old fresh after too many hours at the stewpots. Off-duty waiters, sports jackets over their tuxedo pants, rushing up the street to their neighborhood bookies, ready to risk their fat tips on a hot tip. The perpetual motion of bootblacks snapping their cloths, valet parkers running for the cars they've stashed alongside fireplugs, bicycle messengers scooting about like waterbugs, scattering pedestrians, rubbing traffic the wrong way.

★ ★ ★

The city, a place to play games that nobody wins but it doesn't matter. It's the playing that counts, and everybody has a part, everybody is a star, everybody gets to take a bow and get out.

May 12, 1985

Move over, Chico, or, boy, are we spoiled in San Francisco! Floyd Hollenbeck forwards a copy of the Cincinnati Post which devotes an acre of newsprint to 41 restaurants participating in "a gourmet celebration" called "A Taste of Cincinnati." Some of the restaurants and their unique taste treats: Champs at the Hyatt Regency: apple pie. Zino: surf & turf kabob. Black Forest: Sauerkraut balls (well, that has a certain eclat). Pompilio's: fettuccine sundae (pass). Fifth St. Market: chicken fingers, onion strings. House of Hunan: hacked chicken (I know that feeling). Riverview: mini chocolate eclairs (awwww). Barleycorns: Potato skins, chocolate Brownies. Restaurant critics in Cincy must make like bananas and split.

June 3, 1985

Shocking news from Dr. Robert T. Mendle! He forwards page 43 of the June issue of New Republic magazine wherein we read, with mounting disbelief, that Marvin Stone, former editor of U.S. News & World Report, wowed a banquet crowd in Washington by saying, "I've been in Washington a long time. It was a very different city when I got here. You used to find Velveeta cheese in the gourmet section of the supermarket." Comments New Republic's reporter: "There were laughs, but more important, a lot of people—including three at my table—took out note pads and wrote the joke down so they could use it later themselves."

⋆ ⋆ ⋆

Forgive me while I try and collect myself. As you long-suffering scanners of this space know, the Velveeta-supermarket joke, laid in Chico, has been a running staple of this column for what—10? 15 years?—and to see it applied so crassly to Washington is a blow. Also reprehensible. I'm so furious, in fact, that I'm going to run three items I've been holding in the "Maybe" file. First: Lee Nye, program director of KK105 in Sacramento, is about to make a fortune in Chico with his new product: Velveeta on a rope for those who get hungry in the shower. Second: Ken McEldowney is ecstatic that Velveeta now comes in extra-thick slices. "Now," he goes on, "if only someone would market white bread with the crust already trimmed." Third: Len Sullivan of Palo Alto checked into the Royal Windsor in Brussels and ordered the continental breakfast, which arrived with only one cheese. Yup, Chico, your magical smell is everywhere!

★ ★ ★

Let's keep Velveeta jokes where they belong. In this column and in Chico, where the cognoscenti spell it "Cheeko." *June 6, 1985*

During the George Moscone memorial dinner at the Hyatt Regency, his widow, Gina, lost an earring under the speaker's table so she got down on all fours and disappeared under the tablecloth. Presently she was joined beneath the table by dean Bert Prunty of Hastings College of the Law, who wanted to help. A moment later, they looked to their left and found a third person on his hands and knees. It was Mario Cuomo, governor of New York and the evening's principal speaker, who smiled, "What's going on? Is this some crazy game you California people play?"

June 20, 1985

A Day in the Country

"I'm lost and nobody knows it. I'm really missing and nobody misses me."

These are terrifying thoughts. Panic city. Flopsweat time. No food, no water, no sense of direction. As the eerily silent hours pass, exhaustion takes over. Under the broiling 120-degree sun, the brain fries and starts to sizzle with wild imaginings: you know, a person could actually die up here—especially a city slicker who can't tell North from East, up from down.

As I trudged ever higher in the wrong direction, a pair of buzzards circled overhead. They can smell flopsweat miles away. All alone in the ominous stillness, I was almost glad to see these signs of life—and death. Only one thing detracts from this melodrama titled "Missing!" I didn't get into this predicament through the vagaries of fate or outrageous misfortune, but simply because I am dumber than a cow.

At least the few cows I saw weren't lost.

★ ★ ★

Starting at about 11 a.m. last Saturday, I was lost for 24 hours in some of the highest, hottest, loneliest hills in Sonoma County. These are on Prentis Hale's ranch, which is big enough to qualify for a seat in the UN. At least 10,000 acres, 9,999 of which are uninhabited save by coyotes, wild boar, deer and, for what seemed like an eternity, one dumb columnist, a redundancy.

As most of my friends and several ex-wives can testify, I have less sense of direction than a weathervane in a hurricane. However, the Hale adventure started simply enough. The foreman's wife, Mrs. Black, checked me in through the front gate and I started up a winding road to the main house. Typically, I missed the turnoff and continued straight ahead. I went through two gates spaced so far apart that the most doltish 10-year-old would have said, "Wait a minute, this doesn't seem right. Better turn back."

Your mulish correspondent forged ahead. It wasn't until he came to a padlocked gate, far up the hills, that his oxlike mind registered "Tilt." I swung around and, already panicking but unaware of it, took a narrow dirt road I thought would return me whence I came. In Gold Rush San Francisco, some streets were described as "Impassible, not even jackassable." This one was Jeepable but definitely not Jagable.

The jackass took it anyway.

* * *

My boy scout training stood me in bad stead. "Keep going downhill." Rocks bouncing off my undercarriage, I kept driving downhill. Then I took an even narrower road going even more steeply downhill. Certainly I would see the Hale house any minute. What I saw was a herd of cows blocking the road. I backed up and tried to turn around. The back wheels spun in the loose dirt. I was trapped between two high embankments, with no traction. The car wouldn't move an eighth of an inch forward or backward. I was well and truly imprisoned in the otherwise trackless wastes of 1,000 feet above the world. "Hello!" I cried out. The cows moved off without replying.

* * *

"Be resourceful," I said querulously, stuffing wood and rocks and even my suitcase under the back wheels. No go. I tried to clear out a space but only forced more dirt and rocks under the car. At last I locked it, quavered "So long, Old Bess," and set out. For hours, I walked in all directions, down trails that suddenly went up or around the next mountain. I kept shouting, if only to break the maddening silence. I yelled "Hello!" at regular intervals, a word echoed back contemptuously by the oak-studded hills. I tried "Chloe!' for laughs. Nobody laughed. At last, with some embarrassment, I hollered the word I'd been trying to avoid. "Help!" It got the same results as “Hello, Chloe.”

★ ★ ★

The day grew late. I was seriously dehydrated. The front of my shirt was white and stiff with salt. At last I found my way back to the car, my immovable home. Nearby I found a dry stream and followed it till I heard a trickle. There was plentiful evidence that the cows had discovered this stream long before I but it was no time for niceties. I dunked my head in a noisome pool and drank deeply of Eau de Vache. As darkness settled on the hills, it became obvious that I would be sleeping in the car. I lay there on the reclining seat, thinking of the festivities below at the Hale house. A good group was there. Kirk Douglas, famous movie star. Terence McEwen, famous impresario. Douglas Cramer, famous TV producer. Jeremiah Tower, famous chef. I dozed off, figuring a search chopper from the Sonoma Sheriff's office would clatter overhead any minute. Or a kindly Deputy would shine a flashlight into the car, asking “You OK, sir?” Or Kirk Douglas would arrive at full gallop with the Seventh Cavalry. With my luck it would be the Night Stalker. I locked the doors.

★ ★ ★

Next morning at dawn, frozen stiff, I drank some more Sparkling Bovine and decided to keep walking, no matter what. Every road still went the wrong way, but at last I saw a cow trail heading downhill. My last chance. I took it, slipping and sliding through cowflop all the way down to the highway, where the two greatest guys in the world picked me up and dropped me at the Hale entrance. I had gone five miles in the wrong direction. “What happened to you?” asked the famous people. “Dunt esk,” I replied. When I described the two wonderful fellows who'd picked me up, Sonoma Deputy Sheriff Will Conner said, “Hey, those are the two poachers we've been trying to pick up for weeks!” It seemed a fittingly surreal ending to an unreal adventure. Another thing. It has been years since I spent 24 hours alone with myself, and frankly, I wasn't impressed.

August 28, 1985

Without stooping to “Only in Marin,” I will simply report that Mike Cunningham was playing at the Mill Valley Gold Club when, at the 15th hole, his caddy laid down his bag and said, “Sorry, I have to go to a wine tasting in Tiburon.” *September 4, 1985*

MAYOR AS PINCUSHION

A lot of people, including her loyal and loving husband, wonder why I keep needling Mayor Feinstein, and I wish I could explain it without having to spend many an expensive hour in psychoanalysis. It may turn out that I am secretly in love with her and am forced to express my frustration with little digs and jabs, a truly Freudian figure of speech. Or perhaps I am jealous of Richard Blum, a tall, handsome, rich man with a gift for climbing icy peaks in exotic locales. Actually, it is hard to be objective about our Leaderene, a term the British satirical magazine Private Eye uses about Margaret Thatcher. Although I carelessly referred to Mayor Feinstein as "The Ice Queen" a few columns ago—some critics consider her chilly under that cool and composed smile—she is a much warmer person than Thatcher, definitely more attractive, slightly more liberal and the best dancer ever to occupy the mayor's office, having the gift of natural rhythm. I speak from experience, although, on second thought, I can't recall dancing with any other S.F. mayor except Roger Lapham.

★ ★ ★

The foregoing happened at a debutante party in the Burlingame Club—it was the year I came out—and as I was about to sweep Mrs. Lapham into my arms, she having accepted my gallant invitation, the then mayor interceded roughly exclaiming, "I don't want you dancing with that" (several words censored here). Picaresque fellow that I am or was, I grabbed Mr. Lapham around his WASPish waist and attempted to lead him in a waltz. Like Queen Victoria, whom he resembled faintly when wearing a doily on his head, he was not amused, nor, as a ballroom dancer, could he follow. Perhaps I should have let him lead, which is what mayors are all about, or should be.

★ ★ ★

Getting back to an objective appraisal of Dianne—I'm entitled to call her that since I knew her when she was a very young girl—let us agree that we are fortunate to have her in the front office. She is industrious, dedicated and, in the words of her husband, "busts her ass for the city." I'm sure that is true. When she rises to her full six feet to address an important audience—the visit of Queen Elizabeth II and Prince Philip comes to mind—she makes you proud to be a San Franciscan. She speaks well, with charm, conviction and sincerity. Her sincerity is so palpable, in fact, that, in comparison, she makes Mother Teresa seem just a little shifty. Add to this the fact that she is a beautiful woman with almost perfectly formed features and you have a formidable figure. In fact, she put a chokehold on me one recent night—all in the spirit of fun, of course—and I had a sore neck for hours.

* * *

Perhaps it is Dianne's earnestness, accompanied by a slight deficiency in the humor department, that makes her an irresistible target for slings and arrows; just about the worst thing you can say about a person is that he or she has no sense of humor, but I can't remember her ever getting off a funny line. When she had the Board of Supes over to her Presidio Terrace mansion one recent night for dinner, the entertainment consisted of community singing—another example of her intense civic-mindedness. At times she reminds me of the young Shirley Temple. I can see her clenching her baby fists, stamping her tiny feet and saying resolutely, "By golly, we'll do it, gang! We'll get the job done and it'll be fun, too. Gee whillikers!" Actually, that little-girl quality is quite appealing. The hair stylists and dressmakers who consistently sabotage her good looks might keep this in mind. Her adversary, Li'l Wendy Nelder, would be in an absolute snit, drowning her anger in fluoridated water.

* * *

One of Mayor Feinstein's favorite photos of herself, I'm told, shows her in a police jumpsuit standing with her legs apart at the top of a hill, her police cap at a rakish angle, her pleased expression implying, "Go ahead, make my day." I can understand why she would like this picture, with its powerful macha quality and its celebration of her as guardian of law, order and morality. Dianne would very much like to be one of the guys, and gives it a good try, but she is naturally quite reserved and proper, more at home balancing a teacup on her knee than a shot of red eye in a North Beach saloon. She likes the USS Missouri and detests the Mitchell Brothers, a perfectly reasonable viewpoint. Missouri clean, Mitchells dirty. Her unresolved dilemma arises when the Missouri sailors head, with a whoop and a holler, for the Mitchells' sleazy porn parlor on O'Farrell.

* * *

Let's try to keep things in perspective. Ms. Feinstein is a good enough mayor, and some day we may look back upon her reign as a golden age, even though the city is deteriorating alarmingly. Given some of her odd decisions and appointments, she should consider the occasional jab a form of affection. Overall, she has been treated like royalty by the press, and if she dislikes being called Princess Di Fi, too damn bad. *September 8, 1985*

Those newish signs on the back of cars that read "Baby on Board" are a real pain in the bazoo, for some reason—especially, as Ralph Duncan says, when Mrs. Chic Housewife in her Audi 5000 has the windows up and is puffing on a king-sizer. *September 16, 1985*

Believe-it-or-noddity! Barbara O'Hara, who drives a Chevy Malibu with the license plates "RUMRRYT" ("Are you Mr. Right?"), drove into a car wash in Westlake last Sunday, glanced into her rear-view mirror and discovered that right behind her was a Pontiac with license plates—no! yes! "MR WRYT." Could this possibly be the magic moment, the meeting and mating of the plates and and who knows what else? Heart pounding, she drove out of the wash and waited for Mr. Right to emerge. He, of course, had noticed her plates and was all smiles. Not only that, he turned out to be tall, youngish and good-looking. "Hello," he beamed sticking out his hand. "I'm David Wright of Burlingame." Then he turned and pointed toward his car. "And that's my wife and our baby daughter." Wave bye-bye. *September 18, 1985*

The updated pitch: At Hallidie Plaza last Friday, Pat Leckey was approached by a panhandler who said beguilingly, "I need a quarter to scratch off my lottery ticket!". . . Lunching at the most excloo of all S.F. men's clubs, the Pacific-Union: Brayton Wilbur, pres. of the symphony, and his guest, John Molinari, pres. of the Bd. of Supes, who said "Y'know, this is the first time I've ever been here but my grandfather used to drop by every day." Brayton: "Oh? Was he a member?" John: "No, a garbage collector". . .

October 14, 1985

A day when worlds come crashing to an end: It was on a Monday that Dan White murdered George Moscone and Harvey Milk. It was on a Monday that a jury returned its verdict of manslaughter. Yesterday, too, was a Monday and in the afternoon, the dizzying world of San Francisco came to a sudden stop.

"DAN WHITE IS DEAD." You heard it up and down the streets, in a series of insistent phone calls, most of them ending in "Why did he do it?" or a sick joke: "Up to now I've liked all his victims." A few callers said nastily, in various ways, "You won't have Dan White to kick around any more," as though I had persecuted him; in fact, I wrote very little about him, considering his importance as a symbol of various sicknesses, pressures and tragedies in this explosive community. Like San Francisco, like the still uneasy relationship between the straight and gay worlds, like the never-ending war between "right-thinking" conservatives and "bleeding heart" liberals (the bleeding was considerable), Dan White was a man with unresolved problems. He tried to solve some of them with a gun and he paid a price even he might have thought a bargain (two liberals for the price of one short jail term). Under that impassive exterior, an angry man seethed and fumed and tore at his own vitals—we know that from talking to his friends. Slowly, it must have dawned on him that there was no life left for the man who had taken two in an act of what he might have thought of, crazily, as biblical vengeance. Now he has taken his own, irreligiously, having come to a dead end in his tortured life. A chapter is closed. The long story of people like Dan White and their feelings about people like Harvey Milk and George Moscone—that story goes on. *October 22, 1985*

The subject of "Marin, Only In" is a closed file, but nevertheless, it was at the Bel Aire School in Tiburon that Ms. B.J. Davis asked her fifth-grade students to list the food they don't like. Some of the replies: "I hate pâté." "I don't like escargot because it's icky." "Chocolate mouse is too rich." What happened to poor as a church mousse? "I won't eat octopus because it's too slimy. Whenever we go to Hawaii I don't go to a luau because that's where I first had octopus." "I hate squid—when I look at that orange stuff I gag." Other hates: Water chestnuts, raw sea urchins and frog legs. Those overprivileged kids are mighty picky. *October 28, 1985*

As long as we're in the boonies, the Cop-Out Lounge in Modesto advertises "Free Chile During Monday Night Football." Like, depose Pinochet at halftime? *November 6, 1985*

Mr. San Francisco

I am no more obsessed with death than the next dissembler. How can one argue with a fact of life? If you are a True Believer, it could even be the start of something big, like the hereafter. Not being a T.B., I prefer the here and now to the hereinunder, just as I prefer Ocean Spray cranberries with the dumb yet noble holiday bird, and Best Foods mayonnaise with next day's sandwich on gummy white bread. Despite what might be construed as a plug, I would appreciate if Ocean Spray and Best Foods would not favor me with a sample of their excellent wares. Just send them to the charity of their choice, preferably Native Americans, without whom there would be no four-day weekend for those who are not stupid enough to be six-day columnists. Even a turkey is smarter than that, but not THIS turkey.

* * *

But back to death, a lively subject on this unlikely weekend that (hark!) heralds the Christmas season, with all its love and speciousness. I am having intimations of immortality, which shows how far gone I am. Here today, gone tomorrow seems like a silly way to live. Here today, here tomorrow and also the day after, that's the way to go—or rather, stay. The only thing wrong with immortality is that it tends to go on forever, but what's wrong with that, really? My ancient contemporaries always say, gallantly, "Who wants to live forever?" as though it were being put to a vote. Put me down as voting "Aye" for an "I." Almost everybody I know is dead already, but as long as they keep moving around, hardly anybody notices.

* * *

I think it was Plato who said, "The life which is unexamined is not worth living." If he were alive today, he might have punned, "The life which is Examinered is not worth living," which begs the obvious topper, " 'Tis better to have been Chronicled." Plato must have gotten off a good one because that line of his keeps coming up as something deep and worth pondering, although it is perfectly obvious that most lives cannot stand up under close inspection. We didn't ask to be born, we're stuck with what we got and press on as best we can, against the tide. Some of us get a better shake than others, but no matter how diligently we examine our lives, we never know why or how.

* * *

You may wonder why this piece of tripe à la mode de Caen—a poor thing but mine own— is titled "Mr. San Francisco." It's because I'm a serious student of the obituary column, the only one deader than this, and I keep running across wonderful material. A few months ago I read the obituary of a chap who seems to have led a fine and possibly examined life—marrying early, having a lot of great kids, scoring well in business, running up an honorable war record, joining the "right" clubs, living in a nice house. It all added up to "A Charmed Life," which I called the column I put together from the bare facts of his long and impressive obituary.

* * *

Now I have read the obituary of a San Franciscan who led a much different life from that of the clubby chap. Yet this fellow—Jerome Angelo Vernazza, born in 1903 on Telegraph Hill—was also a "Mr. San Francisco." I never met him, either, but his obituary also tells the story of a life and a city that no longer exists. We read that he "played on the Poly basketball and baseball teams and swam regularly at the Old Lurline Baths and the Sutro Baths at the Cliff House." Remember the marble slide at Lurline? The rank smell of chlorine at Sutro Baths? Jerry Vernazza did, this kid from North Beach. He played baseball in the S.F. Winter League, where "some of his teammates were Frank Crosetti, Tony Lazzeri, Joe Cronin and Lefty Gomez." Jerry must have been pretty good. "He grew up in Cow Hollow" and joined the Elks Club in 1924. Jerry played three-cushion billiards, one of the toughest of all games, for the Elks, and "the Billiard Sportsmen's Creed always hung by his desk: 'The memories of companionship linger long after the score is forgotten.'"

* * *

Hail and farewell, Jerome Angelo Vernazza, who may or may not have led an unexamined life. We have now had a chance to examine it, and there is the fine full flavor of old San Francisco about it—white baseball rolling across the fog-wet grass of Big Rec in the Park, kids swinging from the rings at Sutro, Jerry hanging out at the Elks. He probably knew Lefty O'Doul, another "Mr. San Francisco" for the ages. Jack Rosenbaum reminds us that Lefty's gravestone at Holy Cross reads, "He lived in good times and he had a good time living." That's the way it was in the old town, where we never thought about Plato but examined life through a glass, brightly, and found it sweet. It should go on forever, like a well-hit ball sailing over the eucalyptuses into an infinity of tomorrow.

December 1, 1985

Bob Quinn confides that Mayor Feinstein is too modest to disclose her greatest success in Russia: "She made the best-dressed list there."

December 19, 1985

★ ★ ★

1986

★ ★ ★

The city was uncharacteristically quiet yesterday morning. Traffic moved slowly, pedestrians walked with their heads bowed. Foghorns moaned in the distance as a huge shroud enveloped the skyline. Seven people had just died in a fiery explosion and the impact seemed universal. A tragedy, a waste, a black day for American technology. (For sheer prescience and timing, no journalist will top our financial columnist, Donald K. White, who, yesterday morning, had his character Adele saying "I'd cancel the space shuttle program. It's all expensive show biz now, what with congressmen and schoolteachers going along for the ride"). Only the faceless voice of bureaucracy was unchanged by the horror. The bureaucracy is unflappable, stripped of emotion, bloodless. As the shuttle burst into fatal final flame, the voice of NASA said coolly, "We obviously have a major malfunction." That is one way of putting it. The sad silent faces of San Francisco said it more eloquently. *January 29, 1986*

Dept. of utter confusion: What happened to Joel Pimsleur shouldn't happen to a dog, and it didn't. It happened to Joel, the veteran police reporter for this very journal.

How innocently it all began! He went to florist Bob Bell's Marina Greenery on Steiner and bought some wildflowers, honeysuckle and jasmine, to plant along the bare wire fence behind his house on Lyon, alongside the Presidio wall. Next thing he knew, a Presidio MP was holding a .45 Colt automatic to his head, another MP was handcuffing him and three other MPs were surrounding him, looking grim. Serious stuff.

Let us now follow a weird chain of events. The wife of the Sixth Army commander had reported "a suspicious-looking character" (that's Joel) parking his car and taking out "a box with some wires." The wires, were, of course, tendrils, but to Presidio security, this was an "explosive device." When the MPs peered into Pimsleur's car, they knew they were onto something: a two-gallon watering can—containing rose fertilizer that had turned the water pinkish—had to be "liquid plastique." A radio speaker wire was mistaken for a lead to a detonator. A warning was then issued not to open the car doors because the vehicle undoubtedly was as booby-trapped as Carol Doda.

While all this was going on, Joel's neighbor, Connie (Mrs. Robert) Lurie, was screaming from her window, "Don't arrest that man—he lives here!" Eventually, the MPs removed the cuffs and shambled off, mumbling apologies, but we can all sleep better these nights, knowing they are on our toes out there at the Prissidio. *March 12, 1986*

You won't believe this. Mark Jennings, owner of Shanghai Kelly's at Polk and Broadway, threw a big party there Tues. night for the Giants' opening game of the season, televised from Houston. At the very instant Rookie Will Clark hit his dramatic home run in his first major league at-bat, there was a simultaneous crash outside: a motorist had run a red light and ploughed into a car driven by Henry Bracco, whose passenger was—Joe DiMaggio! Nobody was injured, but, while Henry dickered with the other driver, Joe sauntered into the bar, signed autographs and generally charmed the adoring crowd. To round off this believe-it-or-noddity, DiMaggio and Henry had been en route to the Oakland A's opening night game when the accident occurred. They got there—eventually. *April 11, 1986*

I am adamantly opposed to those dratted "Baby on Board" signs and all variations thereof, but I agree with Joe Brennan that THIS one, on the back of a foreign car, is amusing: "Baby on Board—Carries No Cash." *April 28, 1986*

Onward: Hey, my mean-spirited campaign against those icky "Baby on Board" car stickers has paid off! Last Friday, at Stanford Shopping Center, Neil Hansen saw a blue Toyota van with this sign in the back window: "Well, Herb, I Hope You're Happy—My Husband Sold the Baby." *May 5, 1986*

Steve Silver's amazing "Beach Blanket Babylon" passed the 4,000th-performance mark with all flags flying Sunday night and the cast got a standing roaring ovation from Carol Channing and Mary Martin, among others. In fact, as a veteran "BBB"-watcher, I would have to say this is the best edition yet; never have so few (10 performers, six-piece band) entertained so many with such artistic enthusiasm; and while everybody is sensational, Val Diamond is even better. Of course Cyril Magnin was there. "It may be the 4,000th performance," said Tex Mailliard, "but Cyril has seen it 6,000 times." La Channing to La Martin: "Did you see Val Diamond's makeup, all purple, green, pink and magenta? I'd like to wear that." Mary, acidly: "You're wearing it now, dear." One of the better nights in show-biz history. *May 20, 1986*

A Hemingway award for grace under pressure to Ken Hildebrand, the superb pianist at Masons in the Fairmont. Feeling a heart attack coming on, he managed to get off a chorus of "There Goes My Heart" before collapsing. He is now back at work, playing the best background piano in a town that is otherwise full of crash-bangers who think they're stars. *June 4, 1986*

Let's Dance, Sadly / Herb Caen Remembers the King

I returned to the office from lunch yesterday afternoon to find a stack of messages from radio and TV stations, disc jockeys and obituary writers. They all carried the same mournful message: "Benny just died— any comments?" I couldn't think of anything penetrating or perceptive at the moment. Sure, he'd been under the weather for the last couple of years, surviving a major operation, but one had the feeling Benny Goodman and his clarinet would go on forever, as of course they will on millions of records.

At 77, he had just made his first big band album in years, and whereas the band itself didn't swing particularly, he did. He used himself sparingly and wisely, playing only half the notes he would have blasted out in his prime, yet they were, as usual, the right notes. The tone was thinner, yet unmistakable. And now the man behind the sound has blown the last lick on what we adoring alligators crudely called his licorice stick. He deserved better than that. A shy and difficult man, he hated the title of "King of Swing" and usually looked owlishly surprised at the roars of approval his music generated among so many different kinds of audiences for so many years.

★ ★ ★

As the phone kept ringing with requests for comments I couldn't seem to come up with, I sat down and stared at a double photograph on my office wall. The top photo shows Benny, Jerry Bundsen (my longtime aide, now retired) and me in 1937. The picture was taken one afternoon in Oakland, a few hours before the Goodman band was about to break records at Sweet's Ballroom. Benny is standing there, wearing a sport shirt and slacks and that trademark crooked smile, his arms folded across his chest. Jerry and I are looking awed, which we were. Before picking him up at the airport, we had phoned KRE, then the hot swing station, and told a disc jockey friend that we would have "B.G.," as we called him, in the car and the radio tuned to that station. As we drove into town, with one Goodman record after another blazing out of the primitive speaker, he said "I had no IDEA I was so hot around here!"

The second half of the photo was taken 35 years later, in 1972, when Benny played at Concord with a small group. We re-created the pose—Benny in the center, his arms folded across his chest, the smile still crooked. Jerry had put on a little weight and I had lost 20 pounds of hair, but the feeling is the same as it was in 1937, a feeling of love and admiration for a guy who was a factor in our lives, and the lives of so many, for 50 years or more, depending on when you first picked up on B.G.

★ ★ ★

Benny Goodman. Even the name has a nice swing to it, unlike the more popular (at one time) Al Goodman, or Ben Pollack, his first bandleader boss. There are those of my generation to whom Satchmo was king, Duke Ellington more significant and the clarinet of Artie Shaw more lyrical, but for me it was always Benny. From the time (early '30s) of those first blue Columbia records, when he had Jack Teagarden in his band, hardly a day or week went by that I didn't get my Goodman "fix." The sound of his clarinet became as familiar as Crosby's voice, and later Sinatra's. In the odd swing lingo of the times, "Benny sent me." If I was depressed, which was often enough, I had only to throw "King Porter Stomp" or "Get Happy" onto the turntable for an immediate lift. Even at his worst, he was the best. At his best, which was most of the time, nobody could touch him.

* * *

The swing era. It lasted such a short time, but never before or since were so many gifted musicians working together in so many bands and cutting so many records. "If I'd known it was an era," the big band singer, Helen O'Connell, remarked a few years ago, "I'd have paid more attention. All I remember is sleeping in the back of the bus," but millions of us were paying attention, comparing Benny with Tommy or Jimmy Dorsey or Charlie Barnet and especially with Artie Shaw, and arguing over who was cutting whom. I remember the day that Kirk Torney, a good friend and fellow swing addict, invited me over to his house to hear "the guy who will knock Goodman out of the box." With a smug smile, he put on Shaw's brand new "Begin the Beguine" and settled back. The band was good. The arrangement was brilliant. The saxes were a perfect blend. Artie played well. I felt so threatened I yanked the tone arm off the record, scratching it. My buddy Kirk swung on me and I flailed at him and we fell to the floor, rolling around as hundreds of records fell on top of us. "This is ridiculous," he finally said, and so it was, but that's the way we felt about our bands and a friendship had ended.

* * *

Sacramento in the mid-1930s. The airwaves were full of dance music, most of it corny, or, as we "hepcats" said, "icky" and/or "Mickey Mouse." Guy Lombardo was Number One, with his own radio program. Wayne "The Waltz" King was a star. Anson Weeks was sort of jazzy but basically "square," and Dick Jurgens, Sacramento's other "name" bandleader, was busy copying Ray Noble's English band, note for note. In the middle of all this mush came a three-hour Saturday night radio show featuring a straight band (Kel Murray's), a rumba band (Cugat's) and—Benny Goodman! After all these decades, it's not hard to recall how clean, clear, solid and driving that band sounded. The pied piper had arrived on the scene with his magic clarinet and we were ready to follow for the rest of our lives. And his.

* * *

Along with his genius, Benny was shot through with luck. Although he'd been around for years, he put together the perfect band for the times, with brilliant Fletcher Henderson arrangements and a showman-drummer, Gene Krupa, who was the ideal foil for the reserved, bespectacled Benny. There was the professional Goodman, playing his impeccable runs, turns and "hot licks," and there behind him was the dashing Krupa, sweat and hair flying, Zildjian cymbals crashing, tom-toms throbbing to a jungle beat. No casting director could have done better. Meanwhile, there was that first great group doing the rest—Bunny Berigan on trumpet, Toots Mondello on alto, Jess Stacy on piano, all giving the band a sound of precision unlike any other.

Not that it was all so simple. The band—"too loud!" complained the headwaiters—had bombed in the East, but when Benny came to McFadden's Ballroom in Oakland in 1935, he knew for the first time that he was a hit. The smallish ballroom was jammed with every musician in the area (plus a kid who had driven in from Sacramento). From the first note, the place was in an uproar. Benny looked dazed. When I dared request "Sometimes I'm Happy" during an intermission, he looked at me quizzically. "How come all you people out here know our stuff?" he asked.

He hadn't realized that the "Let's Dance" show, on late in the East, came to the West Coast at the perfect time. You couldn't go to a fraternity house party those Saturday nights without finding everybody crowded around the radio. The boys, that is. The girls, as usual, were pouting and saying "Doesn't anybody wanna dance?" This was something new, too. It was more important to listen than dance. We lost a lot of girls that way.

⋆ ⋆ ⋆

Benny was a hard man to work for, a perfectionist who demanded perfection, a tyrant famous for "The Ray," a long look that he would direct at an offending musician till the latter dissolved or walked out, shouting "I quit!" Difficult as he was, the best men in his band (Stacy, Hymie Shertzer, Krupa, Harry James, Ziggy Elman, Chris Griffin) stuck with him for years. After a rehearsal of the quartet, at which Benny had been particularly abusive, I asked Krupa how he could stand it. "I can't, sometimes," he said, "but how many chances do you get to play with an authentic genius?" Jess Stacy once complained, with justification, that "Benny hogs all the solos," but then, he did play better than anybody else. Stacy quit after four years to join Bob Crosby, and he said to me one night at the Mark Hopkins, "What a pleasure it is to play for a real gent. If I feel like playing five choruses, it's OK with him." Pause. A look into the distance. And then, "But God, when that Goodman band was really swingin', there was nothing like it. Nothing, man."

★ ★ ★

Those few unforgettable years. Unless you heard the band in person, you don't know what I'm talking about. There you were crowded in front of the bandstand saying to your girl, "No, I don't WANNA dance." Then Krupa came on, to a burst of applause, nervous, fiddling with his cymbals, playing a soft roll. James, Elman and Griffin, three perfectly matched trumpets, filing into the top row. The rest of the rhythm section—Stacy, guitarist Allen Reuss, bassist Harry Goodman, Benny's talented brother—setting up in a corner. The brilliant sax section, led by Shertzer and featuring the wild tenor man, Vido Musso, settling down in the front line.

★ ★ ★

An expectant silence and then Benny snapping his fingers and muttering "One-uh-two-uh-one-two-three-four" and the crowd roaring to the lilting swing of the best of all theme songs, "Let's Dance," based on Weber's "Invitation to the Dance." From then on, it was bedlam, Krupa riding his high hat like a dervish, James puffing out his cheeks till surely they must burst, those saxes playing as one, the rhythm always burning and churning and driving you out of your mind, and then, just when you thought nothing could get hotter, Benny's clarinet rising like a burnished bird out of the tightly-controlled maelstrom and soaring to the heavens, outscreaming even the crowd.

Orgasmic, yes. And then, after all the hours that went too fast, the plaintive melody of "Goodbye," Goodman's closing theme, and the audience, spent, filing out reluctantly in a sort of post-coital depression.

★ ★ ★

We heard sounds we would never forget, sounds that would run through our lives, a steady throbbing beat that would be the background music for births, deaths, divorces, hangovers, all the joys and vicissitudes. As though it were last night, I can see Bunny Berigan, already a little drunk, rising out of his chair to begin "King Porter." I can see Harry James coming down front to play those little licks in "Sugarfoot Stomp." I can hear Stacy playing the opening chorus of "Stealin' Apples" and pleading to play another and Benny giving him THAT look and then reeling off 12 unbelievable choruses in a row as even Stacy shook his head in disbelief.

★ ★ ★

The phone keeps ringing. Because I knew Benny for so many years—through his sessions at the 1939 Fair on Treasure Island, through his Mozart with the Budapest String Quartet at Mills College, through the sometimes painful changes in his embouchure and fingering—because of all that, a lot of people want a comment and I can't think of a thing except, "There was nothing like it, there was no band that played with such verve, there was no other musician who could have dominated so many stars." Now I think I'll go home and make a stiff drink and go through the hundreds of Goodman records and pick out maybe—yes—this 1942 air check from the New Yorker Hotel, when Krupa and Stacy returned to the fold and Benny played an entire lexicon of swing licks on "Stealin' Apples." The King is dead. No use adding "Long live the King," for he will rule the kingdom of swing forever.

June 14, 1986

Katy Butler found the graffito of the week at Haight and Fillmore. "Stop Graffiti," it reads. *June 20, 1986*

How the Kid Got Lucky/ It All Began 50 Years Ago...

If you had been a seagull wheeling over a white Southern Pacific car ferry one June morning in 1936, you'd have seen a skinny young man, wearing a hat with the brim turned up in front, shaking his fist at the San Francisco skyline, looming straight ahead.

The skinny young man was me, an eager greenhorn fresh out of Sacramento. Fresh as a ranch egg and cocky as a rooster, I was saying as I shook my fist, "I'll lick you yet, San Francisco!," a variation on a cliché then popular in movies about country bumpkins taking on the big town. Since I was standing alone on the forward deck of the ferry, nobody heard me get off this bit of silliness, but the gods of the heavenly city must have been listening, offended by such brashness.

They dispatched a gust of wind that plucked the hat off my pointy head and whirled it into the bay, where it bobbed forlornly and helplessly. The wheeling seagull who'd been observing this scene swooped down, pecked frantically but futilely at the chapeau, and then flew off as it sank out of sight.

Thus disappeared the first hat I had ever owned, a $5 number purchased only a day earlier at Sacramento's leading clothing store, Albert Elkus ("Every Man Is Odd But We Can Fit Him"), a sign the high school graduating class had once stolen in the middle of the night and installed over the entrance to a lower J Street whorehouse. I bought the hat to celebrate my entrance into big-time journalism, and I turned the brim up in front because a comic strip character named "Front Page Farrell" wore it that way.

Front Page Farrell scooped the world at least once a week, and I intended to do equally as well in the magic San Francisco of 1936.

★ ★ ★

Amid a squeaking of pilings, the ferry eased into its slip at the Ferry Building, and I drove my 1934 Hudson coupe across the wooden planking into a world of excitement. My hands were wet, my heart was pounding and my 20 pounds of curly hair, released at last from the hat, flared out as though I'd been electrocuted. Cautiously, the greenhorn from the valley inched forward into what he would later dub "The Roar of the Four," the metropolitan madhouse of four lines of "iron monster" streetcars squeaking around the loop in front of the Ferry Building. "C'mon, move it, kid," hollered a cop, unaware that he was addressing a steely eyed newsman determined to shake this old town to its very foundations.

Dizzy with excitement, I drove up Mission toward the Gothic magnificence of The Chronicle building, its tower then encrusted with carvings. I couldn't believe my incredible luck and kept yelling "WOW!", frightening several pedestrians. All my adolescent life, a period that was to go on indefinitely, I had dreamed of becoming that most favored of mortals, A San Franciscan, and the dream was coming true. Not only that, I was going to work for The Chronicle's fabled "boy wonder" editor, 27-year-old Paul C. Smith, a glamorous and charismatic figure. There wasn't a young newspaper person in the West who wouldn't have given up his best typing finger to work for Paul. He was already shaking up the staid old sheet, hiring eager-beaver kids and becoming the talk of the "game," as we called the newspaper business then.

I parked my Hudson across from the paper—spaces were plentiful and bus zones (and buses) unknown—and marched into Paul's office. Like all real and fictional characters of that era, Paul had a salty-talking, red-haired Irish secretary named Dorothy McCarthy. She took one look at my Medusa-like tresses and said, "Migawd, now they're sending us kids with fright wigs!" "I'm the new radio editor," I said in a wee voice. "YOU'RE the new Dinty

Doyle?" she said incredulously. "I don't believe it. Well"—doubtful shake of the head—"go on in. Paul's waiting for you."

Against all the laws of probability or even logic, I was about to be admitted into the magic circle of "Paul's boys," dedicated to him and making a sacred vow that we would take The Chronicle from fourth place in a field of four (The Examiner, The Call-Bulletin and The News were the others) to No. 1. "The Clan," as Paul called us, had no idea it would take so long. He and many others of the original group would die along the way. The rest of us would grow old in the process of helping Paul's dream come true, but it was worth every headache, backache and heartache.

* * *

As I sit here today, slumped as usual over the old Loyal Royal staring out the window at the space where I parked my Hudson coupe, I find it hard to believe that 50 years have spun by. It seems like day before yesterday that Dottie McCarthy opened the door to Paul's office, and he said warmly, "Welcome aboard, kid." He employed Naval terms constantly, being in the reserve (he entered World War II as an officer, chucking the finery to become a Marine private). Everybody called me "kid" in those days, and a lot of people still do, since I have refused to grow up.

"How come you hired me, Paul?" I asked, and he replied with a half-smile, "Because I wanted somebody on the paper younger than I am. Hell, even the copy boys are older. I'm getting tired of the old fogies. Say, how old are you, anyway?" "Twenty-two," I lied. "You're 20," he twinkled. "I looked it up. Well, good luck. Give 'em hell." The interview was over.

* * *

Let's rewind the film to 1932 in Sacramento. Herbert Hoover, later to become a Stanford tower that leans to the right, is still president, barely. Depression time. A huge "Hooverville" of shacks across the river. My old man is in big financial trouble, but I am shot through with luck, as always. Job-hunting, I walk into the Sacramento Union, the morning paper, just as Steve George, the dapper sports editor, is looking for a new assistant. He has lost his right-hand guy, Kirt MacBride, a real pro, to the city side, and he was desperate.

"Can you type, kid?" he asked. "Yep," I said with the overweening confidence of a 16-year-old fresh out of Sacramento High. To prove it, I flailed away at the ancient Underwood with two index fingers. "Hm," murmured Steve, a dear man. "Well, you're hired. Eleven bucks a week, six days a week, OK?" You bet!

"Uh—write me a piece about the football prospects at Sac High this fall." He read it, sighed and said, "Put your byline on it—I'd hate anybody to think I wrote it." My first bigtime byline! "By Herbert Caen," I wrote in longhand. Steve scratched out the "ert," sniffing, "Whoever heard of a sportswriter named Herbert?" I got lucky there, too. Suppose he'd made it Bert Caen?

My preparation for professional journalism was a couple of years of writing a column called "Corridor Gossip" for the high school paper, the X-Ray. Pretty thin stuff, but it taught me something I'd never forget: People love to see their names in the paper. I even got the first heady taste of power: Big Men on the Campus and beautiful girls fawned a bit, hoping to find their names in type. During two years at Sacramento Junior College, where I slept in class while working nights at the Union, I wrote an even deeper column called "Campus Chatter," detailing who was cutting classes to neck in the parking lot or seen disappearing into the shrubbery of William Land Park. I was becoming a sort of celebrity without knowing it, not that I was aware that journalism would be my entire life. I still yearned to be an architect, a job at which I surely would have starved to death.

And now, students, another lesson: Be a Boy Scout. Take on extra jobs without asking for extra pay. In fact, forget about money, because there isn't much in newspapering unless you own the presses. Remember people's names, and they'll never forget you (forget, and they'll never forgive). As a teenager, I undoubtedly was a major pain in the neck, but a point is being made, so pay attention.

It was great working for the Union, which called itself "Mark Twain's Newspaper" (he wrote his wonderful Hawaiian pieces as its traveling correspondent). A battered desk in a dusty corner was labeled "Mark Twain's Desk." According to rumor, it would be sold every year to a Twain buff, to be replaced by another battered $25 desk. Thus the paper survived against the mighty Sacramento Bee. The small underpaid staff worked like beavers and did everything except peddle the product on street corners.

After a delightful year with Steve George, I was transferred to the city side, where life was harder. I discovered the luncheon club beat, putting my stomach to the ultimate test and interviewing celebrities like Sunny Jim Rolph, a great San Francisco mayor who was miserable as governor. Then I went on the police beat, covering a double murder and suicide the first night. Slightly ill at the sight of so much blood, I phoned the story in to city editor H. Lee

Watson, an old pro out of Chicago, and learned another lesson. When he found out they were Mexicans, he said, "No class, gimme a paragraph." "Three people dead!" I wailed. "No class," he repeated, hanging up.

I was broken into the police beat (presstitutes are "broken in," prostitutes are "turned out") by the aforementioned Kirt MacBride, the epitome of the well-seasoned newsman, peppery and salty. He introduced me to the cops, the speakeasies along J Street, and the various houses of prostitution, where he was welcomed with excited cries. I waited for him in the foyer, and when he came out, the girl said "No charge, Kirt. Man, you are one great ———!" I looked at him with fresh respect. It takes a pro to know one, and obviously Kirt was a champ.

Now, about the Boy Scout part. Although there was occasional excitement—I covered three hangings at Folsom Prison when I was only 18—it was generally quiet at night on the police beat. So I whiled away the time by writing a radio column. Free. I didn't know anything about radio, but I wrote sassy things about Fred Allen, Jack Benny and Bob Hope anyway. The Union was happy enough to print this stuff, and I was delighted to have a daily byline.

There was no long-range plan here—in fact, I've never had a plan in my life—but it was this dumb radio column that got me out of Sacramento and into the city of my purple dreams, the city I would one day dub "Baghdad-by-the-Bay."

★ ★ ★

In 1936, The Chronicle had a hot radio columnist (think of this as the equivalent of today's TV columns) named J. E. "Dinty" Doyle, a tough-talking, hard-drinking, colorful and irascible Irishman. In fact, he was the hottest thing in the paper, which Paul Smith had not yet had time to transform. There were no other local columns. The slant was drearily Republican. The old editor, a grandfatherly sweetheart named Chester Rowell, nattered on. David Lawrence wrote boringly about Washington, which, in his pre-FDR view, was indeed boring.

So Dinty was a star, and Mr. Hearst lured him away to become radio editor of his New York Journal-American. Everybody in the state wanted his job here. It paid $50 a week, princely at the time. Paul sifted through dozens of radio columns—including a few of my freebies brought to his attention by the late Harry Elliott, then CBS' publicity man in San Francisco. "This guy is fresh," said Harry, meaning smart-ass. "Sort of a style, all right," said Paul, not quite sure, but he liked the fact that I was a kid.

To Dinty Doyle's anger, I got the job over a host of candidates who could outwrite me seven different ways and knew a lot about the radio scene, besides. Dinty's personal choice was a buddy who worked for the Oakland Post-Enquirer and wrote like an angel, but Paul found him "too stuffy—I want something brighter."

Before leaving for New York, Dinty was asked to "break me in." He took one look at my mint-condition '34 Hudson, with running boards, sun visor and cut-glass vases, and rasped, "Get rid of that heap, kid. That's for old ladies." (I graduated to a Plymouth as soon as possible.) "Now, we're gonna make the rounds. Lissen good—writing the column is only part of the job. You gotta make yourself into a celebrity. I go to the fights, ball games, night clubs. I want people to say, 'Hey, there's Dinty Doyle!' Then they'll read my junk because they figure I'm important, see? Now come on, I'll introduce you to the head waiters at the Palace, the Frantic and the Mark, and we'll eat at Jack's or some other swell place."

We made our first stop at Hanno's, a true newspaper bar across the street from the Chronicle, run by a fine gent named "Pop" Hanno. Dinty strode in to be greeted with a chorus of cheers and rounds of drinks, for he was indeed a gregarious fellow and master storyteller. Like a little lost child, I'd tug at his sleeve every now and then—"Hey, Dinty, shouldn't we be making the rounds?"—but he was deep into his cups and regaling the crowd with Irish humor.

At about 11 o'clock, he looked at his watch and said, "Holy ———, I gotta get out a column. Damn near forgot. Let's go." At his office, he put his head into the wastebasket, made awful noises, and emerged greener than the sports section. "Hey," he said thickly, "I can't make it. You write the column, OK?" So, frightened and baffled, I batted out something about Jack Benny's superiority to Fred Allen (Doyle loved Allen and hated Benny) and wrote across the top "By J. E. (Dinty) Doyle."

Thus did I first appear in The Chronicle, as the ghostwriter of the worst column Dinty Doyle never wrote. He never forgave me, either.

* * *

Dinty departed soon thereafter, and 50 years ago today, the new radio columnist appeared, nervously, bringing with him the city's first taste of three-dot journalism. "Dot's Aplenty," it began—a weak pun on an old jazz classic, "That's Aplenty." There were strange subheads, such as "DIALectics" and "ETHERaves" and coinages like "radioracles" (Walter Winchell's influence was never far away). I ran seven days a week, and on Sunday I threw in a gossip column titled "Radio-Man-About-Town," filled with local items related vaguely, if at all, to radio. "Mayor Angelo Rossi, an avid Fibber McGee & Molly fan, will announce tomorrow that he's running for re-election." "Mrs. Adolph Spreckels, whose proud boast is that she has never listened to 'One Man's Family,' is giving another great painting to the city." Oh, and LOTS of items about bandleaders, the reigning celebrities of the day. These ran under the catchy subhead, "BANDANDIES," and guaranteed me a ringside table in the hotel supper clubs. As Dinty Doyle said, "You gotta get around, kid," and I did, even to an Oakland hangout that had only just changed its name from Hinky-Dink's to Trader Vic's.

Dinty Doyle fans were not too pleased with his replacement. Whenever I made a gaffe, which was often, they'd write, "You can take a boy out of the country, but you can't take the country out of the boy," which I thought a pretty clever line the first 50 times. When I wrote glowingly about the city, they'd bring up my Sacramento heritage. I responded one time by pointing out that I had been conceived in San Francisco since my parents had spent the summer of 1915 at the Panama Pacific International, and I had been born in April of 1916. "Were they in the sideshow?" someone asked cruelly.

Once again, I hit it lucky. In 1938, The Chronicle and a few other papers decided to drop radio columns as giving "too much free publicity to the competition," and Paul Smith asked, "Well, whaddya want to do now, kid, write feature stories?" "I'd like to do a column about San Francisco," I said, and he replied incredulously, "Every DAY?" When I nodded, he shrugged, "What the hell, let's give it a try." A couple of weeks later, he sent me a memo that read, "Not bad. Keep going!"

And that's what I've been doing ever since, never ceasing to marvel at the blind luck of the kid from Sacramento who has led the most charmed of lives—writing for a paper I like in a city I love. As I said when my hat blew off on that ferry in 1936, "I'll lick you yet, San Francisco!" but it may take a few more years.

June 23, 1986

"Mr. Millionaire" lives!: Few days ago, a stocky, baldish fellow with a twinkle in his eye walked into the office of Judy Langley, development director for Goodwill Industries, and said "I'm here to make your day"—with which he handed her a check for $10,000, no strings attached. The beardless Santa Claus turns out to be Joe Kane, retired cofounder of United States Leasing, who has homes in Sausalito and Coronado—and had a rich aunt named Florine Friedlander, who died at 99; she left $2 million and a will allowing Joe to spread the money among charities at his discretion . . . "Am I having fun!" he beams, having already handed out $1.3 million in $10,000 to $25,000 chunks to groups ranging from Guide Dogs through the AIDS Foundation to Glide Memorial, St. Anthony's, Shanti, Salvation Army, UC and onward. "I still have about $700,000 to go," he says happily. "The funniest thing about it all was that my aunt was tight as a tick. I couldn't get 10 bucks out of her." *September 2, 1986*

The Miracle of Geary Street! You know how true believers are forever seeing images of Christ on shrouds, soybean oil tanks, rutabagas and other unlikely objects? Well, Mike Ryan points out there's a much more "miraculous" likeness of Christ in the veined marble facade at 12 Geary, above a jewelry store. Whoever it is, he seems to be in mourning, possibly for the people waiting below for the Muni, or he could be blowing his nose. If it isn't Christ, maybe it's St. Francis of Assisi with an allergy. Definitely worth a look from across the street, where you can have your shoes shined at the same time. *September 4, 1986*

A Night to Dismember

It's still the same old story, a night of snores and glory, a case of do or diet. I speak, of course, of the San Francisco Opera opening, the annual passion play at which the gentlefolk of our community play dressup, wearing mommy's jewels and granddaddy's tailcoats. After 64 years, the event has become as ritually stylized as a Japanese Noh drama. The players have their lines down pat: "See you at the bar." "Hey, you look great!" "Can you believe she got ANOTHER face lift?" The faces do change but the names remain the same, from Hale to Hills, from Hearst to de Young, Walker to Wattis, Tinker to Evers to Chance. The reportage could be carved in granite. Opening nights are always "spectacular" and the audience is "glittering," far eclipsing the show on stage. Four and a half hours of background music by Verdi. Pretty classy.

★ ★ ★

It was 40 years ago that the late Jose Zellerbach ran a finger around the inside of his stiffly starched wing collar and said, "Do you realize we'll be doing this every year for the rest of our lives?" Everybody winced and laughed and a few said, "No way, Jose" (that's how old THAT line is), but Jose was correct. The opera opening is not only the city's leading tradition, topping cirrhosis of the liver, it's one of those events you wouldn't be caught dead at but go to anyway because "I gotta catch up on my sleep," a ritual remark. Except for a much too rare exception—say, Leontyne Price's debut in "Aida"—it is considered bad form to say you enjoyed the show. The established protocol is to complain about the heat, the slow service at the bars and the person seated next to you whose deodorant failed at 9:05 p.m.

★ ★ ★

The opening night fare fed to the troops by the demonic general director, Terence Adolf McEwen, was "Don Carlos," the tale of a simple Spanish prince in love with his stepmother, with a barbecue of heretics by the Inquisition thrown in for laughs. It's one of those operas you can't take but could leave alone. It starts slow and stays that way for what seems like four or five hours and is. As Harry de Wildt once said about opera in general, "there's too much singing." There definitely isn't too much acting, and with the soporific Sir John Pritchard in the pit, not much pace, either. At the end of the first period, with the audience leading 15–3, a glum McEwen was heard to mutter, "Denise (Hale) already told me she doesn't like it." If it will make Mr. McEwen feel better, she slept through the first act. So, by the way, did one of the tuxedo'd guards hired to keep a watchful eye on some of the glitterati's borrowed jewels. (Mrs. Hale wore her own.)

★ ★ ★

"Don Carlos" is usually performed without the first act, but Mr. McEwen decided San Francisco was entitled to the full treatment. Thanxalot, Ter'. Not that it doesn't have something going for it, in this new production apparently sponsored by the Bath Bazaar and Safeway. Center stage was covered by a huge shower curtain. The rest of the scene, depicting the forest of Fontainebleau in midwinter, consisted of miles and miles of Saran Wrap, simulating snow and sleet. Presently the shower curtain rose to reveal idyllic AstroTurf, spring flowers and, in the middle, Pilar Lorengar, the redoubtable Spanish soprano. Geddit? Pilar, as Elisabeth de Valois, a socialite of the time, is such a doll that wherever she walks, flowers bloom. Overhead, the supertitles reveal that she is in love with Don Carlos, the Infante, but has to marry his dad, King Phil Two. Richard Tam describes supertitles as "fortune cookies," but it's not easy to boil down 10 minutes of bad French into one-sentence bursts.

★ ★ ★

Right about here somebody is starting to write a letter saying, "If you hate opera so much why don't you give your ticket to somebody who appreciates it?" I do appreciate it. Grand opera is the splendid anachronism and a major part of San Francisco lore, going back to Enrico Caruso being thrown out of bed during the '06 earthquake and saying, "I will never set foot in this city again," a line that would make a fine supertitle and a 15-minute aria. I like the spectacle of hundreds of limos converging on the Opera House, like the funeral of an Oakland drug king, and the spectators outside saying to the media what they have said for the past 40 years: "I enjoy looking at the gowns, the jewels and the hairdos. It perks me up as I totter back to my dreary little room in the Tenderloin." You think the newsmen make up those quotes? Don't any of these people say "I think the whole thing is sickening"?

★ ★ ★

I especially admire the intermissions, when the standees sit and the sittees stand, applaud briefly if at all (it's hard to get an ovation on opening night) and head for the mezzanine bar. Why is that bar so tiny in relation to the grand theater? Because the Opera House was built during Prohibition and the culturati stayed in their boxes and seats, drinking out of their silver flasks. As usual, the mezzanine bar Friday was wall-to-wall bods, overlaid with rare and exotic perfumes, such as "Cocaine," "Joy," "Poison" and Selix's Eau de Mothballs. As Alistair Cooke put it, the crowd was "wan with chic, arthritic with poise." Ann Getty took one look and whispered "Let's get out of here," and it was only the first act. John Traina said about the opera, "I've heard better French from a Corsican cab driver." You think it doesn't pay to travel?

★ ★ ★

By 1:30 a.m., eight hours after the first drink, it was all over. As I headed for home, my boiled shirt creaking like a ship under full sail, I reflected that the members of the "Don Carlos" cast not only had to stay awake all that time, they had to sing, too. No mean feat.

September 8, 1986

The San Franciscans

Proud. That's what we are. Humbly proud, modestly superior, naturally weird, sourly optimistic, brightly pessimistic and any other oxymoron you'd care to dredge up. Proud of our heritage, even if we had nothing to do with it. Pleased daily and sometimes nightly that pioneers—the dregs and the illustrious—came here only a few years ago, as eternity is reckoned, and founded the impossible, implausible city on mountains and molehills, swamps and shorelines, marshes and muddy streets. The San Franciscans, reciting the grand old names like a litany of buildings and labels—Flood and Crocker, Levi Strauss and MJBrandenstein, Huntington, Sharon, Stanford and Phelan. We know their descendants and they are only human, having their problems, even as you and I. But they are descended from giants and are to be treated with care, as relics of a gilded age in the gelded age.

⋆ ⋆ ⋆

The San Franciscans. All sizes, shapes, colors, creeds and ways of death, some of them better left unexplored. White punks on dope (a classic by the Tubes), on skateboards, on motorcycles, on the thin edge of self-destruction. The San Franciscans live dangerously. Traffic is a snarl, with facial expressions to match. The bars are chockablock with people setting fire to cigarettes and drinking the transparent white killer with an olive or twist, only a few steps away from the embalmer. It's the San Francisco way to go, the ignoble tradition, the earthquake mentality that flowered in the flames of Ought Six. The Big One could come this very minute. If you wake up the next morning with a hangover, you have paid the price for being alive another 24 hours.

⋆ ⋆ ⋆

The San Franciscan is more than self-admired. He (and she) is known around the world. From out of the mud he and his forebears, principally the former, have built a glittering city admired from afar, if not always from anear. San Francisco, temple to tolerance, haven for the misbegotten, safe harbor for the lost souls of faraway tragedies. Al Jolson sinks to one knee and sings "Open up your Golden Gate, California heeeere I come," but it isn't quite like that. The old San Franciscan, he of the Brooks Bros. button-downs with mind to match, feels swallowed up as he gulps down his healer on the rocks. All of these new people—I mean fine, but aren't things getting a little out of hand, Charlie? Not that I don't admire Them, mind you. Hard workers. Bright kids. They raise our scholastic average, you know. But Charlie, WE are the minority now. Imagine being a minority? Still, they'll never take over the clubs. Last line of retreat and all that.

* * *

The San Franciscans, filled with prejudices, generosity, good booze, fine wine and a reasonably expansive outlook on life. They keep the "worthwhile" things going—you know, opera, symphony, the like. The San Franciscan is getting used to the homeless and the drunks passed out on the sidewalks, but the sight still makes him nervous. It shouldn't happen in the city of St. Francis. Money is a partial solution. We've got a problem there, Charlie, but let's bury it under greenbacks if we have to. This is San Francisco, a civilized place. No riots, no barricades, no cops clubbing the desperate. What did Janis Joplin used to sing? "Freedom's just another word for nothing left to lose"? Well, you know what I mean.

* * *

A great and endless show, the San Franciscans, music by Muzak or Sony Walkman. Endless sound effects: sirens, squealing brakes, laboring buses spewing death-dealing fumes. A constant movement up the hills and down the valleys, along the boulevards, through the tunnels and alleys, across the vastly tiny city that changes character from block to block with a different language for every one. The polyglot. Let us never lose it, these constant pipings from faraway lands, transplanted and still going strong, the various voices of other worlds enlivening this hurly-burly whirlybird of a city. A passing show: nutty messengers on bikes, lonely oldsters feeding flocks of pigeons (love is where you find it), women execs striding along in their walking shoes (high heels in Gucci bags), chess players pondering their pieces on a hard bench in Hallidie, bug-eyed kids clinging to cable cars and each other, hotel doormen blowing cab whistles in vain, and the joggers, always the joggers, leaving a whiff of eau de armpitz in the salty air.

* * *

The San Franciscans, headstrong and hidebound, nervous in the service of the myths and legends they themselves created and love to repeat. Yesterday was a dream, today is a bitch and tomorrow we don't care to think about, not while there is a tonight with so many places to go, things to do, old friends to drink with on the altar of a restless city that lost its way. Why does it all have to be so complicated, Charlie? *September 28, 1986*

Lurline Matson Roth's death at 95 reminds Barnaby Conrad of the time he was at her house in Hawaii to do a piece for Architectural Digest. As he and the photogger were waiting, the butler said, "Just got a radio-telephone call from Mrs. Roth. She's on the other end of a 500-pound marlin and wants you to start without her." She was 90 at the time. *October 10, 1986*

A man walked into the new Edmund G. Brown State Bldg. at Van Ness and McAllister yesterday afternoon and said to a guard, "Is this the Edmund G. Brown building?" Guard: "Yessir." Man: "Does it have his name written on it somewhere?" Guard: "Uh—no." Man: "Is there a picture of him somewhere around here?" Guard: "No." Man: "Are you from San Francisco?" Guard: "No—Pittsburgh." Man: "Well, I'm Edmund G. 'Pat' Brown and you really should have a picture of me somewhere in here."

October 15, 1986

Bay Bridge madness! Late Tues. night, a chap wearing an Emperor Norton uniform and driving a mint '37 Cad convertible with the top down was stopped by a cop at Fifth and Howard on suspicion of being under the influence, thereby thwarting a noble ambition. Thus delayed, the driver was unable to hit the Bay Bridge toll plaza at 12:01 a.m. Wed. to become the first person across the bridge on its 50th birthday. Alas indeed . . . However! The emperor's passengers, Llewellyn Phelan and Cinda McConnell, boarded Phelan's motorcycle, stashed nearby, and roared across the bridge, swung around and got a receipt stamped 12:05 a.m. Nov. 12, 1986, from Paul, the toll-taker at booth No. 3, who advised, "Take it easy and you might be around for the 100th anniversary."

★ ★ ★

And for moments of hysterical and historical, let us not forget Alberta Luchetti Cieri Schwengher, member of an old S.F. clan, a Merola opera singer and now a social leader in Reno. On the bridge's opening day in '36, young Alberta Luchetti, at the wheel of her dad's Franklin, became the first driver to run out of gas on the bridge. Charles Dondero of Oakland, a biggie in the marble business, driving HIS dad's Packard, was behind Alberta and pushed her all the way across to S.F. Franklin? Packard? I thought everybody was poor in those days of the Great Depression.

November 13, 1986

BRIDGES

A lovely word, bridges. Crossings, connections, the dramatic closing of gaps. Bridges bring people together. In the case of the Golden Gate Bridge, people all too often come together violently, in head-on crashes, but bridges are not always benign. Doyle Drive, the San Francisco approach to the Golden Gate, is a deathtrap, but nothing is done. Are we nibbling around the edges of a shaky metaphor here? Let's see, supermen designed and built the Gate Bridge and the San Francisco–Oakland Bay Bridge, whose 50th anniversary we celebrated all last week. The supermen departed, leaving their works of art to be lessened, if not desecrated, by ordinary men who came along to improvise toll booths and fool around with traffic patterns and—yes, OK—build a second deck and add an approach here and there to create commuter gridlock.

* * *

The bridges in their original pristine state were dreams made real. All of us who vividly remember the great events leading up to 1936 and 1937 could hardly believe what was taking place, 24 hours a day, day and night. The vast and bridgeless bay, its surface crisscrossed for decades by the invisible tracks of ferries and barges, was being conquered, and we were alternately sad and excited. The ferries were well-loved. They did the job and smelled great besides. As children, we marveled at the "walking beams," steel arms pumping, gangplanks lowering with a crash, pilings creaking, seagulls screaming for food and doing what seagulls do. If you were hit, you were given a white lapel pin to wear and solemnly inducted into "The Seagull Club." On foggy days, sometimes you were selected to "model" a life jacket during the drill, an incident that was thrillingly embarrassing. As for the corned beef hash, could it possibly have been that good? Probably.

* * *

From the hills, we watched the great spiders spinning webs toward each other. The roadway's arms began reaching out like yearning lovers. A huge and mystifying concrete monolith rose between Yerba Buena Island—still "Goat Island" then—and mainland San Francisco. "Center anchorage," we learned to say, knowingly, not knowing it contained enough concrete for a 65-story building, more than enough for Cheops' pyramid. (Insiders call it "Moran Island" for its indomitable designer, Daniel E. Moran.) The impossible was taking place before our eyes. Eras were ending and beginning, a dizzying experience as we sat around at Izzy Gomez's on Pacific or the original Trader Vic's in faraway Oakland, discussing the future that was at hand.

* * *

The Bay before the bridges was slowly fading. Now it was becoming difficult to conjure up the old Golden Gate, unsullied by a man-made object, however magnificent. That was a landmark of the old city—a clipper ship bending to the breeze as it pranced into the bay, an ocean liner heading out, trailing a plume of smoke. The miracle unfolded relentlessly, seeming almost to pull the city out of its blessed, misty isolation and toward the mainland and the problems of progress, which, by the way, would be more complicated than even we contemplated over that second martini in the Mark's Lower Bar. Fortress San Francisco was being breached, allowing the great world easy access, and things would never be the same.

* * *

For all its fame and growth, San Francisco has always struck me as a rather shy, self-effacing city, chary of being thought as "pushy" as That City Down South. It is or was a city that accepted as its due the praise heaped upon it by young lovers and acolytes but essentially preferred to be left alone, once the last tourist dollar had been spent. Now, gradually and then suddenly, the city was to be home to two of the greatest landmarks in the world to go along with our more modest Ferry Building, cable cars, Alcatraz (not a landmark we were particularly proud of), Coit Tower and, well, Seal Rocks, almost too minimal to mention. The triumphs of the engineer-mystics, making real the dream of the mad Emperor Norton, would go into the history books as authentic wonders and become among the most celebrated of tourist attractions. "Little San Francisco," with its ferryboats carrying singing hikers to Sausalito each Sunday, was well and truly dead.

* * *

Bridges, a poetic concept, a symbol San Franciscans live with daily. The Bay Bridge, its night lights spilling onto dark waters, its incredibly long main span—two suspension bridges—arching across your living room window, if you are among the lucky, or appearing tantalizingly between tall buildings that have blocked so much of it. We cross it and recross it through the years, always marveling, always impressed at the city's skyline exploding out of the bay so far below. We walk the Gate Bridge, the wind caressing or tearing at us and pause to look down as so many have just before they leaped, their last view being the pinkish-white flank of the soft hard city. Bridges to other worlds and sometimes to infinity—the city's glory and heartbreak, man-made, impossible, triumphant.

November 16, 1986

Speaking of weird, I'm browsing a newsletter called Executive Productivity, a self-cancelling phrase, and discover that you can now get computer software that sends subliminal messages to employees on their computer screens. Yep: "You can tell employees how valuable they are, what a fine company they work for, or even that they are making quite enough money already. The conscious mind can't read the messages because they come and go so quickly but they sink in and can change behavior without the subjects knowing why" . . . That's why I still use a manual typewriter. And why the other people working around me on computers are lined up at the boss' door, pleading for pay cuts. *November 28, 1986*

In Oakland, Carole Vernier passed a red Corolla license-plated "Zen 911" and her sis, Darryl, yawned, "I wonder if that's Gertrude Stein's emergency phone number?" *December 8, 1986*

If you can draw the cartoon I've got the caption: After her goldfish jumped out of the bowl during her absence and perished, Andrea Leiderman of Stanford was heard to cry, "He committed sushi!"

December 9, 1986

I phoned city archivist Gladys Hansen to inquire "Why do we have 11 supervisors?" "Because we couldn't stand 12," she shot back, justlikethat. *December 10, 1986*

'Twas the night before Christmas, and all through the house, not a creature was stirring, not so much as a martini. No, I have never seen a mouse make a martini, but many a pussycat is good at it. Trouble is, if you order a martini these days you have to answer more questions than Hasenfus in Managua. "A martini, please." Yessir, gin or vodka, imported or domestic, up or over, stem glass or regular, olive, olive with pimiento, twist, onion, orange slice (oh, the heck with it, gimme a straight shot of Old Overalls with a water back). It was simpler when there was only one proper martini—three-to-one Bombay Gin with Noilly Prat, chilled and straight up. "Glass of white wine, please." Yessir, Chardonnay, fumé blanc, Riesling, or we have a very unusual (fergeddit). "Cup of coffee and I'm in a hurry." Yessir, regular, decaf, regular espresso, decaf espresso, cappuccino, decaffuccino—made that word up myself—French roast, cafe au lait, that's fractured French for "Shall we eat first?" or we have this new blend from ———. Don't ask for tea. You'll be in real trouble, starting with herbal Darjeeling mixed with Lapsang Souchong.

December 23, 1986

★ ★ ★

1987

★ ★ ★

Grateful Dead, Hot Tuna, Jefferson Airplane, Quicksilver Messenger Service, etc. There was a time when we thought those names of local rock groups were unusually weird but it's a new world, again. Sylvia Massy, sound engineer at CD Presents on Grant, has lately been recording Verbal Abuse and Raw Power, plus Mojo Nixon and Skid Roper singing "I Ain't Gonna Pee-Pee in a Cup" and the Stirups' rendition of "Dildos Are a Girl's Best Friend." Over at Berkeley's Boner Records, where she also works, Sylvia has engineered and produced such greats as Doggie Style, the Sea Hags and Malibu Barbie. We won't even mention Dayglo Abortions and Christian Death . . . I say, bring back The Doors!

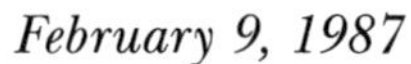

February 9, 1987

Grand old-timers: From tomorrow on, the downtown streets will be different. No more Dapper Dave Falk, shoes shined, hair slicked down, pocket handkerchief just so, making his rounds from Bardelli's to John's Grill to the St. Francis, and, in between, selling more clothes than any 10 salesmen half his age. "I've outlived 'em all," says Dap, the city's most famous suit salesman for 57 years. "First Berger's, then Roos Brothers, Roos-Atkins, Richard Bennett and now Grodin's," of which he was vice-president. It folds Sat., and Dave is retiring, a sad day for waiters and bartenders. As the old-time saying went, "He goes to his pocket pretty good."

February 19, 1987

I see that Fortune magazine is offering, for a mere $24.95, a computer program called Compusit that "generates" seating arrangements at dinner parties. You have to like that kind of language. For 25 bucks, you can "generate" something nobody needs. At dinner parties, it's boy, girl, boy, girl, a time-honored system that is only slightly more challenging for San Francisco, with its odd sexual orientations. The other rule is that married couples are split up and placed at opposite ends of the table, whereas singles or extras may sit next to one another. I once knew a young woman who married the biggest bore in town so she wouldn't have to sit next to him at dinner parties. It helped, of course, that the bore was rich, which is so often the case. You won't find out things like this from programs like Compusit. One last word of advice: Don't bring Lulu! *February 22, 1987*

Passengers boarding the Muni's 44 O'Shaughnessy in the Richmond were told by the lady driver to take their own transfers "because I just finished painting my nails and they aren't quite dry." *April 20, 1987*

Steve Carey is worried about tomorrow night's Black & White Ball. He's afraid Ted Turner will try to colorize it. *April 30, 1987*

That was one weird news story—the one about the male jogger shot in the head and found floating off Stinson Beach with a Sony Walkman and a Mario Lanza tape on his person. "Foul play is not suspected," announced the S.F. coroner's office, but Bob Levitt is not swallowing that. "OK, maybe he shot himself in the head and threw himself into the ocean," he concedes, "but anybody who jogs to Mario Lanza tapes has GOT to be involved in foul play." *May 14, 1987*

We bring you now three sartorial excloos on the G. Gate Bridge's 50th anniversary party! On opening day in '37, Albert Birsinger walked across in a pair of brown and white Bostonian shoes, warning his wife, Charlotte, through the years that followed: "Don't throw those out—I'm going to wear them when I walk across on the 50th anniversary." Albert didn't make it but his shoes will. His son, Robert, will wear them Sunday . . . Joseph L. McReynolds, pres. of Corporate Security Services Inc., who walked across the bridge in '37 in his Cub Scout uniform, will do it again, wearing a facsimile run up for him by Rochester Big & Small (Joe is now 5' 10", 200 pounds) . . . Don't go away! In '37, Paul Dolan, then in the Navy, thought it would be a kick to cross the bridge in a tuxedo, so he bought one from Selix. He then handed it down to his son Patrick, asst. mgr. of the S.F. Hilton, who will wear it Sunday . . . The party is definitely shaping up.

★ ★ ★

Oh joy: Golden Gate Bank, getting in on the bridge madness, is putting on a banquet next Wed. to present its Golden Gate Award to "the individual who has brought the most favorable recognition to San Francisco during the previous calendar year." Among the 11 nominations: Roger Boas, Dianne Feinstein, Cyril Magnin, Charlotte Mailliard, Coach Bill Walsh, James Thacher, Ian White and Judy and Brayton Wilbur. The award includes a $10,000 cash prize. I hope one of those needy people wins it. *May 21, 1987*

A Walk Through Time

Happy birthday, old beauty. Or rather, ageless, not old. You will outlive us all, especially those who remember the great day 50 years ago when we spent the day dreamily walking back and forth across your broad expanse, seeing views we had never seen before, hearing sounds that were new to us, feeling a living thing beneath our feet. We were overexcited and hypersensitive and trying very hard to capture the essence of those moments. It is not often that one is so intensely aware of being privy—almost literally a footnote—to history in the making. We held hands and looked at one another with shining eyes. The words didn't have to be said aloud, through the kind of fog and wind we had never experienced. Our expressions said it all: "We are walking across the Golden Gate on the greatest suspension bridge ever built!"

★ ★ ★

Fifty years is not very long in the life of a wonder of the world. History does not indicate that there was a 50th birthday party for the great pyramids; some Cheopshot artist probably Tut-tutted, "Fifty years, big deal." But in our time, The Disposable Age, 50 years IS a big deal, imbued with a reasonable amount of sentiment. Many if not most of us who were around at the beginning can try to recapture the magic, compare old photos, laugh at our own callowness and "funny" clothes. And, if all goes well, those who have been hearing all their lives about—oh no, not again!—the now historic First Walk may feel the living pulse of the lithe structure, freed for two hours from the buzz and fumes that constantly assail it.

★ ★ ★

Carried away by the great occasion of 50 years ago, engineer Joseph Baerman Strauss, destined to die almost a year to the day later, said, "This bridge will stand forever!" (He did not, of course, anticipate the bridge's board of directors when going on to list the unlikely catastrophes that might destroy it.) For most of you, the Golden Gate Bridge HAS been standing forever, a part of everyday life and yet never quite taken for granted. The mystical structure, with its perfect amalgam of delicacy and power, exerts an uncanny effect. Its efficiency cannot conceal the artistry. There is heart there, and soul. It is an object to be contemplated for hours, if one but had the time, and to be viewed from its various angles, all of them forever shifting in the various lights it refracts so elegantly.

★ ★ ★

Engineer Strauss died on May 18, 1938. His ashes are inurned at Forest Lawn cemetery in Los Angeles, behind a bronze plate depicting the Golden Gate Bridge. His wife, Ethelyn Annette Strauss, died on Oct. 13, 1961. Her ashes are next to his, behind a plate that shows the Golden Gate BEFORE the bridge was built. No one at Forest Lawn is able to explain the significance of her choice.

★ ★ ★

This 50th anniversary is an exercise in nostalgia, a sentiment that seems in especially short supply in Marin. This is somewhat understandable: From the start, the idea of bridging the Gate was San Francisco's, and stern-looking men with fierce moustaches fought it through, against considerable opposition. The environmentalists of the time, whatever they were called, argued that the open Gate was sacred and significant, not to be cluttered; they also argued that a bridge would "significantly" increase auto traffic, a patently ridiculous prediction. Today, between the BCDC, environmental impact reports, puny politicos and inflation, such a bridge would never get built. Part of the nostalgia is for the old town's "can do!" spirit. We rose from the ashes, we built the two greatest bridges in the world, we dredged the bottom of the bay to create a setting for a world's fair celebrating the feat, we had a bustling harbor, and we lived in a city beloved by all. In the middle of a great depression, we were astonishing the world. We would never ride so high again.

★ ★ ★

Those who don't seem to get the idea at all keep wringing their hands (it is their necks that should be wrung) over the "sadly diminished" birthday party, as though a $20 million job would be preferable. Much has been made of the "bickering" among the groups involved; I suppose the fashionable headline would be "Trouble Over Bridged Waters." But as long as the traffic keeps moving, somehow, it doesn't much matter what happens today. Like the great arched span itself, less is more; there is no fat on the bridge except between the ears of certain directors. Indeed, "every prospect pleases, and only man is vile," as demonstrated by proliferating and ugly toll plazas, head-on collisions, Doyle Drive's destruction derby and childish traffic control.

★ ★ ★

But there is no stupidity great enough to ruin the majesty of the Golden Gate Bridge. It has been the subject of terrible poetry and worse paintings, but it rises easily and grandly above the mundane, its towers poking through the fogs, natural and man-made. Don't worry about the party. The bridge is its own celebration, today and every day and, in Joe Strauss' word, "forever." *May 24, 1987*

We discovered a lot of things last weekend, didn't we? There are reservoirs of affection for the Golden Gate Bridge that hardly any of us were sufficiently aware of. We knew that everybody "loves" the Bridge, as everybody "loves" San Francisco, but now we know it is undoubtedly our most precious symbol. We look at it now in new ways, sharply aware of its specialness. Paris has its Eiffel, New York has its statue, we have the best of the lot, pure and simple in its simple purity. Up at Grace Cathedral last Sunday, Dean Alan Jones spoke of the celebration as a "quasi-religious event" commemorating "heroic materialism," a felicitous phrase. It is a structure only visionaries could have conceived and only heroes achieved.

★ ★ ★

We settled a few other things, too. For decades, various groups have been pushing for a "West Coast Statue of Liberty" on Alcatraz. Who needs it? The Bridge already plays that role, enriching the entrance to the world's greatest landlocked harbor. Let Alcatraz remain what it is, another kind of symbol, even though it is, in the words of one of our leading developers, "primo real estate." That's the way developers think, in terms like "primo." Land is real estate. Something should be DONE with it. I say certain things should be left alone. We can also forget those people, mainly newcomers, who say as though for the first time, "Why isn't the Golden Gate Bridge painted gold?" These people really think that's a clever idea, even though any painter could tell them different. International Orange was a masterstroke.

* * *

Questions that will never be answered, probably: How close was the bridge to collapsing under the weight of all those bodies on Gridlock Sunday? Those who were there felt the tension, the nervousness, the "flopsweat" (the late Howard Gossage's great term) of panic. Later we all laughed a little hysterically that "it was an unforgettable experience." The magnificent behavior of the crowd was due in part, I think, to the respect we felt for the bridge itself. Even when the crush was at its worst, even when there was no movement for what seemed like hours (and no information, only rumors), we knew it was a privilege to be on the roadway of "our" bridge. A lot of things were royally screwed up, but we were damned if we'd make the move we would always regret. I used to wonder if the San Franciscans of today could respond to catastrophe in the way our predecessors did after the 1906 earthquake, and now I'm sure of the answer.

* * *

A visiting New Yorker read the local papers after the bridge celebration and shook his head. "You people," he said with a hard little smile, "certainly know how to congratulate yourselves." Guilty, but somebody has to do it. San Francisco-bashing is very much in vogue, but even St. Andreas can't fault the bridges. Kindly rise for one chorus of our anthem, "The Car-Strangled Spanner."

May 31, 1987

No, I don't know why his obituary wasn't on the front page yesterday morning. All I can say is, two bad weekends in a row. First we almost lose the Golden Gate Bridge, and then, last Sat. night, an authentic giant topples over, never to rise. Turk Murphy, dead at 71, his place in S.F. musical history already secure but not worthy of page one, apparently. A great San Francisco name, right up there with Lefty O'Doul, Sunny Jim and Billy Ralston. A terrific guy, soft-spoken, gentlemanly, kind; I never heard him swear or lose his temper except maybe at thickheads who called his music "Dixieland" or requested "When the Saints Go Marching In," a number he detested to his dying day, I'm sure. He played New Orleans jazz, happy jazz, Frisco jazz, every number burnished to perfection, bouncing right along with the most infectious of beats. Typically, San Francisco took him as part of the scenery, somebody who'd be around forever, a treasure to be ignored, but at Carnegie Hall he got standing ovations. If San Francisco seems different today, it's because one of the authentic sounds of the city is gone to where the saints go marchin' in. Sorry about that, Turk. Sorry about everything. *June 2, 1987*

This was to have been Arnold Batliner's big day. If his name rings a slight bell, it's because he's "the world's only coin washer"—the man who keeps the Hotel St. Francis' small change bright and shiny, a gimmick that delights the tourists and gives the natives a link to the past (the late Dan London, the hotel's most celebrated mgr., began the custom in 1938 when Real Ladies wore white gloves and complained about dirty coins soiling them). Today is Arnold Batliner's 83rd birthday and his 25th year on the job, so the hotel had planned a big party, with champagne and cake, but now all signals are off. While he was walking back to his Mission Dist. apt. after grocery shopping, he was mugged. His wallet, filled with dirty money, was stolen. And he is now in Kaiser Hospital. Happy birthday anyway, Arnold. *June 17, 1987*

You should've been aboard the Muni B Express as it thundered down California St. yesterday morning. I mean you shouldn't have been. Roderick George was on it, and he reports it was pandemonium, with men screaming, children crying and strong women turning pale beneath their beards. This particular bus—3495—was crawling with cockroaches, many of which also began crawling onto the passengers. These poor souls wound up standing in the middle of the aisle, staring in terror as the roaches did everything except scrawl graffiti. Maybe a roach could be elected mayor. "Cocky" Roach. At first you don't like him but he grows on you. By the way, the driver of the infested bus was philosophical. "Happens all the time," he assured passenger George. We don't call it the Muniserable Railway for nothing. *June 19, 1987*

The Sunday Soporific

A lot of people say to me, "You're living in the past," as though it were an accusation. What's wrong with it? The present is tense and future indefinite—but ah, the past! Pluperfect! If I could only get that hippie kid out of my mind, the one who said to me years ago after yet another "That Was San Francisco" piece, "Why do you keep writing about the old days? I mean, what GOOD does it do?" He said that some time during The Summer of Love—an awfully corny label, when you stop and think about it—and I couldn't answer him. It doesn't do any good at all, judging by what has happened to the most attractive smallish city in the land. When there's a quick buck to be made, nobody thinks about anything but the quick buck, another item that ain't what it used to be.

* * *

I have plenty of evidence that writing about the past makes the old-timers happy—apparently they can read endlessly about the tragedy of the ferryboat Peralta and about the one-legged gull called Pete and the vending machine outside the Ferry Building that dispensed collar buttons (yes! collar buttons!)—but the old-timers are a vanishing audience, by definition. The reading audience itself is vanishing. "Chewing gum for the eyes"—who said that about TV, Fred Allen or Marshall McLuhan?—is gumming up the mind, although when Wimbledon is on the tube, I'm all for it. Time is short. The Earth spins ever faster. Suppose you commit yourself to a big fat $21.95 book and it's no good? A column is no big deal. Read a paragraph, turn the page. 'Byeeeee.

* * *

The idea behind writing about the past is to keep memories alive, but that dratted hippie kid was right. One man's memories are another's nightmares, and besides, the attention span keeps getting shorter and nostalgia isn't even a pretty word. Sounds like a disease, which it can be. Neuralgia is an ache in the nerves, nostalgia is a pain in the brain, a pang in the heart, a clutch at the throat. Ah, how simple and satisfying it is to run on like that, but yeah, kid, what good does it do? Where does nostalgia begin these days? Janis Joplin drinking Southern Comfort for breakfast at Enrico's? Jim Morrison emptying a bottle of Remy Martin cognac before going onstage with the Doors at the Cow Palace? To show off my own prodigious memory, a moment's silence for Benny Horne, a reporter for the old San Francisco News, who invented the term Cow Palace a good bit more than 50 years ago.

⋆ ⋆ ⋆

Living in the past is fine for a guy like Peter Mintun, who "tickles the ivories" (ah, very 1930s) in the L'Etoile bar, a popular Nob Hill hangout. I go into a little detail there because maybe some people never heard of L'Etoile. We regulars call it L'Etoilet, but lovingly, as we call the Wash. Sq. Bar & Grill the Washbag and the St. Francis the Frantic. Peter decided long ago that nothing of interest has taken place since the 1930s, so that is where he lives, wearing 1930s clothes, surrounded by 1930s objects, driving a 1930s Buick and playing only songs of the 1930s or earlier. For him it works. He looks 1930 years old.

⋆ ⋆ ⋆

Roger Boas, a candidate for mayor, keeps warning in sepulchral tones that the city is falling apart and in danger of becoming another Venice. That doesn't sound so bad. Maybe we can lose some ugly new buildings for a change, instead of just lovely old ones. A canal down Bush St. would be nice. Wouldn't you like to go to work in a gondola? Getting it back up Pine might be a problem, but we can always install a cable, sort of like the Chute the Chutes at old Playland at the Beach. The memories are always close at hand. I can hear Laughin' Sal and her manic cackle this very moment, and an ugly sound it is, causing small children to cry. Was there ever more fun than climbing all those stairs in the Fun House and coming down that beautiful wooden slide on a pair of gunny sacks, one for your bottom, one for your feet? You were sure you'd get a sliver up an important part of your anatomy, weren't you? What were we talking about, anyway? Right. Venice. Atherton Macondray Phleger, a lawyer with a real S.F. name, said to John E. Robinson III the other day, "Do you really think we're becoming another Venice?" John: "Venice began its decline about 1600, and when was the last economic summit held in Milan or Turin?"

⋆ ⋆ ⋆

Maybe the decline and fall of Baghdad-by-the-Bay began when we let Playland at the Beach be torn down. Or perhaps you decline to see a fall at all, preferring to dwell on our excellent weather, our magnificent bridges and eternal vistas, some of them now eternally blocked. It is not altogether inaccurate to say that San Francisco and Boston are the best of what is left of the great American cities—for the same reason: the flavor of the past, memories that bless and burn, the fast-disappearing evidence of a simpler yet richer life. If you have an especially salubrious experience today, store it in your memory bank. Fifty years down the line, it will add a wistful fillip to an otherwise gloomy day, believe me.

June 28, 1987

Harmonic convergence works! More than 55,000 fans converged harmonically on Candlestick Park Sunday to watch a game that was as good as baseball can get—great pitching, fancy fielding, clutch hitting and a Giants win over a Dodgers team that bears little resemblance to the great ones. Still, they wear Dodger blue, and Tommy Lasorda, the man with the lasagne eyes, still wears a belly that resembles the one on Garfield the Cat, so it made for a perfect afternoon in a sunny, windless 'stick. Roger Craig, who is much trimmer, called an almost perfect game except for a suicide squeeze that everybody in the park knew was coming. It didn't work. The crowd itself was warm and friendly and also almost perfect. Late in the game it went into a "Wave," which is so bush as to be embarrassing. The real fans booed or hid under their seats . . . If you got there late, you missed the old-timer's game, a re-enactment of the last game of the '62 World Series. You also missed, then, the sight of No. 24, Willie Mays, running out of the dugout and trotting to center field. It was a moment frozen in time, to be treasured with moist eyes, a lump in the heart and a glob of mustard on your shirt. We will not see his like again, and that scene may never be re-enacted. *August 18, 1987*

Sing, You Sinners

Last night, the vicar of Christ on earth slept (soundly, one hopes) in heaven on earth. Welcome to the city of St. Francis, O Patriarch of the West! It is sad that you cannot linger longer in this Paradise of the Pacific, this baffling but never less than coruscating Baghdad-by-the-Bay—part devout, part barbaric, a vastly tiny corner of the uncivilized world where God and Mammon are served equally and the dollar-topped spires rise even higher than those crowned with crosses. A city founded on a mad love for gold and silver and growing up bad, happy, silly, sappy. A city that loves a parade, a winner and an event, and your princely presence is definitely an event. For 24 hours, San Francisco is going crazy, as it will go crazy when the Gigantics, a local baseball team, get into the playoffs, and as it went crazy when a bridge turned 50 and—mirabile dictu!—survived the onslaught of 1.6 million feet, give or take a few.

★ ★ ★

Yes, a small place, Pontiff of the Universal Church, but expansive as well as expensive. A city "where the winds of freedom blow" across the hills and through the valleys, ruffling hair and minds, clearing foggy heads and sharpening the eye. A Catholic as well as a catholic city. A place where your dogma chases my catechism, or vice versa. Some old-timers and even historians call them the best years of San Francisco's life—the long era when Irish Catholics ran the show, dominated the political life, monopolized the police and fire departments, presided over the various treasuries. But nobody runs a headstrong city like this for long. She is still untamed. A wild streak of rebellion simmers and stews just below the surface, refusing to conform to the orthodoxies of religion and society. That is why San Francisco is a mecca—that non-Christian term—for those who have been cast out from lesser temples.

★ ★ ★

From its beginnings, San Francisco has been called a wicked city, your holiness. "Sodom and Gomorrah" is a favorite charge, leveled by frightened people who fear (as the old saying goes) that somewhere, somebody may be having a good time. AIDS, they cry, is the vengeance of the Lord, a thought that could be conceived only by a mind sicker than the victims of the disease they loathe. Fire, earthquakes, epidemics, pestilence—the city of St. Francis has gone through it all and emerged shining in the rising sun or glowing like a gray pearl under foggy skies. Yes, there are homeless people sleeping on our streets and yes, there are people given to the worst kinds of excesses. But there are also people—many of them young people—who are dedicating their lives to helping. In the most sectarian definition of the word, San Francisco is blessed. There are monumental sins of omission, but very little ingrained evil. "There may not be a Heaven," as Ashleigh Brilliant wrote on his most famous Pot-Shot card, "but somewhere there is a San Francisco."

★ ★ ★

With due respect, Bishop of Rome, I think of you on your present trip as a man in a cage. Transparent, but a cage all the same. Your familiar face smiles out from behind bulletproof glass wherever you go in public, and sad it is. Also instructive. By coincidence, you arrived on the 200th birthday of the signing of the Constitution, the world's greatest secular document, our Ten Commandments (plus amendments), our Torah, our Koran. It is an inspiring document, holy in its own way, setting standards of perfection for an imperfect country in a messed-up world. Yet we go on trying to live up to its teachings and those of your religion and all the others. The measure of how greatly we have failed is summed up in your cage, the one you ride in, the one you preach from.

* * *

"The test of a good religion," G.K. Chesterton may have remarked, "is whether you can make a joke about it" (we do know this "good Catholic" wrote that "The Christian ideal, it is said, has not been tried and found wanting; it has been found difficult and left untried"). This being an irreverent city populated by "perfectly mad people" (Kipling), the jokes have been coming sick and fast, Holy Father. In fact, if volume counts, Catholicism must be the best of religions, being the butt of both cheap humor and such profound observations as "The last Christian died on the cross." Last night, there was a "Pope Look-alike" contest at the Oasis, a disco. One of our better-known spots is the Holy City Zoo, a comedy club, of course. Since Rosh Hashanah is next week, Noah Griffin called out "Good Yontiff, Pontiff!" but of course you didn't hear him. However, you may have heard the line before. Discussing your appearance at Candlestick Park today, Jim Archer insisted yesterday that Oral Roberts is already standing at third base, "waiting to be called home." And Forrest Patten thought the archdiocese should have hired Barbra Streisand to perform. Why? "Well, she could sing, Papal, papal who need papal." I agree, O Primate of Italy. Flebilis!

* * *

Only 22 hours in a mysterious city that takes more than a lifetime to learn about. Its secrets live shadowy lives, even as the views open out to heavenly expanses. And yet it is a religious city, as 450 churches attest, and 3,000 saloons question. Not a proper balance, your holiness, but neither the churches nor the saloons are always crowded. Perhaps Samuel Butler (1835–1902) had this city in mind when he wrote "If a new edition of the church catechism is ever required, I should like to introduce a few words insisting on the duty of seeking all reasonable pleasure and avoiding all pain that can honorably be avoided." Words to live by! Pax et amor.

September 18, 1987

I'm a geezer. I stop at red lights and signal at least a quarter of a block before I turn. Even in the heat, I wear a hat, a suit, a necktie with my shirt (changed twice daily) and a pocket hankie. My shoes are polished because I approve of shoeshine stands run by geezers. My fingernails are short and clean (buff, no polish) because I approve of what geezers used to call manicuties. The only reason I wear a hat is because Dr. Jack Owsley ordered me to; I'm bald on top and prone to skin cancers. I play geezer tennis: chops, slices, drop shots, lobs. Geezer softball: a dead pull hitter who sometimes lofts one clear over the shortstop's head. On a crowded Muni bus, I rise to give my seat to pregnant women and elderly ladies who turn out to be younger than I; they look me up and down and refuse my offer—gently. When a woman enters the elevator, I take off my hat and place it over my heart, as I used to see my father do; only elderly ladies notice the gesture. I'm a geezer. I love old days, old places, old friends, old jokes, old manners and customs. I'm as out-of-date as the 78-rpm records I play, but I'm not so out of it that I'm not rooting for the Giants or happy to be alive in the city I christened Baghdad-by-the-Bay long before I became a geezer. Just don't call me "spry." That's the last thing a geezer wants to hear about himself. *October 11, 1987*

Bang the drum slowly: The sun shone brightly over beautiful San Francisco yesterday. The air was crisper than a new 10-dollar bill, for what it's worth. Old Glory fluttered above awesome financial institutions whose leaders fluttered hands and hearts. There was big-D Depression in the streets. Traffic was oddly light, the sidewalks almost empty except for beggars, with more to come. People gathered around corner newsstands as though reading war bulletins; "DOW DROPS 508" was bad enough. At Jack's and Sam's and the other stockbroker hangouts, you heard "Gimme another martini over, what the hell." There were dumb jokes about falling bodies. The guessperts on TV might as well have been singing Cole Porter's "Just One of Those Things"; its best line—"too hot not to cool down"—explained the stock market crash as well as anything.

Memories of Herb Hoover in '29: Treasury Secty. James Baker tried to place part of the blame on the Democrats for talking about a tax increase!

Forget about the bulls and the bears. It's the chickens that have come home to roost, as we knew they would. It was just a matter of when, and it is fitting, if not proper, that it happened during Mr. Reagan's "watch" (he likes military terms). The proud U.S. of A. a debtor nation; billions upon billions in budget and trade deficits; more billions for Krazy Kap Winebargle and "trickle-down" for the poor, the ill, the needy. Even an economic illiterate (guilty) could predict a maiden voyage to disaster.

Yesterday the bag ladies of Mission and Market were going about their business as the bagged brokers of Montgomery were walking away, exhausted, from theirs. The downtown sycamores are turning the colors of fall, and a great fall it is, like that of an earlier October. "Prosperity is just around the corner," said Mr. Hoover. So is winter. *October 20, 1987*

Wonderful Town

I'm a geezer who likes the youngies, and not necessarily the chicks or foxes or whatever they're called these days. By assiduously hanging out on weekend nights at certain bars favored by The Bright Young Things (thankya, Evelyn Waugh), I have come to know many of them well enough to feel reasonably confident about the future. To put it simply, the kids are terrific! If they aren't the way we were at their age, so much the better. They seem bright, funny, amused and very much involved with, and concerned about, what's going on in the town, the country, the world. And wow, are they good-looking! Unlike us geezers, they've had the benefits of what used to be called the affluent society—orthodontists, vitamins, good food and, I suppose, decent swimming and tennis instructors. The guys are tall, thin but not skinny, white of tooth and thick of hair. I can't tell you too much about the young women for fear of Dirty Old Geezerdom—you know, staring. The impression I get, however, is of a rare perfection, the classic profile marred only slightly by the bottle of Corona clamped between the ruby reds.

★ ★ ★

A Saturday night ago, I was pinned to the bar of the Balboa around midnight, surrounded by these godlike creatures. The noise was at supersonic levels and the body contact just short of illegal, but the vibes were excellent. Also the aroma. All those deodorant ads on TV apparently pay off. Hundreds of kids, with much banter between the Cals and the Stanfords, the yacht crews and the rugby crowd, the bowlers and the softballers, the lovers and the lonely. If all the Sperry Topsiders were placed end to end—well, they were, bringing to mind Dorothy Parker's remark that if all the Vassar girls were laid end to end, she wouldn't be surprised. I felt as though I were trapped in a beer commercial, playing the Bob Uecker role, but I was content, talking nose to nose with perfect strangers, and who said, "How come only strangers are perfect?" Or even, familiarity breeds.

⋆ ⋆ ⋆

Contempt was not what I was feeling. Listening to the feverish and generally literate conversations, shouts, grunts, bellows and clichés ("How about another, big guy?"), I reflected that maybe our schools aren't so bad, after all. It is possible, of course, that the Balboa crowd is made up exclusively of youngsters who went and go only to private schools, but there must be a fair sprinkling of public schoolers, too, and they come off as reasonably educated. Aside from an unfortunate addiction to "you know"ism, they are what used to be called well-spoken.

⋆ ⋆ ⋆

Toying with my second Corona, hold the lime, I found myself wishing these young San Franciscans would hurry up and take over. Shades of poet John McRae and "In Flanders Fields": "From failing hands we throw the torch." The ancients have been running and ruining the town long enough, and there's an election Tuesday that doesn't promise to change anything. Fortunately for the Establishment, the young aren't as revolutionary as some of their predecessors; no loud cries of "Throw the rascals out!" but that day will undoubtedly come. There is always a streak of youthful idealism that, one hopes, will never die in cynicism. One also hopes that the recent unpleasantness on Wall Street will hammer home the lesson that money isn't everything. You say, "It'll do till something better comes along"? Cynic.

⋆ ⋆ ⋆

Around 1 a.m., the crowd started filing out, to gather in knots on the sidewalk, yelling, laughing, chattering away. The Young San Franciscans, in the glow of health, the time of their lives. The mood was still as mellow as the weather, as redolent of the city's long history as the foghorn that sounded occasionally. I thought briefly of my own youth, of making the rounds in The City That

Was, hitting the after-hours spots, "slumming" (what a word) in Fillmore District jazz joints where a guy named Jimbo served up booze in a thick coffee cup; I thought of dawns at Ocean Beach and breakfast at a rather formal Cliff House, with waiters in wing collars and proper, if spotted, tuxedos.

★ ★ ★

Gradually, the young crowd moved off in all directions, and I wondered if they thought about the miracle—too strong a word?—of being San Franciscans, building up their own memories of a city that one day will seem strange and changed to them, too. We oldsters are burdened with the most beautiful yesterdays, a swirl of gingerbread ferryboats, one-buck Italian dinners, a bridgeless bay, trains on Mt. Tamalpais, safe streets, heroes in high places (hiya, Lefty O'Doul!), Laughin' Sal, and the amazing Fox Theater. These kids will have their own memories—Joe Montana, Saturday nights at the Balboa, Bay to Breakers—but I wouldn't trade mine for a thousand tomorrows. Uh, let me think about that, OK?

November 1, 1987

Drifting Shadows

From the window of my study—grandiose name for a wall of books, a desk, a 30-year-old typewriter—I look out on the teeming crest of Nob Hill, where the garish mansions of the nouveaux riches once blossomed. A bus labors up the Sacramento St. grade, flopping down at the top with a gasp. On California St., time and traffic signals stand still as a cable car rattles into the past it never left. I see a slice of the Fairmont, with its endless double-parked tour buses and trucks. The Pacific-Union Club, its only sign of life a sign of death—the club flag being lowered to half staff. The beautiful, open-faced facade of the Mark Hopkins, the Beaux-Arts charms of 1001 California and the Huntington's parapets, Grace Cathedral's carillon showering silvery notes across Huntington Park. It is all so authentically 1920s, San Francisco under glass, a perfect period piece preserved in amber. If we're lucky, forever amber.

★ ★ ★

A San Franciscan. A proud title, going back only a few years, as eternity blinks, but filled with excitement, passion and a certain madness. I am a San Franciscan, attuned to the stirring of ghosts in taffeta that peek shyly from between velvet draperies in a house long ago turned to dust. I never saw but will always remember the bowler-topped dandies with their muttonchop whiskers, ogling the beauties along the Kearny St. "cocktail route" and then turning into the Waldorf on Market for a drink with the lads and a thick slice of pink Virginia ham on a warm Parker House roll, compliments of the house. On a still night, I hear the rattle of carriages over cobblestones, except, of course, in front of the houses of the ill and dying, where sacks are laid over the stones to muffle the sound. Gaslights cast a golden light, turning the scene to sepia.

* * *

I am a San Franciscan, steeped in the cobwebs of the past, nervous about the present, hopeful for the future. A new mayor will soon be installed. Let us hope he has a sense of history, a feeling for the magnificent strangeness of this city—strange in that it has captured the imagination of so many for so long. Yes, "special" is the word. Sometimes it is especially bad, evil or merely naughty. Sometimes, in its greed, it turns ugly and destroys or blocks its most precious assets. Sometimes it kicks up its heels and is great fun—zany and headstrong. It can be and is cruel and thoughtless, talking a great game of "tolerance" and "freedom" and not doing a damn thing about it. A spoiled, vain city with many a fault more dangerous than the San Andreas.

* * *

A new mayor has much to cope with and much to live up to. One major task: keeping alive the spirit of San Francisco, the spirit that carried it through the catastrophes, that built bridges and opera houses, that has to be rallied if this city is to remain truly alive. We will never have another Sunny Jim Rolph, who reigned for 20 years over a city the likes of which will never be seen again, but we can have our eyes opened to the magnificence that lives to this day. There are danger and degradations in streets that were once innocent and even beautiful. It will take all the strength that a strong leader possesses to make San Francisco whole again. It was once a family, moving to one rhythm, one harmony. The discords grow louder as privilege and poverty move farther apart.

* * *

A San Franciscan. It's a great thing to be if you can afford it, but it still means something even if you're looking for jobs that aren't there, living on handouts. We invoke the spirit of the prizefighter Willie Britt, who said he'd rather be a busted lamppost on Battery St. than the Waldorf-Astoria. It's a tough city to be broke in, but the city is broke, too. The views are thrilling, but not when you're looking down. The boulevards are beautiful, but not when you have holes in your shoes. In "The Picture of Dorian Gray," Oscar Wilde has Lord Henry saying to Dorian about Basil's disappearance: "I suppose in about a fortnight we shall be told that he has been seen in San Francisco. It's an odd thing, but everyone who disappears is said to be seen in San Francisco. It must be a delightful city, and possess all the attractions of the next world." The next world is sometimes hell. But the next mayor must remember that San Francisco once excited the cognoscenti of the world.

* * *

Perhaps the last kind of words ever written about politicians were contained in the Ephebic Oath, a rarity unearthed by Madeleine Tress, Esq.: "To bring no disgrace to the city by dishonest act. To fight for the ideals and sacred things, alone and with many. To desert no faltering comrade. To strive unceasingly to quicken the public sense of civic duty. To transmit this city not less but better and more beautiful than it was transmitted to us." Ah, days of innocence! Many a San Francisco politico pledged to support that oath in 1912, when, Madeleine Tress points out, "there were true city lovers." We are all the caretakers of San Francisco. It is not too late to bring the past into the future. *November 8, 1987*

Hitting bottom: Before the stock market unpleasantness, the three-car garage of a certain Sonoma house contained a Bentley, a Porsche and a pickup truck. A neighbor, retired Air Force Col. John C. Stewart, sends me a photo showing that garage today—empty except for a bicycle with a sign on the back reading "Thank You, Paine Webber." *November 18, 1987*

Here is my final solution for the baseball stadium crisis: roof Candlestick with Latex and call it the Condome. And of course the bases should be covered with the same material in the name of safe sacks. *November 23, 1987*

Let's see, nasty crisis in the Fire Dept., lethargy in the Police Dept., crisis among the homeless, minority anger over the rehiring of the Muni boss, major flap over the design for a "new" Civic Center, huge budget deficit. Is Art Agnos having fun yet?

January 15, 1988

Sunday Punchdrunk

Being a fun-loving San Franciscan (redundant), I play a lot of games in this hallowed space—self-cancelling phrases (working press), namephreaks (Fran and Bill Flesher own a nudist resort near San Berdoo), cuuuute firm names (the King Kong Window Washing Co., and thanks, Bunk Sicotte) and ever so many others that have dismayed readers for 51 years (everything keeps for a long time in S.F., even columnists). We've had the "You know it's gonna be a long day when" game (example: when you get dressed in the morning and your shoes are still warm). There's the "You're in big trouble when" game (Dr. Herman Schwartz submits: "When your wife, after having surgery, asks the doc, 'Will I be able to have sex?' and he replies, 'Yes, but only with your husband—I don't want you to get too excited.'"). And Agnes Pritchard enters the lists with, "You know it's gonna be a bad day when you see your name on a street sign."

★ ★ ★

This last one calls for some explanation. Lawrence Ferlinghetti, esteemed dean of beatnik poets, suggested recently that certain S.F. streets be named for writers, artists, dancers and so on, including even the oversigned. The public works committee of the Bd. of Supes is going along with the idea but has decided that only dead people should qualify—Saroyan, Dashiell Hammett, Kerouac, Frank Norris, Isadora Duncan, Bufano and (I'm throwing this in on my own) sculptor Ralph Stackpole. Hence the point of Agnes Pritchard's sharp little line. The only good writer is a dead writer. I don't think anybody can argue with that.

* * *

In dashing off his plan, poet Ferlinghetti created a bit of doggerel with the suggestion that Mary St., a one-way alley that runs alongside Fortress Chronicle, be retitled Herb Caen Lane, redolent of daffydills, Sweet Williams and forget-me-nuts. Since I have to die to achieve this immortality, I say thanks but no thanks. Besides, I was honored a bit more substantially a few years ago in Sacramento. At a ceremony that drew a goodly crowd of used-car salesmen, bartenders and lobbyists, my birthplace at 10th and O sts. was affixed with a handsome plaque headlined, "Local Boy Makes Good." Bands played, pigeons flew, rocks were hurled and relatives cheered. One week later, the house at 10th and O was torn down for a redevelopment project . . . Footnote: Since there is already a Gold St. over there near Montgy. and Jackson, it appears that novelist Herb Gold has it made, dead or alive.

* * *

Further aside: An enterprising reporter, doing a man-in-the-street number on Ferlinghetti's plan, discovered that hardly anybody had heard of William Saroyan or Frank Norris. To paraphrase Santayana, those who cannot remember the past are not doomed to repeat it, and that's too bad. San Francisco is a city of yesterdays and Saroyan was a charmingly noisy part of it, laughing at the human comedy he created.

* * *

Santayana puts one in mind of another famous esthete, Bernard Berenson. After I wrote the other day about the three great cities of Europe—Paris, London, Venice—John E. Robinson III recalled these words of Berenson about Venice: "The richest, and most exquisite, artifact in the history of civilization because she has been spared by that great and beneficent goddess, Poverty. For a century, the Venetians have been too poor to build anything new." So the flight to L.A. of all those go-go companies may eventually be all to the good-good. Market St. will never be another Champs Elysees, but given the S.F. penchant for deferred maintenance, it could easily become as flooded as the Grand Canal. Then, as that wonderful supervisor once recommended, we could buy two gondolas and let nature take its course.

★ ★ ★

Getting back to fun & games, so-called, Judith Turgendreich says, "You know you're in trouble when a letter arrives from conductor Herbert Blomstedt explaining the new modern work to be performed that week by the S.F. Symphony. Then, when the composer walks onstage to explain it further, you know you're really in for it. Of course, the reason for this is so the audience will know that the preconcert warm-up has ended and the next work is beginning." Bang-on, as the Brits say. Our chief music critic, Robert Commanday, has done a commendable job of trying to keep the town musickers from rehearsing onstage in full view of a disgusted audience, but to no avail. What a treat it is when an orchestra like the Vienna Philharmonic is in town. The guys walk onstage at the appointed hour, sit down and start playing. And WHAT playing!

★ ★ ★

One-sentence newsflash in the London Telegraph, culled by Tom Rooney: "Chili powder is to be spread over farmland in the Queen's Windsor Castle estate in an attempt to deter pigeons." You think this might work in Hallidie Plaza and Union Square? Or maybe giving the feathered rats a hotfoot is not cricket. Just keep them out of Herb Caen Lane, by golly. *January 24, 1988*

I have sadness in my heart over the death of Kurt Herbert Adler, whose cloaked, bemedaled figure floats like a phantom over the Opera House. In a city that has lost a lot of characters as well as character, Kurt was a standout—tough, talented, funny, feisty, haughty and surprisingly warm when you least expected it. He was and is the San Francisco Opera, no matter who's in charge. When he entered the mezzanine bar on opening nights, you knew somebody had swept in. He looked great in white tie and tails, his decorations glittering, his eyes darting around, taking in everything. There was no fooling Kurt. "Great opera, Kurt," the phony millionaire would beam. "Phony millionaire," Kurt would mutter, pushing on. His successor, Terry McEwen, resigning for health reasons (I believe that story, even if a lot of "insiders" don't), is a huge loss, too. Terry is also unique, a character, a man you love or hate (Kurt was the man you loved to hate). He tells great anecdotes in half a dozen languages and dialects and is the life of every social occasion, an art form he dotes on. We might get somebody twice as good but I'll bet he or she won't be half as amusing, and we're in this thing for the laughs, aren't we? *February 15, 1988*

Sightem at a red light on Van Ness and Pine: a youngish guy in a BMW yelling at the woman driver in the car alongside, "Would you MIND turning down that damn radio—can't you see I'm on the phone???" *February 25, 1988*

Sodden thoughts: Do you think the person who invented "music on hold" also came up with car burglar alarms, the authentic voice of urban insanity? *March 21, 1988*

Real estate inflation note: The brokerage fee on Harry de Wildt's outer Broadway mansion, which sold for $4.2 million, was larger than the amount he paid for the house when he bought it 14 years ago. *April 26, 1988*

When Newsman Kevin Leary told me yesterday that Cyril Magnin died, I blurted, "I don't believe it—he'll go on forever." Even now, in the face of incontrovertible evidence to the contrary, I figure he's still among us, playing the role he loved most, that of "Mr. San Francisco." He was a glad-hander without being a pain in the neck about it, a boulevardier who looked incomplete without a beautiful girl (much MUCH younger) on his arm, a first-nighter who loved show biz and show people in an open-mouthed starstruck little-boy way. And yet he was also sophisticated and shrewd, a tireless fund-raiser, a business success and a people person. All kinds of people liked him because he liked all kinds of people, never making an unkind judgment. With his passing, the title of "Mr. San Francisco" is retired, at least until another octogenarian swinger comes along who can sit through "Beach Blanket Babylon" night after night, sing a song or two for the nightcappers in the Mark Hopkins bar and rise the next morning to write a check for a charity nobody ever heard of. Cyril, you done good.

* * *

Caenfetti: You noticed, of course, that Jesse Jackson carried S.F.

over Dukakis and Bush; this proves again that there is no place like our home, which is why we come up with people like Cyril Magnin . . . *June 9, 1988*

What's the Big Deal?

So I've been writing a 1,000-word column six days a week for 50 years. Hasn't everybody? Or couldn't anybody? All it takes is time, a certain lack of imagination and not much interest in doing anything else. Critics, of which I have a satisfying number, maintain that I've been writing the same column for 50 years, and I wish that were true. There is no doubt in my mind that some have been even worse than others. Another critic and confrere, the late columnist Charles McCabe, said I kept writing about a city that died 20 years earlier. He wrote that about 20 years ago, so I guess I am now writing about a San Francisco that died circa 1948, which I recall as a very good year. The city was still small, manageable and quite elegant.

★ ★ ★

The column was born—or, at least, first saw the dark of print—on July 5, 1938. It died somewhere along the line, but nobody is quite sure when. Like a dog in one of those old Russian experiments, it keeps limping along, occasionally showing signs of life, to the surprise of its creator, if that is not too grand a term. If it had a golden age, it must have been before Pearl Harbor, which changed the city forever. Thousands of people who had never heard of San Francisco discovered our magical little secret, and many of them stayed. Up to then, we had a club, and I was the only one writing about it every day, this big little city where nothing and everything happened.

★ ★ ★

Just a lucky kid, a fresh and fresh-faced greenhorn out of Sacramento, suddenly granted the signal honor of recording some of the goings-on in his dream city, the city he had been in love with since he was old enough to think about cities, hotels, restaurants, glamorous people, the excitement of metropolis. At the age of 22, there was his name in fairly big type in a fairly big paper that was destined to get bigger and better. No wonder he dashed around in an endlessly happy daze. He was the kid in the candy store, Dorothy in Oz, Alice in Wonderland, Tom Swift and his Electric Column. He worked like hell for peanuts but it was all great and exciting fun, and anyway, peanuts went further in those days of the 15-cent cocktail and one-buck dinner.

* * *

My timing was as good as my luck. The Great Depression was still on, but San Francisco was an exciting place in 1938. The two greatest bridges in the world had opened, and an island was being created in the bay for a world's fair. The 1939 Golden Gate International Exposition on Treasure Island was all that anybody could talk about—that and Harry Bridges' grip on the waterfront, Anita Howard's latest affair, William Saroyan's latest short story, the nightly fights at the Black Cat over Matt Barnes' and Luke Gibney's latest paintings, the courtroom triumphs of the hot little lawyer, Jake (The Master) Ehrlich, with his starched white collars and cuffs, his starched white handkerchief, his starched blondes twice his size.

* * *

A marvelous city to write about. Like a snake, it sheds its skins, changes its shape, wanders off in unexpected directions. A hard city for sentimentalists, which most writers are. Beloved landmarks disappear, manners and mores change, "unforgettable" characters die and are forgotten. The 1950s: jazz, convertible Cadillacs, too much drinking. North Beach is the hangout, thanks to the Beats and Banducci. The 1960s: Rock rocks the world, and San Francisco rock is right up there; Vietnam, the hippies and the Hashbury (farewell to North Beach); we all marched for peace. The 1970s: the rise of the high-rises, the wild ride of the entrepreneurs; the city is twisted out of shape. The 1980s: We have problems. We don't have solutions.

* * *

Fifty years of columns, setting down pieces of the unfinished story. Historians a century hence might find a nugget or two amid the dross. Meanwhile, I think I'll try for another 50. Where do we go from here?

July 10, 1988

Things to Come and Go

In any list of the world's most memorable viewing experiences, this certainly has to rank close to the top: the moment when you burst out of Marin's "rainbow tunnel" to find a rising river of white fog roiling around the towers of the Golden Gate Bridge and gradually swallowing them, red warning lights and all. Maybe that's the best part—the cherry atop the sundae. Unsated by this feast—there isn't that much to eat on a bridge tower—the gauzy boa constrictor slithers on across the Bay, gobbling up sailboats like so much plankton, ingesting Alcatraz without a burp and lunging hungrily at Treasure Island. The Bay Bridge is next to pay the toll, and yes, I agree that this entire mishmashterpiesh is out of control.

★ ★ ★

The change of metaphors from "rising river" to "gauzy boa constrictor" is definitely not worthy of a Sacramento High School honors graduate. Instead of "gauzy boa," how about "feathery," suitable for wearing to the opera? Furthermore, a whale is much more likely than a boa to consume plankton. "Your no doubt good intentions will not preclude my giving you a failing grade," quoth the professor.

★ ★ ★

I was more or less amusing myself with the above exercise while driving from the 100-plus heat of Napa through the warmth of Sonoma and Marin and on into the sudden coolth of San Francisco, the once and forever magic city. I was thinking that more bad "poetry" must have been written about the Golden Gate, its bridge and the incoming fog than any other landmark. You know, the kind of poetry in which every other sentence starts with "O." O, twin sentinels of the western sea. O, framed in the mists that veil thy Gate of Gold. Ina Coolbrith and George Sterling, our poet laureate, were good at, O, that sort of thing-o, and I'm not poking fun, not this Baghdaddy-by-the-Bay. It was the style of the time to wax florid, but then came the wane. Oddly, the view from the Bay Bridge doesn't cause the poetasters to salivate all over their parchments, and yet there is much to be said, and badly, about the skyline reaching O, for the heavens and the streets climbing to the stars. Halfway.

★ ★ ★

The irresistible lure of the lore of the city. In March, 1776, a brown-frocked padre stood on the northernmost tip of the peninsula, overlooking "the port and its islands . . . the mouth of the harbor and all that the sight can take in as far as beyond the Farallones." He was Fray Pedro Font, friar of Lt. Col. Juan Bautista de Anza's expedition. "Indeed," Father Font continued, "although in my travels I saw very good sites and beautiful country, I saw none which pleased me as much as this. And I think if it could be well settled like Europe, there would not be anything more beautiful."

★ ★ ★

A man of vision, the friar, and already falling under the spell of a city that had yet to be built. I extracted his words from a remarkable small (128-page) paperback titled "Almanac for Thirty-Niners," put together by the Federal Writers Project in 1938 as part of the buildup to the 1939 World's Fair on Treasure Island, a piece of land dredged from the bottom of the bay. I mention this because it suddenly occurred to me, as I drove across the Golden Gate Bridge, through "O, the striving billows' reach," that the next Very Big Deal around here will be the 50th anniversary of the entrancing exposition that opened so bravely on the eve of war and that ended, late in 1940, as the world we knew began going up in smoke.

* * *

It was with a feeling of relief and pleasure that I discovered a tattered, discolored copy of "Almanac for Thirty-Niners" tucked away in my messy bookshelves. Having survived the flowing boa constrictive fog of the bay, I was soon lost in the world of FDR, his WPA, a "$50,000,000 fantasy" of a fair dedicated to the completion of our two mighty bridges, and the simple good humor of that era. Since at least 10 WPA'ers, led by editor W.M. McElroy, worked on the "Almanac," it is hard to know who wrote what, but the little book definitely bears reprinting. It was in its pages that I first read Miriam Allen de Ford's quatrain—"Oh, give me a big silver dollar/To throw on a bar with a bang;/A dollar all creased/will do for the East,/but we want our money to clang!" And I believe it was Margaret Wilkins who wrote, "Much surprised—in fact, agog—/We would put it in this log/If there chanced to be no fog/In San Francisco in Aug."

* * *

The book is indeed laid out in almanac style, and here's the entry for Jan. 4, Wednesday: "Said Oakland's Daily Transcript on this date in 1869: The police in San Francisco arrested 488 drunks last month, only 8 of which were 'common' ones. Drunks in that town are generally of a remarkable character." O vile Oaklanders, forever mocking us! Onward, O avenging fog, to smite with fire and ice the dread Piedmontese! *September 11, 1988*

This is positively the last time! Every 10 years or so I print my favorite toast, and readers clip it out, lose it and ask for another copy. So here it is again, and this time take care of it: "Here's to the roses and lilies in bloom, you in my arms and I in your room, a door that is locked, a key that is lost, a bird and a bottle and a bed badly tossed, and a night that is 50 years long." Cheers!

September 18, 1988

The first novel written by Herbert Gold—or anyway the first one I read—was called "The Man Who Was Not With It." A catchy little title. Today, I am that man, trapped by my invention of a place that may have been as mythical as Oz or Atlantis, or, in this case, Pacificus. I am much more excited by photographs of the faded old city than by drawings of a skyscraper soon to rise, not that this is too difficult. A glimpse of Yesterday Town starts the juices flowing and the mind racing. What was it really like, this upstart place with its oversized grand hotels, it's equally oversized grande dames riding in their carriages, the cobbled streets alive with vested dandies with fierce moustaches. Maybe it was like the Real Baghdad—dirty, dusty, smelling of horses and abuzz with flies.

★ ★ ★

The man who is not with it: Nowhere man, a liberal living in the past, canceling himself out. For decades, it was very important for me to be With It, first with the latest, picking up on the new slang word and slinging it around, hitting the hot spots, the darling of head waiters and the occasional debutante, Right This Way Mr. First-Nighter and take this table by the band. The country bumpkin became the city slicker, dressing carefully in double-breasted suits and shiny shoes that matched his nails. I would be more San Franciscan than The Born and Raised, showing my respect for the beloved objects by dressing to the teeth and writing love letters. I would get to know everybody who mattered and a lot of people who didn't, and maybe one day I would be mistaken for a Real San Franciscan, if I had to make up the definition myself.

★ ★ ★

Well, Baghdad-by-the-Bay changed but I didn't. I wear the same kind of clothes as I always did and am stared at oddly by the young people who are With It and who, I must say, look mighty fine. They are doing most of the same things I was doing once upon a time, but, as a young lady said loftily, "We're doing them NOW." Ah yes, Nowhere Man in the Now Society. I drive through the streets, looking around at unfamiliar sights and sounds, playing the tapes that fix me in time: Clancy Hayes and Bob Scobey, a little Benny Goodman in Moscow, some Mozart, Oscar Peterson playing his musical profile of Frank Sinatra (another Yesterday Man) and the new Quicksilver Messenger Service and the old Jefferson Airplane. I like rock, I like the heavy beat. I liked the Eagles and Lynyrd Skynyrd and The Who. I don't like boom boxes disguised as cars, cruising past, polluting the air. When I get angry enough, I say "Holy cow!" or "Jeepers!"

* * *

Baghdad-by-the-Bay: A magic carpet afloat on a misty sea, a faraway near-at-hand secret garden of unearthly delights, a place of mysterious lights high in dark buildings or floating in the invisible bay that once knew oyster pirates and shanghai'd sailors crying for help. To think of a city in those terms, you have to live in the past, and Lord knows I have plenty of that. *October 2, 1988*

Yupward and downward in Marin (classified ad in the Independent-Journal caught by M. Lundquist): "Killer garage sale, overloaded yuppie simplifying lifestyle." Mill Valley, of course.

October 27, 1988

Days of Our Years

November, month of mournful anniversaries. Ten years ago, two delightful, valuable and well-loved men, George Moscone and Harvey Milk, were shot to death by a cold-eyed loser. An excruciating lesson was learned: Always be wary of the uptight. When they snap and crack, a madman emerges. The 10th anniversary of Jonestown, one of the most bizarre tragedies in American history; Jim Jones was another madman waiting to explode through his facade of sweet reasonableness. The 25th anniversary of the assassination of John F. Kennedy, who will live through history as the eternal enigma. We will never be quite sure who he was or what he might have become; what we feel forever is an aching sense of loss. "Who Killed Jack Kennedy?" The conspiracy peddlers will not let the question die, but, as experts on such matters say, "If there are several conflicting theories, the simplest is usually the correct one." I'm willing to accept that Lee Harvey Oswald was the lone killer. There is always a madman, ready to explode, and we never know what will trigger him.

* * *

November, an overcast month of occasions and celebrations. Armistice Day, a solemn "holiday" that has died along with almost all the survivors of the first World War. No, it wasn't called World War I at the time; it was the war to end all war. The ritual of Thanksgiving, and what a noble bird is the turkey. Truly, the national bird. Have you ever tried to eat an eagle? Neither have I, but it seems inadvisable. On Thanksgiving, there is food galore for the homeless and hopeless as the Haves rush to assuage their guilt. "A thousand points of light," as our president-elect puts it. They glitter brightly at Thanksgiving and Christmas. By January, it is only the quiet, dedicated ones, as usual, who go about their good works, their light under a bushel. Meanwhile, the shopping spree has begun. Downtown traffic is terrible and getting worse, which means that business is good. The pre-Christmas sales are on. When you live in San Francisco, it's Christmas all year 'round anyway, unless fate has been unkind.

* * *

Saturday, a perfect November day, with a high autumn haze of timelessness. I take a well-worn path, across the Bay Bridge, left to Berkeley, up University Ave. toward one of the great landmarks, the Campanile on the Cal campus, graceful, ingratiating, perfect. By contrast, the Hoover tower at Stanford is a clunker, which is appropriate, considering some of the clinkers it houses. Don't get me wrong: Berkeley's University Ave. is no grand boulevard. It resembles some of the less attractive aspects of L.A.'s Sunset Blvd., except maybe for the Santa Fe Bar & Grill, which has the best homemade potato chips in the Bay Area. After nondescript University Ave., the university itself seems even more grandly impressive than it actually is. No, I'm not a Cal man, except in spirit, and it is one of the great regrets of my life, but in the depression year of 1932, a steady job seemed more important than two years of college. Wrong!

* * *

It's Big Game Day, one of the happy November rituals. "They call it the Big Game because it really is," I wrote a thousand years ago, but the detractors tend to downgrade it now as just another game between two teams that aren't going anywhere. It's a classic, they say, only for the old grads who remember the heroes of their youth, from Andy Smith's Wonder Teams to Stanford's cocky Vow Boys, from Vic Bottari, Sam Chapman and Jackie Jensen to Ernie Nevers, Biff Hoffman and Frank Albert. True and false. There is something special about the Big Game, and the memories have a lot to do with it. The players sense that they are part of the mythology, and rise to the moment. I've seen my share of Big Games, but seldom a dull one. Something wild and crazy always happens, the melodramatic ending as the clock winds down and the shadows grow long across the stadium floor and you know that another chapter is ending in the long story of a fascinating rivalry. Could two schools be more different than Cal and Stanford? Yet, it works.

★ ★ ★

The mood on the Cal campus on Big Game Day is always mellow. Excitement but not tension. Strangers become friends. At the tailgate parties, the old-timers have that special look about them, the look of people from another civilization, from the era when they and the world were young and life was simple and predictable, every move preordained. They are the lucky ones. They knew what they wanted and most of them got it, to judge from their demeanor, their talk, their clothes, their style. Not only that, they know how to do the tailgate parties in the sacred lots close to the great stadium. I had a couple of Bloody Marys with some strangers who soon seemed like my dearest friends. Such is the atmosphere of Big Game Day, but "strangers" is the wrong word. There aren't any on such an occasion. "It's too bad," sighed one Old Blue, "that Big Game comes only once a year." Good feelings, friendly rivalries, all the wonderful cornball stuff that keeps a way of life from falling apart.

★ ★ ★

I don't know what the sportswriters and other experts will say, but I thought it was a marvelous game, exciting all the way and providing the usual stunning finish that characterizes so many Big Games. It ended in a 19–19 tie that didn't quite measure up to the 20–20 tie of 1924, perhaps the best Big Game ever played, but it was a dandy. As I walked out through the quiet crowds, I couldn't help thinking how much Jack Kennedy and George Moscone would have enjoyed it. *November 21, 1988*

Sometimes it all gets a little too surreal. For example, at Glide Memorial tomorrow, the poor and homeless will be treated to a gourmet meal AND a fashion show. What to wear while rummaging through garbage cans? *December 23, 1988*

★ ★ ★

1989

★ ★ ★

The Moving Finger

"Ever-changing never-changing San Francisco," I used to call it in my callow youth, but of course no city stands still, even one as set in its ways as this one. Yesterday morning, in the beautiful white fog that blotted out the high-rises and made 1989 seem at least 30 years younger, I drove past the corner of Broadway and Kearny—surely a major intersection—and discovered that all four corners are dead. The Galaxy topless joint, closed. The place across the street that once housed the thriving Swiss Louie, papered over and padlocked. On the north side of Broadway, Enrico's coffee house, empty of everything except ghosts. And on the fourth corner, Vanessi's, once the powerhouse of the entire neighborhood, gone with the garlicky winds. The traffic was as thick as old Joe Vanessi's minestrone—"You can stand a spoon in it," he used to boast—but the traffic doesn't mean anything but trouble. The soul of a once-great street has departed and the emptiness is palpable. This stretch of old Broadway is shellshocked, pockmarked, burned out.

★ ★ ★

I was away when I heard that Vanessi's had folded. The news wasn't unexpected. Business had been slow there for a long time for a variety of reasons: Bawdway had grown sleazy, parking was expensive, the police were too zealous about towaways, and the topless gimmick fell flat a long time ago, not to mention the bottom falling out of the bottomless pit. Still, the whole country thought we were crazy and even wonderful for a while: topless waitresses at the Off Broadway ("Get your—uh—left one out of my salad dressing"), the topless shoe shine stand on Columbus, "Topless Mother of Eight" at El Cid, and of course the queen of the strip, Carol Doda, whose heroic cleavage was our own Silicone Valley. But nothing lasts forever, even with the help of silicone injections, and the boom finally went bust. The few rubes and bumpkins who still exist no longer come to ogle and goggle. "We're cleaning up Broadway!" Enrico announced gamely every few months, but Broadway had lost its identity and was dying.

* * *

Nevertheless, Vanessi's closing came as a slight shock. This place was an institution, an ex-bootlegger who once ran a speakeasy at 77 Broadway called the Cairo (his real name: Silvio Zorzi), knew everybody in town and everybody went to to Vanessi's—politicos, sports people, show-biz stars, socialites. Customers stood three deep for a seat at the counter, to watch the cooks threaten each other with cleavers in mock fights. The big bar was always jammed. The place stayed open till 3 a.m., its "in" back room studded with bandleaders, headliners, comedians. Jerry Lester did his routines in the aisle, the Ritz Brothers waited on tables, Dancer Tony DiMarco was there every night. For a columnist, it was the last stop on the way home.

* * *

Down the street stood New Joe's, a few years older than Vanessi's, just as busy, and celebrated as the birthplace of Joe's Special (the Joe was a gambler and night club owner named Joe Merello, who wore a white hat and a chorus girl on each arm). The city was divided between "Vanessi people" and "New Joe's people." Fists flew over which served the better hamburger, North Beach style—thick slabs of great beef between slices of sourdough that had been hollowed out, filled with butter and tamped down on the grill till they were as one. When a localite returned from a long vacation, he headed immediately for Vanessi's or New Joe's for a hamburger. That was considered very S.F.

* * *

We used to needle Joe Vanessi as "Benito." He was an admirer of Mussolini and a bit of a racist, as was most of the old North Beach crowd. Vanessi's got into trouble in 1947 when Paul Robeson, appearing in a show here, was refused service. Robeson, never one to take an insult lightly, filed suit and Joe paid off. "Why didn't somebody tell me he was a celebrity?" he complained. However, it seemed that nothing could hurt business. For 40 years or more, Vanessi's was jammed day and night. Then Joe died and something died with him. For all his faults and crassness, he was genuinely colorful and always attentive to the quality of his food. The last good chef there, Giovanni, left to open his own place farther up Columbus. Vanessi's partner, Bart Shea, tried to keep the restaurant going, but there were always seats at the counter, space at the bar, empty tables. The time had come.

⋆ ⋆ ⋆

After Vanessi's closed (New Joe's died long ago), the usual cry of "North Beach is dead!" was heard, but Broadway hasn't been North Beach for a long time. Old Broadway was that terrific cigar stand selling Marca Petris at the corner of Columbus. Fior d'Italia stood between Vanessi's and New Joe's, and over at Lupo's, Frankie Cantelupo would fall to his knees, beseeching you to try his latest pizza. The Manger, the Backyard—they were part of Broadway when it was North Beach. Lupo's still lives on as Tomasso's, and there's Little Joe's. Across Columbus, the Columbus Cafe is the last place in that block that hasn't become Asian. In the next block, Des Alpes struggles on. A couple of Basque places still exist, even if the Basque sheepherders have disappeared. But North Beach will always be alive, as long as there's a clove of garlic, a Verdi aria being sung badly in an upstairs flat, an accordion school, and old black-hatted gents on the benches in Washington Square, talking about their childhood in Lucca.

⋆ ⋆ ⋆

Broadway today is just another wide street with too much traffic. North Beach is just around the corner, as charming and irresistible as ever. *January 18, 1989*

Yes, that was songwriter-entertainer Bobby McFerrin standing forlornly alongside his broken-down Saab 9000 on Portola Drive last Wed., waiting for a tow truck. And it didn't help that passing motorists who recognized him slowed down long enough to holler, "Hey Bobby, don't worry, be happy!" *February 1, 1989*

An "only in San Francisco" grand slam in spades, doubled and redoubled (headlines on a press release rec'd yesterday): "San Francisco AIDS Foundation Set to Kick Off National Condom Week With Safe Sex Cable Car Tour." Couldn't they find a way to squeeze in Tony Bennett as the singing gripman? *February 10, 1989*

Deep Down Inside

Gut feelings. Like you, I get them regularly, and not necessarily from overindulging. Or call it a hunch, something so strong you'd stake your life on it. There is nothing scientific about this. It can't be analyzed, explained or compressed into a formula. It's just—There. Thirty seconds after meeting a guy, you know he's a phony. The alarms start ringing, but you're not sure why, except you know you're right. Ten seconds after that, you know it so strongly you walk away. Same thing with women. Thirty seconds after meeting this lady, you know something, yep, wonderful is going to happen. Maybe not in the next minute but—soon. So you don't walk away. Not that you're always right. When this hot dame turns out to be married to the phony, you may be wrong on both counts. Or neither.

* * *

Gut feelings. With 40 seconds to play in the Super Bowl, you'd have bet your right arm that Montana would find a way to win it. If you'd made the bet, you'd now own 1783 right arms, all from Cincinnati. Kirk Gibson's homer in the first game of the Series. You felt it coming, down there where it counts, in the pit, right under the breadbasket, where the butterflies of excitement hang out. It's a great, mysterious, mystical, metaphysical feeling. Such fun when you're right! Cal should've won the Big Game, but you KNEW that guy would miss the short field goal.

* * *

Your gut may lead you astray, but it's never wrong. You have to have the guts to act on it. When you don't and the moment passes, you forget about it, but the gut remembers that you were a gutless wonder. In gut we trust. Political hunch: You knew Dukakis was going to get whipped, no matter what the polls showed, or when. It was time for a Democrat, but he was the wrong one. Democrats were relieved when Dukakis lost. My gut tells me George Bush will turn out to be a pleasant surprise, despite his Iran-Contra numb-fumbling and his disastrous nomination of John Tower. You take one look at John Tower and what does your gut tell you? Believe it. Same with Jim Wright, the Texas Democrat who's Speaker of the House. Tip O'Neill, where are you? Your gut tells you Jim Wright is yet another snake oil salesman in the Year of the Snake. Gung hay fat chance. Texas Democrat is a self-cancelling phrase anyway.

⋆ ⋆ ⋆

I love San Francisco. That comes from the heart, not the gut, but I knew I was right from the start. When I was a kid of 10, the place got to me right in the old viscera. I was so dizzy with excitement, I didn't know what had hit me: the smells, the sounds, the downright noise, the people—demigods—on the streets. Palatial hotels, smart restaurants, chauffeurs and doormen, exciting bells and horns along the waterfront, the wail of the winch, the kick of the donkey engine, the metallic rattle of an anchor chain. My gut told me, "This is it! This is where I want to be." Like Professor Higgins, I've grown accustomed to its charms, but it still charms, even without a teeming waterfront, without a heavenly, smelly produce district where the rats chased the cats by midnight.

⋆ ⋆ ⋆

It doesn't take a gut feeling to know that the city has changed for the worse, but such is the way of cities when they grow up, grow old and are forced to face reality. My gut tells me we're not doing enough about the homeless or AIDS, both disgraces, but I have a hunch we never realized the magnitude of the problems. By comparison, the 1906 earthquake was easier. Now take Art Agnos, to whom a city looks for leadership. Jack Molinari might have made a better mayor, but he had the wrong campaign manager. My gut tells me that Art Agnos is a good man, a nice man. Heart in the right place and all that. My hunch is that he won't be able to handle all the problems he fell heir to, but maybe nobody could. He has a real plus in his camp. His wife, Sherry. It took my viscera less than 30 seconds to tell me that.

⋆ ⋆ ⋆

No wonder people get ulcers, heartburn, the shame of acid indigestion. And whatever happened to Carter's Little Liver Pills? They made the bile flow, and pretty soon "Happy Days Are Here Again!" What does your poor, overworked gut tell you about the Stealth bomber? Right. We're going to blow billions of dollars on a winged bummer. For that kind of money, you'd think we'd get a body and a tail, too. The abortion issue. What's the issue? A woman has the right to do what she wants with her own body, and nobody has the right to question it. Intellectualize it all you want, but down there where it counts, where it burns, you know from their track record that the "pro-life" types care deeply about babies—right up to the moment they're born.

⋆ ⋆ ⋆

I'll have to stop now. My stomach's killing me and we haven't even got around to the Giants and the acoustics at Davies Hall and what to do with the Presidio. Gimme a shot of Gaviscon with a Maalox float. *February 12, 1989*

Well, some progress is being made. I note that the graffiti on Muni buses now include actual words. Frexample, the rattler I rode on Wed. had "Comik" scrawled in several places. Definitely a step ahead. Teaching the comiks to spell is the next problem.

March 3, 1989

The Alaska oil spill must have reached San Francisco. At Sam's, the waiter asked whether I wanted my petrale leaded or unleaded. Or is it petraleum? *April 25, 1989*

Here comes a bike messenger, peddling furiously against the traffic. Horns honk and he flips a quick bird. He looks terrific: skinny, wiry, strong, and all on a diet of junque food, if that. I watch him run a light and do a skidding turn onto the sidewalk, where he almost hits a guy who shakes a fist and curses. People hate the bike messengers. I love 'em. They're dangerous and they live dangerously, all in the service of capitalism, consumerism or whatever you want to call it. OK, business. These kids are possibly radicals, and here they are risking life and limb—theirs and ours—to get those papers, packages and messages from one office to another, as fast and unsafely as possible. Devotion to duty, by golly. They've got it. That, and something that is fast disappearing from our drab little corporate world of paper-pushers and bean-counters. They are colorful.

⋆ ⋆ ⋆

San Francisco's bike messengers may be an endangered species in more than the obvious way. It's apparent that fax machines, the new menace to a leisurely, uncluttered life, can get a message from one place to another faster than even a suicidal messenger hunched over his pedals. The biggies in the package delivery business—UPS, Federal Express—do a bang-up job, and I'm not talking about fenders. And there are even "nice" messengers who wear uniforms. The heck with 'em. I'll take this crazy guy who wears his baseball cap backward and shouts at intersections. His socks and shoes don't match, his T-shirt is four sizes too large, his pants are so tight he looks like a beetle. Throw in a tattoo, a necklace and one earring and you've got A Look, as in terrific.

★ ★ ★

A fashion writer on one of those little S.F. magazines that come and go phoned me one day before hers went, never to be seen again. She was making a list of the city's 10 best-dressed people, and she wanted my nominations. Make your own list, it'll be as good or bad as anybody else's. Anyway, I said, "Any 10 bike messengers." She thought I was kidding, but I'm serious. They look right in the city of today. They go with all of it: the graffiti, the wavy traffic stripes, the signal-shooters, the double-parkers, the feelthy pigeons, the dirty streets, the eternal jackhammers, the fishy white bodies taking the sun on the grassy slopes of Union Square—a square, by the way, that could use a good lawn-mowing. In fact, I like the way all the young people dress these days. Street fashion is fun to look at. I enjoy the wild combinations, the anything-goes air, the pants that are too baggy and the shoes that are too heavy. A pretty girl in clunky shoes—who'd have thought that this could look sexy? But it does. *July 30, 1989*

For a cuuute firm name, how about Shut Up and Eat? That's comedian Jeff Hendricks and Don Rickard's newish cafe at 25th and Valencia. Michael Masry of Palm Springs ran across a dandy in Riverside: the Sweet Sleep Casket Gallery. With a layaway plan? He didn't ask. And Judy Lindberg found Cute Name heaven at the St. Louis Centre in that city. There, she lunched at Lettuce Quiche You, ordered pizza from First Federal Frank and Crust Co. (I say!) and bought candles at Wicks and Sticks.

But the foregoing are merely a buildup to the zinger, a new firm in Orinda called Sweet Revenge that supplies cow manure gift-wrapped in a bakery box for $18.75 plus $3 shipping charge. The bovine bouquet is just the thing to send to somebody who's been acting crappy lately, with a card reading "Have a nice day!" Co-owner Jennifer Sanders (her partner is Gayle Massey) says business is "fantastic." The plops, which they buy at nearby ranches, are "clean and nonsmelly" and approved by the Post Office and Dept. of Agriculture, if not Miss Manners. Did I hear you say, "Cow about that"? Moo. *August 14, 1989*

My spies tell me that Grace Cathedral has been experimenting with a product called Hot Foot to rid itself of pigeons, and what would our patron saint, Francis of Assisi, think about this? According to contemporary accounts in the Assisi three-dot columns, St. Francis loved birds and was often seen covered with pigeons, a saintly gesture at a time when dry-cleaning establishments were unknown. Hot Foot, so called because it burns pigeons' feet just enough to make them stop roosting, would undoubtedly bring a disapproving scowl to St. Francis' benign countenance. "It is not God's way," he would say, probably in Italian (he was born Giovanni di Bernardone, about 800 years ago). By the way, since pigeons love to roost, why aren't they called roosters? What?

* * *

A lot of people ask me if I hate pigeons, and the answer is no, even though I sometimes write disparagingly about their beastly habits. I hate no living things. I do hate inanimate objects, many of which are to be found at cocktail parties, holding highball glasses. Pigeons are preferable. Except for a certain body function that is perfectly natural, if overdone, they are helpless and lead a miserable claw-to-mouth existence. Do pigeons walk man-toed? No, but they do walk a lot on the hard pavement, which makes for sore feet. Last Tuesday, in front of Nordstrom on Fifth, I saw two pigeons limping badly. They probably had been shopping all day and couldn't find a thing to wear to the opera opening, which is Verdi's "Foulstuff," underwritten by Charles Squab. Squab is often served financiere.

* * *

Nevertheless, two facts must be faced: San Francisco's tourist business is off, and we have too many pigeons. Therefore, we should import peregrine falcons and install them on rooftops around Union Square and other places where pigeons hang out, smoke crack and exchange dirty jokes. This would create a terrific tourist attraction. Have you ever seen a falcon swoop down on its prey at 200 miles an hour? A thrilling sight, and one that is drawing crowds to the Las Vegas Hilton. That hotel has installed four peregrine falcons on its roof plus video cameras so guests can watch the attacks on their room TVs. Yes, it's nature in the raw and not for the fainthearted, but neither is trying to hit the hard eight at the craps table, where you are the pigeon, puss.

* * *

Well, pigeons are not an inexhaustible subject. Cheers! As the original dirty bird, they are roundly and even squarely disliked. They lead a hard life in a cold city. Perhaps they could be trained to carry messages, but who'd want to put the much more colorful bike messengers out of business? Getting the pigeons to go away is a major minor industry, but the late famous S.F. architect, Timothy Pflueger, solved the problem long ago. He designed the I. Magnin building at Geary and O'Farrell to be pigeonproof, and so it remains to this day, with no remains to be seen. There are absolutely no ledges for a squab to squat upon. Give a pigeon an inch and it'll take a youknowhat. Anyway, that's why pigeons shop at Nordstrom. *September 3, 1989*

A San Franciscan's priorities: Jacqueline West just bought a half-ounce bottle of Ferre perfume at I. Magnin—$110, plus tax—to add to the earthquake emergency kit she keeps at the front door of her Marina flat. *September 13, 1989*

If you were aboard a Powell cable climbing Nob Hill at around 5 p.m. Tues., you enjoyed a treat. Among the passengers was the great jazzinger, Margaret Whiting, who'd been shopping at Nordstrom with pal Denny Klein. As they rattled past Union Square, the gripman rapped out "clang clang clang went the trolley," whereupon Margaret sang "The Trolley Song" all the way up to California St. Now that is entrancing transit. *September 21, 1989*

Clichés updated: Nothing is certain except death and faxes.
September 24, 1989

Bay Area Rapid Typewriter

OK, let's talk baseball for a change.

I have before me a copy of the PG&E Progress, the monthly newsletter published by that struggling monopoly. The big black headline reads, "New Home for Giants," and under that, the bell-whopper: "Radiant Heat to Warm Fans at Night Games." Ah, the dreams, the hype, the bushwah.

The date on that issue of the Progress is August, 1959. Slack-jawed, we read on that "Candlestick Park, the beautiful new home of the San Francisco Giants, is designed especially for the Bay

Area's unique climate." Right, cold. "The pear-shaped park, nestled in a cove with a breathtaking view of San Francisco Bay, has been built at a cost of $11,000,000." It was especially breathtaking when the city dump was on the other side of Bayshore.

"From a standpoint of beauty and function," the Progress goes on, "it has been truthfully called one of America's most attractive athletic centers." Rivaled only by the recreation yard at San Quentin.

"It will be the only large stadium in the nation with radiant heating . . . A natural gas-fired boiler will send hot water through 35,000 feet of three-quarter inch pipe laid immediately below the precast concrete seats."

Fire the boiler. It never worked. Not a single patron suffered hotfoot. Chilblains, yes. Fortunately, despite the preceding paragraph, the seats weren't actually made of concrete, although, on cold nights, they felt that way. St. Bernards roamed the aisles with little casks of antifreeze hanging below their jowls and saved many lives.

The Progress article concludes: "Architect John S. Bolles took advantage of the terrain to deflect prevailing winds from the playing field and stands. Nestled against Bayview Hill, the stadium has a concrete shell baffle, shaped like a boomerang, to provide wind protection."

Worked like a charm. The wind boomeranged out and came right back, utterly baffling the shell.

★ ★ ★

And so life began a couple of decades ago in America's most maligned ballpark, the icy butt of so many bad jokes. The Froze Bowl, the Polar Grounds, the Diamond in the Dump, Candlestink and worse. The first Giants to play there were heroes. I never heard Mays, McCovey, Marichal or Cepeda complain about the cold. Johnny Antonelli beefed a lot, but he was a chronic whiner as well as winner. The club owner, Squire Horace Stoneham, survived with massive infusions of Dewar's White Label. He has been living in Arizona for many years now but still hasn't thawed completely.

As the years drifted by, the brute of a park became sort of lovable, if you like pit bulls and alligators. It is definitely grumpy, with no redeeming features, but when you sat through the full nine innings on an arctic night in the wind tunnel, you felt you had been tested and found insane. When the Giants began to win, the place sometimes seemed bearable, as in polar bearable.

During the series against the Cubs, of course, the weather

turned as balmy as the fans, and victory was sweet. But even with the flags drooping and the temperature at 80, old Candlestick looked as mean and ugly as ever. Grouchy to the end, it glowered down on the scenes of victory, steadfastly refusing to take part in the tribal rites. The place has character, no doubt of it.

* * *

So now, thanks to the miserable 'stick and the Giants' great home record, we are champions. Not yet world champions but champions nonetheless. As the toast of the National League, we San Franciscans are entitled to stand tall, walk with a swagger and even spit on occasion. It is considered gauche to spit in public, but baseball is a spitting game. People ask me why ballplayers spit more than other athletes. Football players can't spit because they're wearing face guards. (Bobby Hebert tried it in last Sunday's 49er game, to disastrous effect on nationwide TV.) Basketballers are too busy running. They could run into their own spit. Tennists are too polite. Baseball players spit because they're always chewing something, and it's either swallow or spit. The old-timers chewed a lot because the fields were dusty and their mouths got dry. The moderns chew because the old-timers did. I like everything about Will Clark except his chewing bubble gum. Bubble gum is for bubbleheads, not future immortals.

* * *

And so we head into the final golden days of a memorable season. My problem as a fan is that I can't hate enough. I tried to hate the Cubs, but they were sort of appealing, as are all gallant, doomed warriors. You knew they'd lose, and they knew you knew it. The A's are different, being infused with cockiness, success and talent, and are at least dislikable. The Giants do it with soul, spirit and the crazy devil-may-care attitude exemplified by Will Clark. I admire the Giants and am trying to detest the A's, but then I remember that San Franciscans are supposed to be cool. So all I will say, in a well-modulated voice, is, "Gentlemen, give them the old what for."

October 15, 1989

Days of Our Years

April 18, 1906. October 18, 1989. Yesterday dawned bright and beautiful—April 18, 1906, was said to have been a gorgeous morning, too—but there the comparisons stop. In '06, what reporter Will Irwin described as "the most pleasure-loving city of the Western continent" was destroyed by the fire that followed the earthquake. As of yesterday morning, San Francisco was surviving the great shake of 5:04 p.m. the day before, but make no mistake.

It is not the same city it had been up to a split-second before the earthquake struck with devastating force. The people of what is still "the most pleasure-loving city" were as badly shaken as the rest of the Bay Area. Suddenly and terrifyingly, they came face to face with the reality of life in this most fragile of cities. It CAN happen here again. And yet again. The price we pay for being San Franciscans is the never-ending threat of instant danger.

* * *

Nostalgics have romanticized the 1906 earthquake and fire into some kind of golden age, peopled with supermen and heroic women who never flinched and never cried. The legends lapse into caricature: Almost like characters in a musical comedy, our forebears whistled while they worked to rebuild the city, a task they performed almost overnight. San Franciscans ever since have been haunted by the tragedy and triumphs of '06. Would there be another major quake, and if so, how would we measure up against these heroes?

Well, 5:04 p.m. on October 17 was not quite like 5:13 a.m. on April 18, '06, but it did teach a lesson. There is nothing romantic about a massive earthquake. Given the choice, avoid it. It is sheer terror, followed by horror. Nobody is untouched. You may laugh, you may cry, you may congratulate yourself on your luck, but you are still emotionally drained. And, yes, there undoubtedly are heroes around. Perhaps the survivors of the Great Earthquake of '89 will start gathering 50 years hence at Lotta's Fountain at 5:04 p.m. to celebrate them.

* * *

Tuesday was a perfect day for baseball. One couldn't help thinking of old Ernie Banks, the perennially upbeat Chicago Cub, who was famous for beaming, "What a beautiful day—let's play two!" In the morning, we were joking about how the Oakland A's had beaten the Giants twice in San Francisco weather, cold and overcast. Now the A's were on our side of the bay, and the weather was unaccountably balmy, as it had been for the playoffs. Nobody talked about "earthquake weather." As Dr. Richter of The Scale has taught us, there is no such thing.

The Giants fans crowding into Candlestick were fired up after hours of partying in the parking lots. "Oakland fans are wimps," said a guy on the escalator. "We're gonna make some real NOISE, we're gonna root the Giants to victory!" His eyes were shining. In fact, as the stadium filled, there was already a roar. The energy and the excitement were palpable.

At 5:03 p.m., Sandy Walker and I were standing in a long line for beers. A minute later, we were reeling and hanging on to each other for support. "Earthquake!" I hollered. In the crowd's sudden silence, you could hear the old concrete structure grinding away, its steel bones bending but not, thankfully, breaking. The floor rippled and shook for what seemed like 30 seconds.

The terrified young women behind the beer counter stood rooted under swaying signs. They were statues with bulging eyes, holding empty glasses. Candlestick slowly settled back into place, more or less. There was an instant babble of excited talk. The guy at the head of the line pounded on the counter and complained, "Hey, what about our beers?" His remark seemed like a return to normality but in retrospect, it had a surreal quality.

⋆ ⋆ ⋆

I am also surprised to recall that Sandy and I continued to stand in line for our beers. After we got them, we wandered down into the stands. At that point, nobody realized the size of the quake or its seriousness. Nervous jokes were flying around. "Was it a 6 or what?" "When it gets to 7—sell!" A girl sang "Shake, Rattle and Roll." The word heard most often was "eerie." The swaying light towers, their power off, were definitely that. So was the sight of Jose Canseco and Mark McGwire, nervously playing catch in lieu of something better to do.

Gradually, the realization grew that there would be no game. The party was over. Perhaps the Series was over. Maybe the quake had saved the Giants. The crowd began heading for the exits, to jeers from the diehards: "Chicken!" Outside, one of the all-time great traffic jams was building up. Once you had left the briefly festive atmosphere of the ballpark, it became apparent that something awful had happened. The laughter stopped. The jokes died. The mood turned somber. People were glued to their radios. Commentators said that the earthquake "put things into perspective." Right. There is more to life than baseball. Death, for instance.

⋆ ⋆ ⋆

When the power is out and an emergency is on, there is nothing like radio. On KCBS, that great pro Jan Black was anchoring a remarkably fast and frightening report on the disaster. No doubt the TV people were doing equally well, but I had no way of checking. We drove inch by inch toward a city that looked stricken—very few lights, no traffic signals, the constant sound of sirens, street corner flares and volunteer traffic controllers. On the whole, people behaved well at the intersections, crossing alternately, but there are always the few who refuse to play the game. Watch out for them during the next catastrophe.

At one intersection on Third St., a young jerk in a white car refused to back up, thereby blocking hundreds of cars. A bearded man walked over to him from the sidewalk and said, "Brother, you are causing gridlock. Why don't you let these people through? You're not going anywhere anyway." "F—— 'em," said the young jerk, hunkering down behind the wheel. The bearded man tried a few more times and then gave up. Shaking his head, he said, "May God be with you, brother," and walked away.

★ ★ ★

Yesterday morning, the city was in a strange holiday mood. The neighborhood streets were filled with people enjoying a rare day off on a beautiful day. They sunbathed on the sidewalks or drove around in open cars, jeering at the tourists checking out of the Nob Hill hotels: "Whatsammater, afraid?" Hundreds were drawn to Fillmore and Broadway, with its view of the hard-hit Marina. The bar at the Balboa was jammed. Everywhere you looked, there were knots of people in summer clothing, comparing notes, answering the inevitable question, "Where were you when ———?" There was the feeling of family that comes with shared experience and the mood was upbeat. We had come face to face with the beast. And here we still were, filing memories for future reference.

October 19, 1989

Literal namedrop: The shake knocked an array of memorabilia off the top of a bookcase in my office, revealing an item I'd forgotten—a real can of Campbell's Tomato Juice autographed "To Herb—Andy Warhol." That must be worth something. Not even a line? . . . Add sightems that stick: Japanese tourists aiming their cameras at windowless (except for the ground floor) I. Magnin. Shopping? . . . Further eyetem: people congregating on stoops, steps and sidewalks. At a time like this, they hate to be alone. On Sacramento Street, an attractive widow I know only slightly said, "I've been alone in my apartment all day, feeling so lonely. PLEASE give me a hug."

★ ★ ★

Speaking of all alonely, Clara Shirpser, the 88-year-old onetime member of the Democratic National Committee, has been trapped on the 10th floor of 1201 California. No power, no water, she couldn't raise the building manager, and "I'm too crippled to walk downstairs." Grace Cathedral promised to send help . . .

October 20, 1989

Can the events of the past few days, plus the postponement of the World Series, be summed up in three words? Maybe so. Yesterday, Phyllis Winter of Lagunitas found herself driving behind a car sporting the old environmental bumper sticker: "Nature Bats Last" . . . A great woman, Phyllis. She's the first in her neighborhood to sport a T-shirt inscribed "Thank You For Not Sharing Where You Were When The Quake Struck" . . .

★ ★ ★

. . . All in all, Tom Rooney is not too displeased with the events of the week. "Survivors of the 1906 earthquake have to be up at 5:13 a.m. to observe the anniversary," he says. "We can have our reunions at 5:04 p.m., just in time for cocktails.

October 21, 1989

Disjointed thoughts: It's Sunday and you can still hear the sirens. Only five days have passed since E-Day but the little world of San Francisco has changed. We look at the city and each other in a different way than we did before 5:04 p.m. last Tuesday. Life as we lived it seems to have taken place years before. Did we really get that worked up about graffiti? Or care so desperately about the Giants and A's? We did, and perhaps we will again.

The unlikely cry of "Play ball!" will ring out at Candlestick on Friday. The World Series must be completed, if only because nature abhors a vacuum (and seems to have mixed feelings about this area, providing beauty and disasters). Besides, maligned Candlestick rates a tribute for having stayed in one piece, and the fans deserve the games for having behaved in exemplary fashion. And slowly, the native wits are returning to action.

"If God had wanted the Giants to have a new stadium," says Tom Youngblood, "He wouldn't have let Candlestick survive." A miracle indeed: If the top deck had dropped, as seemed likely for those chilling few seconds, thousands would have perished. Gary Hanauer thinks Jose Canseco got off a quote for the ages: "I was in right field. At first I thought it was another of my migraines but it was just an earthquake."

★ ★ ★

. . . During a memorial service at Grace Cathedral yesterday, Dean Alan Jones predicted that "Even at the end of the world, somebody will be selling T-shirts." *October 23, 1989*

Steve Schaer's T-shirt: "I Went to the Series at Candlestick and All I Got Was This Lousy Earthquake . . . *October 24, 1989*

We Are the New Survivors

Outwardly, it looks almost the same, this misty city clinging to the edge of the world. The joggers are back on Chestnut St. in the Marina. To cheers and applause from passers-by on slanty California St., the cable cars went back into service with a cheery clang, proceeding at precisely the same speed—nine miles an hour—they'd achieved in 1872, when they were invented.

At lunchtime, the dice cups rattle and bang in dozens of old-time eating and drinking establishments; shaking for the check is a lusty San Francisco tradition that no amount of shaking can halt. South of Market, South o' the Slot, the ancient paint-starved wooden buildings lean against each other for support along the alleys named for such long-gone but no doubt admirable ladies as Clara and Clementina, Jessie and Minna.

Let's hear it for these rickety old wrecks! For years now, their skinny frames have hung out over the streets, looking as though one good push would topple them, let alone a 7.1 earthquake, but they still stand, defying gravity, the odds and the inspectors. Truly they are the spirit of old San Francisco—bent but not broken, tipsy but on their feet, stubborn as sin and almost as defiantly ugly.

Yes, we have survived the heaviest hammer blow since the dawn of April 18, 1906—a day that has haunted our dreams—and we have reason to congratulate one another on having survived. That's what those who lived through the '06 firequake proudly called themselves—"The Survivors." They were the aristocrats of this earthly paradise, this treasure that Mark Twain once called "heaven on the half shell."

We have lost much—too much—but we have gained much, too. The ghosts and demons of 83 years ago have been exorcised.

Our city is not going up in flames but lives have been lost, buildings have come crashing down and the damage is being counted in the billions.

The chain of hellish, difficult and sometimes even amusing events that began at 5:04:30 on Tuesday, October 17, continues to keep our small world off-balance, but we have handled it well. The question that has tormented generations of San Franciscans—could we face a major catastrophe with the cocky courage and elan of our forebears?—has now been answered.

At last, and at great cost, we have been validated as San Franciscans. We are the new survivors.

⋆ ⋆ ⋆

People live here by choice, knowing the risks. "San Francisco" and "earthquake" are almost synonymous in the minds of millions around the world, which accounts for the tremendous media interest in this city's travails—and those in Oakland—almost to the exclusion of even more stricken parts of the quake area. From the Gold Rush onward, San Francisco has been a fascinating object.

The pioneers set the style and tone that exist to this day. Those that had it spent it—and not always wisely, splurging fortunes on hideous huge houses, on demimondaines that were at least preferable to their horsey wives, and on suckers' schemes to make another fortune.

There was and is a certain wildness in the air, a "tomorrow we die" attitude based on the unspoken awareness that the earth could open up in the next instant and swallow it all—from the baroque palaces of Nob Hill to the gaming houses of the Barbary Coast. That attitude has carried over to this day. It may account for the city's hedonistic devotion to good food and strong drink (the old town's fabulous eating troughs were famous around the world long before the idea of a "celebrity chef" was born).

The knowledge that disaster lurks just below the earth's crust may account for our high incidence of alcoholism, of suicides off the elegantly aloof Golden Gate Bridge, of wild excesses in our ways of living, laughing, lying and dying. Under its polished overlay of cynical sophistication, San Francisco is still a frontier town. The narcissism that so annoys and mystifies "the outsiders," a term of derision, comes from self-awareness. We know we are different. We like being different. Sometimes we go to outlandish lengths to be different, simply to shock "the outsiders."

We don't think we are odd for living right here in Quiver City.

We think people like Jesse Helms, Jim Bakker and Dan Quayle are odd.

* * *

It has been a long—what is it now?—nine days. Nine days that shook our snug and sometimes smug little world and allowed the outside world, the one we like to keep at bay, to come in and look us over with its Cyclopean camera eye. We are not the same city or the same people we were the instant before H-Hour on Q-Day.

It is considered hip or at least fashionably insouciant to reiterate that it was not The Big One, it was just the Almost Big One or the Little Big One. For those who died and those who lost everything, it was The Big One, period.

In some ways, the day after the earthquake did seem like the first day of the rest of our lives. The people held up admirably and worked together with spirit and strength, but everyone was in shock. The city we love had taken a blow to the head that left it groggy. Still on its feet, yes, but the haymaker came frighteningly close to a knockout.

When our vision cleared, we saw San Francisco in a clearer light. It was like rediscovering our feelings for this unpredictable, wild and wildly fascinating place. We realize afresh the joys and dangers of living here, and we reaffirm our belief that it is worth the gamble, however great. We know the pluses—the history, the traditions, the laughter on the hills, the freshness of the constant winds of change. And we have been reminded, with a sharp jolt, of the minuses.

These we can do something about. "Earthquake preparedness" is no longer a phrase to glaze the eyes. Too boring, my dears. Yes, killingly so, old chums. Now let's buckle down and see if we can atone for our sins of omission. Our sins of commission we know all too well.

I suppose we look a little different now to "the outsiders," who made fun of, and often seriously criticized, our wicked, wicked ways. Perhaps we look "better," whatever that means, but who cares? We like ourselves pretty much the way we are, and we are proud of the way our amazingly varied population rallied around. Hemingway would have admired the grace under pressure, the gallantry of those who worked around the clock, the generous spirit of the volunteers.

The city is different now. Quieter, sadder. Too many have died who needn't have. There has been carelessness, some of it to a scandalous degree. To those who were in the wrong place at the wrong time, a salute and silence. Life is a lottery, and it doesn't even out. We speak of fate and we talk of miracles but it is all blind luck, a cosmic joke in the worst possible taste.

It is time to heal the wounds and get on with the life of this great place on the edge of forever. There is much work to be done. The playing can come later, when we come to grips with what really happened and what we might have done to prevent it.

October 26, 1989

Yes, the quake was felt even in hushed Hillsborough, where Ann Lane dashed across the living room and, like Jerry Rice in the end zone, caught a valuable vase in mid-air. When told of this incident, their friend, Frosty Knoop, inquired, "Did she spike it?"

November 8, 1989

Life Is an Item

Items are my game. Items are stories boiled down down to the bone. Some are pseudo-stories, the shorter the better. Somebody said something to somebody that sounded funny at the time. In cold type in the cold light of the morning of the cold cereal and the cold coffee, it doesn't read funny. It lies there like the oat bran in the bowl. Maybe nobody will read it anyway, any way at all. The paper comes out and vanishes. Forgotten by 10, dead by noon, pulped by dark. And there's always tomorrow. That's the hell of it. All these wonderful people slaving desperately to put out the paper each day, a prodigious achievement, and by 11 a.m. you see it fluttering down the street. More clutter for litterbugs. Please use the trash container. Thank you.

* * *

Life is an item. You can write it either way, long or short. A beginning, a middle and an end, not necessarily in that order, as writer Herbert Gold said. Some lives end at the beginning but take on a false life of their own and continue to the end, which is always the same. Curtains, fadeout, The Big Sleep (Raymond Chandler). In San Francisco, life can be sweet. All the ingredients are here. Good people, good places, good attitude. These are generalities. The luck, she has to be running good (fake Hemingway). Nevertheless, San Francisco is good for most people. For others, life can be

Hobbesian, nasty, brutish, short. A long judgment with short words. My kind of item.

* * *

San Francisco, a small, well-crafted item, rare, expensive, sparkling, depressing. A city you can wear on your charm bracelet or around your neck. A pet of a city that will turn on you without warning. Housebroken but not tamed. Housebroken. A word that lends itself to jokes about the housing shortage, the high price of housing, the oxymoronic joke of affordable housing. Or hosing. San Francisco: a problem, a conundrum, a place you love to hate and hate to leave. Deadly, as only a female can be deadly (not even Mickey Spillane). "I love San Francisco." No item. It's something people have been saying since the beginning of Pacific Standard Time. How do you love a city? You love her essence, her midnight song as she nibbles your ear. She is seductive, she can shimmy and shake, she can sing "Drunk With Love," but she doesn't always return your phone calls.

* * *

It gets dark earlier now. No item. I walk the streets, spiral-bound notebook ready. Items all around, unfit to print. Dead and not so dead bodies in doorways and strewn on the sidewalks. Disposable but not recyclable. Dregs on drugs, wacks on crack, moochers on the make. Item: The Tenderloin is getting no better. It is getting no worse. It just is, an endless source of misery, joy and fascination. A place for voyeurs with notebooks and cameras. Sure I am fascinated by the Tenderloin. Hookers of all sexes speaking in tongues. Skinny guys with automatic weapons, right there on the street. Dark laughter in the underbelly. These people love each other right up to the moment they kill each other. They embrace, they kiss, they walk arm-in-arm in the fraternity of the damned. They die with a smile, happy.

* * *

Item: San Francisco is the most beautiful city in the world that has suicide and cirrhosis among its top 10 killers. It is a city where everything and nothing happens. Millions are collected for the homeless, and the homeless proliferate. Nothing gets done. The guy with the spiral-bound notebook calls various people in charge of these things. "We are doing the best we can," plaintively, in the voice of a guy who is late for lunch. Good town for lunch. It is a city that votes right but still gets everything wrong. A city with a unique voting record: McGovern, Mondale, Jesse Jackson, that Greek fellow from Massachusetts with the wife, yeah, that one. In

San Francisco, courageous people can demonstrate against the outrages of the right wing in El Salvador and still get clubbed by the police.

* * *

The night comes early now. Even in the dark, the new Marriott Hotel, the Palace of Ming the Merciless, glows like a living thing. St. Ignatius Church shines on its hilltop, a beacon of hope and beauty, but let us not discuss freedom of choice. Did the fisherman of Galilee say, "Don't rock the boat"? Not in so many words. The big holidays are with us now through the end of the year. The big holidays and the big depression. Item: San Francisco is a great party town. We may have forgotten everything else, but we can still throw parties, maybe the best in the world. Short days and long nights for dancing till dawn. Then the big hangover, the big depression. The trip to the bridge. The sun is rising out of Contra Costa. The city looks golden, fresh, alluring. What the hell, give it one more day.

* * *

Life is a bad item, short but pointless. You stand at the bar and play liar's dice with fate. It's the San Francisco way. You might win, and even if you lose, the scenery's great and the weather isn't too bad.

November 26, 1989

You Must Remember This

Yes, tonight's the night. At midnight we sing "Auld Lang Syne," whatever that means, and embrace perfect strangers. Why is it that only strangers are perfect? Once you get to know them, they're like the rest of us. Flawed. Remember the joke about the young lady who went over to this bachelor's apartment and discovered he had no furniture? "Boy, was I floored!" she said. But, being English, she said, "flawed." I'm struggling here to say something about New Year's Eve, another holiday that floors me. I mean, what exactly are we celebrating? The fact that wine and horses are a year older? So are we. After you reach a certain age, this is hardly a cause for celebration. That's why we drink so much on New Year's Eve, and what is there to be said for a year that starts with a hangover?

* * *

This one is Important, however, with a capital "I." It's the end of a decade, even though the purists can prove that it really isn't.

Who cares? Accuracy can be so tedious. The newspapers have been busily—yes, and tediously—recapping the '80s, which actually have a year to go, but it's the numbers that count. Personally, if I had the nine years of the 1980s to live over again, I'd be delighted. My favorite memory is provided by a septuagenarian lady of my acquaintance who said shortly after Mr. Reagan took office: "I'm about the same age he is. Every now and then he must walk into the Oval Office and say to himself, "Now what did I come in here for?" Turned out it didn't matter. Nancy ran the country and Joan Quigley, the San Francisco astrologer, ran Nancy, so the country was being run out of an apartment up there on Nob Hill. Isn't that scary?

★ ★ ★

People go on making New Year's resolutions as though they really believe they can change overnight. Forget it. Once a frog, always a frog, even if you're a prince of a fellow. However, a few resolutions are in order. In the immortal words of the great orator, Chauncey Depew, "I am not at all superstitious, but I would not sleep 13 in a bed on a Friday night." In 1990, the last year of the 1980s, I will stop picking on Art Agnos. He hasn't done anything. I will be nicer to the pigeons. They are only doing what comes naturally. I will double the daily allowance of my favorite street people from one buck to two. I will stop drinking Stoli on the rocks. A splash of soda can't make that much difference. I will get some new batteries for my flashlight, in case there's another earthquake. Oh, speaking of my favorite street people, I've lost track of the guy whose sign read "Spare Cash For White Trash." Anybody seen him?

★ ★ ★

For the line that best sums up the Reagan-Bush years, Jack Bunzel nominates Oliver North's testimony that "As best I can recall, I can't recall." A lot has been written about greed in the '80s, but so what? Greed is a great motivator, said Ivan Boesky, who motivated himself right into prison. For me, the lowest form of greed is displayed by athletes who charge kids for their autographs. Hard to sink much lower than that, and I don't care what the rationale is. OK, so some of those guys have a hard time writing. That brings to mind Pete Rose, who got into trouble for betting on Steve Garvey in the Breeders' Cup, or something like that. I also think of Jose Canseco, who did a commercial for an Oakland booster group. Mr. Sincerity! "Living and working in Oakland is more of a thrill than hitting a home run," said Mr. Canseco, who lives in

Florida. At the beginning of the season, he spent more time in a police lineup than in the A's'.

* * *

Old '89 had more ups and downs than a cable car, still our best form of transportation. Of all the technological advances, I still say one-hour photo developing is the greatest. Don't knock the quartz watch, either. For the best cute firm name, I nominate the House of Ill Compute, a computer repair shop. There were lots of Dan Quayle jokes but he himself was hard to top. Steve Baker got off the smile of the year: "As badly attended as a Salman Rushdie look-alike contest." One of our really distinguished writers, Wallace Stegner, turned 80 and said, "If you're going to get old you might as well get as old as you can get." Bumper snicker of the year: "It's Great To Be Alive in Colma." Button worn by a punkette cashier at Tower Records: "If We Ate What We Listened To We'd All Be Dead." Enrico's Coffee House closed and I still miss those three little hamburgers.

* * *

We survived an earthquake in grand style, we voted the Giants out of town and we learned to live with voice mail, Roseanne Barr, Valentines via fax and car alarms that go off in the middle of the night. At midnight, I raise my glass to you and say "Cheers, old friend. We've been through a lot and a lot has been through us. Let's keep doing what we're doing—it seems to work." See you in a couple of weeks—I'm goofing off. Happy New Year and let's meet at the Super Bowl. *December 31, 1989*

1990

Now then: Tear down the Embarcadero Freeway! There, I feel better already. For years, I wanly defended the undoubted eyesore because it provided a nifty view from the upper deck and a speedy way to get from The Chron to North Beach for lunch with Don Sherwood and Barnaby Conrad at Enrico's or Vanessi's. But times and minds change. Enrico's and Vanessi's on Broadway are closed, Don Sherwood is dead and Barnaby has moved to Carpinteria. I think what finally got to me was lobbyist Rose Pak's specious and tedious complaints that the freeway's closure hurts business in Chinatown. Don't kid a kidder, Rose. The freeway is a lot more important to North Beach, and nobody there is putting up that argument, besides which who drives to Chinatown? So tear it down. I'll be happy to see the last of that stub end, which nobody ever had the decency to cover with a giant Band-Aid.

January 23, 1990

What is there to say? You saw it all, even if you didn't believe what you were seeing. It was not the Superbore from Hell, it was Super Bowl XXIV from New Orleans, the San Francisco killers vs. the Denver meatballs. Here, in one of the world's great party towns, Joe Montana and his mates committed murder and mayhem. Down the drain went two weeks of buildup and baloney, replete with warnings about overconfidence and predictions that "it could be closer than you think." The experts who made the 49ers a huge favorite were right all the way, erring only on the conservative side.

Denver, the mile-high city, must be feeling even lower than John Elway. It's San Francisco that's the mile-high city today, riding a mile high over the world of football, wherein Montana is king of all he surveys. He may still be looking for the Denver defense. Meanwhile, he has four Super Bowl rings, the Niners have won two in a row, and a legend has been born that will live forever wherever football filberts gather to play trivia.

Montana, Rice, Craig, Rathman, Taylor, Jones, Ronnie the Lott and the rest of the lot. They blew out the Broncos and they blew CBS' TV ratings off the air. By the fourth quarter, the Superdome was emptying fast and up there in the broadcast booth, Pat Summerall and John Madden wore the expression of people who knew they were talking only to themselves. *January 29, 1990*

For those who are tired of football stories—shake, pal—let me tell you about Scott M. King, who lives on Monterey Blvd., and Scott R. King, who lives on Montgomery St. For years, of course, they have been getting each other's mail and phone calls, but that's only the beginning of the coincidences. Scott M. owns Sugar Happy, which delivers supplies to diabetics. Scott R. is president of Thymax Corp., a research group seeking a cure for diabetes. Not only that, both Scott Kings are diabetics themselves, something they found out when they finally met, for the first time, at a UCSF conference on diabetes. Both are in their early 30s and have quite enough in common to become good friends.

February 1, 1990

A graffito for the '90s, spotted in Berkeley by Albert Levy: "I wept because I had no shoes. Then I met a man who had a fine pair of shoes. So I beat him up and took them for myself."

February 7, 1990

Hide and Seek

She's still out there somewhere, hiding behind the infernal towerings, dancing across concrete meadows, cackling like Laughin' Sal as she dashes into the rollers at Ocean Beach, getting her white silk robes wet and dirty with sand.

Sometimes we see her flitting across the lawn behind Coit Tower, throwing a kiss to almost-forgotten artists who wore berets and worked for the WPA. Now she's doing figure eights around the Ferry Building tower, where she once played as a girl, and then she blazes across the hills and flatlands to the Palace of Fine Arts, posing for a laugh alongside Bernard Maybeck's weeping figures.

She is elusive, a wisp, a misty dancer doing a slow Castle Glide as Art Hickman's band plays his classic hit, "Rose Room," at the St. Francis. In the marbled and pillared lobby, she is moved to laughter as the eccentric architect, Willis Polk, tries to stand on his head. Brushing a kiss he never felt across his furrowed brow, she drifts through the revolving door and twinkles her way along Chinatown's alleys, pausing at the spot where Little Pete was gunned down by a rival tongster.

* * *

North Beach is closing down as she floats dreamlike up Columbus Avenue. The opera stars—Mary Golden, Schipa, Martinelli—have stopped their drinking and singing at Papa Coppa's, where an inscription on the wall warns that "Paste Makes Waist." It is near dawn now and the bakeries are aglow with rising loaves of sourdough. She sniffs appreciatively.

As the sun rises over the bridgeless Bay crisscrossed with ferry tracks, she draws her white robes closer around her, pulls her hood over her head and disappears into her favorite hideaway, the Golden Gate Park of Uncle John McLaren. Swanlike, she glides across a secret, still lake, admiring her reflection. She is loved, she is carefree, she is admired by all the world.

* * *

She is San Francisco, once the girl of our dreams, now a woman grown old. The white robes, all satin and silk, are dirty and frayed. She hides from the bright sunlight. The years have been kind, but the long nights have taken a toll, not to mention the terrapin imported from Maryland and the magnums of Bollinger, the scandals and disasters, the earthquakes and fires that had her running for her life in red slippers torn to shreds.

Yet she is still a beauty. There is something about the way she carries herself. The eyes are old, wise and sad. She gazes constantly into the far distance but she is seeing all the yesterdays, the friends who made her laugh and spoiled her to death, the enemies who were jealous of her beauty and fame.

* * *

She is still alive, an aging little girl lost trying to find her way through the canyons and concrete forests of the new city. Now and then her laugh has its old, sexy tingle as she recognizes the places where she was young and eager. At Jack's, she looks long at the corner table, under the steps, where Louis Lurie sat behind a big cigar and bought a city. She is pleased to see her old friend Willis Polk's Hobart Bldg. but laments the passing of the Fitzhugh.

She worries about the old Palace Hotel, the hangout of so many of her ardent admirers—John Francis Neylan and Garret McEnerney, Paul Smith and Clarence Lindner, Colonel Kirkpatrick (the inventor of Oysters Kirkpatrick) and the extravagantly dressed Lucius Beebe, wearing his diamond gardenia boutonniere. Few people loved her more than Lucius, or drank champagne more often from her red slippers. Silently, she makes her ethereal rounds through the new restaurants and bars, approving of a few, curling her nose at others, the ones that lack the style. San Francisco was all style. She liked the mansions and the peak-roofed houses of the Mission, she liked to steal rides on the iron monster streetcars with their real leather seats and proper motormen. She liked the swagger of Sunny Jim Rolph as he danced with his Hollywood movie star friend at Edgewater Beach, she liked the strutting Jake "The Master" Ehrlich, with his starched handkerchiefs that flowered from his breast pocket.

For a while she liked the hippies, especially doomed Janis Joplin and honest Jerry Garcia. She misses the noisy fun of El Prado restaurant at noon, with all the ladies in their flowered hats imploring a perspiring Walter Glinsky to find them a table, any table. There is no scene like that around Union Square any longer. She is no longer happy in Union Square. And she is downcast on Broadway, remembering the Mastersounds at the Jazz Workshop, Woody Allen lunching alone at Enrico's newfangled Coffee House ("Don't you dare call it a coffee shop!") and the young socialites, wild as she was once, carousing at Barnaby Conrad's Matador.

* * *

Every day we gaze out at the city, looking for San Francisco. Sometimes we think we see her, here and there between the high-rises, or perhaps along the Embarcadero or in the hideaways of the Arboretum. We know she is still alive, living on in memories and wondering if she is still loved. Loved she is. And too often missed.

February 11, 1990

Front-page Chron headline: "Hockey Team Interested in Oakland." Give it to them. *February 12, 1990*

To our list of timely warnings (sleeping pills labeled "May Make You Drowsy," hair dryers that caution, "Do Not Use While Asleep") add this notice on the cloth towel dispenser at Luxor Cab: "Do not attempt to hang from towel or insert your head into the towel loop. Failure to follow these instructions can be harmful or injurious." Right. If you want to kill yourself, just step in front of a cab.

February 13, 1990

Jack London's 90-yr-old dghtr, Becky, was at the Palace of Fine Arts yesterday for the 75th annvy. of the opening of the 1915 World's Greatest Fair; asked to say a few words, she shivered, "My heavens, it's cold. If Jack were here he'd have left!"

February 21, 1990

WHERE ELSE?

Where else but in San Francisco would you find four guys wearing white-tie and tails and baseball caps playing Bach and Mozart on saxophones while seated on a busy downtown street corner? Don't ask me. I can't be everywhere at once. Maybe they have saxophone quartets in Snohomish, Washington, or Chillicothe, Ohio, and if so, I'd like photographic evidence.

Meanwhile, it was Saturday. The city was experiencing its usual 100 microclimates per minute, from rain to sunshine to icy winds direct from Kodiak to waves of fog crashing silently over the Heights. A day for trench coat and sunglasses. Rich kids drove around in their Volkswagen Cabriolets with top down, heater on and stereo blasting ka-boom ka-boom. I walked down Powell alongside a cable car with a flat wheel. It was going ka-boom ka-boom, too. A cable car with a flat wheel sounds like a toothache.

I window-shopped my way along the Post Promenade to Grant, which was where I discovered the San Francisco Saxophone Quartet playing outside Brooks Bros., with about 100 people listening respectfully. Along with wearing tails and baseball caps, these guys are artists, which most street artists aren't. They were playing the haunting slow movement of Mozart's quartet No. 15 (K. 421) and a tear trickled down my grizzled cheek. At the end, everybody applauded warmly and rushed forward to throw green stuff into a box on the sidewalk.

The S.F. Saxophone Quartet is composed of David Schrader, soprano; Bill Aron, alto; David Henderson, tenor; and Kevin Stewart, baritone. Fred Tice, mgr. of Brooks Bros., said: "I wish I could hire them on a permanent basis—they're good for business." They also provided one of those increasingly rare "only in San Francisco" moments. As I said earlier, there may be equally talented sax quartets in Snohomish and Chillicothe but I'll have to check it out.

* * *

It was a good Saturday downtown. Lots of people, including tourists consulting maps. Maybe They are back at last. Oh, bless Them if They are. We welcome Them with open palms. I trudged up the stairs from Stockton to Bush, alongside the Stockton tunnel. The graffiti is worse than ever. Kids, this is really boring and also uncool and unhip. Graffiti-scrawling has died out in New York—to be replaced by something worse, no doubt—and here we are still afflicted with it. "Graffiti artist"—there's a self-cancelling phrase. Humming the opening bars of Mozart's symphony No. 29, I puffed up Bush past Burritt St., where Brigid O'Shaughnessy gunned down Sam Spade's partner, Miles Archer, in "The Maltese Falcon." At Powell, I paused to admire the Kenilworth Apts., named for the racehorse that won some long-forgotten Derby and paid enough to build that landmark. Oh, it's one colorful city and I don't mean Chillicothe.

* * *

All in all, a salubrious weekend in this small wonder of the Western world, trembling on the brink of spring. Cut out the trembling. Let us not scare Them away again. Early on Saturday eve, the Hard Rock Cafe was the place to be for some serious people-watching. The Hard Rock is loud, the service is terrific, the food is affordable as well as edible, and the crowd is all duded up, the dudes eyeing the chicks and the chicks pretending not to notice. There were guys in crazy haircuts wearing tuxes and ladies in what we used to call "formals," loading up on burgers, beers and burps because it was—Bammie night!

Even though rock hasn't gone anywhere since the Eagles, Foreigner and maybe even the much-despised Journey, the Bammies are one of the great S.F. shows of the year, the others being the opera opening, the Black & Blue Ball and the Dandelion Festival at Strybing Arboretum. Comedian Doug Ferrari, wearing tails, of course, was the emcee and did a remarkable job under the circumstances. The mike was on. Only kidding, Doug! I took note of the really important things, such as Bonnie Raitt's wheels, which are excellent, and tried to figure out why rap is sort of a hit. Rock may have run into a wall but if rap is the answer, forget the question. We've gone from four basic chords to one and soon, if we're lucky, there may be none.

I do believe the tourists are back. Sunday, Chinatown was jammed with the camera-crested beauties, spilling off the narrow sidewalks and dodging crazed drivers looking for parking spaces that no longer exist. I dropped in for a healer and some pot stickers at the Imperial Palace, the only restaurant in Chinatown that still has a uniformed doorman and waiter captains in tuxedoes. Only in Snohomish.

★ ★ ★

I don't think this is an excloo, but spring is here! Moe Gavam was the first to remind me that it arrives today at precisely 1:19 p.m., a matter of interest to Moe because that also marks the beginning of Persian New Year (happy 1368) and he is Persian. Actually, spring arrived Sunday night when I turned on Ch. 2 and discovered the baseball lockout, strike or whatever is over and we can begin arguing again over really important matters, such as Clark vs. Canseco, Lurie vs. Haas and so on. The Ch. 2 reporter was interviewing the stoned and stunned regulars at Lefty O'Doul's, a place he described as being on "Geary Boulevard." Geary Street, please. The so-called boulevard begins at Gough and continues out to the fog bank.

Spring is here but we didn't earn it, which diminishes the sacred moment. We didn't struggle through a long hard winter, unfortunately. The rains never came but the tourist drought may be ending. One last thing: It's OK to eat fresh tuna. A lot of coastal fishermen have been hurting because of the save-the-dolphins boycott, but their tuna is correct in every way, including the ingestion thereof. *March 20, 1990*

Let's hope this is a trend. At Washington and Polk, Betsy Day and David King ran across a scruffy kid on a skateboard carrying a boombox that was blaring Sousa's "Stars and Stripes Forever."

March 21, 1990

Into the mist: He was a great guy—lean, mean and salty, with a bit of a swagger. For years, he cast a long shadow over San Francisco waterfront, for better or worse but definitely for history. To his followers, he was a hero; to his enemies, "the man who killed the Port." Either way, he was a hard-boiled original, a man of integrity, a chapter in the San Francisco legend. It was hard to watch Harry Bridges growing old and harder to learn, on Friday morning, that he had died at age 88. "He outlived his friends and enemies, or most of them." said his widow, Nikki. "I hope they met him at the pearly gates with a hot tub. Near the end, all he dreamed about was a hot tub. He had nerve damage and couldn't bend his legs so he could never take a bath. It became an obsession." Harry fighting the bosses on the waterfront, Harry beating the government that wanted to deport him, Harry dancing the night away at La Fiesta on Bay, Harry lunching at a shocked Pacific-Union Club with a mischievous editor Paul Smith, Harry smoking, smoking, smoking. Yes, another victim of emphysema, like his sometime drinking buddy, Don Sherwood, but he and his lungs went a long way. Mr. Bridges, your bath is ready. *April 2, 1990*

With the 84th annvy. of the 1906 quake approaching, Jim McRory was doubly touched to run across this heartbreaking obit in last Sunday's Monterey Herald: "John James McDonald, 90, died Friday at the Monterey Convalescent Hospital, where he had been hospitalized with injuries he received in the October 17 Loma Prieta earthquake. Born February 7, 1900, in San Francisco, he was orphaned in the 1906 earthquake that devastated the city. He leaves no known survivors" . . . Orphaned by one quake, killed by another and nobody left to mourn. I'll propose a toast to you, John James McDonald, at the annual April 18 convocation of quake survivors at Lotta's Fountain. *April 12, 1990*

George Adamson checks in with the sightem of the week: a Postal Service jeep parked outside the San Jose main post office with a "For Sale" sign in the window, on which someone has written: "If this runs like the post office, who needs it?" *April 16, 1990*

Anything that begins with getting out of bed is likely to be a mistake, and so it turned out. Yesterday, full of beans and Shredded Wheat, I jogged down to the old Chron, or rather, parked in the lot and walked briskly to the office, and faced the world's greatest living typewriter, my Loyal Royal, to bat out yet another 1,000-word epic for the ages. Only I didn't. Because I couldn't. After 32 consecutive years, the world's greatest living typewriter had—yes—died.

Whether it is terminally dead or simply lying doggo depends on good old Matt Venezia, ace repair man at The Typewritorium. For all these 32 years, Matt has nursed it and rehearsed it and kept the Loyal Royal operating, even when parts became rarer than Model T Fords, which the Royal resembles. "I don't know if we can save it this time," he sighed yesterday morning, lugging the beloved machine off to the hospital. As tears welled up in my squinty, astigmatic eyes, he patted me kindly on my swayed back. "Brace yourself, man. This could be the end."

I got Matt by dialing 911. The emergency began when I rolled some copy paper into the old beauty and began pounding the keys. They wouldn't pound. It was an awful feeling, like being run over by your own car. To the merriment of the staff, I use a typewriter because I hate all things electronic and because I have always felt I could repair a typewriter myself, if I had to. I had to. I couldn't. I am bereft.

* * *

Answering your next question, of course I have a backup. I am writing these imperishable words on an ancient Smith-Corona that belonged to Erskine Caldwell, giant of American letters. Erskine—"Skinny" to his friends—lived here for several years and we got to be good friends. Shortly before he died in April of 1987 in Scottsdale, Arizona, he said to his fourth and most charming wife, Ginny, "I want my typewriter to go to Herb. He's the only guy I know who still uses a manual and four-letter words."

Ginny lugged the heavy beast of a machine to S.F., where, over a long and liquid lunch at Trader Vic's, she presented me with Caldwell's typewriter. This is the first time I've used it. As the French say, it marches well. Between sentences, I think of all the dirty words that Erskine typed on it. The author of such classics as "Tobacco Road" and "God's Little Acre" was famous for them, even having his works banned on occasion. Nevertheless, he was one of the five great 20th century American authors, the other four being Hemingway, Faulkner, Wolfe (Thomas, not Tom) and

Fitzgerald. Malcolm Cowley decided that, not me, so take your complaints to him. Yeah, I'd throw in Steinbeck. *May 24, 1990*

Golden days by the Golden Gate. Well-scrubbed skies, breezes running their fingers through your hair, if any, and foghorns mooing at midnight like lovesick cows. Not only that, the tourists are definitely back, overloading the cable cars and looking in awe at the sights we take for granted. If Gorbachev's visit didn't signal the end of earthquake phobia, how about last week's convention of 7,000 petroleum geologists from every state and 46 countries? As Bo Jackson knows football, geologists know earthquakes, and yet here they were, their very presence an implicit endorsement of our seismic safety—or irresistible charms. *June 12, 1990*

Never on Sunday

Today I have good news for people who hate The Sunday Column.

This is the last one.

The bad news is that I will go on writing five columns a week, Monday through Friday.

Not that everybody hated The Sunday Column. It's just that the guy who liked it died last week. His last words were: "It seems to me I read this before somewhere." Right here.

Why do I call it The Sunday Column, in caps? Because that's the way I always thought of it. A little heavy and too often pretentious, with an attempt to sound Important. Sunday was serious.

The daily column is more me. Mister Monkey Mind, bopping along from subject to subject on a wave of three-dottiness, one-liners, puns, a wisp of fog, a sprig of news, the more than occasional correction, a lot of corniness about the sophistication of the great gray city, here a plug, there a knock and the inevitable Agnos needle. Art's OK! When he is pricked, does he not bleed?

If there's anyone still around who prefers the Sunday to the daily effusion, apologies. I'll try to throw a Sunday column in there one of these Thursdays, when portentous things are happening that require my special brand of missing the point.

★ ★ ★

Of course I feel a pang over the passing of The Sunday Column. I've been writing one more or less regularly since July, 1938, give or take a war and vacations. If you want to count the radio columns I wrote for two years before that, we have a lot of Sunday columns down the drain and long forgotten. When we hacks talk about our "deathless prose," we are making ze little joke. Dead by noon—that's the fate of a newspaper column. A morning one, anyway. Others die by sundown. A whole hell of a lot of them die unread, but we don't talk about that.

Entre nous, I've had a clause in my contract for years that allowed me to cut back from six to five columns a week whenever I wanted. I didn't want to. It would be a sign of weakness. I fancied myself an iron man. For a couple of years there, just before World War II, I was writing seven columns a week. I was a tireless young buck, burning the scandal at both ends, and oh, how I loved seeing my name in the paper. Classically insecure, I took short vacations in those days for fear I'd be forgotten. Who remembers Winchell or Pegler or Oscar Odd McIntyre?

Hardly anybody writes even six columns a week any longer. There are prima donnas, especially on the New York Times, who do two a week. I know people who do one (OK OK, so it's a good one). The norm is probably three. Getting back to my insecurity, I did six on the premise that I may stink today but tomorrow I might be better. In most cases, tomorrow never came, but a lot of generous readers kept hoping.

⋆ ⋆ ⋆

A decade or so ago, somebody at the Columbia School of Journalism, a man who described himself as "a column buff," phoned from N.Y. to say, "Congratulations—you are now the country's longest-running six-day-a-week columnist. You just passed Winchell's 37 years." That made me feel pretty good, but they don't give Pulitzers for longevity. It may not even be a record. There may be some geezer on a paper we never heard of who's been pounding one out every day for 75 years, and how ya doin', old-timer?

Record or not, it is now broken. I'll admit, it made me feel good when someone would say, "Six columns a week—how do you do it?" "It's nothing, really," I would respond in all truth. The question was always counterbalanced by people who said, "Six little columns a week—what do you do with the rest of your time? Sell insurance, or what?"

It was the deadlines that finally got to me. "In the old days," a phrase that always struck terror into the hearts of readers of The Sunday Column, in the old days I could write Friday for Sunday, which meant that if I had stumbled onto a piece of actual news, I could use it. Sunday Punch, however, goes to press on Wednesday night, meaning I had to write The Sunday Column on a Monday or Tuesday, along with the daily one.

* * *

I never did get a handle on The Sunday Column. Nostalgia was a logical subject, given that five-day lead time, but only old-timers seemed to enjoy it. Not a growing market. Talking about how great Old San Francisco was exposed me as the crank and grump I was becoming. The Baghdad-by-the-Bay stuff—"the fog slithering through the harpstrings of the bridge, gobbling up Alcatraz and, like a great python, settling down under the Bay Bridge to digest" A ROCK?—wore thin as the city changed.

So, farewell, faithful Sunday readers. We'll meet again: There's a plan afoot to run old Caen columns in this space, and I'll read them with great interest, wondering how I got away with it. Thanks for being there so long and complaining so little. *June 17, 1990*

Summer and smoke. Midsummer and the smoke of a thousand barbecues. Smelly sweatsocks, damp shirts, whiff of chlorine from the pools of fools who don't know there's a drought on. In the background, sun-dried hills, cracking. Foreground: bloody Marys and a charred charburger that drips blood down your front and onto your new Reeboks. Midsummer. California perfume of dust, underbrush and pine, merging on a hot afternoon punctuated by the champagne pop of well-stroked tennis balls. Stately eucalyptuses like filigree against a pink dusk. Murmured conversations, glow of cigarettes, on old hi-fi playing even older Sinatra. Wonderful world of midsummer, forcing you to count the days, count your blessings, count the ways in which I love thee, California, tousle-haired beauty dancing through poppies. Homemade peach ice cream. Driving back toward the city on 101 in a sea of boats being towed; anybody remember Willie Nelson's line about what that girl could do to a chrome bumper hitch? The midsummer half-moon disappears in a gentle fog that lops the head off the Golden Gate Bridge towers. "Thank you," said the tolltaker. No, thank YOU.

July 31, 1990

This old town: Yesterday-and-today sightem caught by Nikki Lastreto at Ellis and Larkin: a cop on horseback talking on a cellular phone.

August 2, 1990

You've gotta like these guys! How California can it get? A weekend ago, Erik Rosenquist and Steve Taylor of Menlo Park's Etak Inc. and their Berkeley pal, "Stretch" Armstrong, rented a car and drove through all 58 California counties in a nearly nonstop 60 hours—and they have goofy photos taken at each county line marker to prove it. Explains Rosenquist: "California is the greatest state in the union and manic psycho trips are the most satisfying way to travel." Best county: Plumas. Worst: Orange or El Dorado. Rosenquist: "All those yuppie west side Tahoe towns are indistinguishable from the paved-over ennui of Irvine." Best of all: not a single speeding ticket. Caengrats, gents. It's history.

August 13, 1990

The portentously named "Crime Beat" column in the Sonoma Index-Tribune carries this blood-curdling flash: "A woman reported that a man she hired to pick her peaches sat down and ate one when he finished the job." That's the way it goes. You try to be nice to people and they take advantage of you.

September 4, 1990

Well, we all have to make sacrifices during the Gulf Crisis so I'm dropping Baghdad-by-the-Bay for the duration. Please, no applause. We can all live without it. I concocted the phrase back in 1940 when, in my fevered not-long-out-of-Sacramento mind, it described perfectly the magic and mysterious city of that era—a place of minarets, intrigue, perfumed passion and the occasional thief on a flying carpet, fleeing the eunuchs. Even then, people more worldly than I warned, "If you ever saw the real Baghdad, you'd realize you are not paying San Francisco a compliment." I now understand that and may the fleas of a thousand camels invade the armpits of Saddam Hussein.

September 7, 1990

Strange de Jim resurfaces: "I got so tired of my parrot squawking "Polly wants a condo" that I taught her "Here, kitty kitty."

September 21, 1990

Mary Alice Bengston of Oakland saw it on 580 North—a beaten and battered car dying at the side of the road. Its chilling license plate: "5 04 PM". *October 16, 1990*

THE DANCE OF TIME

Daylight-saving time ends. We're back on God's time, and just in time. November approaches, signaling pre-Christmas sales. We are going to give an election to which not many people will come. Too many propositions, not all of them honorable. Yeah, I guess I'll vote for Dianne. After all, she's one of ours. Stanford and all that. She was schooled in politics by her late uncle, a wonderful S.F. character named Morrie Goldman who manufactured ladies' coats and gave the best ones free to the town's models, which shows a lot of heart. A model's life is not an easy one. They've got to stay skinny and learn how to teeter up and down a runway without falling over the side. Sure, a lot of models had Sugar Daddies who bought them fur coats, but that was a long time ago. Now furs, models and Sugar Daddies are endangered if not extinct.

★ ★ ★

Morrie Goldman was a jolly type with curly gray hair and a penchant for gambling. He and guys like Joe "The Silver Fox" Bernstein and Benny Jackson, the prince of Powell St., used to hang out on the third base side at Seals Stadium and bet on every pitch. The cops knew but looked the other way because that was The San Francisco Way. Dianne isn't much like her Uncle Morrie, but she gets my vote in his memory. Besides, she is definitely more colorful than her opponent, who is almost invisible in his facelessness. Eight years of Deukmejian followed by eight years of Wilson? Does California deserve this? Another good thing about Dianne: She has weird taste in clothes. After her TV debate, with her purple Nehru jacket and just-so hair, I said she looked like Michael Jackson, but I was wrong. More like Khadafy. Definitely.

★ ★ ★

Wise people keep saying "You can't turn the clock back" but that's what we did as daylight-saving ended. Somewhere in the middle of the night, we got back the hour we lost last April, or did we? I don't feel like we got an extra hour's sleep, do you? When an hour's gone it's gone and that's that. Anybody who tells you different is just another lying politician. I prefer the beginning of daylight-saving because it happens in the spring, baseball is around the corner, the saps are running, the juice is rising and you only have to advance your clocks and watches one hour. When it ends, you turn the clocks back, and if they're electronic, it's not all that easy. You have to go all around the dial, and turning a watch back is supposed to be bad for the works. I've got about 20 clocks and watches so I spent a busy Sunday. So did a lot of other people, all of them dialing "POPCORN" for the correct time and not getting through because (chimes) "All circuits are busy." I'm so old I still dial Rochester 7 and any four digits for the time. OK, I don't "dial" it, I "touch" it. Oooh.

* * *

Now that we've demonstrated it's possible to turn back the clock, why don't we keep turning it back to the good times? As in a bad movie, the scene gradually changes as the hands whirl around in reverse. Magically, we are young again. Hair grows on Mt. Baldy! There are parking spaces everywhere, even on Market, with its streetcar tracks and dozens and dozens of splendid trolleys. There are rich people and poor but not so many of them. Now and then it even rains. The city smells clean again. You can throw a silver dollar on the bar of the Techau Tavern, order a martini and get six bits in change. Six bits. That's a term as dead as a silver dollar, which, by the way, were almighty and respected the world around, the same globe that was covered by Sherwin-Williams Paints. Cable car gripmen still clang "Shave and a haircut, six bits," but not too many passersby catch the drift.

* * *

As long as we're about it, let's turn the clock back to tea dancing. As a social and presexual exercise, the tea dance was an excellent idea, a civilized way of getting together. A drink and a dance at the end of the day—is that so bad? During the '20s through the '40s, this town went in big for tea dancing, from the great hotel rooms and their big bands to racier places, like Marquard's on Geary and the Lido on Columbus, next to Gerun and Martinelli's Bal Tabarin. The guys wore their hair pomaded and their suits nipped in at the waist and were known as "snakes." The flappers showed lots of garter and loved to Charleston. I remember tea dancing at the St. Francis, where bandleader Ted Fiorito had a very young, blond singer named Betty Grable. We all agreed she had terrific legs. One of the best things about tea dancing was that hardly anybody drank tea. We could live without the creamed chicken in patty shells, too.

⋆ ⋆ ⋆

Yes, my eyes are glazing over. Daylight-saving has ended, the spell is broken, the streets are back to being dirty and there's that damn election coming up. The weather continues to be relentlessly perfect. Blue skies and not a cloud in sight, not even one bigger than a man's fist. We are getting a dose of fog, tumbling over the Marin hills and sidling through the eucalyptus groves of the Presidio. When the fog arranges itself just so, the bay looks like the most dazzling lake in the world, the equal of Como or Garda or Maggiore. The light keeps changing as you move along, in and out of the sunshine. From minute to minute, a complete microseason. No wonder the tourists are still fascinated by San Francisco. No wonder the old-timers never fall out of love with her, even when she breaks your heart and sometimes your head.

⋆ ⋆ ⋆

And so we head into deep fall, which doesn't mean necessarily that winter is around the corner. Not in this city. Forget about the time and season and live it the way it was meant to be lived—day by day. See you at the tea dance. *October 30, 1990*

'Twas the Day Before

I like Christmas but I don't want to get involved. When I hear the hypocrisy and read the Little White Lies, my reaction is "Don't kid a kidder." We've heard that tune before and it's getting tinnier every year. A couple of decades ago, my dear departed friend Howard Gossage started to address Christmas cards and then suddenly swept the whole pile into the wastebasket, announcing, "Dammit, I'm not going to let Christmas ruin my Christmas this year." If you succumb to the pressure, Christmas is almost as much trouble as going skiing, a sport with no redeeming features unless you're a masochist. Make lists of gifts for people you barely know, read the ads, watch the commercials, walk the streets, scan the windows, shake your head and try to hang on till January 2, always the best day of the year. It's all over and you survived another one. This year, of course, there won't be any post-Christmas clearance sales. This year they had them before Christmas.

★ ★ ★

It's the only holiday that's a season, which is another problem. Thanksgiving comes and goes in a few hours and, except for the leftovers and the dyspepsia, can be forgotten till next year, but Christmas is a megillah, the whole enchilada. It starts just after Labor Day and by Thanksgiving, the tinsel is already beginning to look tired. Lug the decorations out of the basement, find a tree that costs much more than a mink, string the lights, have another drink. Christmas lasts three months and ends in a hangover, followed by a stack of bills for items your friends and relatives have already returned. If you can get through the season without hearing "The Little Drummer Boy" once, you've won the game. "Jingle Bells" holds up because it can be jazzed and swung and played every which way. "Joy To The World" has the proper exultant tone. We need that end "Come All Ye Faithful" to remind us that there is something to be celebrated that has lasted 2,000 years against all odds and oddballs.

★ ★ ★

The real trouble with Christmas is that it is altogether wonderful. If we didn't have it we'd have to invent it, which is actually what we did, for various good reasons. It's good for the church business. It's good for the business business, which is also sanctified. It is a delightful mishmash of fables, legends, traditions and geographical conundrums, with a jolly German Santa Claus plodding through the snow to honor the desert child on the burning sands. This year the star shining in the East casts its glow over hundreds of thousands of American troops, ready to do battle for oil that is holy. Hold the myrrh and frankincense, O three wise men, but the gold we can use. The armed forces of this constitutionally secular country are there to fight for those who consider us infidels but nobody ever pretended that organized religion makes sense. To be kind and generous is enough and there is no reason not to worship a tree.

★ ★ ★

The two Christmases, the sacred and the profane. Well, we've been through that waltz a number of times, restating the obvious in various ways that fill the space with portentous emptiness. Yeah, Xmas is about department store grosses and about the infant Jesus and about sincere and spurious sentiments and about our hopes and anxieties. No wonder it's a whole season, a third of a year. We couldn't go through all these traumatic delights in a single day. In the first place, we have to revert to childishness, in the best sense of the word. We search for the eternal simplicities: good and evil, sad and glad, beautiful and beastly. We try to unclutter our minds and psyches and return to innocence, when we thought we could make a difference and even shed light in dark corners.

* * *

If Christmas can do all that, and it can, it is worth the bother, which it is. I marvel at the trouble people go to, the energy and money expended in the name of spreading holiday cheer. Colored lights strung in the window of somebody's tiny and maybe even awful room in a Tenderloin hotel—a touch that makes you choke up a little. The unbounded generosity of anonymous people who feed the helpless and clothe the homeless and lug turkeys to the free food places and work in the soup kitchens—all without the recognition they don't want or need. Tonight they can turn out their lights and read the newspaper by the light of their halos. You have to believe that somebody is keeping score and putting high marks next to their names. If you don't believe that, the game is up and the party's over. He knows when you've been naughty, he knows when you've been nice, is it not so, Sire?

* * *

The rich city of San Francisco at Christmas. From a vantage point on Telegraph Hill it's a magnificent sight—the Bay Bridge a mammoth Meccano set, the Ferry Building tower a beloved toy, the reasonably mundane buildings of Embarcadero Center transformed into dreams by thousands of lights that out-twinkle the stars. Ah, the magic of oil-driven energy! There are carols in the streets, trees in the windows, enticing packages festooned with bows. The gift of wrapping gifts is not a minor one, and it is with a pang that one rips off the artistry. But there is the everlasting guilt among the gilt, the most egregious conflict of the blessed and damned season: the haves and the have-nots, the winners and the losers, the Scrooges and the scrooged. The charities have done their best and millions have been raised but it is still not enough, it is never enough, it never will be, and that is the shame of the richest country.

* * *

Merry Christmas to the beautiful city and its people. The air is crisp, the vistas endless and hope eternal. *December 24, 1990*

★ ★ ★

1991

★ ★ ★

Girls Just Want to Have Fun

Suffering from equal parts of nausea and nostalgia—naustalgia?—I recently reminisced about the great madams of San Francisco and their elaborate maisons de joie, most notably Sally Stanford's Gothic castle on the Taylor St. crest of Nob Hill. The delicious part was that Sally rented the quite magnificent spread—a dozen bedrooms, each with a working fireplace—from Paul Verdier, the snobbish owner of the City of Paris department store, who would only say with a sniff, "She pays the rent regularly. I am not concerned with her morals."

Sally's place became so celebrated, I recalled, that it became a regular call on a special Yellow Cab nightlife tour. A wide-eyed kid from Sacramento, I first paid a visit to Mme. Stanford's in 1938 under the auspices of John Pettit, a Yellow Cab official who was helping break me in as a columnist. Prostitutes are "turned out," presstitutes are "broken in," and both have other things in common, of course.

When the young ladies filed down to the drawing room to meet the gawkers over champagne, I wrote, they were "as proper as Junior Leaguers in their silk wrappers"—perhaps I meant negligees—and each wearing a gardenia corsage. That's the way I remember it, but maybe I just imagined the corsages.

★ ★ ★

My reminiscence produced one positive result—a letter from one of Sally's girls from that era, when San Francisco was as wide open and exciting as any city in the world. She signs herself simply "Lorrie W." and writes in a free flowing hand:

"Honey, we did not wear 'silk wrappers.' We weren't candy! Nor did we wear gardenia corsages. Having worked for Miss Stanford (Marsha Owens) for five years in the old mansion and then on Pine St., I would be qualified to correct you.

"As for being as proper as Junior Leaguers—yes, and I might add that three of us are still members, due to excellent marriages. One lives in Sausalito, one (my best friend) is married to one of the OLD S.F. family hotel owners, and another (Diana) lives in N.Y. and France, married to a big tobacco company owner.

"One of us was really lucky—me! I married a rich Armenian farmer who treats me like a queen. Knows all about me and could care less! A lovely condo, house in Palm Springs, so what more do I need?

"We girls see each other around Xmas for lunch in S.F. or N.Y. and let me tell you, it would make a movie—diamonds, homes, cars, furs, money and talk! So, dear, we did what we had to do at the time. The results were great, thanks to the wonderful 'landladies,' as we called them.

"Most of us worked for Sally, Lorraine Fontaine (on Franklin), Edna on Green St., Mabel (Malotte) on Bay, Ethel and Billie Doyle in the old Castle Apartments, eighth and ninth floors, on Geary. Plus Mabel kept a room at the St. Francis for years for 'out calls' and Lorraine sent all her cab action out to a place in the avenues, near Masonic Hospital.

* * *

"I see you often at lunch time when I'm in S.F. shopping. Le Central is my favorite for lunch. Years ago (dating myself) the Palace Court—what a place! And of course the lower bar at the Mark Hopkins Hotel, a natural for a 'bill' ($100) or more.

"Jake Ehrlich, Lou Lurie, Pat Brown, Dave W. (meat business), Grover Magnin (Fridays), D. London (Sundays!), Walter, Dick, Charles I and II of the Burlingame Country Club. I played golf at the club many many times. What a laugh!

"In case you're wondering, I still look good, thanks to a wonderful plastic surgeon in S.F. And the frosted hair helps, plus designer clothes, furs, shoes, the works. So what else do I need? Not a gardenia corsage, that's for sure!"

* * *

Lorrie W.'s letter made me feel good. Here, obviously, is a happy person and also something of a rarity—a "working girl" (that's what hookers call themselves) who seems to have come out of "the business" with all nerve endings intact and in place. Perhaps it has to do with the benign atmosphere of this small city of the late '30s and early '40s.

The police ran the town and quite well. Payoffs were made in an orderly fashion. The "landladies" were celebrities, of sorts, and there must have been hundreds if not thousands of "working girls," keeping the oldest profession alive in shadowy Tenderloin hotels, musty apartment houses that smelled strongly of disinfectant (old S.F. line: "Is your sister married or does she live on Bush Street?"), neat little flats in the Marina, cottages on Ocean Beach—by golly, they were all over the place, till Pat Brown (see above) became district attorney and shut everything down, even the slot machines that clattered all night at the Old Press Club at Powell and Sutter.

I remember a lunch with Sally Stanford and Polly Adler at the Mark Hopkins shortly after they both retired. "I'm delighted to be out of the business," said Polly. "Yeah," nodded Sally. "You know the madam's lament—'Everybody goes upstairs but us.' It's a relief to open the front door and not have to look at the guy's shoes first." Polly: "Yeah. How come cops have such big feet?"

⋆ ⋆ ⋆

Polly was in town to plug her best-selling book, "A House Is Not a Home," and Sally was already at work on her memoirs, "Lady of the House."

In the lobby of the Mark, they ran into the well-known S.F. newsman and author, Robert de Roos, who first asked how their books were doing and then uttered the classic lament of "working girls" about those who don't play for pay:

"You amateurs are ruining the business!" *February 4, 1991*

Just a Lucky Guy

This is it, folks—the big seven-five. Yes, The Sackamenna Kid has reached the considerable age of 75, which in itself is not much of an achievement. People are living longer than ever, or does it just seem that way? No trick to it at all. Just keep breathing in and out, not necessarily in that order. "What is the secret of your longevity?" the young interviewer once asked William Saroyan. "Not dying," replied the famous writer. That's about the size of it.

Warm birthday cards from Harry Gluckman, who runs a business down the street on Mission: "Do you know what's really funny about someone your age having another birthday?" Turn page. "Absolutely nothing." It's true that 75 doesn't lend itself to the wry, dry humor of, say, 50, when I was able to joke that I was "halfway there."

Still, it is necessary to keep trying. Like the heroes of my generation, D'Artagnan and Scaramouche, we must perforce spit in the eye of the devil, and vow never again to use a word like "perforce." In honor of Hemingway, we strive for grace under pressure, suavely rejecting the last cigarette and glass of brandy and placing the target over our hearts with steady hand and sardonic smile.

Mark Fontana, famous maker of "monuments" in the marble forests of Colma, has sent me a miniature granite headstone inscribed "Caen . . . " It's the three dots that make it eloquent. A thoughtful gift and useful as a paperweight on my cluttered desk.

* * *

Jokes about age, an American tradition. Nobody will ever top comedian Joe E. Lewis' "If I'd known I was going to live this long I'd have taken better care of myself," one of the most plagiarized lines in history. "Just think," soothed Scott Beach, "when Mozart was your age he'd been dead 40 years." Mary Lou Colton quotes Isabel Russell's poem to E.B. White on his 75th: "Hardly a person is now alive/Who really looks forward to seventy-five." My cheery friend Winston Cock, pronounced "Cook," smiles "Remember, you're only 10 in dog years." At 75, I am 24 Celsius. That has a nice ring to it. "How old are you?" "24 Celsius." Willie Mays' number, a lucky one. Or I could think of myself as a French 75, the drink (cognac and champagne) the doughboys invented during World War I. Trouble is, nobody drinks French 75's any longer—it was named after a French gun—and I am only half-French, at best.

* * *

At 40, I put away a lot of dreams, such as becoming the oldest rookie in major league history. A 39-year-old rookie was faintly possible, but a 40-year-old one, never. At 75, the horizon is much more limited: far too old for early retirement, still too young for the national 80s tennis competitions (one of the champs, Bob Seller, lives right here). My tennis mentor, Sandy Walker, has just about convinced me that my fadeaway slice, plus my natural cunning and guile, would put me right up there among the octogenarian hackers. "You can still run," he marvels, sending me around the court one more time.

* * *

My patient and tireless assistant, Carole Vernier, has presented me with a front page of the April 4, 1916, Chronicle, so I'd know what was going on in the world the day I was born. It was a heavy news day. A major war was raging in Europe. The French and Germans were fighting over Verdun, a mistake. General "Black Jack" Pershing was chasing Pancho Villa in Mexico. There was, however, no story about a star shining in East Sacramento, where people stirred uneasily and muttered to one another, "That's all we need—another columnist." The Caen family of 1916 lived in a small but sumptuous house at 10th and O streets. My German-born mother, the amazing Augusta, or "Gussie," was from Zweibrucken, which means "two bridges." Thus was my eventual move to San Francisco foreordained. Gussie, an excellent operatic singer with a powerful mezzo-soprano, was obsessively clean, strict and a hausfrau par excellence. From her I inherited all those lovable German characteristics of stubbornness, rigidity and punctuality, which is why I am always right (well, almost always) and never miss a deadline (well, almost never). My father, Lucien, from Lorraine, was a dashing chap with a moustache, brocaded double-breasted vests and a taste for wine, restaurants and the good life. My kind of guy. When he had it, he spent it. When he didn't, he spent it anyway. He believed the only honorable way to die is broke, and he achieved his goal. He was only 72. I can now say "only."

★ ★ ★

My fate: growing old without growing up. The Peter Pan of the Pusillanimous Pun, the fallen arch remark, the flat one-liner. I expected at 75 to be a white-haired, apple-cheeked, twinkling-eyed old darlin', with grandchildren tumbling around my feet and people coming to me with words of wisdom. Sort of a Sage of San Francisco. If I were still writing a column, which seemed unlikely, and still does, it would be serious and reflective, filled with words like "trenchant," "insightful" and "meaningful." The conscience of the city, firm but fair.

Instead, I'm just as silly and light-hearted as I was at 25, dropping funny names, picking up on odd license plates, mongering the gossip and making the rounds. At deadline time, I still get butterflies, wondering if I can get away with it one more time. When stuck in the middle of a column, with the clock ticking, I can feel the ulcer that never quite grew. But I have wonderful friends, enemies I'm proud of, readers with saintly patience, a paper I enjoy working for in a city I love, and a cast-iron stomach with brain to match. A lucky guy.

* * *

The good news is that this is the last column I will ever write about my age. However, if I make it to 100, all bets are off.

April 3, 1991

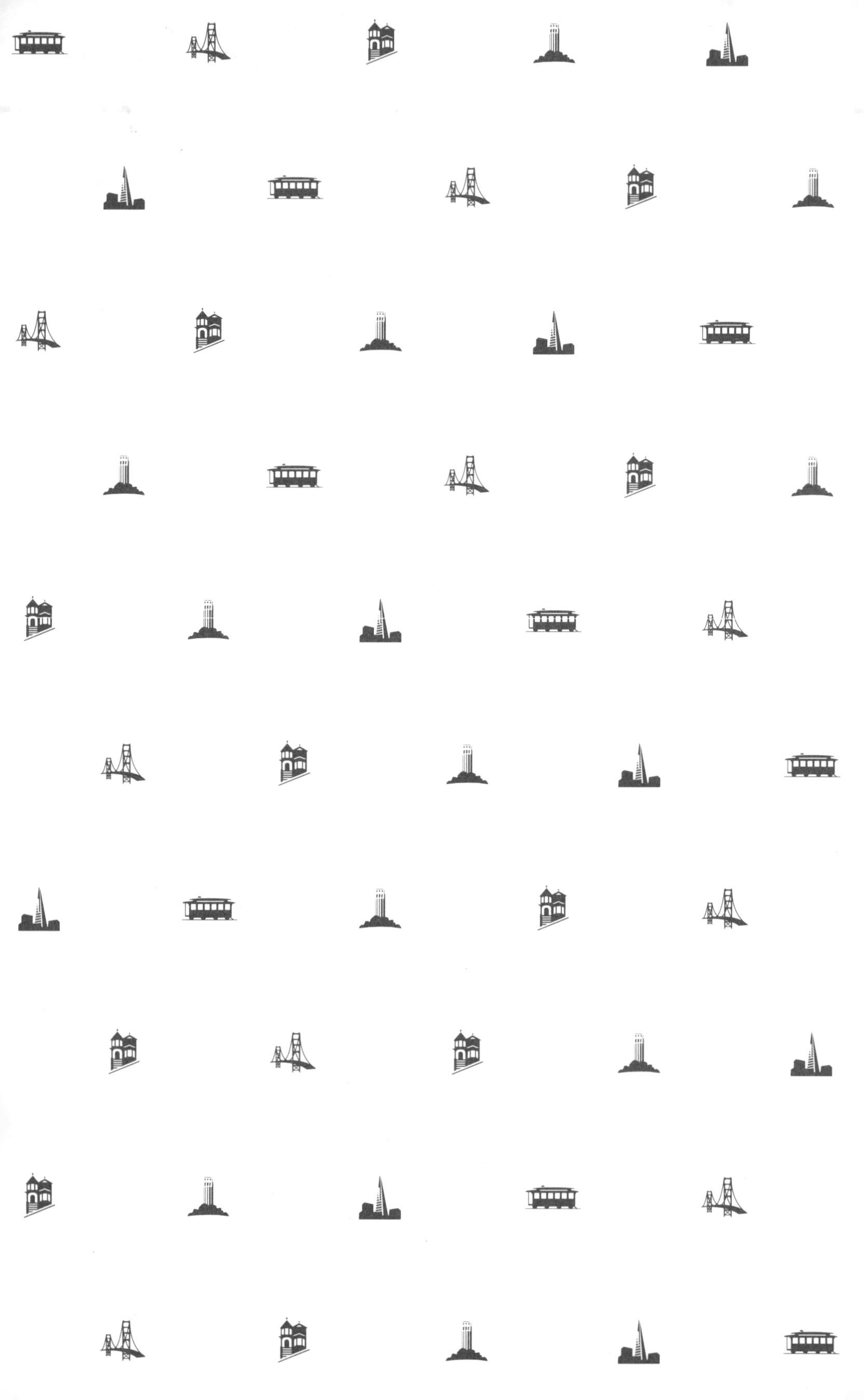